Steal My
Breath
Away

Other Works by Sarah Castille

The Sound of Us

Steal My Breath Away

Sarah Castille

BRAMBLE

TOR PUBLISHING GROUP · NEW YORK

STEAL MY BREATH AWAY

A Bramble Book
Published by Tom Doherty Associates / Tor Publishing Group
120 Broadway
New York, NY 10271

www.torpublishinggroup.com

Bramble™ is a trademark of Macmillan Publishing Group, LLC.

The Library of Congress Cataloging-in-Publication Data is available upon request.

ISBN 978-1-250-28992-6 (trade paperback)
ISBN 978-1-250-28993-3 (ebook)

Our books may be purchased in bulk for promotional, educational, or business use. Please contact your local bookseller or the Macmillan Corporate and Premium Sales Department at 1-800-221-7945, extension 5442, or by email at MacmillanSpecialMarkets@macmillan.com.

First Edition: 2025

Printed in the United States of America

0 9 8 7 6 5 4 3 2 1

For the lost and lonely and anyone who has ever wondered where they belong. I've got you.

Steal My Breath Away

CHAPTER 1

Haley

Good morning, Chicago. This is Hidden Tracks *on WJPK, coming to you from the basement of Havencrest University's student center. I'm your host, Haley, and welcome to a brand-new year. We'll be uncovering the unheard voices of the music world and exploring the stories behind the songs that inspire and heal.*

Do you ever feel like you're just going through the motions? Like you're on a path, but you're not quite sure if it's the right one? Today's playlist is for anyone who's ever felt lost on the journey, anyone trying to find their rhythm in a world that sometimes feels out of sync. It's for those of us struggling to find ourselves and stuck between who we are and who we're supposed to be.

We're going to start off with Eddie and the Hot Rods's *"Do Anything You Wanna Do." Stay with us and remember—sometimes the most beautiful melodies are born from discord.*

I cued up my next few songs and sat back in the studio chair. I'd been hosting *Hidden Tracks* for two years, playing an eclectic mix of lesser-known music from various genres including indie, alternative, folk, acoustic, and experimental tracks. My focus was on emerging artists and underground bands. It wasn't easy to break into the music business, especially for solo singer/songwriters like me. I'd been singing since the age of four, playing guitar since I was eight, and I'd written my first song when I was ten years old. I'd grown up performing in school musicals, talent shows, and community events, with the occasional foray into local television and radio, but success continued to elude me.

I caught motion through the glass in the opposite studio and saw Derek putting on his headphones to prep for his show. Tall, thin, and always dressed in black leather, Derek had joined the radio station as a volunteer at the same time as me and we'd moved up through the station ranks together.

"Did you talk to Dante yet?" he asked through the mic.

Dante was one of the interim station managers, sharing the role with longtime volunteer Siobhan so he could spend more time developing his career as a session bass player. I'd been thrilled when he'd asked me to join his band, Dante's Inferno, hoping the exposure would boost my career. He'd invited Derek to play keyboards, and another station volunteer, Nick, to play guitar. His friend Jules kicked ass on the drums. I'd never played with a band before, and the experience was beyond anything I'd ever imagined. Aside from the fact that we got along well and had fun together, there was a level of energy and excitement that I couldn't match as a solo singer. We had a synergy that made every performance electric, and from the number of bookings we'd had since our first gig, Chicago thought so, too.

"He sent me a message asking me to come and see him after the show. What's going on? Did a big-name producer call him up and ask to sign us?" My heart kicked up a notch. I knew the chances of that happening were slim at best, but that didn't mean it wasn't possible. I'd wanted to be a singer ever since I could re-member. My dream had always been to pursue my music career in LA after graduating high school, but life didn't go the way I'd planned. The summer before senior year, my brother Matt died while serving in the air force and my world spun off its axis. I didn't want to be alone in a new city without any support. My mom had my stepfather, Steve, to comfort her. I gave up my LA dream and followed my best friend, Paige, to Havencrest instead.

Derek's gaze dropped to the soundboard, and he shrugged, making the skin on the back of my neck prickle. "It's better if he tells you."

I would have pumped him for information, but my set was

almost up, and I was about to move into the segment where I invited listeners to send in requests or stories about how certain songs had impacted their lives. I tried to catch his attention again to visually express my disapproval, but he knew me well enough not to look up again.

After the show was done, I headed straight for Dante's office. When Noah had been station manager, the hallways had been crammed with boxes filled with old CDs, magazines, electronic equipment, and music memorabilia. He'd just walked away from everything last year, disappearing without saying goodbye. I was pretty sure Dante and a few others knew what happened to him, but if they did, no one was talking. Dante and Siobhan had taken over and cleaned everything up, including Noah's disaster of an office. They had also modernized the station, framing the band posters on the walls, changing out the worn furniture in the lounge, and arranging proper storage for Noah's extensive music library overflow.

To be honest, I preferred the chaos. I loved walking down the hallways and seeing something new each time. My bedroom in the house I shared with Paige and four other students was always a sea of clothes and books, half-written songs, and fast-food wrappers. Every so often, Paige would make me tidy up, and although I loved the sense of calm that came with being able to see the floor, I couldn't keep it that way for more than an hour.

"What's up?" I poked my head into Dante's office. "I got your message. Derek came into the studio looking like someone had broken his keyboard."

Dante ran a hand through his thick, dark hair. Tall and intensely handsome with an angular jaw, dark eyes, and a strong chin, he had a dangerous vibe that always made me nervous, but it hadn't put off my friend Skye. They'd hit it off from the moment they met, and six months later, they were still going strong.

"I've been offered a chance to do some session work with a band in LA and a gig with an international artist who is touring the US," he said. "I'll be in and out of the office to help Siobhan manage things and to hire a new station manager, but I won't have time for rehearsals or gigs." He let out a heavy sigh. "I'm going to have break up the band."

Whoosh. My heart didn't just sink in my chest, it crashed, taking my breath away. With Dante's star status—he also DJ'd WJPK's biggest show—the band was my best chance of being discovered. Playing with Dante's Inferno had been the best eight months of my life, and now it was over. Just like that. I'd be back to open mics, occasional gigs at the cocktail bar where I worked for stage time, and my usual Sunday-afternoon busking on Michigan Avenue.

Breathe. Breathe. You're fine. Lock it away. The mantra had gotten me through my father's death when I was twelve years old, and the loss of my mother's emotional support when she'd poured her grief into a new career in politics. It had sustained me when Matt had followed his best friend Ace into the military and my mother had gotten remarried, to a man I couldn't stand. And it had been holding me together in the two years since Matt died, when I'd felt totally and utterly abandoned.

"Congrats on the contract." I mentally pushed the uncomfortable feelings into my mind's black box where I kept everything that was too much to process. I was the happy one, the chatty one, life of the party, always on, ready for anything, capable of handling anything life threw at me with a smile. "That's amazing. I'm really happy for you."

"It's been in the works for a few weeks," he said. "I asked Skye not to tell you until all the paperwork was signed. I don't want you to think she—"

"I would never think anything bad about Skye." I cut him off with a wave. Skye was one of my closest friends. She was a journalism major who ran a news show at the station and wrote for the *Havencrest Express*. We worked together at the Buttercup Bakery Café, and I liked to think that I'd helped her and Dante through the ups and downs of their relationship with the psychology I'd learned in my classes.

"I'm really sorry," Dante said. "I know how it feels to try and make it in the music industry. I've got all your demos and I'll be sharing them where I can."

"It's fine." I opened my mouth and just rambled while another part of my brain was putting a lock on my pain. "Really. I'm good. I've got lots of open mics and a few potential gigs lined up for the rest of the term. It was an amazing experience getting to be in the band with you and everyone else. It's made me a better musician."

Dante hesitated, frowning. "Are you sure? I've been in bands that have split before, and it was almost like a relationship breakup. It hit hard."

Yeah, it hit hard. Too hard. I'd been riding the high of enthusiastic crowds and screaming fans for eight months, and the thought of going back to the grind of small, cramped bars and disinterested audiences was like a punch in the gut. The public validation that had come with my brief brush with fame had filled some kind of void inside me, re-creating the warm, fuzzy feelings I'd had when my whole family used to come out to watch me sing.

"I never expected it to be a long-term thing," I lied. "It was only a matter of time before the world discovered your musical genius and stole you away."

It was a master performance. By the time I'd crossed campus to the coffee shop on the ground floor of the main library where I worked with Skye, I'd even convinced myself that losing the band was no big deal.

Skye was already serving customers when I arrived. A former DII basketball player, she was almost my perfect opposite. Her long dark hair was thick and smooth whereas I had been cursed with a wild mane of curly chestnut-brown hair that fell past my shoulders in barely controlled chaos. My high, sharp cheekbones gave my face an angular appearance, and instead of the simple clean lines of the athletic wear she favored, my style was equal parts edgy and bohemian. I varied looks between festival goth, boho rocker, and '70s hippie with a witchy twist. Today, I was channeling Stevie Nicks in my skinny jeans, a white boho-style shirt, and a fabulous long olive velour coat with a red silk lining that I'd found in a thrift shop. It was an utter travesty that I had to replace the coat with a horrific buttercup-printed apron for work.

"Dante just messaged that he'd talked to you." Skye wrote the next drink order on a paper cup while I filled the espresso machine. "Are you okay?"

"I'm fine. It's all good. I never expected it to last."

"You don't have to pretend with me," she said. "I know how much you loved being in the band. Maybe the band could find a new bass player and start over."

"Dante was the real draw," I said. "And it's not like we had regular gigs. It was a nice-to-have add-on to my regular schedule, and to be honest, I was wondering how I'd keep it up with all the open mics I'm planning to do this fall." I didn't like lying to Skye, but she was head over heels in love with Dante, and I didn't want her to feel any guilt about him leaving the band to follow his dreams.

A rich baritone voice interrupted our conversation. "What does a guy have to do to get a drink around here?"

I looked over to see Jason Roach, one of the university's top basketball players, at the counter. Skye grinned and greeted him with a high five. She knew all the ballers on campus from the year she spent playing on the women's basketball team. After she'd been badly injured in a road accident, she'd been forced to give up her dream of making it to the WNBA and embrace her passion for journalism instead.

Jason smiled and reached over to high-five me, too. He was over six foot five, slim, with blue eyes and thick brown hair. We'd met at a bar the previous year, but our conversation had been cut short when Skye's roommate, Isla, had hustled some guys at pool, and we were forced to make a hasty exit.

"I remember you," he said. "Haley. Psych major. You were

analyzing everyone's personality. You told me I had attachment issues."

Cringe. I'd come to Havencrest with no idea what I wanted to study. My mother had pushed me toward political science, hoping I would follow her footsteps into a political career. Instead, I'd taken a wide range of courses, including an introductory psychology course, through which I hoped to find a way to understand and process my grief. The subject had clicked with me. I enjoyed the challenge of learning what made people tick and helping them through their issues, although I wasn't able to apply what I'd learned to me.

"I might have had too much to drink," I admitted. "Sometimes when the filter isn't on, I get overly enthusiastic and too many words come out."

"I saw you singing with Dante's Inferno at the end of last term," he said. "You guys were awesome. Are you on any of the frat/soro booking lists? I'm in charge of entertainment for my frat's first party of the year."

"The band isn't taking any more gigs," I said. "But I take solo bookings. You can look me up online and hear some of my demo tracks."

Jason made a good effort to hide his disappointment, but I could see it in the crinkles at the corners of his eyes. "Yeah. Thanks. I'll take a listen, but we're looking for the high energy you get with a band. Why don't you two come to the party? It's next Saturday and it's going to be great."

"Sounds good." More fake smiles. More aching cheeks. I lifted my hand for another high five. "I've never said no to a party. I'll be there."

Skye looked over at me with a worried expression after Jason left. "Do you remember the frat party we went to last year? They weren't good guys, and Jason's frat is even worse."

"I remember drinking something purple and highly alcoholic from the bathtub and not much else." I added the party to the calendar app Paige had set up on my phone to try and help me stay organized. "You should come. Bring Dante. It'll be a blast."

Or at the very least it would take my mind off yet another setback to the shambles that was my music career.

CHAPTER 2

Ace

A-list actress Jessica Swanson wanted me in her bed.

I knew this because she'd run off to change into something "more comfortable" after we'd returned to her Beverly Hills mansion. She'd been devastated by her loss at the Academy Awards, and although she'd put in an Oscar-worthy performance at the *Vanity Fair* afterparty, the moment we were safely in the limo, she'd crumpled.

I knew then I was in trouble, and it became crystal clear when she swanned into the living room where I was checking the security system and put her hand on my arm.

For me, "more comfortable" meant ditching the suit and tie and pulling on a pair of track pants and my favorite Chicago Bears jersey. For Jessica, it meant see-through lingerie with nothing underneath.

Jessica fucking Swanson.

In the two years I'd been working as a celebrity bodyguard for Stellar Security, I'd seen clients in all states of undress. I'd been propositioned by actresses and singers multiple times, but I had never crossed that professional line, and I wasn't about to do it when my client was in an emotional crisis. Most celebrities, I'd discovered, were very lonely people, prone to making inappropriate attachments with anyone who was a solid, stable presence in their life. It was why I never accepted a job with the same client twice or stayed with a client more than my self-imposed limit of six months. It was why I was going to call my boss, Tony, and ask him to reassign me first thing in the morning.

"Ace, have a drink with me." She tugged on my arm. "It's been the worst night. I can't believe they gave the Oscar to Sophie Louis. It was totally political."

"Ma'am." I gently moved her hand off my arm. "I can't protect you if I'm distracted or under the influence."

Jessica twirled her blond hair around her finger and looked up at me with her big blue eyes. She was a very beautiful woman, and her team had spent the last two days glamming her up for the Academy Awards. I didn't know many men who would turn down an invitation from one of the hottest celebrities in Hollywood, but I was done with hookups and one-night stands. Nothing could fill the black hole in the center of my chest, and I wasn't interested in trying.

"Don't call me ma'am." Her plump lips turned down in a frown. "It makes me feel old. I'm only twenty-nine, and you're, what? A year or two younger?"

"Twenty-four," I corrected her. "And your security file said you're thirty-five."

"Someone made a mistake." She wandered over to the marble minibar in the corner of a room ten times the size of the hotel room I'd lived in between this job and the last. "I can't be over thirty in this industry, or my career will be over. I'll be stuck playing single mothers and divorcees. I've asked Rachel to try and get my birth certificate changed."

Rachel wasn't just an agent; she was a Hollywood fixer. I had no doubt she could get the birth certificate changed. There was no problem she couldn't solve.

Jessica poured herself a shot of vodka, downed it, and poured another. She'd already had a full bottle of champagne at the party. I felt a pang of sympathy for her. I understood all too well the need to self-medicate with alcohol. Despite her star status, Jessica was deeply insecure, and tonight's loss had cut deep. I didn't want to add to her feelings of rejection, but she'd lost her sense of boundaries and if I didn't manage the situation, it would mean trouble for both of us.

"I saw your tattoos the other day when you were working out

downstairs." She pulled on my sleeve, trying to get me to remove my jacket. "Where did you get them?"

"Air force. I spent four years on active duty." I pulled out my phone and pressed Rachel's number. She was always able to calm Jessica down when she was distressed.

"Come sit with me on the couch." She grabbed my free hand and led me to the enormous feather-stuffed sectional in the center of the room.

"I'm sorry, Jessica. I can't stay. I need to go outside and do a sweep of the grounds."

"But you work for me." She patted the cushion beside her. "And I'm sure everything is fine outside. Talk to me. Do you have someone in your life? A wife? Girlfriend? Boyfriend?"

It was ironic that she chose to ask the question now, three months into the contract, and not at the start of the awards season when the house had been full and she'd been everybody's darling. Her previous bodyguard had left to get married. I didn't have a similar excuse.

"No, ma'am. I'm all about the job."

"Then there's no reason why we can't get to know each other better."

"I don't think—"

Her phone buzzed and she picked it up, instantly distracted. "Rachel. Oh my God. I looked everywhere for you after the ceremony. Where were you? What happened? I thought you sent gifts to all the judges. You told me it was in the bag."

With a sigh of relief, I went out the back door for a breath of air. I was done with this assignment. The awards season was over. Jessica didn't have any new projects lined up. The house would no longer be filled with stylists, makeup artists, hairdressers, and the multitude of sycophants who clung to the biggest stars. This was the third time I'd had to turn her down and I couldn't see things getting any better.

I sent a quick message to Tony asking for a reassignment before heading outside to do a sweep of the walled garden, a lush oasis in the concrete desert of LA. Even in the dark, I could make out the symphony of vibrant colors—a riot of pink, purple, and yellow flowers, perfectly planted and groomed until they looked almost unreal. The air was heavy with the sweet scent of jasmine, lavender, and roses. Rich and lush as it was, it couldn't compare to the crisp mountain air and the fresh scent of pine from home.

Jessica had spent ten million dollars to buy the LA mansion and fix it up, including an entire redesign of the landscaping, but in the three months I'd been with her, not once had she walked through the garden. Given the chance, I would have spent all my time outdoors. Before moving to the small town of Riverstone, Virginia, I'd spent most of my childhood alone in run-down apartments while my parents gambled at casinos or got high with their friends. When social services finally caught up with them and took me to live with a grandmother I didn't even know I had, I'd immediately been drawn to the outdoors. Riverstone was nestled at the edge of a forest, and I'd taken full advantage of the natural beauty, swimming in the nearby lake, hiking and mountain biking on the nearby trails, camping with my best friend Matt, and skating and snowshoeing in winter. It was the only place I truly felt free.

My phone buzzed and I picked up the call. "I just talked to her. She's in a bad way," Rachel said. "I need to know you're going to stay up with her. I'm sure Sophie's team bought off the judges. It's outrageous."

"You also tried to buy off the judges," I pointed out.

"I was discreet about it," she said. "And Jessica deserved that award. I cry every time I see that performance."

"My job is to protect her twenty-four/seven," I assured her. "I'm not going anywhere."

"I don't mean just setting the security alarm," Rachel snapped. "Do I really have to spell it out? She needs comfort, Ace. She needs someone to hold her tonight. She's so distraught, I don't know what she's going to do. I don't need you to protect her from strangers. I need you to protect her from herself."

My stomach tightened in a knot. "I'm not going to cross that professional line."

"Damnit, Ace. This has been the biggest blow to her career. She needs to feel loved. She needs to feel wanted. Not one of her previous bodyguards has ever refused her."

"We all need to feel loved and wanted," I reminded her. "One night with me isn't going to make any difference about how she feels about herself tomorrow."

Of course, Rachel didn't give up. She hadn't become the top fixer in Hollywood without reason. "I can't believe you would give up the opportunity to sleep with one of the most beautiful women on the planet." She hesitated and I could almost hear the wheels turning in her mind. "Are you not attracted to women? Or are you with someone? Her last bodyguard had a girlfriend, but he was prepared to step up. It was hush-hush. No strings. No expectations. His girlfriend never knew and now they're getting married, so no harm, no foul."

"I'm not going to sleep with her, Rachel." I bit back my irritation. "I can't do the job and the client at the same time."

"Crude," she said with a sigh. "And disappointing. I'll have to send someone over. He's a friend of a friend who has been dying to meet her."

No doubt the "friend" would come from an escort service and would be paid a huge sum of money to make Jessica feel special. I opened my mouth to tell Rachel that lying to Jessica wasn't going to help her, and that Band-Aid solutions didn't solve deeper problems. She needed a therapist to help her work through her issues. But who the fuck was I to give that kind of advice when I couldn't take it myself? I still couldn't sleep through the night. The things I'd experienced on deployment still haunted me, but worse was the accident I'd witnessed and had been helpless to stop—the one that killed my best friend.

———

Tony Davis, owner of Stellar Security, had served four tours of duty in the army before an injury forced him into early retirement. He was a fiercely practical man who had taken his LA-based private security firm from a three-person operation to a global enterprise with offices across the United States and Europe in the time it had taken me to serve my four years as an airman.

"Why the fuck do you want to be reassigned?" He leaned back in his chair, hands folded behind his head. Tony was shorter than me by a few inches, but still imposing, with broad shoulders, thick arms, and a frame hard with muscles earned from daily workouts in the gym. "Most of my personnel would kill to work with Jessica, and the pay only goes up the longer you stay."

"She wanted to get too close."

"I don't have a problem with 'getting close.'" He punctuated the last two words with air quotes. "Kim K., J. Lo, and Madonna dated their bodyguards. Pamela Anderson married hers. Getting close is a perk of the job. You're taking on a surreal and intimate role in your clients' lives. You're there in their private moments. You're there when they need you. There are few people they can trust to have their best interests at heart. You're like a glorified boyfriend, but with a gun."

I'd never understood how Tony could be so relaxed about some things and so rigid about others. He had rules we had to follow and rules the clients had to follow and extensive training courses that had to be passed, but it was okay to sleep with clients if that's what they wanted. "I'm not interested in being a boyfriend or getting into a relationship with the clients. I want to keep them safe, and I can't do that if emotions get involved. I need that professional barrier, Tony, or I can't do my job."

His eyes hardened, shifting from cool blue to steel gray. "Are you afraid of attachments? Is that it?"

"I'm not afraid of shit." With a wall covered in certificates, commendations, medals, and awards, Tony was clearly not a man who understood fear.

"Then why don't you come out drinking with the team? Why

don't you take time to get to know our staff or the other guards? Why don't you take a break between assignments, make some friends and have a life?" he persisted. "You don't even have a place to live in LA. You stay in hotels between clients. I get the feeling that if someone tried to be your friend, you'd ask to be reassigned to a different city."

I bristled at his questions. "Do you have any complaints about my work?"

Tony shook his head. "You're one of my best, but it's a problem when I have to tell clients you won't do repeat bookings. It's a problem when you refuse to stay past your self-imposed six-month limit, because it means the client has to develop a new bond of trust with someone else. I want our clients to feel that the bodyguard they hire is someone they can form a relationship with, someone who will stay with them for as long as they need. Long-term placements are good for business. They are good for our reputation. They tell the world that our people are solid, stable, and trustworthy, and that means more business."

"If you're saying I have to continue with Jessica—"

"I get it." He kept talking as if I hadn't interrupted. "I've worked with other vets who have issues forming attachments after losing close friends on active duty. And I know it was worse for you because you also lost your grandmother when you were on deployment. I lost people, too. But I took the time to grieve. You finished your military commitment and came straight out here to join the team. You've worked nonstop for the last two years without a break, and you haven't taken the time to see the firm's psychologist, which you promised you would do when you first came to work for me. I think you need to talk to someone, Ace. I'll take you off Jessica's detail, but I'm not going to reassign you until you deal with your mental health."

I'd been avoiding the psychologist since the day I'd started with Stellar Security. I simply wasn't prepared to unpack a lifetime of trauma in front of a stranger, and I had no idea what would happen if I let someone in.

"What if I just took some time off?" I offered. "I'll take a vacation."

Tony gave me a dubious look. "You? On vacation? Where would you go?"

"A beach." I'd never taken a vacation before, but some of my celebrity clients had island getaways where they would go on the pretense of getting away. In reality, it was an excuse to get photos of themselves in swimwear, showing off the months of restricted diets and intense workouts in the hopes they'd be offered a juicy role to revive a flagging career.

"What are you going to do on this beach? You're not a lie-in-the-sun-and-read-a-book kind of guy."

"Surf. Kiteboard. Scuba dive." I'd always wanted to try out water sports, but aside from waterskiing with Matt during summer camping trips, the opportunity hadn't arisen.

He raised a curious eyebrow. "Would you be going to this beach alone?"

I sensed Tony wasn't buying into my beach plan, so I tried to assuage his concerns with a smirk. "I'm sure I won't be alone for long." It wasn't a total lie. I had no trouble attracting women—Jessica was a case in point. But I didn't do relationships. When I did need to burn off some sexual tension, I drove to the coast where the vibe was chill, and it was easy to meet a woman who was happy to spend the night with a stranger who would be gone by the first light of day. It had been a long time since I'd taken that drive.

"Cut the bullshit," he said abruptly. "We both know you're not going to any beach. You're not a beach guy, and don't tell me you'll go to Paris and see the sights, because you're not that guy either." He steepled his fingers in front of his chin. "Maybe I should send you back to Jessica. She likes you. She said you two had a connection. Don't you want that in your life?"

"I don't need connections." Connections meant giving up a part of yourself and living with a giant black empty hole in your chest when the people you cared about disappeared from your life.

"What do you want?"

"I want to get back to work," I shot back.

"I'll make an appointment for you with Dr. Stanford."

My pulse kicked up a notch when he reached for the phone. "I'll go home," I said. "My grandmother left me her house in Virginia when she died. I haven't been there since Matt's funeral, and I've been meaning to go back and fix it up so I can sell it."

Tony knew all about Matt. He knew that Matt had been accepted into dental school at Havencrest U but had decided to follow me into the air force instead. We'd joined the buddy program and planned to turn our four years of military service into four years of fully paid university education under the GI Bill. We had it all laid out. After we'd finished our military commitment, we'd go to the same university, share an apartment, graduate, and return to Riverstone to live our lives—me as an engineer and him as a dentist—and maybe even have families, assuming we could find women willing to marry us. Looking back at my eighteen-year-old self, I couldn't believe I'd been so utterly naive. Fate had a way of destroying the best-laid plans, and only a few weeks before the end of our final tour of duty, it took him away.

"That I believe." Tony put the receiver down. "I think it's a good idea. You need to make peace with the past. Two months."

Two months alone with my own thoughts was nothing less than torture.

"One week."

"Six weeks or I make that call to Dr. Stanford."

Fuck. Six weeks in Riverstone. Nausea roiled in my gut. "Six, but you promise to have an assignment ready for me the day I get back, even if I've worked for them before." I was willing to break my own rules if it meant an early reprieve from a vacation I didn't want to take.

"Done." Tony slapped his desk. "Go home. Get your head straight. Lay the ghosts to rest."

I forced a smile, but I already knew there was nothing for me in Riverstone but pain.

CHAPTER 3

Haley

My dad loved music. Until he died, I can't remember a day when I came home from school to silence. Whether it was the deafening guitar riffs of "Mustang Sally" or the soothing sound of "Georgia on My Mind," our house was alive with sound, and every song was a learning experience. I knew all the music greats and could recite the top-ten bands of every decade before I learned how to write. But through the years, Van Morrison always stood out. Whether it was "Brown Eyed Girl," "Moondance," or any of his classics, every one of my dad's playlists featured a Van Morrison song. We sang to everything from the low bass talent of Johnny Cash to the high treble of Michael Jackson. Dad knew all the lyrics, but I was the one carrying the tune, and there was nothing we loved more than taking to the "stage" during family gatherings to sing and dance to our favorites.

By the time I was eight years old, I was a pretty good singer, and I was all set to be "discovered" after my first solo stage performance at the school talent show. I could play piano, guitar, and curiously the french horn, because bass player extraordinaire John Entwistle played the french horn and Dad thought I should learn it, too. I picked Elton John's "Tiny Dancer" for my public debut because Dad had been playing it on repeat every day on the way to school. He showed up dressed in head-to-toe denim honoring the song's first line and I forgot to be nervous because it made me laugh so much.

Despite my stellar performance, I didn't get my big break that day. Instead, I had to grind it out in a town so small no producer would ever find it, dreaming of the day I could head to LA and make it big as a singer. Dad died when I was twelve years old, and even though it felt like my world had ended, music kept me going. It was a way of keeping his memory alive. I performed in school musicals, the church choir, and at community events and fundraisers. I sang in malls, cafés, and on street corners. I entered talent contests across the state, and when I started writing my own music, I recorded songs and uploaded them to YouTube, Spotify, and social media channels. I was driven to succeed as a singer not just because it had always been my dream, but to feel close to my dad again, to honor his love of music, and to feel the kind of love he'd given me the day he'd dressed in denim.

Matt's death at the end of my senior year threw me off course. With both my dad and my brother gone, the world seemed too unpredictable to navigate alone. I needed support and stability in my life, so instead of moving to LA like I'd planned, I followed Paige to Havencrest University instead.

I tried to stay upbeat even though I felt like a failure. I told myself that I was doing it for my dad. He had never gone to university and had always wanted Matt and me to chart a new path. But even though I'd traded LA for Chicago, my dream wouldn't die. The music was still inside me. I kept writing, recording, and performing any chance I got. I joined an artist collective for tips on finding open mics in Chicago, leads on promotions, venues looking for openers, and the best places to busk on a Sunday afternoon, which is where I found myself three days after Dante's Inferno went bust and my hopes of record deals and world tours with it.

I plugged my guitar into the amp and strummed a few notes while Paige adjusted the microphone in front of me. I'd been busking on Chicago's Michigan Avenue on and off for the last year, when the weather wasn't too cold. Between the regulars with their drums and newbies who didn't know the unspoken rules, it was often a challenge to find a good space, but Paige always managed to find a way to squeeze me in at the best locations.

Her phone buzzed and she checked the screen. "It's my mom."
"Is everything okay?" Paige's mom had been fighting non-Hodgkin's lymphoma for over five years and had been the impetus behind Paige's decision to go into biological sciences and specialize in cancer biology. The complexity and detail-oriented nature of the subject appealed to her analytical mind and problem-solving skills, and aligned well with her organized personality. Above all, however, Paige was driven by a desire to help people. She was the introvert to my extrovert, my emotional anchor, as I was hers. She balanced my impulsiveness with her pragmatism, and I tried to give her respite from her coursework and her worries about her mom by dragging her out for new experiences and letting a little crazy into her life.

"She's good." She studied the screen. "They're considering her for a new clinical trial. I might have to go home if she gets accepted. She'll need help with the paperwork and an advocate for when she talks to the doctors in case she has to make any big decisions."

"Let me know and I'll come with you," I offered. "My mom isn't getting home very often, and she'd be happy to have someone check the house." I hadn't visited Riverstone since Matt's funeral, and I had no desire to go back and be reminded of our childhood. But there was no way I was letting Paige go alone. Her dad had abandoned her and her mom shortly after her mom's diagnosis, and she had no other family to provide support.

Paige repositioned my amp, so it was out of the way. She'd made me a checklist of equipment to bring for every type of gig, but I just wasn't a detail person, and after three gigs in a row when I'd forgotten something critical, she decided it was easier if she just came along. Even more than organizing things, Paige loved to organize people, and I was her favorite project.

"Looks like a good crowd today." I plugged in my portable GK amp. I'd bought it from a musician friend who gave me a deal because it had "fallen off the back of a truck." It was a good size for carrying around, loud enough to be heard on busy Michigan

Avenue and the park behind us, but not so loud that the store owners across the street would complain.

Paige snapped open my portable table and covered it with a tablecloth before setting up my tripod. I live-streamed every performance and posted it on my social media so that I was not only playing to an audience, but also to my online fans. "Do you have everything you need?"

"I forgot my sign."

"Taped to the back of the table." She pulled the sign off with a flourish and set it up alongside the permit that meant I wouldn't be hassled by the police. "And your CDs are in my bag along with your QR codes." She pulled out a few copies of the new EP I'd recorded after getting my first solo gig in Chicago when I thought I had finally hit the big time. When it became clear that open mics weren't the path to riches, I went back to busking and developing my musicianship out on the streets.

By the time I'd finished setting up and Paige had gone to buy some snacks, the street was bustling. My competition included a saxophone player in a fedora, a band with a fantastic marimba player, and three Columbia music students who were playing pop songs on their strings. Paige had set me up as far away from the others as possible within the permit area, hoping the noise wouldn't drown out my voice.

There was nothing I loved better than performing, whether it was on stage or on the street. I opened with my most popular covers and a semicircle grew around me. It was the biggest crowd I'd ever drawn on Michigan Avenue, and everything came together in perfect harmony. The notes flowed through my veins, lifting me from the street and transporting me to a place where the only thing that mattered was the music.

With the crowd hanging on every beat, I finished with Fleetwood Mac's "Dreams" and soaked in the applause. I glanced down to check my set list. When I looked up again, a tall man in jeans and a gray Henley, a baseball cap pulled low over his face, had pushed himself to the front of the crowd.

"Are you Haley Chapman?"

It was an odd question given that I had a table full of merch and CDs with my name on them, but I nodded and smiled, hoping he was a fan and would be generous with his donation.

"Senator Chapman's daughter?"

My smile faded and the skin on the back of my neck prickled in warning. I'd moved to Chicago to put some distance between me and my mom and all the demands and expectations that came with being related to one of Washington's best-known power couples. After my dad died, Elizabeth Chapman had gone from stay-at-home mom to congresswoman in the span of two years and then she'd been elected to the Senate. She'd met Steve, a high-profile lawyer, in Washington and started spending more and more time away until I was practically living at Paige's place during the week and Matt and his friend Ace were fending for themselves in the house. She tried to keep Matt and me out of the limelight, occasionally trotting us out on campaign trails and for victory parties and articles about moms in politics and how successfully they balanced family and career. After Matt died, she stopped asking me to attend public events, and I'd managed to get through a full year at Havencrest without anyone recognizing me.

Before I could respond, the dude tossed a dollar bill into my guitar case and disappeared into the crowd.

I didn't think much of it. The crowd had grown around me, and the energy was electric. Paige returned with some sodas, and I took a short break before starting my second set. By the time the crowds started to dwindle, the sun was setting and my fingers were getting numb from the cold breeze blowing off the lake. We packed everything up, and had just started down the street toward the train station when a white van pulled alongside us.

"Haley . . ."

I glanced over and a man jumped out onto the sidewalk and grabbed me.

Startled, I froze, my brain trying to process what was happening as he dragged me backward. Only Paige's shriek of alarm brought me back to my senses. Heart pounding, I kicked and wiggled, trying to break his hold, screaming as he got closer to the van.

"Let her go." Paige swung the amp, hitting my captor on the side of the head and knocking him off-balance. I took the opportunity to throw myself forward, loosening his grip, and fell onto all fours on the ground.

The man swore and jumped back into the van, shouting at the driver. With a squeal of tires, they sped away, leaving us alone on the sidewalk.

"Are you okay?" Chest heaving, Paige dropped to her knees beside me and pulled me up to inspect my hands. "Did he hurt you?"

I opened my mouth, but nothing came out. I couldn't move, couldn't breathe, couldn't even process what was happening. My ears were ringing, body shaking. Paige was right there but she seemed far away.

A woman ran over to help us, and then a man who had been across the street, and a family who had been standing on the corner. Someone called 911 and after that, everything became a blur. There were sirens and police cars. An ambulance. A paramedic wrapping me in something soft and warm.

"She's in shock," the paramedic said to Paige, who was sitting at the back of the ambulance beside me, holding my hand. "I think you're in shock, too."

"I don't understand," she said. "Why would someone want to kidnap Haley?"

I didn't understand it either, but for some reason I was more upset that I'd scraped my hands in the fall and how was I going to perform next week if they scabbed over?

"How are we doing? Feeling any better?" A uniformed police officer with blond hair and bright blue eyes joined us outside the ambulance, along with his shorter but no-less-good-looking partner.

I shrugged, realizing my brain wasn't as fuzzed as before. "As better as an almost-kidnapping victim can be."

"Humor. That's a good sign." He pulled out his notebook and asked Paige and me to recount everything we could remember about the attack.

"Any idea why someone would want to grab you? Did you have a fight with an ex? Have you had any arguments or disputes? Are you involved in anything I should know about?"

"No exes," I said. "I'm not big into relationships or criminal activities. Also, not a sex worker, if that's what you mean. Do you think it's a human trafficking thing?"

"Honestly, I don't know." He ran a hand over his jaw. "People have been grabbed here before. We'll need to talk to the other witnesses and see if we can track down the van. It's hard to tell if it was opportunistic or targeted until we have more facts."

"It could have to do with my mom," I offered. "She's a US senator and is up for reelection. Her name is Elizabeth Chapman." I told him about the man who had come up to me earlier to ask if I was Senator Chapman's daughter, but the description I gave him didn't match the man Paige had hit over the head.

"I've got your details in case the detective in charge needs to talk to you," he said, handing me his card. "Call me if you remember anything else or if you have any questions."

"We should ask them out," Paige whispered after they walked away. "We could double-date."

"They've got to be at least thirty," I said. "I like my men to have been born in the same decade."

"Did you text your mom?"

I nodded, shrugged. "She wanted to fly out first thing in the morning, but I told her not to. I wasn't hurt, and it would just be awkward. She always has so much to do, and she'd probably bring along a photographer for a photo op of her hugging her almost-kidnapped daughter."

Paige gave me a sympathetic look. "I'm sure she's genuinely worried about you."

"Her first words were 'What were you doing busking on the street?' followed by 'I thought you gave up that silly hobby,' so I don't think my safety was her first concern." For a brief moment, I wished my dad was here. Or Matt. Or even his best friend Ace, who had practically lived at our house when I was growing up, and always seemed to be there to catch me when I fell. It was Ace who came after me when I decided to do a solo hike in the forest during a family camping trip. Ace who saved me when I swam out too far in the lake. Ace who stopped a senior from taking advantage of my naivety at a high school dance. Ace who had been there for me when my father died. Strong, steady, quiet Ace who grounded me and made all the noise go away.

Ace who had broken my heart.

"You always have me," Paige said, giving me a hug.

"There's no one better. You swung that amp like a pro." I leaned into her comfort, but for the first time since Matt died, I wished Ace had been there, too.

CHAPTER 4

Haley

TEN YEARS AGO

I was ten years old the first time I met Ace Murphy. Paige and I were in the kitchen dancing and singing to Martha and the Vandellas with my dad while his grilled cheese sandwiches sizzled in the pan. He was a chef and the owner of Riverstone's only high-end restaurant, a charming riverside bistro named HAM—Haley and Matt. Dad's creative cooking had earned him a coveted Michelin star, but the remote location meant that he struggled to fill tables after the summer rush was over.

"How was school today?" Dad loved all the gossip and had arranged his work schedule so he could be home when we got in from school. Mom left early every morning for work in her law office so Dad fed us breakfast, made our lunches, and sent us off to school. He did his shopping and meal prep at the restaurant during the day, then came home to fix our snack and prepare dinner for when Mom came home. He spent his evenings at the restaurant, often not getting back until Mom was in bed. I never appreciated how well their system worked to ensure we always had a parent in the house, nor did I appreciate what we had—stability, security, and the absolute joy of his presence—until he was gone.

That late-summer day, we filled him in on all the gossip while he nibbled on a dry rice cake. His doctor had put him on a strict diet after his last checkup revealed he was not only overweight, but his blood pressure was too high, and his heart wasn't working the way it was supposed to. When Mom told Matt and me that we had to make sure he didn't sneak any bad food, I pretended it was a game and tried not to think about the family curse. His dad and his grandfather and his great-grandfather had all died young from heart attacks, and the doctor had told him he was heading that way if he didn't look after his health.

Dad had just plated our sandwiches and was about to show us a new dance move when Matt walked in the door with his friend Rafael and another boy I'd never seen before.

"This is Haley and Paige," Matt said behind me. "Don't be too nice to them or they'll follow us around and be a total pain. Everyone, this is Ace. He just moved to Riverstone and he's in my class."

Curious that Matt had brought home someone who didn't know me and Paige, I looked back over my shoulder as Dad twirled me around. Rafael stuck out his tongue like he usually did. Ace just stared. He was as tall as Matt, but lanky, with dark tousled hair and a face so pale it looked like he'd never seen the sun. He wore baggy clothes that seemed too big for his frame and his hands were shoved into the pockets of an oversized jacket.

When the song ended, I turned to properly study the new boy. Our eyes met, locked, and that's when everything went quiet.

My head was always full of noise. My brain jumped from idea to idea and even the smallest thing could distract me. I needed to be doing two or three tasks at once to focus on a single chore, or I needed to be outdoors where there were lots of things going on. Even better I needed people, lots of people, because people meant conversation and I loved to talk.

Ace took the noise away. For a few brief seconds, the world disappeared until it was just me and him in a bubble of calm. I felt a connection with him that I'd never felt with anyone before, and all I wanted to do was get him alone and unravel the mystery of his silence.

Paige pulled me back with a nudge. "Do you know him?"

"I've never seen him before."

"Usually, in this house we greet guests with a 'hello,'" Dad said in an admonishing tone before turning his megawatt smile on Ace. "Welcome to Riverstone. I'm sorry about Haley. She was raised by wolves. Sometimes I think we should send her back."

"Dad." Laughing, I gave him a playful shove. I loved Dad's sense of humor, especially when his jokes were directed at me. "Last time you told someone I was raised by hyenas. Get your story straight."

"Are you thirteen, too?" Paige asked Ace.

It was a strange question, but I understood where it had come from. Something about the way Ace carried himself made him seem much older than Matt and Rafael, older in some ways than Dad.

He nodded but kept staring at me, so I stared back. He had the most interesting eyes I'd ever seen. They were brown and green mixed together, like Matt's favorite marble—the one I wasn't allowed to touch. He had a nice face, but serious, not like Rafael, who always tried to make us laugh. I felt like I knew him, like he'd always been around. I knew things about him that he didn't need to say.

Rafael and Matt headed over to the counter and grabbed their sandwiches, as they did every day after school, seemingly oblivious to the fact that there was nothing for Ace. I took my plate over to him. Dad had cut my sandwich in half and the cheese was oozing from the center. "You can have mine."

Ace shook his head. "Thanks, but I'm not hungry."

He was lying. I could feel it. I could see it in his face. He was hungry in a way I couldn't even begin to understand.

I held out the plate again. "I had a big lunch. Huge. Dad made burritos that were the size of the teddy bear Matt sleeps with at night. I probably won't need to eat for days."

"Don't listen to her," Matt shouted. "I don't sleep with a teddy bear."

Ace's lips tugged at the corners and that hint of a smile softened his face. After a moment of hesitation, he took the plate. "Thank you."

"Maybe we won't have to send her back to the wolves after all," Dad said, ruffling my hair. "I'll whip up a new batch. Looks like we've got a load of hungry kids here this afternoon." Dad walked over to Ace and held out his hand. "Dave Chapman. You can call me Dave."

Dad had never told any of Matt's friends to call him "Dave." Only adults called him "Dave." I didn't understand why he thought Ace was different, but maybe he'd seen what I'd seen—a boy who was world-weary at the ripe old age of thirteen.

A flush of pleasure crept up Ace's face and he shook Dad's hand. "Yes, sir. Thank you, sir."

Dad laughed. "I see your grandmother's handiwork already. She's always been big into manners. Just don't get on her bad side. I heard that when she became head nurse at the hospital, they gave her unlimited access to needles."

Ace smiled and his face went from beautiful to breathtaking in a heartbeat, making me feel warm all over.

"You don't need to make any more, Dad. I'm not that hungry," Matt said piling his sandwiches on Ace's plate. "Ace can have mine, too. You did make us a big lunch."

I stared at him, wide-eyed in surprise. When had Matt ever not been hungry? Matt was always hungry. Mom said he was an eating machine. But he was also kind and generous, even to me, and I was, admittedly, a bit of a brat. It was why people liked Matt and why Mom called him her little gentleman.

"Well, I'm hungry." Rafael stuffed one half of his sandwich in his mouth and blew out his cheeks, pretending to be a chipmunk as he walked away.

"I like the new boy," I said to Paige after the boys had gone to play video games in the basement.

"He's quiet," she said. "Maybe he's shy."

"He's hurting," Dad said quietly.

"What do you mean?" I sat at the counter while Dad buttered another slice of bread. He knew that Matt and I were just being polite and if he didn't feed us right away we'd be in the kitchen scrounging for unhealthy snacks as soon as our guests went home.

"I talked to his grandmother," Dad said. "She was in the restaurant the other day. He's had a hard life but it's not my story to share. Just know he's been through a lot. He needs love, and we have more than enough to give."

That was Dad. He was a big man with a big heart and he loved people. He could see right through to a person's soul.

If I'd known then that the love and friendship I gave Ace over the years would leave me with a broken heart, I might not have given him that sandwich. But I was only ten and Paige had brought her Barbies, so I didn't think any more about it and went to play.

Ace became a permanent fixture in our house, and it wasn't long before Paige and I got his story. He had come to live with his grandmother after social services had taken him away from his parents. Paige had heard her mother whisper "drugs" on the phone and something about Ace's parents leaving him alone in their apartment for days at a time. Once she even heard the word "jail."

I'd never known anyone whose family had been in trouble with the law, and it just added to the mystery that surrounded Matt's new best friend who fit in with our family like he'd been there from the start. Dad offered to have Ace come over after school when his grandmother was working, and Matt was happy to have someone other than his irritating little sister to play with when Rafael wasn't around. When Dad found out Ace hadn't had much of a childhood, he took it upon himself to teach Ace how to fish, ride a bike, and catch a ball. He even paid Ace to help us with our chores so he could earn some extra money. When Matt was at baseball practice or hanging out with Rafael, Dad would give Ace and me cooking lessons and he and I would serenade Ace with Dad's favorite songs from the '50s and '60s.

"You could sing this one for the talent competition," Dad said to me one afternoon as we chopped onions to Nancy Sinatra's "These Boots Are Made for Walkin'." "It's easy enough on the guitar. I could show you the chords."

Ace and I didn't usually talk much, and I'd figured he thought I was just an irritating kid, but he turned to me with interest. "I didn't know you were going to compete."

"Of course she is. She plays guitar and she sings like an angel," Dad said. "She has a natural gift for music. I caught her messing around with my old Stratocaster when she was five years old, so I bought her a guitar of her own and taught her how to play. We did a daddy-daughter duet for the Christmas pageant last year. We sang 'Baby, It's Cold Outside.'"

A smile spread across my face at the memory. Dad had really hammed it up on stage. He loved an audience almost as much as me.

"Let's give Ace a private performance of our act," Dad suggested. "Sing nice and loud. I'm going downstairs for potatoes, and I want to be able to hear you."

I never turned down an offer to sing, so I sang my part while Dad shouted his lines from the cellar.

"You're really good," Ace said, and my face instantly heated for no discernible reason. Matt never said anything nice about my singing. When I told him I was going to become a singer/songwriter when I grew up, he just laughed and told me Mom would never allow it. She expected us to go to college and Dad agreed. He'd learned his cooking skills from working in kitchens in Europe, LA, and New York before finally settling down in Riverstone to open his own restaurant, but he'd told us more than once that he wished he had a college degree.

"You've heard me singing before," I said with an embarrassed shrug.

"I know, but usually Matt is around, and I didn't want to say anything in case he teased you."

I couldn't help the grin that spread across my face or the

warmth that filled my chest. "I think he's jealous. Whenever he sings, he's out of tune. Dad says Matt got his genes."

"My grandmother used to be a singer in a jazz club before she became a nurse," Ace said, "but I've never heard her sing."

Ace never talked about his life, and I didn't know whether to keep quiet or ask questions. But I was a talker and sometimes my mouth moved before my brain could catch up. "Do you have other grandparents?"

Ace diced his onion in silence and for a moment I was afraid I'd been too nosy. "I didn't know I had family until I moved here," he said, his gaze fixed on the cutting board. "My grandmother didn't even know I existed, so if I do have other grandparents, they probably don't know about me either. My parents were eighteen when I was born. They both ran away from home when they found out my mother was pregnant. They didn't want me at first and planned to put me up for adoption, but when they found out that the government would give them money every month for having a kid, they decided to keep me around."

I didn't really understand about the money, but I felt sad for Ace that his parents had kept him away from the rest of the family. "Where did you live?"

"Different cities." He shrugged, his hands frozen mid-slice. "We had to move a lot. Sometimes it was because my parents didn't let me go to school, or they would leave me alone for weeks at a time and social services would get involved. My parents said they didn't want anyone to take me away, so we'd pack up in the middle of the night and a few days later I'd be in a different school, sometimes even a different state. Other times, we'd have to leave because people were after them . . ."

"It must have been hard to leave your friends." I couldn't even imagine the world he described, and his words made my heart ache in my chest. I'd lived in the same house all my life with a family who loved me. I knew my parents would be there when I woke up in the morning and when I went to bed at night. I knew everyone in town, and most of the kids in school had been with me since kindergarten. My world was small, but it had always been safe and secure.

"I didn't have friends," he said. "I always knew we were going to leave so there was no point. When I came to Riverstone, my grandmother promised that I wouldn't have to move again, but I don't know . . ."

He trailed off with a shrug, and I scrambled to think of something to cheer him up again. "How did you become friends with Matt?"

A smile tugged at the corners of Ace's lips. "He wouldn't leave me alone. He kept asking me to come over after school. He chose me as his partner in gym class. He sat with me at lunch . . ."

"Matt's like that," I said, laughing. "Once he sets his mind on something, he won't let it go. I guess he decided he liked you and he wanted you as a friend. You had no chance."

Ace laughed, too. He didn't laugh often, and it made my heart happy that I was the one who had given him that moment of joy. "Your dad said that, too. You say a lot of things like him. You're like the same person except you're a girl."

The way he looked at me when he said "girl" did funny things to my stomach. I'd only just started having crushes on boys, and I felt being a girl in that moment in the context of him being a boy.

I heard the crinkle of a plastic bag and caught Dad listening at the top of the stairs. "Ace . . ." He came over to the counter, his usual warm expression replaced with a seriousness I'd never seen before. "You are very wanted here. Your grandmother was thrilled when she found out she had a grandchild. She called in forty years' worth of favors to have the house updated before you arrived. I even heard she smiled when she was at the school giving kids their shots."

Ace blanched. "I'm sorry, sir . . . Dave . . . sir. I didn't mean to sound ungrateful."

"I don't think you are ungrateful," Dad said. "I think you're one of the most solid, grounded, respectful kids I've ever met, and that's a credit to you because your grandmother told me what it was like for you before you came here. You've been a big help around our house, a good example to my kids, and I've seen how you look out for Haley when Matt's not around. It puts my mind at ease to know there's always someone there for her."

"I'm not a kid." I looked up, annoyed. "I don't need anyone to look out for me."

"Of course not, bug." Dad kissed my head. "I just mean you're a free spirit like me, and sometimes we need someone to make sure our feet stay on the ground. That's what your mom does for me. She makes sure I don't get involved in crazy schemes, paint the house purple, dye my hair orange, or go too wild with the restaurant menus. I won't always be around, so I like to know that someone is checking in on my baby girl."

I loved when Dad called me his baby girl. It made me feel warm inside. I hoped when I grew up and had kids of my own, I'd still be my daddy's baby girl.

"Now . . . I've changed my mind about dinner," Dad said. "I saw a can of beans downstairs and I've decided we'll try mixing beans and potatoes with a little chipotle and create something new. Call me impulsive. Call me crazy . . ."

"But don't call me late for dinner!" I shouted out one of our favorite family sayings.

"I hope you've got a good appetite," Dad said to Ace. "I'm not letting you go home tonight until you've tasted my new dish, so both of you get back to work. We've got a lot of chopping to do, and I'm pretty sure Matt's not going to lend a hand when he gets home."

He was right about Matt. Lately, my brother had been refusing to do a lot of things, and particularly anything that involved cooking. He preferred to spend his time building his model planes, tracking planes in the sky, or playing airplane simulation games in the basement with Ace or Rafael. Sometimes he locked himself upstairs in his room and listened to music so loud it made the house shake. Ace, on the other hand, never refused any request my parents made of him. He dutifully grabbed another onion and got to work.

I glanced over at him as he chopped. I'd never really thought about the fact that Ace was always looking out for me. He'd saved me from a few falls in the playground over the last few weeks, and he'd stepped in one afternoon when Chris Sturgess and his friends were harassing Paige and me after school. He'd even rescued the cookies Paige and I had made for the school bake sale moments before they'd turned into a blackened mess in the oven. I hoped I could return the favor. Maybe someday I could save Ace, too.

CHAPTER 5

Ace

I hated afternoons.

Afternoon meant the 3:00 P.M. arrival of Mrs. Janice Welling, a sixty-five-year-old widow, nurse administrator at Riverstone's only hospital, and my deceased grandmother's best friend. Janice never bothered to knock or ring the bell. She opened the door with the spare key my grandmother had given her years ago and walked right in.

I don't know why I tolerated the intrusion, only that I likely would have starved to death if she hadn't brought me dinner every day. I wasn't interested in cooking. Two weeks ago, I'd come back to my grandmother's small bungalow in Riverstone, locked the door, and started drinking the pain away.

She'd showed up exactly three days after I'd arrived. I went to bed in the darkness and woke up in the light. Janice had cleaned up the garbage, tidied the house, bought groceries, and cooked a meal. "Your grandmother would have done no less for my Dan," she said, referring to her son who had been injured in a car accident and now ran a hardware store in the center of town.

After that, she stopped by every day. I was grateful for the hot meals. Not so grateful for the incessant chatter that accompanied them. Still on my forced "vacation," and with no desire to leave the house, I was a captive audience.

So, every day at 2:45 P.M., I pulled on a clean shirt, ran a comb through my hair, sat at the kitchen table, and persevered to honor my grandmother, who would have been ashamed of the state I was in. I persevered when Janice pulled open the curtains to let in the sun, imagining the moment when she left, and I could plunge the house into darkness again. I persevered when she boiled the kettle and poured two cups of tea. And when she settled down to tell me all the news in town, I persevered, praying she wouldn't mention the one name I most dreaded hearing on her lips.

Perseverance would take me through the one hour and twenty-seven minutes of Janice's daily visit until she looked at her watch and said, "Oh my. Look at the time." And then, as soon as she was gone, I ate the meal she'd prepared, pulled out a bottle of whiskey, and drank until I could slip into a coma where the nightmares wouldn't find me.

At least that's how things usually went. But not today.

"Ace?"

My bedroom door creaked open, and I threw my arm over my face to block out the light streaming in my doorway. Although my grandmother had passed away over four years ago, I still slept in my old bedroom. I'd never had a room of my own growing up, and it was comforting to sleep in a place that had always and would always be mine.

"Janice . . ." I groaned. "What are you doing here so early in the morning?"

"Nine A.M. is not early." Janice marched over to the window and pulled the blinds, searing my eyes with sunshine. "Are you ill?"

I wanted to lie, to tell her I had the plague or some other highly contagious disease, but I was long past hiding anything from Janice. "Jeff didn't show up with my delivery yesterday. It was a bad night."

Jeff was the grocer's son, the grocer being Ben Galloway, a member of my senior class, who had taken over his father's store when his dad passed away. I had a standing order for exactly two bottles of whiskey to be delivered every day at 5:00 P.M. It was the perfect way to end each day.

"Well, today's a new day. You've been locked away in this house for the last two weeks, and now it's time to start living again. You need to take a shower and get dressed so you can eat your breakfast before Senator Chapman arrives. She wants to have a little chat with you."

"Wait. What? Why?" I pushed myself up to sit. "How does she even know I'm here?"

Matt and Haley's mother was the last person I wanted to see. It had been hard enough to talk to her at the funeral. Hard to shake the hand of the woman who had welcomed me into her home and treated me like one of her own. Hard to listen to her tell me it wasn't my fault when I knew I was to blame. Matt would never have joined the air force if not for me. He wouldn't have been in the B52-H that crashed into the Mediterranean Sea during a routine air refueling training mission. He would have come home safe to his family, just like I promised Haley. Instead, he returned in a coffin.

"You'll find out when she gets here." She patted my shoulder and a few moments later I heard her bustling in the kitchen. I briefly considered returning to my bed, but I knew she would be back. Janice didn't take no for an answer.

"Well, that's better." Janice smiled when I joined her twenty minutes later at the kitchen table. She handed me a cup of tea and a plate of bacon and eggs.

I gave a noncommittal nod and took a sip of the bitter brown liquid she'd poured for me. I hated tea. I hated the taste, the heat, the reminder of sitting around the fire in the desert at night on deployment with Matt talking about our plans for a future that would never come to be.

"I was talking to Esme Duncan about you," Janice said. "I told her you were back. She offered to come out and visit to cheer you up. Didn't you two used to date?"

"Briefly, but that was long ago, and I'm not interested in seeing anyone while I'm on vacation. I don't want to give any wrong messages." The last thing I needed was Esme Duncan in my house. I'd dated her in high school. Although I'd ended our relationship before I left home, she'd made it clear that she was willing to wait for me no matter how long it took. I didn't have the heart to tell her it would be forever. There was only one woman I truly wanted—the woman I could never have.

"I think she just meant to come out as a friend," Janice said. "She's engaged to Blake Forester. Do you remember Blake?"

Yes, I knew Blake. He was the quarterback of the football team and the guy I'd beaten up after I caught him taking Haley to "see the stars" during her first high school dance.

As a rule, I didn't do dances. I had two left feet and no sense of rhythm, but I'd heard Haley's name in the locker room after senior football practice, and something about the tone of Blake's voice had made my skin crawl. Matt had dismissed my concerns out of hand. Haley could take care of herself, he said. He was right about that. Haley had a bit of wild in her and wasn't afraid to speak her mind. But she was also trusting and innocent and as susceptible to Blake's considerable charms as anyone else.

I got there just in time.

I heard her say "No," and his crude response. I heard the fear in her voice when she asked him to let her go back to the dance. I don't remember much else. At some point she stopped me from beating him unconscious and Blake got away. That was the first night I held her in my arms.

I was pulled out of the memory by the knock on the door, followed by the whirlwind of energy that was Senator Elizabeth Chapman. She was a short, heavyset woman with cropped curly hair, and she radiated power in her bright pink suit jacket. She looked like she was about to walk into a meeting rather than sit down to tea in my grandmother's worn country kitchen.

"It's good to see you, Ace." She shook my hand across the table, a cold contrast to Janice's warmth, but then the senator had never been an overly affectionate person. I could count on one hand the number of times I'd seen her hug Matt and Haley, and that was only before her husband died.

"Senator." I gave her a nod.

"No need for formalities," she said, taking a seat across from me. "You're family. Call me Elizabeth."

"Yes, ma'am."

Her lips thinned for the briefest moment, but then the smile returned. "How are you? I was in town two weeks ago and I bumped into Janice. She mentioned you'd come home. I'm sorry I didn't get a chance to stop in but it was a whirlwind trip to check on the house and touch base with some party donors. She said you've been working with a security company in LA, looking after celebrities. It sounds very exciting."

"Yes, ma'am."

"Janice also told me you're here on vacation."

"Yes, ma'am. I was thinking of selling my grandmother's house, so I thought I'd use my time off to fix it up."

"Um-hmm." She glanced over at Janice, and I knew right away that Janice had let her know exactly how much fixing had been going on.

"Are you planning to stay long?"

"I'm heading back to LA in four weeks." There was no question that I would go back. What else would I do with my life? I had always wanted to become an engineer, but that was the dream I'd had with Matt, so going to college now was out of the question. I couldn't reenlist. After witnessing the crash that killed my best friend, I'd developed PTSD and the air force had made it clear I couldn't come back.

"Would you consider cutting your vacation short?" She sipped her tea. "I need your help. It involves Haley."

My breath left me in a rush and my fingers tightened around the handle of the porcelain cup so hard it snapped off.

"I'm sorry." I stared at the fragment of porcelain in my palm.

"It's all right." Janice took the cup from my hand. "They were your grandmother's cups, not mine."

"Is Haley okay?"

Senator Chapman nodded. "I'm not sure if you know that she and Paige went to Havencrest University in Chicago after they graduated. She's studying psychology. At least I thought that was what she was doing, but it turns out she is still trying to make it as a singer in her spare time, playing gigs in shady bars and busking on Michigan Avenue." She shared a look with Janice and shook her head before filling me in on the attempted kidnapping.

"Did they catch the guy?" It was an effort to stay in the chair. All I wanted to do was fly to Chicago, hunt the guy down, and make him pay.

"No, it was getting dark and there weren't many people around. The few videos the police got from witnesses are blurry and they haven't been able to track the van. Honestly, I don't think the police are taking it that seriously. I talked to the detective in charge of the case right after Haley called to tell me what had happened, and he thought it was likely an opportunistic grab for a human trafficking ring." She sighed and put down her cup. "I think it has to do with me."

Janice frowned. "How could it have anything to do with you? It happened in Chicago."

The senator's hand trembled the tiniest bit. "The detective I spoke with told me Haley had mentioned that someone had approached her earlier that afternoon and asked if she was Senator Chapman's daughter, but it wasn't the same person Paige saw dragging Haley into the van, so he discounted that interaction. However, last week my husband Steve was attacked while he was running the Mount Vernon Trail in DC. Two masked men grabbed him and beat him up. He got away with a few bruises and a broken rib after some bystanders intervened. He reported it to the police, who wrote it up as a mugging, but the strange thing about it was that they didn't take his phone, credit cards, or his cash. They just wanted to hurt him."

My pulse kicked up a notch. "Do you think the two events are connected? Have you had any threats?"

"As a woman in politics, I get an inordinate number of threats," she said, drumming her thumb on the table. "In the last few weeks, however, the threats have ramped up and some of them have specifically named Haley and Steve. I suspect it's because I'm up for reelection and I'm considered a strong front-runner in

the Senate race. I'm also spearheading several contentious bills
that will likely fail if I'm not reelected. Even so, I wasn't convinced
Haley was truly in danger until yesterday, when I received this."
She held up her phone and showed me a picture of Haley standing behind the counter of a coffee shop. Someone had edited the
picture with a scrawl over Haley's face and the words "Drop out
or she drops dead."

Haley. Danger. My protective instincts flared, and my pulse
pounded in my ears so loud I could barely hear Janice's gasp of
horror.

"I received similar pictures of me and Steve in public places,
and I went straight to the Capitol Police. They are going to provide Steve and me with a protective detail and they suggested we
might want to get the US Marshals involved to protect Haley. The
Chicago police don't have the manpower for that kind of protection."

"Jesus." I was halfway out of my seat before I caught Janice's
stern look and forced myself back down.

"Haley doesn't know about all this yet," she said. "I'm flying
to Chicago tomorrow morning to try and convince her to come
back to DC with me where we can keep her safe, but—"

"She won't go." A statement. Not a question. Haley was too
much of a free spirit. There was no way she'd let anyone clip her
wings, especially if it involved living with her mother and stepfather.

A smile tugged at her lips. "You know her well, which is why
I came to see you. I'm ninety-nine percent sure she won't leave
Havencrest, but I don't think having a US Marshal following her
around is the best solution, especially at college. And you know
what Haley's like . . ."

Stubborn, willful, capable, independent, and yet at the same
time irreverent, funny, and caring. I knew all her qualities. I knew
she was fiercely loyal to her friends, trusting of people who often
didn't deserve it, and I shouldn't know that when she kissed, she
kissed with utter abandon. "It would be a challenge."

Senator Chapman nodded. "The Capitol Police suggested that it might be better to keep Haley's protection low-key. It would send a message that I'm not afraid of the people behind the threats, but she would be safe, and her day-to-day life wouldn't be interrupted."

"They might come for her again if she has no visible protection," I warned. "You could be putting her at risk."

"She's already at risk." Her shoulders slumped. "I never wanted this for her. I've already lost one child. I can't lose another. I need your help, Ace. I need you to protect her. I've come to ask you to be her bodyguard."

Haley. Bodyguard. My brain couldn't process the information. Haley was the only woman I had ever wanted and the one woman I couldn't have. She was my best friend's little sister, three years younger, and my friend, too, at least until she turned fifteen and my feelings changed into something that could have put a rift between me and Matt. I couldn't betray him that way. He was the only true friend I'd ever had. He'd saved me, shared his family with me, and he'd had my back more times than I could count. So, I did what I had to do, put a lid on those feelings, and some distance between Haley and me.

"She would never agree," I blurted out. Haley hated me and I didn't blame her. The night before Matt and I left home, when I thought I might never see her again, I'd given in to years of temptation and kissed her. Then I ghosted her for four long years. I didn't see her again until Matt's funeral. She didn't speak to me that day, and I didn't think she ever would. Not only had I kissed her and walked away, I'd broken my promise to bring Matt home safe.

"I'd like to help," I said. "But—"

"I got in touch with your boss, Tony, this morning," Senator Chapman continued. "He told me you were only two years into the job, but he considered you one of his best—professional, competent, and very good with difficult clients. Apparently, you've developed a stellar reputation in celebrity circles. He said you were taking some much-needed vacation so he offered me someone else." She folded her hands on the table. "I don't want someone else, Ace. I want you."

"I'm sorry. I can't do it. Haley and I—"

"You had some kind of falling-out," she said. "She didn't tell me the details, but I knew there had to be a reason we never saw you again after you left. And then at Matt's funeral you didn't speak to each other. But you were part of our family, Ace. You were a loyal friend to Matt, a joy to have around, an incredible support to all of us when Dave died, and you were always so protective of Haley. I can't think of anyone I would trust more with her life."

Fuck. Janice must have been cutting onions in the kitchen before Senator Chapman arrived, because the fumes were affecting my eyes.

"Tony said he's happy to put you back on duty if you agree, and of course we'll pay you well." Consummate politician that she was, she didn't mention the onions.

I shook my head. "I can recommend three or four good guys from the company. I've worked with them before and—"

"I want you," she said firmly. "I know you, and I know you care about Haley. You understand her in a way few people do. You're also young enough to blend in on campus. There is no one else." She reached across the table and squeezed my hand. "I know you and Dave were close. He always thought of you as the rock in our family. I need you to be that rock for us now. If not for me and Haley, for him."

In the short time I'd known Dave Chapman, he'd been more of a father to me than my own father had been in the thirteen years we'd been together. I'd loved Dave as a father and I'd grieved him. There was nothing I wouldn't have done for him, or for his family. I couldn't let them down.

And this was about Haley. The senator was right. There was no one more qualified to protect her than me.

CHAPTER 6

Haley

Good morning, Chicago. This is Hidden Tracks *on WJPK, coming to you from Havencrest University. I'm Haley Chapman, and . . . well, I'm here.*

You know those moments when the world suddenly feels a little crazy? When the rhythm of your life skips a beat, and you're left trying to find your footing? Yeah, it's been one of those weeks for me.

Today, we're exploring songs about unexpected moments, about the way life can change in an instant. Our playlist is for anyone who's ever felt vulnerable or exposed, anyone who's trying to make sense of a world that sometimes doesn't make any sense at all.

We'll start with a track that's about finding strength when you least expect it and holding on even when you feel like screaming. Remember—even in the darkest moments, music has the power to light the way. Here is Gang of Youths, with "Achilles Come Down."

Almost two weeks after the incident on Michigan Avenue, I was still shaken. Even my usual trick of burying my emotions in my mental black box wasn't enough to make the fear go away. I couldn't be alone. I had to have one of my housemates walk with me on the way to and from school and even then, I jumped every time a white van passed us on the street. I had hoped my weekly radio shows would be a catharsis, but music didn't do the trick.

"When are we going to talk about it?" Paige asked when I stumbled into the kitchen of the house we shared with four other students after another sleepless night. Unlike me, Paige always made a proper breakfast. I was a grab-and-go kind of person, basically eating anything portable I found in the fridge.

"There's nothing to talk about." I forced a laugh. "If you're referring to the kidnapping thing, I worked it all out during Thursday's show. It was actually very helpful when my listeners called in to share their experiences of being vulnerable. Those segments really create a sense of community and resilience."

"I'm not interested in the PR version of the 'kidnapping thing.'" She emphasized the last two words with air quotes. "I'm interested in the version where you share how you feel."

"I feel great."

"So great that you're missing class?" She lifted an eyebrow in censure. "It's ironic that you can use what you've learned in your psychology classes to help your friends, and yet you can't analyze yourself. Don't you get tired of holding it all inside? It was a terrifying experience. It's okay to cry or to be angry or to admit that you're scared, instead of pretending it never happened and telling us that you just want someone to talk to on the way to and from class. I was on the phone with my mom for two hours just getting it all out there and I felt so much better afterwards."

"That's because you were the hero of the story," I retorted. "I just stood there, frozen like an idiot, and did nothing to save myself. I was powerless. That's not something I want to think about, just like I don't think about how I couldn't save my dad, or how I couldn't make my mom stay home, or how I couldn't convince Matt not to join the military, or even how I couldn't tell Ace how I felt about him before he went away. Someday, I'd like to be the hero of my own story, but it's never going to happen."

I was saved from the uncomfortable conversation by a knock on the front door. Still groggy from lack of sleep, my hair a rat's nest of curls, and my emotions all over the place after my discussion with Paige, the last thing I needed was an unexpected visit from my mom and two middle-aged men in black suits.

"Mom? What are you doing here?" I instantly regretted not brushing my hair or changing out of my gym pants and tank before coming downstairs. As usual, she was impeccably dressed in a red jacket over a navy skirt and top, her blond hair perfectly coiffed and her makeup expertly applied.

"We need to talk." Mom gave me a quick hug. It had been so long since she'd hugged me, I automatically stiffened in her arms.

"Who are those guys?" I asked to cover my reaction.

"Security. They'll wait for us outside." She followed me into the house and paused in the hallway, looking around. She had never seen where I lived, and I was pretty sure she wouldn't approve of the '70s-era house Paige and I were sharing with four other students. Decorated with dark wood paneling, high-pile shag rugs, and furniture in shades of mustard and clotted cream, the house was in serious need of updating, but we'd added our own touches to make it a comfortable home.

"Oh, this is . . ." Mom looked around at the brightly colored paintings, patterned rugs, and assorted knickknacks that we'd purchased from garage sales and thrift stores to hide the worst of the wear and tear. ". . . cozy."

I gestured her into the living room, keeping my eye on the basement stairwell in case our downstairs housemates, Chad and Theo, decided to come up in their usual shorts-and-nothing-else morning attire. Paige joined us to say hello. Our roommate, Aditi, was out for a run, and Molly had moved in with her boyfriend the week prior, leaving Paige and me with the onerous task of finding someone to rent her room.

"Paige, darling. It's nice to see you." Mom gave Paige a quick kiss on the cheek. "How's your mom?"

"She's doing okay. She's still working at her accounting firm. She might get into a clinical trial, so fingers crossed." Paige forced a smile, but I knew she was worried that her mother wouldn't be accepted.

"Why do you have security?" I gestured to the window where the two men in black were talking to her assistant in front of a black SUV.

"Let's all sit." Mom took a seat on one of the worn armchairs and gestured to the couch, taking control of the room as if it were her house. "Paige, will you join us? I think Haley will need some support."

"I think the kidnapping attempt has to do with me," she said after Paige settled beside me.

Before I could respond, she told me about the threats she'd received, Steve being mugged, and the pictures of me at the coffee shop where I worked with Skye. "The Capitol Police are now involved, and they think that you're at risk," she continued. "I would really like you to come back to DC and stay with Steve and me, where we know you'll be safe. You can return to Havencrest next year, or you could even transfer to a local university. I'm sure I could pull some strings at Georgetown or Howard."

"Next year?" I drew in a deep, calming breath and tried to let the good energy flow through my veins. Aditi was into holistic medicine and was always giving us tips on how to lead a better, calmer life. "I have classes, Mom. I have friends. I have my radio show, and I have gigs lined up for the rest of the term."

Her lips thinned as they always did when I mentioned my music. "Darling, singing is not a serious career option. I thought you'd come to understand that when you started at Havencrest. I was disappointed to find out you were busking on street corners—not just because of the risk, but also because that time and energy should be going into your studies and not some pipe dream—"

"Singing is not a pipe dream," I retorted. "It's what I want to do with my life. College is my fallback in case it doesn't work out. I'm not cut out for office work. I'd go crazy if I had to spend all day sitting behind a desk."

Mom had been disappointed that I hadn't even tried to get into an Ivy League university, but I'd been so messed up after Matt's death the summer before senior year that it was a miracle I'd filled out any applications. If not for Paige begging me to go with her and insisting on filling in the forms together, I would still be in Riverstone. Havencrest had been our top choice, and the day we were both accepted had been the only bright light in an otherwise dismal year.

"I'm not leaving."

"It's for your own safety," Mom said. "I don't want anything to happen to you."

"Then you shouldn't have put me at risk," I shot back, still reeling from the revelation that the incident had something to do with her.

"I didn't think you'd be at risk out here in Chicago," she said. "But now that you are, I can offer you two security options. First, we can arrange twenty-four/seven protection through the US Marshal Service . . ."

I stared at her in horror. "I don't want some old dude following me around college. It would be creepy." I didn't realize my leg was bouncing—something that only happened when I was stressed—until Paige put a calming hand on my knee.

"The second option is private security," she continued. "I suspected you wouldn't want a US Marshal so I've already found a bodyguard for you. He's ex-military and works with one of the top security companies in the country protecting movie stars and famous singers. He's young enough to fit in at college, and he comes very highly recommended."

"Where would he sleep? At the foot of my bed?" I couldn't keep the sarcasm from my voice.

"We do have an extra room," Paige reminded me. "Molly's coming today to take the rest of her stuff to move in with Jace."

"Paige!" I glared at my bestie, who was supposed to be supporting my refusal to go along with Mom's plan.

"I don't want anyone to hurt you," she said gently. "I also don't want you to leave. This way we won't have to interview for a new roommate. It's not like it's going to be forever."

"Definitely not," Mom said. "The Capitol Police are working with the police here in Chicago to track these people down. I would expect they'll find them in a matter of weeks, and at most after the Senate election, which is what I suspect this is about."

"Why don't you meet him?" Paige suggested. "If not for yourself, for your bestie who hasn't met a decent guy in a very long time and is in the market for someone with mad protection skills."

Paige always knew what to say to bring me around. "Fine," I muttered. "I'll meet him. But I'm not making any promises."

CHAPTER 7

Haley

NINE YEARS AGO

Dad wanted Ace to have a camping experience, so he invited him to come with us on our first camping trip of the season. Matt was thrilled to have someone to hang out with that wasn't his irritating little sister, and I was happy to have Ace around. He was kind and thoughtful and he also seemed to show up when I was about to get myself into trouble. He'd been in Riverstone for less than a year and had already become a fixture in our house, and frankly it would have seemed odd if he hadn't come with us.

Camping was Dad's favorite recreational activity. Every winter he spent hours poring over maps and review sites to pick the best campsites for the summer. Big Meadows Campground near Shenandoah National Park was one of his favorites. Located in a remote forest with three waterfalls nearby and plenty of hikes, wildlife, and mountain vistas, it was the perfect place to pitch a tent.

Ace was the first one out of the car when we reached our campsite tucked away in the middle of the forest. Usually, Matt and I would wander around checking things out while Mom and Dad unloaded the supplies, but Ace had the hatch open before my feet even hit the ground.

"Bruh, you're making us look bad." Matt sometimes got irritated with Ace's enthusiasm for helping out, because it meant he couldn't slack off like he'd started doing when he turned fourteen.

"He wants to get this party started," I said, sticking up for Ace.

Although he'd tried to hide it, Ace was more excited than I'd ever seen him, and I didn't want Matt to ruin his experience.

Ace caught my gaze and thanked me with a smile and a nod of his head.

"Haley, you can help Ace pitch his tent," Dad called out. "Matt and I will take care of the others so we can get this vacation party started."

"Prepare yourself." I looked over at Ace and grinned. "You're about to experience 'vacation Dad.'" I grabbed our spare tent and took it to one of the clearings. "Where did you go on vacation when you were younger?"

"My parents didn't do vacations," he said quietly. "They didn't like to leave the city unless we were moving somewhere new."

"My parents don't like to leave Virginia." It was the first time I realized that we'd never vacationed anywhere else. Paige and her mother were always going on trips to Mexico, Florida, Costa Rica, and California. They'd even gone to Quebec City for the winter carnival, and once they'd gone to London to visit Paige's grandmother.

"If I could camp here all the time, I wouldn't leave either." He helped me lay the ground sheet and I showed him how to peg it down.

"Don't you want to travel and see the world?" I was desperate to get on an airplane and visit other countries. I wanted to experience new cultures, new foods, beautiful buildings, and different people. "I saw a show about Florence and that's the first place I'm going to visit when I grow up. It looks so pretty."

"I want to fly." He glanced quickly over at Matt like he was embarrassed by his admission. "I don't care where I go."

"Fly like a bird?" I teased, trying to lighten his mood. "Or in an airplane?"

"I want to fly airplanes and helicopters." He looked up at the sky, barely visible under the canopy of trees. "I'm thinking of joining the air force when I graduate . . ."

Something told me to tread carefully, that this was a dream

Ace had never shared. "I think that would be very cool. You could see the whole world from up in the sky."

"I'd be free."

Dad had told Matt and me that Ace's parents had often left him alone in their apartment when he was a kid, sometimes for days at a time, and that was why he was quiet, and that we shouldn't think he didn't want to be involved. I didn't know what Dad meant because Ace always talked around us, but in that moment, I got a glimpse into the pain he'd been hiding.

"Think how fast you could go," I said, hoping to pull him out of the memory that had made his forehead crease and his shoulders slump. "Maybe you could fly one of those planes that breaks the sound barrier."

Ace shook off whatever had pulled him into the darkness and smiled. "You'd like that, wouldn't you, bug?"

Ace had never called me by my nickname before, but I liked it. He was like family and that was my family name.

"I love going fast. I can hardly wait to be able to drive." Ever since I'd been little, I'd loved speed, the roar of the car engine when it accelerated, the invisible force pushing me back in my seat, the world racing by so fast it took my breath away. My favorite part of our road trips was when Dad had to pass another vehicle on the road, and I would yell, "Hit the gas!"

"I'd be afraid to be in a car with you driving." He helped me unfold the tent and we laid it on the ground.

"No, you wouldn't." I smiled at him. "You're not afraid of anything, and you like to go fast, too."

Early the next morning, I left the campsite to go for a walk to one of the mountain vistas where I could see the entire Shenandoah Valley. We'd hiked the short trail many times before, and I was confident I could do it alone. I picked a handful of wildflowers along the way for my mom and found a few smooth stones in the creek under a small bridge for Matt to skip in the lake. By the time I reached the lookout, the sun was almost up, and the last streaks of the pink-and-orange dawn were fading away.

I drew in a few deep breaths of mountain air, fragrant with pine, and took in the valley spread out below me. I loved being up high and would happily hike to any mountain peak for the feeling of being at the top of the world.

"This is amazing."

I startled when Ace came up behind me. I hadn't even heard his footsteps.

"Just wait until you see the waterfalls and the view from the top of Blackrock. Dad said we're going to do that hike today."

"Did you tell your parents you were coming up here?" His tone was more inquisitive than admonishing, and I appreciated that he wasn't judging me.

"I thought I'd be able to get back before they woke up. We've done this walk lots of times. It's not like I could get lost." I looked over at him, hands stuffed in the pockets of his jeans, T-shirt uncharacteristically untucked, hair mussed like he'd just rolled out of bed. "How did you know about the trail?"

"I followed you." He shrugged. "I figured you'd be up early and find something interesting to do."

"It gets crowded up here during the day," I said. "But if you get here early enough you can have it all to yourself."

We watched the colors change from pinks and golds until the sun was fully up. It was one of the few times I didn't mind the silence, because Ace was talking without using any words.

"We should get back," he said finally. "Your parents will be worried."

"Not if you're with me." I knew he hadn't followed me because he was looking for something to do. He'd come to keep an eye on me, and it didn't bother me the way it did with Matt. My brother would have shouted at me and dragged me back to camp. But Ace had stayed to enjoy the view. "Thanks for coming."

"Thanks for showing this to me."

I heard a rustle in the bush, followed by the crack of sticks and a huff so loud I knew it wasn't human. Two eyes blinked in the shadows and then a black bear walked out of the bushes and onto the path leading back to camp.

Ace's arm slammed across my chest, and I sucked in a sharp breath. I didn't feel so grown-up anymore. I wasn't supposed to leave the campsite alone. There was no way off the lookout except through the thick forest or down the path, and if the bear charged at us, the only escape was over the cliff.

"I'll run over there and try to get him to chase me." Ace pointed to the side of the lookout. "You get to the path and go back to the campsite."

"You can't run from a bear," I said. "We have to make noise and wave our arms to scare him away." Mom and Dad had drilled us on how to handle a bear, although we were never supposed to go hiking without bells and bear spray.

"Go away," Ace shouted at the bear.

"No. Like this." I dropped the flowers I'd picked for Mom, jumped up and down, and waved my arms. "HEY BEAR!! GO AWAY BEAR!! GET OUT OF HERE!! BEAR!!"

Unimpressed by my efforts, the bear just stared.

"You try," I said to Ace. "You're bigger and louder than me."

"AHHHHHHHHHHHHHHH BEAR!!!!!!" Ace yelled, waving his arms. I clapped my hands and joined in. Still the bear didn't move.

"Do you have anything to throw?" Ace asked.

"I have some stones in my pocket. I picked them from the creek for Matt." I handed him a few stones. "Don't hurt him. We're just trying to scare him."

We shouted some more and threw our stones until Ace hit the bear's nose. The bear growled and shook his head. For a moment I thought he was going to charge us, but he turned and lumbered away into the forest.

"Let's go." Ace grabbed my hand and half ran, half dragged me down the path until we reached the meadow, and I realized I'd left my flowers behind.

"Wait." I pulled to a stop. "I need flowers."

"We need to get back to the campsite." Ace put his hand in his pocket. "I only have one stone left."

"He didn't follow us. We're safe now."

Ace offered me the stone. "At least you've got one left to give to Matt."

"I think you should keep it." I folded his hand around it. "That's a lucky stone. You never know when you might need it."

CHAPTER 8

Haley

Stellar Security's Chicago branch was on the twelfth floor of a tall high-rise in the Loop. Everything about the office screamed professionalism and efficiency, from the sleek black uniforms of the staff to the display cases filled with high-tech surveillance equipment lining the walls. Decorated in varying shades of gray and steel, it was a stark contrast to the bustling city streets below.

"Senator Chapman." A tall man in a dark suit shook my mother's hand. "I'm Tony Davis. We spoke on the phone." Tony was the founder and head of Stellar's US operations. He introduced us to Jordan, who ran the Chicago office, and Maverick, one of their security personnel, before leading us down a long hallway with closed gray doors. Jordan was middle-aged and heavily muscled, his neck so thick he had to fully turn anytime my mom asked a question. Maverick, by contrast, was tall and lean with slightly mussed golden-brown hair and a cocky attitude that showed itself when he winked as he shook my hand. He didn't look older than thirty, and I hoped he wasn't the bodyguard they'd chosen for me, because he reminded me of a guy from high school who had taken me outside during the spring dance on the pretense of looking at the stars, only to make it clear when he got me alone that he was looking for something else.

Thankfully, Tony sent Maverick away to find the bodyguard they'd assigned to me, and I wandered over to the window to look at the view while everyone else took a seat at the boardroom table.

"Darling, could you pour me a cup of tea?" Mom said. "I've been up since 4:00 A.M. and my caffeine buzz is wearing off."

I made the tea at the small snack bar in the corner and turned just as someone walked into the room.

"Ace," I whispered, my voice barely more than a breath as I stared at him in disbelief. A maelstrom of emotions swept through me at the sight of my brother's best friend, my childhood crush, and the man who had broken my fragile teenage heart and then added insult to injury by serving up a heaping dose of humiliation by kissing me and then ghosting me for four years. My hands shook uncontrollably, the cup clattering against the saucer as hot liquid spilled down the front of my shirt.

"Damnit." I plucked at the sodden material, my cheeks burning and not from the heat.

Ace handed me a stack of napkins. "Are you okay?"

God. That voice. That face. I didn't know it would have been possible for Ace to become even more gorgeous, but he'd matured since I'd seen him at the funeral. He'd been lean before, but now his Stellar Security T-shirt nestled snugly against his thick, muscular chest. My eyes trailed down his trim torso to the jeans hugging his narrow hips, and then back to a jaw that seemed more chiseled than before, dark eyes that softened as I stared. Our hands touched when I took the napkins and I could almost feel the electric current between us, the connection that we'd never fully acknowledged, igniting a spark that had been dormant for years.

I was already struggling to keep myself in check, but this was too much. Too difficult to process. A tidal wave of emotion crashed over me, stealing my breath away, and all I could do was run.

"Restroom is on the left, three doors down," Tony called after me. "I'll send someone with a T-shirt for you."

I made it to the restroom and locked the door. *Breathe. Breathe. You're fine. Lock it away.* Hands trembling, I pulled out my phone and texted Paige, realizing belatedly that she was in a lab all morning and couldn't check her messages.

After a few more breaths with my head between my legs, I

could think clearly again. *Get it together, Haley.* At least I had the excuse of almost burning myself with the tea for the hasty exit. I pushed myself up and turned on the tap, splashing water on my face and dabbing at my shirt with a wet paper towel.

"Haley?"

I knew his voice, even muffled by the thick metal door. My chest tightened as another wave of emotion surged again, but I pushed it back down. I was over him. He was nothing to me but a childhood acquaintance who happened to be my brother's best friend, and who had made it clear he wanted nothing to do with me. And since I wanted nothing to do with him, there was no reason why I couldn't act like a normal person instead of a bumbling idiot. I was older now. More mature. I was officially an adult, and I needed to act like one. Swallowing hard, I opened the door.

"I'm sorry for surprising you like that," he said, holding out a blue T-shirt with a white *Stellar Security* label on the front. "I thought your mother told you she'd hired me."

"If she had, I wouldn't have come."

I'd been played. Ace already knew about the assignment, which meant my mother had set the wheels in motion before she'd come to see me. That was the downside of having a mother in politics. She was an expert at manipulation—starting with the obviously unacceptable option of suggesting I move to DC, then the offer of a US Marshal, until the only palatable option was the private bodyguard that she'd already hired. Had Paige been in on it, too? Likely not. Paige was as loyal as they came.

"I told her you wouldn't want me, but she insisted." He shrugged. "You know what she's like. It's hard to say no to her."

I didn't want the reminder that he'd been a part of our family since I was ten years old, or that he'd always had a good relationship with my mom—a relationship I didn't understand. "I'm sorry you had to come all this way for nothing," I said stiffly.

"It's not a problem." His eyes softened, and he tipped his head to the side in a gesture so familiar it made my heart ache. "It was good to see you again. I think they'll assign Maverick to you. He's got more experience than me. You'll be in good hands."

"Maverick reminds me of Blake Forester," I blurted out. I'd had a crush on Blake in freshman year and I'd been thrilled when he came over to talk to me at the high school dance. I honestly thought he shared my interest in stargazing when he asked me to show him the constellations. I wasn't ready for what happened next. But Ace was. He appeared out of nowhere and beat Blake so badly the dude missed three weeks of football practice. I thought Ace would go to jail, but Blake told everyone he'd been mugged. He had a reputation to protect. Even then, people knew better than to mess with Ace.

Ace understood right away. "I'll tell Tony to find someone else."

"How did she find you?" I asked him. "Paige heard through some of our old high school friends that you'd moved to LA."

"I was in Riverstone on vacation. She was in town for some political fundraiser, and Janice mentioned I was there taking a break from security work. Your mom thought it would be easier for you to be with someone who knows you."

Lost in a maelstrom of emotions and memories, I knew I should end the conversation, but part of me didn't want him to leave. "What exactly do you know about me? You hardly paid any attention to me after I started high school, and we haven't spoken in four years."

If my words hurt, he hid it well. "I know that you didn't do mornings but could stay up all night," he said, his voice soft. "I know that you couldn't remember dates or deadlines but somehow you always managed to get your work done on time, that you studied with three screens and one was always streaming a show you'd seen ten times before, that you worked out your feelings through music, that you had a junk food addiction and you loved speed and taking risks that alarmed everyone who loved you. I know that you're the kind of person who would give your sandwich to a stranger, and skip school to be there for a friend who needed you."

It shook me, the things he remembered, the details he knew about my life. Granted, he used to come to our house most days after school and on weekends, and I always studied downstairs at the kitchen table where there were people to talk to and multiple distractions. I'd given my sandwich to him the first time we met, and he was the one who had found me at the hospital with Paige the day her mother collapsed at work and was taken to the hospital in an ambulance.

"I'm also the person you can't stand to be around or should I have read something else into the night you kissed me and then walked away?" It felt good to get those words off my chest. I'd wanted to say them at Matt's funeral, but I was too wrapped up in grief to talk to anyone, especially Ace, who I wanted to talk to the most but couldn't after how he'd hurt me.

"That was a mistake. I don't know what I was thinking. I should never have—"

"I hate you for that."

"I know." Our gazes met, locked. There was too much history there. Too many emotions. I took the shirt from his hand and closed the door.

After changing my clothes, I returned to the boardroom. Someone had cleaned up my mess and made a fresh pot of tea. I offered my apologies as I took a seat beside my mom. Only then did I realize Ace hadn't returned.

"Ace told us you'd prefer someone else," Mom said. "I really wish you would reconsider. He cut his vacation short to help us out."

Ace on vacation. I couldn't even picture it. I'd never seen him chill out and relax except when he and Matt were hanging out together, gaming or playing ball in the driveway. Even when he came camping with us, he was always busy collecting wood for the fire, helping Dad put up the tarps, or chopping vegetables with

Mom for Dad's gourmet camping dinner. "I think it would be better with someone I don't know."

"Ace had some suggestions for people who might be suitable," Tony said. "Unfortunately, they're all on assignment. I think our best bet would be Maverick. Everyone else who is available is at least ten to fifteen years older, and that won't work for an undercover boyfriend."

"Undercover what?" I looked from Mom to Tony and back to Mom. "Did you say boyfriend?"

"We have to keep this low-key," Mom said. "My PR team is concerned it could hurt my chances of reelection if the public knows I'm being threatened, and it gives power to the people behind this. It's not unusual for senators to have security, but if you have a bodyguard, it will raise questions. Tony said some of his bodyguards will play the role of a boyfriend or girlfriend when the clients don't want to draw attention. I thought it was a good idea since you don't have anyone . . ." She hesitated. "Or do you?"

"No, and I'm not interested in having a real-life boyfriend, much less a fake one."

Mom's jaw tightened, and I knew right away I was in trouble. "I'm not leaving until you have some kind of security. If this doesn't work for you, then I'll have to insist that you come to DC."

I'd run out of excuses. Maverick wasn't Blake. It made no sense to turn him down, too. "I'll go with Maverick but I'm not doing the fake boyfriend thing." I sighed. "When would he start?"

"He'll need a day or two to prep," Tony said. "He'll have to do some recon of the college and the neighborhood and the places you frequent the most. We'll have security outside your house until he starts, so you won't be unprotected. Jordan and I will deal with the paperwork. I'll send Maverick in so you can get to know each other."

Maverick joined Mom and me in the conference room after Tony and Jordan had left. While he poured a glass of water, I made a mental list of all the reasons he wasn't Blake—taller by two inches, hair a lighter shade of blond, wider body, thicker neck, Southern drawl, looked like he'd just walked off a military base and wanted to rip someone in two.

"Tell me a bit about yourself," I said after he settled in the chair across from me. It was the first question I asked all our prospective roommates, and a trick I'd learned from my psychology classes. You could learn more about people by just letting them talk rather than asking them pointed questions.

"Twenty-eight years old. Six feet two inches tall. Two hundred and twenty pounds of grade A muscle." With a grin, he flexed his arm and made his bicep pop beneath the sleeve of his T-shirt. "I played high school football and won a state championship in powerlifting. I've trained in four different martial arts and freestyle wrestle in my spare time. I keep my body pristine with no drugs, alcohol, sugar, additives, dairy, gluten, animal products, or processed foods. Go raw or go home." He pumped a fist in the air. Mom and I shared a quick side-eye, and I caught her lips quivering at the corners. We were definitely on the same wavelength.

"I'm also ex-military." Maverick turned his arm to show off his sleeve of tattoos. "Four years in the navy until I decided it wasn't for me, and came to work for Tony. I'm experienced in street fighting but I try to defuse situations before they arise, so I've only really hurt about thirty people since joining Stellar. I've worked with broken bones, acid burns, concussions, and even a few stab wounds—nothing will keep me off the job. I've used crutches and boiling water as weapons and once I knocked someone out with my cast."

"Very impressive," Mom said, filling in the silence while I tried to get my mouth to close. For the first time in my life, I was glad she was in politics and knew what to say in every situation. "I feel very reassured."

"We should go over the rules," he said. "As long as you do what I say, everything should go smoothly."

Do what I say. The words chafed like a polyester shirt.

"Is it really necessary for you to be with me all the time?" I asked. "I highly doubt someone is going to break into my house in the middle of the night and snatch me away."

"They'd probably step it up," Maverick said. "Maybe try to stab you or slit your throat while you're sleeping, put a bullet through your skull, or even kidnap you in a more public place where there's so much going on people won't even notice."

I could feel the blood drain from my face. Even Mom looked alarmed.

"Well, that's very graphic," she said. "And I'm sure none of that will come to pass with you there, Maverick."

"Definitely not." He slammed his fist into his palm, making both Mom and me jump. "I'll bring a full complement of weapons to keep you safe. One creak and you'll be mopping the bastard's blood off the floor for days."

I couldn't tell if he was laying it on thick on purpose, or it was just him, but I still couldn't get the image of Blake out of my head. And where was Ace? Was he done with us? I'd said no and now I'd never see him again?

"Will Maverick be a good fit for you, darling?" Mom asked. "My flight leaves in a few hours and I'd like to get everything settled before I go."

"Yes." I nodded. "I'm sure we'll get along." *Eventually. Probably. Hopefully. Never.*

Maverick kept me company in the lobby while Mom and Tony finalized the paperwork. I kept looking for Ace, but it made sense that he hadn't come to say goodbye. He'd flown all the way to Chicago for me, and I'd turned him down for a man who reminded me of the worst Riverstone had to offer.

"Have you worked with Ace before?" I idly flipped through a brochure hoping to see Ace in the promotional pictures of Stellar Security bodyguards accompanying famous musicians and actors, many of whom I recognized.

"Once or twice," he said. "He prefers solo gigs with female celebrities and doesn't socialize much with the team."

Mom returned with Tony, and after we'd said goodbye,

Maverick escorted us downstairs. He made a show of checking the sidewalk and street before we exited the building, and then again when we neared Mom's car. I could feel the invisible rope that connected me to Ace slowly tighten the farther we walked away.

"Tony said he's never lost a client," Mom said, misunderstanding when she caught me looking over my shoulder.

"Death is a pretty low bar."

"You just seem very worried, but this is one of the best private security companies in the country. I had my people check them out. You're in good hands, and Maverick seems like a nice young man. Very enthusiastic about his job."

My chest ached and my eyes began to water as we climbed into the car. It made no sense. I couldn't forgive Ace for what he'd done, so why was I so desperate to see him again?

"I almost forgot." Maverick leaned into the car and handed me a smooth black stone. "Ace asked me to give this to you. He said it might come in useful."

I rubbed my thumb over the cool, shiny surface and the cord in my chest tightened so hard it made my heart ache. I couldn't believe he'd kept it all these years.

That's a lucky stone. You never know when you might need it.

"Mom . . . ?"

"Yes, darling."

"I've changed my mind."

CHAPTER 9

Ace

I don't know what I expected when I arrived at Haley's house on Sunday morning, but it wasn't her coming down the stairs in a cropped tank top and barely there shorts and screaming "Fuck!" before running back up.

"I'm not sure what you were thinking showing up so early. Haley doesn't do mornings, especially on the weekend," Paige said, watching her race away. "I knew we were in for trouble when I woke her. You're lucky I was up early to call my mom."

I took a step back, keeping a safe distance between us. I didn't know where I stood with Paige yet, and I didn't want to take any chances. "I wanted to go through the house and assess the security system before we had to leave for her class. Your front door isn't secure. Someone could easily kick it in."

"Someone already kicked it in." Paige gestured to the cracked doorframe. "End-of-the-year party. Haley invited everyone she knew, and over one hundred people showed up. You can check out all our police citations on the fridge. We've been making a collection."

"No more parties," I said firmly. "At least not until this threat is resolved."

"Then you can be the bearer of bad news." She lifted her chin in the direction of the stairs. "Our old roommate Molly cleared out the last of her stuff yesterday. Your room is the third door on the right. Haley is the second door, and the bathroom is at the top of the stairs. Aditi and I are on the left. You'll meet her at the time normal people get up."

"I'll take my bag upstairs and get started checking out the house."

Paige folded her arms and leaned against the banister. "By the way, just in case you got the wrong impression from our conversation, I'll never forgive you for hurting Haley. I don't know why she decided to let you back into her life, but I'm telling you right now that if you hurt her again, not even an army of Stellar Security bodyguards will be able to stop me from hunting you down and beating your ass."

"Noted." I'd learned early on not to underestimate Paige. She looked sweet and innocent with her long, braided hair and gentle smile, but her sharp eyes missed nothing, and when it came to Haley, she was fiercely protective. Matt never teased Haley when Paige was around. Either he'd get a vicious tongue-lashing, or he'd be plagued by mysterious misfortunes—his bike would get a flat tire, his shoes would go missing, and once he found ants in his bed.

I dropped my bag in the spare room and took a moment to check out my surroundings. Bed, dresser, desk, worn corkboard, a few odds and ends left behind by the previous roommate. I'd gone straight into the air force after high school, so I'd never had the college experience. With all the catching up I had to do, school had always been a struggle, but the air force offered exactly what I was looking for—structure, discipline and purpose. After spending my childhood alone, I wanted to be part of something. I wanted to feel needed. The air force had given that to me and more. If not for Matt's accident, and the PTSD that came with standing on the tarmac helplessly watching his plane crash, I would have continued on active duty until I couldn't fly anymore.

I checked the window, noting the rotting wood around the frame and the broken lock. A quick walk around the house revealed more of the same, including doors without dead bolts and a sub-roof that could give an intruder easy access to the upstairs floor—to Haley.

Every muscle in my body tensed, rage surging inside me.

When I thought about what had happened to her, how close the kidnappers had come to taking her away, about what could have happened if Paige hadn't been there . . . High school boys who wanted to show her the stars were no longer her biggest danger.

After completing my sweep of the house, I found Haley and a dude in a leather jacket at the kitchen table. His long hair was tied up in a ponytail and he had a collection of beaded bracelets around his wrist.

"This is my friend Sam," Haley said as if we'd had a proper greeting at the door instead of a shrieked swear word followed by her racing up the stairs. "He's in the music program and he sometimes helps me find songs for my show."

"Friend with benefits." Sam put his arm around Haley's shoulders while he stared at me. I recognized the gesture for what it was—not a show of affection but staking his claim. "I take it you're the bodyguard."

I didn't like Sam. I didn't like the fact that he shared an interest in music with Haley. I didn't like his leather jacket or his long hair or his bracelets or the fact that he was touching Haley in a way that made her smile. I particularly didn't like the fact that he'd slept with her, but several of those problems were easily addressed.

"Ace." I held out a hand at an angle that meant he had to release Haley to shake. I squeezed maybe a little too hard and made his face pale. "Unfortunately, until Haley's safety is assured, we can't have any guests in the house."

"He's here so often, we've been thinking of charging him rent," Haley said. "We can make an exception for him."

I folded my arms across my chest. "No exceptions."

"Except Sam," she said.

"Not Sam."

"I'll let you guys work that one out. 'Not Sam' has to get to a band rehearsal." Sam leaned over to kiss Haley on the lips and then looked over his shoulder at me with a smirk. "My money is on Haley in an argument, so I'll probably see you soon."

I pulled out a chair and joined Haley at the table. "I meant it about guests. We need to keep the circle of people who know about me small. It's better for everyone if this is handled discreetly."

"Better for my mother, you mean." She raised an eyebrow. "I personally think it would be better if you wore a shirt that read 'Haley's Bodyguard. Touch her and die.' You'd be an effective deterrent. Not that I seriously think I'm in danger anymore. Nothing has happened since the incident on the street, and there's no real link between that and the threats Mom received. We learned in one of my psych classes that most people who make threats don't act on them. The biggest danger is the people you don't see coming."

Typical Haley. Burying the pain away. "All the more reason for me to stay invisible."

"Funny," she said, unsmiling. "When did you become such a funny guy?"

"I'm a serious guy, and you need to take this seriously. You can't pretend it's not happening like you always do."

Her jaw tightened. "How would you know what I always do? You completely ghosted me, as if the friendship we had when we were younger meant nothing, as if we were two strangers meeting at a party and then going their separate ways. You made it clear you wanted nothing to do with me when I started high school and even more clear when you left. It changed me, Ace. I'm not the girl I was when you left."

Guilt speared through me the way it had back at the office when she'd mentioned how I'd disappeared from her life. Not only had I encouraged Matt to join the air force with me, making me partially responsible for his death, I'd also abandoned her emotionally when she needed me the most. I had a chance now to be physically present for her in ways I wasn't before, and maybe even make up for any emotional harm I'd caused—if she'd let me.

"I know you've changed. We both have." She hadn't been a girl since the summer she turned fifteen and walked into the backyard in a tiny bikini, sporting curves I didn't know she had.

I shifted in my seat, trying to think of what else to say. I had an introductory speech I gave all my clients, but I couldn't remember the words. It was awkward, the distance between us. Things had always been easy with Haley. She talked. I listened. We had adventures together. Sometimes we shared our feelings. She was never uncomfortable with my silence, and I was never irritated by her need to chatter.

"Do you have any other boyfriends I should know about?" I asked, trying to steer the conversation away from painful topics.

"I don't really do boyfriends," Haley said. "Sam and I probably meet up once or twice a month, have sex, and then he leaves. Is it really going to be an issue?"

My stomach tightened and I reminded myself that I was over Haley. I'd put all those feelings behind me long ago. So why did I keep having a visceral reaction every time the idea of her with other guys came up?

"If it's important to you, we can make it work." I had to force the words out. "But it would be better to keep visitors to a minimum. Can he not handle a few weeks without . . . benefits?"

A slow smile creased her face. "You mean sex? Can Sam not go a few weeks without sex? Maybe he can, but I can't."

"Dammit, Haley," I spluttered. "I'm just trying to keep you safe."

"And I'm trying to live my life," she said. "This whole bodyguard thing is OTT and I only agreed to it because it's the first time since my dad died that my mom has acted like a mom. I'll bet the kidnapping attempt was just a one-off, the threats will turn out to be nothing, and you'll be free of me and back to protecting all your famous actresses and singers in no time."

"Until then I'll do my best to keep you safe." Haley had changed in some ways—she was a woman now and not a girl, and she'd lost her wild edge, but her need to talk through her concerns out loud was still the same.

"Are you going to pretend to be a student or stand conspicuously at the back of the class?" she asked.

"It depends on the classroom setup." I fiddled with the worn strap of the watch Haley's father had given me for my first birthday in Riverstone. He'd been like a father to me, encouraging my interest in mechanics by letting me help him fix things around the house, and even finding me a job with his friend at the local auto body shop when he noticed my interest in engines. "I met with campus security yesterday, and they took me to your classrooms, the radio station, and the coffee shop where you work. For the most part, I'll be able to watch you discreetly."

It definitely wouldn't be a hardship. Not a day had gone by that I didn't think about Haley. I had tons of pictures of Haley and her family on my phone—camping trips, holidays, barbecues, and one of Haley and her dad before he died. They'd kept me going during my darkest days. I'd never met anyone like Haley. From the day I first walked in the door to find her singing and dancing around the kitchen, to the family dinners where she entertained everyone with her nonstop stories, and the camping trips where her innate curiosity always got her into trouble, she had been a light in my life. I'd been utterly drawn to her and for some reason she liked spending time with me.

"I like that you're quiet. You make all the noise go away."

I could see the memory, right there between us, hear the music from the carnival rides the day I'd taken her to the summer fair. I'd known she was going to sneak into town the minute her parents said no, and I made sure I was outside her house first thing in the morning. Haley couldn't resist a fair. I told myself I was there to look after her, but really, I wanted to share her joy.

I pulled out a silver necklace with a flower pendant and held it in the air. "I have a peace offering."

Haley stared at me in stunned silence. "You bought me a necklace?"

"Stellar Security bought the necklace. The pendant has a GPS tracker and a locator button hidden on the back. If you push it twice, it will text me and the team to let us know you need help. The text message sends a link to your exact GPS location and the tracker will let us follow you even if you don't have your phone. You have to promise to wear it anytime we leave the house."

"It's so pretty," she said softly. "It's a violet, isn't it?"

I'd chosen the violet because it was her favorite flower back home. She used to collect them from the dry shale banks around the nearby pond in spring. "I'm not really a flower person."

She looked at me and smiled. "I think you are. Can you put it on me?"

I walked around the table and swept her hair to the side, letting the silken strands slide through my fingers. Her breath caught and for a few blissful seconds I touched the smooth, warm skin of her neck, breathed in her fragrance of wildflowers and something sweet.

I heard the thud of feet and the low murmur of voices just after I fastened the clasp. A few moments later we were no longer alone.

"Everyone wanted to meet our new roomie," Paige said, shooting daggers at me with her eyes until I'd moved a respectable distance away from Haley. "This is Aditi." She gestured to a slender girl with waist-length black hair who promptly struck a pose by the doorframe. "And these two idiots who live in gym pants and spend most of their time gaming are Chad and Theo."

Chad was an inch or two shorter than me, blond and blue-eyed with a square jaw and the lean, toned body of an athlete. He introduced himself as a journalism major who played soccer for the Havencrest Warriors and ran the sports programming at the campus radio station.

Theo, a short lanky dude with glasses, grabbed the doorframe and tried to pull himself up with one arm for no clear purpose other than to demonstrate his insecurity. "I could have handled security if anyone had asked me," he wheezed. "I could wire this place with cameras and sensors that would go off if anyone even sneezed. I also know a guy on the dark web who could set us up with some serious firepower."

"Are you kidding me?" Paige snorted a laugh. "The only weapons you've ever handled are virtual."

Theo jumped down and grabbed his crotch. "I handle this weapon every day and there's nothing virtual about it."

"There are so many things I want to say," Paige responded, "but we have a guest. I'll verbally eviscerate you later so you can cry in private."

"I'm heading to the gym," Chad said. "You coming, Theo? Maybe do shoulders and arms today?"

Theo nodded and flexed a thin arm. "Let's go lift some weights. Sweat it out."

"Any questions?" I asked the group. "I'll be installing a security system. It's been okayed with your landlord. I'll have to show you all how to use it when I'm done. Other than that, I'll try to stay out of your way. If you see anyone suspicious hanging around, let me know. We'd like to keep my presence quiet, so don't tell anyone outside the house why I'm here."

"This is going to be a trip," Haley said. "Me showing up at Havencrest with a bodyguard. Maybe people will think I've finally made it big as a singer and they'll flock around me begging for my autograph."

"They'd better not," I warned. "Because I won't let anyone near you."

Her eyes widened slightly, a flicker of warmth passing through them, and I could swear the corners of her mouth twitched with the start of a smile before she caught herself. Maybe I'd imagined the softening in her expression, the subtle shift that betrayed a mix of surprise and something deeper, more complex.

Quickly composing herself, Haley raised an eyebrow. "That's the job."

"That's the job," I repeated, but it wasn't just the job. It was something else entirely. I could redeem myself for the sins of my past, not only by protecting her but also by finding a way to make up for the harm I'd caused. It was a second chance. For both of us.

CHAPTER 10

Haley

I walked into the kitchen Monday morning to see Aditi, Paige, and Molly sitting in a row on one side of the kitchen table, staring out the window. Aside from the fact that Molly had moved out a few days prior, and Aditi was usually out and about by 10:00 A.M., the entire scene was odd because there was nothing on the other side of our window except the garage of the house next door.

"What's going on?"

"Shhh." Molly put a finger to her lips. "Ace is installing a security system."

"And?"

"And he knows his way around a hammer."

"You cannot be serious. You're sitting here watching him hammer nails? That's objectifying . . ." My voice trailed off when I caught a glimpse of Ace outside the window. His biceps bulged beneath his shirt as he pounded a nail into a piece of wood, and a bead of sweat trickled down his temple.

"Paige?" I looked at my bestie, shaken by the betrayal.

Paige shrugged. "I hate him for you, and I'd happily put crumbs in his sheets or thumbtacks in his shoes, but it doesn't mean I can't help Aditi do some research for her next art unit, which is a study of the masculine form."

"The whole form?"

"Every inch." Aditi grinned. "We had to find models for the class. The problem wasn't finding male volunteers; it was narrowing down the field. You can't imagine how many guys want to pose in the nude."

"I wish I'd taken art." Paige sighed. "There are no worthy specimens of the masculine form majoring in biology."

"What about you, Molly?" Half Swedish and half Dutch and just over six feet tall, Molly had despaired of finding a guy with whom she could wear heels until she met Jace, a philosophy major who was six inches taller than her. "I thought things were going well with Jace."

"They are," she said. "I came by to pick up a few odds and ends, and Aditi dragged me in here to have a chat."

"You're having a chat sitting side by side and staring out the window?"

"Jace is an intellectual," Molly said. "I love him for his mind, but sometimes a girl just needs to watch a little hammer action. It's no different from you watching that TikTok guy with the ax."

"I was learning about different types of axes," I said, bristling. "Who knows when I might go camping again and I might have to make my own kindling?"

Aditi patted the chair beside her. "Have a seat."

"I don't need a seat. I have to get to class. I'm shocked at all of you. Literally shocked." I wasn't shocked. I was tempted. I couldn't imagine many of my friends would pass up the opportunity to watch Ace play handyman, and he certainly didn't need me to pump up his ego.

Of course, right at that moment, when I was about to walk away, Ace looked up and caught my gaze. A smirk tugged at his lips. I wanted to die.

That same smirk was on his face half an hour later when we left for campus. Ace had changed into a Havencrest Warriors T-shirt and a pair of jeans that were a feast of seams in all the right places. He'd added a ball cap and backpack to his student "disguise," and given he was only a few years older than most undergrads, he fit right in.

"Aren't you going to ask me how you look?" I asked as we made our way down the quiet residential street. Our house was a fifteen-minute walk to campus. In winter when it was bitterly cold, I usually took the bus, but we were on the tail end of an unseasonably warm fall, and I wanted to enjoy my last chance to walk down the sidewalk kicking leaves.

Ace scanned the street as he walked, his head swiveling from side to side. "No."

"Is that because you know you have mastered the appearance of a Havencrest University student or because you don't care what I think?" I was irritated he hadn't taken the bait, which could have led to an interesting conversation about people on campus and what they wore and their various ages, the type of people who bought Havencrest merch, and assorted other topics that would keep us entertained for the walk.

"I studied the student population during my recon with campus security." He sounded so stiff and formal, unlike the Ace who had just smirked at me through the window. I didn't know what was going on with him, but I didn't like it and I was determined to make him smile.

"That sounds slightly menacing," I said. "Like you were studying them for nefarious purposes or a nature documentary instead of just wanting to fit in, which you do, by the way. Good job on the disguise."

Ace gave me a curt nod of thanks. "We need to go over some rules," he said after a painful heartbeat of silence. "I wanted to talk through everything last night after I got back from running errands, but Paige said you'd gone to bed. Since when do you turn in early?"

Since I needed some time to process the fact that Ace was in my house, protecting me, and sleeping in the room next door. If someone had told fifteen-year-old me that this is where we would be five years later, I would never have believed it.

"I had homework and I thought it would be better to keep my door closed to focus." There was no point pretending I'd gone to sleep at 9:00 P.M. Ace knew I was a night owl. I did my best work when the world was quiet and still and there was nothing to distract me. I couldn't sleep if there was even the remotest possibility that something exciting might be going on. Even as a kid, I would go and go and go, regardless of the time, but the moment my head hit the pillow I was out like a light.

"I bought a lock for your door," he said. "I was planning to install it last night, but I can do it today. It's got two keys so I can get in if there is any trouble. You should keep the door locked at all times."

Ace opening my door at night, coming over to my bed, watching me as I slept . . . I couldn't stop the pictures racing through my mind. *Bad.* I wasn't fifteen and madly in love anymore. Or seventeen and desperate for Ace's attention. Ace had firmly crushed those feelings out of me a long time ago.

"So, you left me alone to run errands?" I lifted an eyebrow. "I should call Tony and let him know you didn't even last a few hours."

Ace took it in stride. "I arranged for two guards to come and watch the house. They'll always be there if for some reason I can't be with you." His arm slammed into my stomach, and he pushed me back moments before I stepped into the busy street. I hadn't even noticed the light was red. I often didn't notice the light was red. Usually, it was because my brain was busy trying to sort through the noise. This time the only noise in my head was him.

"I was about to stop," I protested.

"Just being cautious. It wouldn't look good for me if I lost my client on the first day."

My stomach tightened in a knot. He could have teased me the way Matt used to do, but he was letting me save face. He knew I often got lost in my head. My parents were always amazed I could make it to school without being run over. To be honest, it used to amaze me too.

When the light turned green, Ace moved his arm from my stomach to my back and guided me across the road. I didn't need help crossing the road, especially now that the light was green, but I couldn't get the words out of my mouth. My entire focus was on the press of his hand against my back, his firm touch, the warmth seeping through my shirt, and the tingles rushing through my veins.

"I'm safe now." I gently moved his hand away as soon as we hit the sidewalk, and instantly felt bereft.

We walked past the athletic center and through the main campus square. Although the sun was shining, the wind had picked up, and the cooling temperature warned that winter was coming.

"You were saying something about rules?" I said when the fifteen-year-old Haley inside me stopped screaming in excitement that Ace had touched me.

"First rule is, you do what I say."

"Is this from the Stellar Security rule book? Maverick also mentioned that as rule number one. You know how I feel about too many rules."

"That's why I'm making sure you remember that one." He paused mid-stride, turned to me, and cupped my jaw in his warm hand, tipping my face up to look at him. "I'm not joking about this, Haley. You do what I say when I say it."

The sudden intimate gesture froze my brain, and the world became still. I told myself he meant it to emphasize his point. That this was so serious he had to touch me like that to command my full attention. That I shouldn't be thinking about the way he'd held my face like this once before, but tenderly and with two hands and two lips and the press of his body against mine.

"Um . . ." I swallowed hard and moved his hand away. "That didn't seem very professional. Do you do that with all your clients?"

"No." He quickly dropped his hand. "But I know you, and I know you need something more than words for rules to sink in."

"It seems to be a blessing and a curse," I said, trying to lighten the mood. "But you're forgetting I'm not a kid anymore. I am, in fact, aware of the need to take your advice into serious consideration in the event of danger."

"I need more than your consideration. I need action," he said.

"You have a high tolerance for risk. That's why you need to trust that if I say run, you run, or if I say a situation is dangerous, you follow my lead."

"Because you have a lower tolerance for risk?" I asked.

"I have a zero tolerance for risk when it comes to you."

We walked past the library and made our way to the social sciences building. I still hadn't decided which friends I should tell about Ace and which ones I should leave in the dark.

"You're quiet," he said. "I hope that means you're giving serious thought to rule one."

"Actually, I'm just trying to figure out who can know you're a bodyguard and who gets relegated to the B team. I have a lot of friends and it feels wrong to lie to them."

"The more people you tell, the less chance it stays a secret," he pointed out.

"My roommates had to know, of course. And Sam, because he would have been upset if he came by for a hookup and I told him I had a bodyguard in the room next door. I'll have to tell Skye because she's one of my closest friends and we work together at the coffee shop. That means Dante will know, because they're dating and he runs the radio station and would probably need to know anyway. And, Isla will have to know because she lives with Skye, and if Isla knows then Nick will need to know because they're dating. And if Nick knows then Derek will know because they live together . . ."

Ace gave a grunt of irritation. "That's too many people."

"Everyone I mentioned except Isla works at the radio station," I said. "We're like a big family."

"An incestuous family," he grumbled. "You all seem to either be living with each other, working with each other, or dating each other. Even you—Chad's living in your house."

"Nick, Derek, Dante, and I were in a band together with one of Dante's friends," I said. "It was amazing. The energy was incredible. I never feel anything like that when I sing solo. But it was Dante's band, and he had to break it up because his career took off and he got gigs and session work and might even be going out on tour—"

"Living your dream," Ace said.

"Yes." I sighed. "I don't think that will ever happen for me. The band was my best chance. Dante drew a lot of attention. He's an amazing musician."

"So are you."

I looked over at him, so calm and confident. "You've never really heard me sing except in the school talent shows and at community events or in the kitchen at home and—"

"Online," Ace said. "I follow your socials. I downloaded all your music and listened to it when I was on deployment every chance I got."

For the first time I could remember, I had nothing to say. "You listened to my music?"

"I'm not a big music lover," Ace admitted. "I like music, but I wouldn't be able to tell you the difference between pop and rock or blues and jazz. I don't spend hours making playlists or analyzing the lyrics of songs. I hear something I like, and I enjoy it in the moment, but your music I've listened to again and again. Matt listened to it, too. He had it downloaded to an MP3 player for when he didn't have internet and he would play it for his unit or before he went out on a mission. He was so proud of you."

Ace listened to my music. Matt listened to my music and shared it with his friends. Matt, who used to laugh when I played him a new song. Matt, who used to tease me about my painfully awkward lyrics. A wave of grief crashed over me, sweeping my breath away. I doubled over, trying to get it under control. *Breathe. Breathe. You're fine. Lock it away.*

"Haley?" Ace crouched down in front of me. "Fuck. I'm sorry. I shouldn't have brought him up. Are you okay?"

"I need . . . space. I need to be alone. Just . . . just for a minute." I backed away, waving my arms. Too much. Too many emotions. I needed to get away, to find a quiet space and stuff them all back in the black box with everything else that I had yet to process.

I didn't have time for emotions. I didn't want to deal with all that pain. Better to put the past behind me and move on with a cheerful face.

"I can't. I can't." I couldn't breathe, couldn't think. The tide surged around me, threatening to pull me under.

Ace gripped my shoulders, his touch firm. "I can't let you leave. I need eyes on you at all times." His hands slid down my arms to my hands and he wrapped them around his waist. "Hold on to me."

I hugged him tight, buried my face in his chest, closed my eyes, and breathed him in. He smelled of autumn leaves and fresh mountain air. He smelled of home.

"I've got you." His deep voice rumbled in his chest as his arms tightened around me, holding me safe.

I don't know how long we stood in the middle of the quad, but the noise faded, and the silence came until all I knew was the warmth of his body and the steady beat of his heart.

CHAPTER 11

Haley

EIGHT AND A HALF YEARS AGO

No one was around to take me to the Riverstone summer fair. It was a busy time for Dad at the restaurant; Mom had a trial; Matt was away at scout camp and Paige's mom had taken her to New York to visit her aunt. I had just made the decision to break the rules and go by myself when Ace rode up the driveway on his bike.

Two years of good meals and stable living had changed him since I'd first laid eyes on him. He'd filled out everywhere and he'd grown taller than Matt by several inches. Dad said Ace was going to be even taller than him.

"What are you doing here?" I tried to act casual, like I wasn't about to bus it across town and wander alone through crowds of strangers.

"Taking you to the fair." He parked his bike against the side of the garage and nodded at the bag I'd hidden behind my back. "Looks like I got here just in time."

My cheeks heated and I slipped the bag over my shoulder. "Did Dad send you?"

"No."

"Mom? Matt?"

Ace shook his head. "I just knew there was no way you'd stay home alone when there was a fair in town. Music, people, chaos, noise, unwinnable games, dangerous rides, candy . . . It's your kind of thing."

I couldn't help the smile spreading across my face. Ace was

right. There was nothing I loved more than the excitement of a fair. "They've got three new rides this year, and I've been practicing for the ring toss and fishing for ducks. This year I'm going to win a jumbo panda bear."

"We'd better get going then," Ace said. "We don't want to miss out on those prizes."

I didn't know many fifteen-year-old boys who would give up a Saturday afternoon to take the tweeniest of tweens to the fair, but Ace didn't care what people thought about him. He took me and Paige to the movies when no one else in the family wanted to watch cartoons. He talked to us in public, something Matt would never do. He mowed our lawn without his shirt on, even though most of the girls in the neighborhood would come out and stare. He sometimes even waited for me and Paige after school and carried our backpacks home.

Ace had never been to a fair and he was more than willing to go on every single ride, walk through the fun houses, and play all the prize games. We ate corn dogs and cotton candy, pink popcorn and mini donuts. It was only when I caught him smiling at himself in one of the twisty mirrors that I realized he was having as much fun as me.

"We only have a few tickets left," he said, when we'd started to flag despite the endless sugar supply. "What about the haunted house?"

I'd never been through the haunted house without my dad. Usually, he sat beside me and I held his hand or buried my face in his shoulder when creepy things popped up from dark corners or the ghosts and witches screamed. I opened my mouth to suggest we ride on the Spider instead when it occurred to me that Ace probably had never been in a haunted house before, and really, was there anything more fun than being scared out of your mind?

Ten minutes later we were sitting in our own little car, painted with spiderwebs and skulls and decorated with sticky fingerprints and wads of gum. I held tight to the bar, taking one last longing look at the sunshine before we plunged into the darkness. The first skeleton came out of nowhere and I screamed.

"I got you." Ace put a comforting arm around me and gave me a quick squeeze. He was warm and solid, and he smelled of popcorn and candy. He'd never touched me before and the feel of that brief hug did strange things to my stomach. But nothing compared to watching Ace in his first haunted house. His walls came down after that first scare and then he was shouting and laughing and jumping along with me. Once I think he even screamed. When our car burst through the final doorway his face smoothed back to an expressionless mask but now, I knew what was underneath—Ace loved a thrill as much as me.

I didn't want to go back into the haunted house. My throat was hoarse from screaming and my heart was still pounding, but as soon as the ride stopped, I looked over at Ace and said, "Let's do it again."

We went through the haunted house three more times before finishing the day trying to win prizes in the rigged games set up at the edge of the fair. For all my practice and the research I'd done to understand the tricks behind the games, I came away with only a palm-size dolphin and a set of plastic bracelets. I couldn't hide my disappointment.

"We need to get back before my parents get home," I said, looking back at the giant panda bear that I'd been coveting for as long as I could remember.

"I still have some money left." Ace waved me over to the shooting game where bull's-eye targets moved slowly across the back of the tent. He handed over his cash and took the gun, checking the different parts like he'd been handling weapons all his life. His first shot went high, but the next two hit the target and the owner gave him the option of a keychain or playing again to trade up. Ace played again. Won again. Traded up and up and up until a crowd had gathered in front of the tent and the only thing left for him to win was the panda.

"How did you learn to shoot like that?" I asked as the carnie pulled down the second-largest prize, a three-foot-high brown bear with sleepy eyes.

"It was the only thing my dad taught me," he said. "And it was because he and my mom had a habit of stiffing their dealers and they needed me to defend them if they were high."

Ace had never been so blunt about his past. I didn't really understand what it meant to stiff a dealer and I had no idea what happened to people when they were high so that they would need a kid to use a gun. But I knew from the tone of his voice and his sudden blank expression that it wasn't something that good parents asked their child to do.

"You want to give this up?" The carnie held out the bear to Ace. "Your girlfriend seems to like it."

"I'm not his girlfriend," I blurted out. I'd never thought of Ace that way. He was Matt's best friend and a part of our family. He made me feel safe and happy and I liked spending time with him because he listened, and he cared. He was curious about the same things as me, and he was always up for an adventure. I looked over at Ace, who was waiting for my answer, and suddenly saw him as if I hadn't seen him before. He had a handsome face and a nice smile. Paige had had two boyfriends already, but there were no boys in our class who were as cool as Ace. Twelve-year-old boys were gangly and smelly and acted like jerks. Ace was . . . different.

"What do you think?" Ace asked.

I shook my head and saw Ace again as I knew him. "Go big or go home."

"I knew you'd say that." He fired a perfect shot.

I got my panda.

Dad met us on the driveway when we rolled up just before sunset. "Why do I see three kids instead of two?"

"Ace won the giant panda!" I jumped off my bike. "You should have seen him shoot. I'm going to put him on the chair by the window so he can look out into the forest. I've named him Pandy."

"If Ace paid for the game and won it, then he belongs to Ace."

Dad shared a look with Ace that I didn't understand, but it made Ace smile.

"I want Haley to have it, sir." Ace lifted the panda off the bike and handed it to me. I staggered under the weight of it, smothered by fluff. Somehow, he'd managed to balance it on the cross rail of his bike, and I'd laughed all the way home.

"Thank you, son. That's very generous, and thank you for looking after my baby girl," Dad said. "I'm sorry she harassed you into taking her. I told her we'd all go tomorrow."

"I didn't ask him," I protested. "He just showed up when I was about to . . ." I trailed off, realizing I might implicate myself in a crime Ace had just saved me from committing.

"I came to see if anyone could show me around the fair," Ace interjected. "I hadn't been to a fair before and when Haley offered to take me, I was grateful for the company."

My heart swelled with gratitude. Dad was pretty easygoing, but I didn't like to disappoint him.

"Hmmm." Dad lifted an eyebrow. "Well, since Haley has already been to the fair, she can mow the lawn tomorrow instead of coming with her mom and me."

My heart sank into my chest. I loved going to the fair with my parents, but it was clear he'd seen right through our story.

"I could use the extra cash if you need it mowed," Ace offered. "I could come by in the morning." Dad used to do all the mowing, but the doctor said he wasn't taking good care of his heart and he had to take special medicine that meant he couldn't do activities that made him out of breath. He paid Matt and me to do the lawn as part of our chores, and if we were both busy, he paid Ace to fill in.

Would the wonders of Ace never end? How come Matt wasn't like him? Ace was everything I'd always imagined a big brother would be, but more. So much more. I got that strange feeling in my stomach again. It made me feel warm and quiet inside. Ace was supposed to go to the fair with Matt tomorrow. I couldn't let him take the fall for me.

"It's my job," I said. "I'll do it."

"Good decision," Dad said in the tone of voice that told me I wasn't off the hook. "You go on into the house. I want to have a word with Ace."

Of course I didn't go into the house. Instead, I hid behind the car parked on the driveway and listened to them talking. Dad told Ace he was a good man and that he was grateful for all the things Ace did to help our family. He thanked him for looking after me and for giving me the panda. He told Ace that if he'd been Ace's dad, he would have been proud to call him his son.

The next day I mowed the lawn early and then took the money Dad gave me and waited for Ace on the driveway when he came to meet Matt. "Take this," I said, handing him the money. "It's for looking after me. I'll give you Pandy, too, when you get back tonight."

Ace shook his head. "I don't need to be paid. I wanted to go to the fair with you. I knew you'd make it fun. And I won that bear for you."

"I'll take good care of him," I promised. There was that strange feeling again, like being wrapped in a hug. "And thanks for trying to save me."

"Anytime."

I waved as he and Matt rode away and wished that "anytime" would come more often.

CHAPTER 12

Haley

Good morning, Chicago. This is Hidden Tracks *on WJPK, and I'm Haley Chapman. Today's show is all about those moments when you think you've got things all figured out and then bam! life throws you a curveball.*

Maybe you're ready to bundle up against the cold, only to have the temperature shoot up like it did this morning, and you're ditching your sweaters and pulling out your tees. Or maybe you think you know someone and they do something that makes you see them in a whole new light. That's our vibe today. We're diving into tunes about those "whoa, didn't see that coming" moments, and how people and situations can flip the script on us when we least expect it.

This playlist is for those of us who've been blindsided by a plot twist in our own life story and are now struggling to keep our head above water. We're kicking off with a track about just riding those waves when you discover there's way more to the story than you thought. This is Alabama Shakes with "Hold On." Stick around and remember—just when you think you've got it all figured out, life loves to shake things up.

Ace and I fell into a rhythm over the next two weeks after a somewhat rocky start, going from classes to work and then to all my clubs. He tried to stay in the background, usually standing or sitting at the back of my classrooms, grabbing a table in the corner of the coffee shop, and hanging out near the door when I was at my clubs. Only at the radio station did he seem ill at ease. I wasn't sure if it was the chaos and the noise, or the fact that he thought it was a security nightmare with people constantly coming and going, hanging out in the hallways or racing from room to room. It was also impossible for him to be inconspicuous standing outside the studio while I did my show, because he was constantly in the way.

I liked seeing him outside the door. I liked knowing he was listening. I tried to play music I thought he might enjoy, and imagined I was talking just to him. My show vibe was funny, sassy, sarcastic, and sincere. I tried to be the fun, smart, yet down-to-earth best friend everyone wants to connect with.

Halfway through my show well into our second week together, I opened as usual for requests and comments. Sometimes I invited listeners to call in or text and share something personal about their lives that vibed with the theme of the day. The station feed lit up with a message and I clicked to open it only to wish I hadn't.

We're coming for you

At first, I thought it was the title of a song or an album I didn't know, but the only tracks that popped up after a quick search on Spotify were heavy metal or didn't vibe with the theme. I uploaded a new track to give me time to respond and clarify the request, but before I could send a reply, another message popped up on my screen.

This time you won't get away

I felt a shiver down my spine, and I glanced over at the window to see if Ace was still outside. I'd had some uncomfortable messages over the years, mostly sexual or suggestive, a few threatening enough that Noah, the previous station manager, had contacted the campus police. Of course, they couldn't do anything, because they couldn't trace the messages, and after a few days they would close their file. Over time, I'd become numb to the invitations and suggestive comments, but this was different.

This time meant there had been another time, which had to be the incident on Michigan Avenue.

Should I tell Ace? The obvious answer was yes. He was there to protect me, but how could he protect me from something that couldn't be traced? They were just words, and maybe I was wrong and the message didn't have to do with the kidnapping attempt. Ace also tended to overreact, and he would likely demand that we go home right away. He might even insist that I stay there or go to a safe house where I couldn't see Paige and I wouldn't be going to college at all.

My brain got stuck in that track and wouldn't let go, muffling the logical part of my mind that said this was panic talking and I just needed to take a breath and talk to Ace. I didn't want to fall behind in my classes, or miss work, or let down the clubs I'd joined to meet people and keep busy on campus. There was recycling that needed to be picked up with my environmental group. I was going to try some new fencing techniques, and my music group was planning a big event in a few weeks, and I had to rehearse. I didn't want whoever was behind the messages to think they could control my life. I'd tell Ace later, maybe when we were at home, maybe not at all if it didn't happen again. The show had to go on and all that jazz.

Resolved to put the messages behind me, I muted the request line, played my final tracks, and took a few deep, calming breaths before I joined Ace in the hallway. He took one look at me and scowled.

"What's wrong?"

"Nothing." I forced a smile for Chad, who was waiting to get into the studio for his show. "Hey, Chad. What's up?"

"You're not looking so good," Chad said. "You're kind of pale, and your eyes are huge. Did you catch that bug Theo had? He's been hogging the toilet for two days."

"I was having issues with the mic, and it threw me off. You know what it's like."

Chad nodded. "I heard last week Derek had to change his mic out in the middle of the show. Dante said he was going to order new ones. I guess they haven't arrived yet."

"I'll ask him about it the next time I see him." I walked quickly down the hallway, forcing Ace to almost jog to keep up.

"What's going on?" Ace reached ahead to pull open the door. His arm brushed my shoulder, and that brief moment of contact soothed the anxiety that had my heart pounding in my chest.

"I told you. Nothing." I jogged up the stairs so fast, Ace had to take them two at a time to keep up.

"Is it Chad? Did he say something? Did he hurt you? Is he harassing you?" Of course he wouldn't let it go, and he was over-reacting just as I'd suspected he would.

"No, of course not. Chad's a good guy."

I pushed open the door to the main floor of the student center, and Ace put a hand on my shoulder, holding me back so he could assess the area before we were fully in the open. I took the moment to make my own sweep of the area, the students lined up for fast food, the cafeteria-style tables bustling with activity, and the small shops selling spirit wear and school supplies. No suspicious people lurking around. My chest rose and fell with my breaths. I was momentarily overwhelmed with the need to hold his hand for the simple comfort of his touch, but I managed to push the feeling away and follow him through the door.

Was it real? Was I truly in danger? Was there a connection between the incident on Michigan Avenue and the threats my mother had received? What would Ace do if I told him? It was too much to process, so I tried not to process at all.

We walked out into the overcast day, and I shivered as a cool breeze licked my skin. I tried to think about cozy fires and winter sweaters and my upcoming tests, and didn't realize I'd forgotten to tell Ace about the change of classroom until he grabbed my shoulder, pulling me to a stop.

"Where are you going?"

"There was a flood in the building. The lecture was just moved to an auditorium in the arts center."

He gave an irritated growl. "You need to give me some warning of any changes in the schedule."

"I literally just got the message." I held up my phone. "I'm not trying to hide anything from you or sneak away. But just to be clear, if I did want to run away, you'd never catch me. I'm skilled at subterfuge."

He glanced over at me, amused. "Is that right?"

"You and Matt saw to that. I had a life to live that didn't involve staying in my room playing Barbies like a good little girl. I couldn't have the two of you interfering all the time." I fell easily into the conversation, grateful for the distraction.

Another growl. A frown. "I don't think I want to know what trouble you got up to."

"And I don't think I want to tell you."

We made our way to the new classroom, and I went to sit beside Aditi in the middle row of seats, instead of sitting at the back like usual where Ace could hover like a mother hen. He followed me down and took a seat on my other side, putting his body between me and the aisle.

Safe.

I masked my audible sigh of relief with fake irritation. "Why aren't you standing at the back like good bodyguards are supposed to do?"

"This auditorium has three exits. I can't reach you fast enough if I'm at the back and someone comes in from the front."

"It would be hard to snatch me away from a classroom," I protested. "I don't think a van could get through the door." I forced a smile and my voice wavered. Instantly, Ace's eyes narrowed, and I began to suspect he could see right through me.

"You never know where the threat is going to come from." He

stared at me with an intensity that had me squirming in my seat. "Or when."

I stiffened and dropped my gaze. His tone said it all. He knew something was up. I couldn't hide anything from Ace. Maybe I shouldn't have agreed to a bodyguard who knew me so well.

"Is there something you aren't tell—"

"You don't have a laptop or a notebook," I said, cutting him off. "People are going to wonder what you're doing here."

As if on cue, the girl beside Aditi leaned right over her to talk to me. "Who's your friend?"

"Ace." I knew exactly why she was asking and what she wanted, and my fake irritation became real.

"I'm Isabel." She flashed Ace a smile, showing off a row of perfectly white teeth as she introduced her friends who were sitting around her. "I haven't seen you in class before."

"Late registration." He smiled back, and my hand curled around the armrest, fingers tightening until my knuckles turned white.

"Don't encourage her," I muttered under my breath. "You're with me. Flirting isn't allowed."

"I said two words," he protested.

"You smiled."

"Should I have frowned?" He tipped his head in query. "I have to keep myself busy since something clearly happened at the station that you're not sharing with me, which means I can't do my job."

Damnit. I had hoped after so long apart he would have forgotten everything he knew about me. Clearly, I was wrong. "There are some things I can handle myself."

"Things that scare you are my job." His body stiffened when the door at the bottom of the auditorium opened. He relaxed again when he recognized my professor from the class earlier in the week.

"I wasn't scared." I opened my laptop and settled back in my seat.

"I went through a haunted house with you five times in a row," he whispered as the professor set up at the podium. "I know when you're afraid."

CHAPTER 13

Ace

Isabel and her giggly friends were waiting outside after class.

"We're going to Shakers for happy hour and then heading out on a pub crawl," Isabel said to me. "You should come."

"We can't." Haley glared at Isabel. "We've got somewhere to be."

Isabel frowned. "Are you two together?"

Haley sucked in her lips and then sighed. "He's my . . . boyfriend."

I shouldn't have liked hearing that as much as I did, but it brought back some of the feelings I'd had in high school when I realized I cared for Haley more than just as a friend. She had been an important part of my life ever since I'd moved to Riverstone, and now that I was with her again, I felt the distance between us like an ache in my chest. I missed the connection we used to have, the easy conversation and the comfortable silence. I may have tried to bury my feelings out of respect for Matt, but I had never stopped caring for her.

"She's my girl." I dropped my arm over Haley's shoulder, and she stiffened, looking up at me with a grimace.

"I thought you didn't want a fake boyfriend," I said after Isabel was out of earshot.

Haley pushed my arm away. "I just don't want to have to deal with women constantly hitting on you," she snapped. "This is easier. People have already noticed you following me around. I'm just waiting for someone to report you as a stalker. It would have been helpful if you weren't so gorgeous that you attract attention."

Haley thought I was gorgeous. She wanted me to be her fake

boyfriend. This was everything I didn't want as a bodyguard and everything I had wanted as a man before I royally screwed up. I didn't know if there was any coming back from what I'd done, but damned if I wasn't going to try. At the very least I could protect her body, but maybe I could also heal her heart.

"I'm happy to know you find my appearance acceptable," I teased.

"Just . . . try not to attract attention," she gritted out. "Do you own a baggy shirt? Or a pair of those jeans that ride below your boxers? For someone whose job is to be inconspicuous, you really stand out."

My lips quivered with a smile. "I'll try to dress down tomorrow," I assured her, putting my hand on her waist to steer her clear of an opening door.

"And just so we understand each other, I don't really want a boyfriend. Boyfriends mean feelings and feelings mean attachments and attachments lead to pain when the person you care about leaves you, which they all do, at least in my life. This is just a safety issue. I don't want you to be distracted when you're supposed to be protecting me."

Her dad, her mom (emotionally), Matt, and me. I'd left her, too. The only stable person in her life was Paige. No wonder she'd followed her best friend to Havencrest. "I'm not leaving you, Haley, and nothing will distract me from keeping you safe. This isn't an ordinary assignment for me, but I need your trust."

"I do trust you." She pulled open the door to the arts building and I followed her through.

"If you trusted me, you would tell me what happened at the station."

She shuddered and suddenly I'd had enough. Something had spooked her and I couldn't just let it slide. Haley had never been able to deal with strong emotions. When her father had passed away, she'd tried to bury her pain, and it had come out in destructive ways. The moment I saw an empty classroom, I yanked open the door and pulled her inside.

"Tell me what's going on," I said, as the door swung closed be-side us. "And don't say it's nothing. That might work for a stranger, but I know you, Haley. I may have been hired to protect you, but that doesn't mean I can't also be here for you as a friend."

Silence. She pushed past me and reached for the door handle. For a moment, I thought I would have to let her go. She could be almost as stubborn as me. Finally, she turned around and pulled out her phone. "I got these messages on the station account when I was on the air."

We're coming for you

This time you won't get away

Fire scorched my veins. All thoughts of being a supportive friend flew out the window in the face of imminent threat. I slammed my hand against the door above her head, as much for the support as for the fear that she might walk away. "Why didn't you tell me? What if he was in the studio? Or in the student cen-ter? What if he followed you to class?" My voice rose as I thought about every damn thing that could have gone wrong, the danger she could have been in if her attacker was waiting outside. "I'm here to protect you and you tied my hands by not giving me the information I needed when I needed it."

"Don't raise your voice with me," Haley snapped.

Guilt knotted my stomach. My job was to remain cool and calm at all times, but this was Haley and my emotions were all over the map. It didn't help that in this position, I could smell the fragrance of her perfume, see the swell of her breasts at the vee of her shirt, feel the heat of her body so close to mine.

"I understood the danger." She let out a shuddering breath. "I was just worried you'd overreact and pull me out of the studio, and I didn't want to give him the satisfaction. The show had to go on."

Haley had never been a coward. She had shown the kind of professionalism that I was lacking in that moment.

"And afterwards? Why didn't you tell me as soon as the show was done?"

"Honestly, I didn't want it to be real," she admitted. "I'd convinced myself that there was no connection between the incident on Michigan and the threats my mother received, and she was just being overly cautious hiring you. That was working for me until I got the texts. I forced myself to finish the show and then I just needed time to process before I had to deal with . . ." She gestured vaguely at me. "All this."

"This is real, Haley," I said evenly. "Very real. This is an escalation. I can't do my job if you're not going to let me know what's going on."

Haley sighed. "I know."

I hated myself for noticing the blush on her cheeks, and the way her soft lips were pressed together. A long time ago, her dad had asked me to protect her. Now, her mom was paying me to guard her. There were a million reasons why I needed to keep my distance, but there I was, adrenaline pounding through my veins, thinking all the wrong thoughts, allowing buried emotions to resurface, reminding me that I'd never stopped truly caring for her, when the only thing that should have been in my head was keeping her safe.

"It's hard for me to rely on people," she said looking up. "Very hard to trust, especially when it comes to you." Her voice came out in a husky whisper that I felt down to my very bones. I was almost overwhelmed with the need to hold her. But more than that, I burned for her. My time in the military and losing Matt had made me realize how short and unpredictable life could be—too short to hold back feelings I'd repressed forever.

"I treated you badly, and I wasn't there when you needed me," I said. "Not a day goes by that I don't regret those decisions. But I'm not the same man anymore and I'm going to work hard to show you that I'm worthy of your trust."

She looked up at me and the intensity of her gaze told me I wasn't the only one who was aware of the heat sizzling between us. But this was the wrong time. Wrong place. I shouldn't have felt what I was feeling. I shouldn't have been thinking of wrapping her hair around my hand, tugging her head back and kissing those soft lips. I shouldn't have been imagining what it would be like to slowly strip off her clothes and run my hands over her curves. But I was, and I did, and I couldn't stop.

"Ace . . ." She leaned up and pressed her lips to the hollow at the base of my throat, my name on her breath a plea I couldn't refuse. I cupped her cheek in my palm, and kissed her.

Our first kiss had been a sweet kiss, a gentle kiss, a taste of what I'd wanted and thought I would never have again. But this was entirely different. Adrenaline was still pulsing through my veins, a mix of fear and fury, a longing too deep for words, and hot, brutal lust. I kissed her hard and deep, my tongue sweeping inside her mouth, touching, tasting, marking every inch as mine. She wrapped her arms around my neck, pressing her body against me. I tasted honey on her tongue, heady and tempting, felt her softness against the hard ridge beneath my fly. She was the one. The only one. I wanted her right there, up against the wall, her legs wrapped around me, breasts bared, her lips bruised from my kisses. We were alone in the classroom. There was no one to stop us . . .

I tore my mouth from hers and buried it against her throat. "Damn it, Haley. We can't do this."

"Shut up and kiss me again." She grabbed my shirt and pulled me down for another kiss. My senses flooded, nerves snapped, pulse pounded. I was no longer thinking *I can't*. I was starving for her. If I had to, I would beg. Our lips crashed together, and the moan that escaped her throat was at once a torment and a sweet temptation.

I heard footsteps in the hallway, voices outside. I drew her away from the door just as it opened behind her.

"Wrong classroom," I said, grabbing her hand and leading her past the white-haired professor staring at us in stunned silence.

"We shouldn't have," Haley said as we emerged into the hallway, her cheeks still flushed, lips swollen from my kisses.

"Definitely not."

She bit her lower lip, dragging it between her teeth. "It can't happen again."

"It won't." I was her bodyguard. Not her lover, or even her friend. The past was still an open wound between us. She hadn't forgiven me, and I hadn't redeemed myself for the emotional pain I'd caused.

Still, neither of us moved. Tension curled in the air between us.

"Ace . . ." Her gaze drifted from my eyes to my lips, and I wanted her all over again.

"Haley . . ." My voice cracked, broke and I forced myself to take a step back. "Let's get you to class."

CHAPTER 14

Ace

What the fuck did I do? By the time we returned to Haley's house,
I was drowning in feelings of guilt and self-recrimination. First,
Haley had been threatened on my watch and hadn't trusted me
enough to tell me. Second, I'd broken my number-one rule about
getting involved with clients. And that's what Haley was. A client.
Our past shouldn't have been a factor. Where was my self-control?
Gone out the damn window, along with any sense of profession-
alism I'd ever had.

Haley went straight to her room to study, and I called Tony
to brief him on the threat situation. I was tempted to tell him I'd
crossed a line, but I was pretty sure he'd pull me off the assignment, and I wasn't leaving until I knew Haley would be safe.

"We need to trace those messages," I said. "I called the station manager, Dante, and he said he'd get in touch with their IT
department. I also spoke to Haley's mother, and she passed the
screenshots on to the Capitol Police. I doubt they'll do anything
because we're not in their jurisdiction and they're busy dealing
with the recent threats she received."

"I saw on the news that someone threw a rock through her
window," Tony said. "She's really ruffled some feathers."

"I still can't believe the police closed the kidnapping case."
I sat on the bed, partly listening to Tony and partly listening
to Haley walking around her room. "I called the lead detective
and he said they couldn't get any CCTV images of the van or
any leads from the witnesses. Can you fucking believe it? Her
mother is a senator and they couldn't be bothered to keep digging." My hand tightened around the phone. "We need to

get involved. Someone out there wants to hurt Haley, and the threats are escalating."

"It's not our job," Tony said. "Our job is protection. We have to leave the investigating to the authorities. You can't protect her effectively if you're distracted."

"If someone actually investigated the crime and caught the guy then she wouldn't need protection," I spat out. "We need to do something."

"I think you're getting too involved."

"Seriously?" I was still reeling from the fact that Tony wasn't as incensed as I was about the lack of follow-up on the attempted kidnapping.

"I'm very serious. You've been there for almost two weeks without a break. I think you need to take a few days and get some perspective."

"There's no way." I pushed off the bed and paced the length of my bedroom. "She's just been threatened, and you want me to leave?"

"I want you to clear your head," he said. "I'll ask Jordan to send Maverick over. Take the weekend or however long you need to get focused on why you're there and what you need to do. I had reservations about letting you guard someone you had a history with, Ace. Don't even think about telling me you won't leave, or I'll pull you out for good."

Maverick arrived an hour later with a duffel bag in one hand and a hotel keycard in the other. "Sorry, bro. I know this wasn't your idea. Tony set you up with a hotel room, so you'd have a place to sleep. Take all the time you need."

"I don't need time. I need answers." I took the card from him and went back upstairs to knock on Haley's door. She'd gone to take a nap after we got in, and although I'd sent her a message and knocked gently a few times over the last few hours, she hadn't responded. When she didn't answer, I sent her another message letting her know what was going on and went back downstairs to brief Mav.

Chad and Theo walked into the kitchen just as I finished show-ing Mav the security system. "We're heading to the gym," Chad said. "Are you interested in working out? Theo's good for company but not so good for spotting. He can barely lift a bag of Doritos."

"Fuck you." Theo gave him a playful slap on the head.

I'd been using the gym equipment in the basement to keep up my fitness, and the idea of doing a workout in a real gym and blowing off some steam held serious appeal. I made sure Mav had all the information he needed, sent a last text to Haley, and then forced myself to leave the house with Chad and Theo to start my mandatory break.

"I heard what happened to Haley during her show," Chad said later while I was spotting him on the chest press.

"How the hell did you hear that?"

"You told Dante. He told Skye. She told Isla. She told Nick. He told me. It's the station, bro. There are no secrets. When Dante and Skye got together, they thought no one knew, but we all did. We just kept quiet about it until they'd worked out all their is-sues. Same as you and Haley." He pushed the weight up, holding it for a few seconds before lowering it again.

"There is nothing between me and Haley."

"C'mon, dude." He laughed. "The way you two look at each other . . . I don't need to be a chemistry major to know there's some-thing there. Life is short, my friend. Don't give up that opportunity."

"You've got it wrong," I protested. "We knew each other a long time ago. I was good friends with her brother. That's it."

"She has a brother?" Chad sat up, frowning. "She never men-tioned him."

I couldn't believe Haley had never mentioned Matt. Although they'd had their differences over the years, Matt and Haley had a good relationship and there was nothing he wouldn't have done for her. "He was three years older. We joined the air force to-gether, in the buddy program." I hesitated, reluctant to share. But it had been a day for crossing lines. Why not cross one more? "He didn't make it back," I added.

I was there. I watched his plane go down. I see it every night. Over and over and over again.

"I'm sorry, bro. I lost my older brother in the military, too."

Too. I didn't know if the word was purposeful or inadvertent, but he captured what had hurt me the most. Matt had been like a brother to me. His family had been my family. And yet I'd repaid him by encouraging him to do something that had cost him his life.

"Every time I read about a coast guard rescue, I think of him," Chad said after I offered my condolences. "He was trying to decide between the army and the coast guard—he loved the water—and I told him to choose the army because I had dreams of being a war correspondent and I wanted to interview him in the war zone. It sounds crazy now, but I was young and so, so naive. Even now, I can barely think about it without feeling sick. It never leaves you."

Fuck. He got it. The few people I shared my truth with had been quick to assure me that it wasn't my fault. They were right that I hadn't been flying the plane, nor had I even worked on the engine. But Matt wouldn't have joined the air force if not for me. He would never have been on that plane.

"Matt wanted to be a dentist." The words came spilling out before I could stop them. "He was a smart guy. I told him the air force would pay for his training if he completed his four-year commitment, so he joined up with me. If I'd kept my mouth shut, he'd be filling teeth and handing out toothbrushes right now."

Chad nodded in understanding and for a long moment we were united in grief and loss and a guilt that would never go away.

"We should go rescue Theo," Chad said finally. "Last time we were here he dropped a weight on his foot and broke his toe. He's not really a gym guy, but I drag him out for the company and because it can't be healthy sitting in the dark most of the day staring at four screens. He's super smart and at the top of his computer science program, so for a challenge he spends his time hacking or gaming. We've got a bunch of guys coming over to play a little *Grand Theft Auto* tonight. You should join us, or do you have to be out of the house on your break?"

"I don't think that would be a problem. I'm just supposed to be off duty. But I used to play that game all the time with Matt. I'll kick your asses."

"Mine maybe." Chad laughed. "But not Theo. It's like he can see right into the internet. Sometimes I think he's part of the code."

Something niggled at the back of my mind. "Could he trace the messages that were sent to the station or hack into CCTV cameras? Or is that kind of stuff just on TV?"

"I'm pretty sure he can hack into anything," Chad said. "Companies pay him to break into their systems, so they know how to fix them. But that kind of thing is legal. I don't know if he would do any black hat hacking. We can ask. What are you looking for?"

"I think the guy who tried to grab Haley on Michigan Avenue is the same one who sent the messages to the station. The local police have dropped the case, and the Capitol Police won't take jurisdiction. Her mom has been trying to get the FBI involved, but who knows how long that will take? I wanted to look into it because it seems to be escalating, but I was told I have to focus on protection."

"Something doesn't sound right to me." Chad racked his weights and wiped his face with a towel. "A senator's daughter? You'd think the police would be all over that. The press, too."

"Her mom is up for reelection soon so her team is trying to keep it out of the press because it would look bad for her campaign."

"Now I'm intrigued," Chad said. "Do you mind if I do some digging, too? I still haven't declared my year-end project, and this has all the juicy political stuff my investigative journalism professor loves."

I could imagine Tony's face if he found out he'd pulled me off duty so I'd focus on protection and instead I found two guys to do the investigation instead. "I'd be grateful for any help."

I heard a thud, and then a shout of pain. Chad looked over at the free weights and shook his head. "There goes another toe. Let's get Theo back to his computer. If his mother finds out I let him get hurt at the gym again, she's going to kill me. I'm not supposed to bring him anywhere he might try to be physical. I took him to a Bears game one time, and he got a shiner. He was trying to measure the velocity of the ball with an app he'd made and got in the way of a dude who was trying to catch a fly. Are you a Bears fan?"

"Hell, yeah. I never miss a game, although I've never seen them play live." My parents weren't interested in sports and I didn't know much about any teams until I met Haley's family. I was a Bears fan because of them, because of the way they made me feel when they kept a seat for me every time a game was on, like I was part of the family.

"I get comps to a lot of games through the station," Chad said. "It would be great to have someone to go with who actually understands the game and isn't so busy staring at his phone that he misses a fly. I'm not taking no for an answer. The next time my tickets and your schedule line up, we're going, and if you've got any friends who are Bears fans we can bring them, too." He pumped his fist in the air. "Bear Down, Chicago Bears!"

Chad reminded me so much of Matt it was almost painful. My first week of school in Riverstone, Matt had decided we were going to be friends and he wouldn't let up. No matter how hard I resisted, he was right there in my face, inviting me to play soccer, partner with him at the gym, be his bench buddy in science, and finally, one day, he convinced me to come to his house after school. I walked into music and laughter and chaos, and never wanted to leave.

Haley and her dad singing and dancing around the kitchen using wooden spoons as microphones was a kind of joy I'd never experienced before. They were totally in sync, utterly uninhibited, almost the same person except that Haley had the kind of voice that you can feel deep inside—rich, powerful, almost too big for such a little girl. She was ten years old and I was thirteen, too young to fall in love, but I felt something watching her, a tug in my heart that had never gone away.

"I'll let you know."

"Too bad there's nothing this weekend," he said. "But a little *Grand Theft Auto* will take your mind off anything."

It felt good to laugh. "It will when I kick your ass."

"My money's on Theo," Chad said. "But we'll see what you've got."

"Thanks for getting me out," I said as I racked my weights. "And for . . . everything."

Chad shrugged. "Anything for a friend."

CHAPTER 15

Haley

What just happened? I hugged the stuffed pig I'd had since childhood, wishing Paige had chosen a different weekend to go and visit her mother. I'd been locked in my bedroom all afternoon with my headphones on and my phone off, scribbling lyrics on sheets of paper that now littered the floor. Paige's go-to for stress, breakups, and emotional issues was ice cream and rom-coms. Mine was music—specifically writing songs—and I'd spent the entire afternoon composing.

I was afraid to leave my room. Afraid to see Ace and hear that our kiss was a mistake, just like the one before. He hadn't said anything since we left the empty classroom. He'd stood at the back of the class, and then walked me home in total silence, almost colder than the day I'd seen him at Matt's funeral.

My hand went to my mouth. I could still feel the press of his lips against mine, the warmth of his palms on his cheeks. The Ace who had kissed me in the classroom wasn't the same Ace who had kissed me at a party in Riverstone four years ago. Old Ace had been soft and gentle, his kiss hesitant and tender. New Ace was hard and demanding, his kiss desperate and filled with passion. It thrilled me, that kiss. It made my heart pound and my knees weak. Even though I was opening myself up to being hurt all over again, I would have done anything in that classroom. If he'd wanted to have sex, I would have stripped off my clothing myself.

By the time I'd worked through my emotions, it was almost midnight. I could hear Aditi talking to someone in the kitchen downstairs, and I could feel the house vibrate from the speakers

blasting the sound from whatever game Chad and Theo were playing in the basement. I opened my bedroom door and saw Maverick
outside the door to Ace's room.

"What are you doing here?"

"Ace is taking some time off," he said. "I'm his backup."

I couldn't take it in. Ace had kissed me only a few hours ago
and now he was gone? "How long is he going to be away?"

Maverick shrugged. "He didn't say much. You know what he's
like."

Yes, I did. The last time we'd kissed he'd left on deployment,
and I never saw or heard from him again until Matt's funeral.
Clearly, nothing had changed.

"He didn't tell me."

"Well, that's Ace." He gave me a sympathetic smile. "He gave
me your schedule and briefed me on the alarm, and how things
generally work at the house. I might slip up here or there but I'm
sure we'll work it all out."

When I didn't respond, he gestured to the stairs. "Aditi made
spaghetti . . ."

"I'm not hungry . . . but thanks for being here. I'm glad it's
someone I know." I walked back into my room and grabbed my
phone. Ace had left a few messages telling me he had to take some
time off and I could contact him if I wanted to talk. No apology.
No explanation. Nothing about the kiss. My stomach clenched
into a knot. It was just like what happened before. New Ace was
old Ace after all.

Breathe. Breathe. You're fine. Lock it away.

"Haley."

I heard my name as if it were far away, each syllable punctuated by a knocking sound that grew progressively louder until I
heard a rattle and then a rush of cool air.

"Haley? Wake up." Ace's voice pulled me out of the darkness
and his firm hand on my shoulder brought me to my senses. I

opened my eyes only to discover I was lying face-first in a sea of papers on the cold, hard floor of my bedroom.

"She's okay," he said to someone over his shoulder. "Text Paige and let her know. I put her number in your phone before I left. She threatened to claw out my eyes if I didn't break down the door."

"I could have handled this." I recognized Maverick's Southern drawl. "You aren't supposed to be here."

"Just go and deal with Paige," Ace barked, gently flipping me onto my back. "I'll make sure she's okay and then you can take over."

"What's going on?" I put my forearm across my face, shielding my eyes from the blinding light.

"You haven't been out of your room in almost twenty hours," Ace said. "You didn't respond to Paige's messages, and you didn't answer your phone . . ." He ran his hands gently over my body, searching for injuries, and the warmth of his touch made me melt into the floor. "The last time anyone spoke to you was Mav yesterday evening. Paige didn't know Mav was filling in so she got in touch with me with all sorts of threats of bodily harm if I didn't check in on you. She's very creative."

"She is in biology," I said. "It comes with the territory."

"What are you doing on the floor?" He gently helped me to sit and peeled away a piece of paper that was stuck to my cheek with drool. "You didn't answer when we knocked. I had to use the emergency key."

"I was sleeping." I pulled myself up, struggling to maintain my dignity with my face smushed from sleeping on the floor, and my hair stuck to my cheek.

"Why aren't you in the bed?"

"I couldn't sleep so I've been writing songs."

"That's what this is?" He gestured to the sea of papers. "I didn't know you were still writing your own songs."

"They're not very good so I've never shown them to anyone, and I can only compose when I'm . . ." I sighed. "When bad stuff happens. I stayed up all night writing and I guess at some point I fell asleep. I don't know why everyone got so worried."

"You didn't come out of your room to eat or use the bathroom. You didn't go to class . . ."

"Oh God." As soon as he mentioned the bathroom, I had an urgent need to go. I pushed myself up and raced down the hallway. After washing up and making myself look semi-presentable, I returned to find Ace sitting on my floor reading the lyrics I'd been writing all night long.

Unlike many songwriters, I had no control over the creative part of my brain. I couldn't write on demand. I couldn't force the lyrics. I had to wait for a trigger and then the words came in a tidal wave that demanded my full attention. I didn't eat. I didn't sleep. And apparently, I didn't pee.

Threats and kisses, it seemed, were more of a trigger than being manhandled into a white panel van.

"These are very good." He looked up from the papers on his lap. "Did you write all this last night?"

"Yes." I snatched the papers away. "But they're private."

"The top one is about fear. Is that why you couldn't sleep? You're afraid?"

I sat across from him, leaning against the bed, my arms wrapped around my knees. I was still trying to wake up and shake off the brain fog that was making it difficult to remember why I'd been so angry with him.

"I'm fine."

"You're obviously not fine if you can't sleep, you write songs all night long without food or water until your fingers bleed—"

"My fingers aren't bleeding." I held up my hand. "I pick at the skin around my fingernails when I'm stressed and sometimes it bleeds. It's a thing with a name I can't remember right now. I would love to write until my fingers bled. It sounds very romantic. I'd feel like a real composer, so fully into the music I would let it destroy me to be free."

Ace chuckled. "You have an interesting view of romance."

My gaze flicked to his lips and away. "So do you."

He sat beside me, leaning against the bed, and lifted my hand, looking at the mess I'd made of my thumb. "I don't like to see you hurt, even if you're the one doing the hurting."

"I don't feel it." I didn't feel anything. I'd basically been numb since my dad died.

Ace brought my hand to his lips and kissed my fingers one by one. I couldn't move, couldn't breathe, couldn't cope with the sudden rush of emotion that flooded my senses at his touch.

"Stop." I yanked my hand away, but I could still feel the soft press of his lips on my skin, the gentle stroke of his finger.

"What triggered you?" he asked, seemingly unaffected by my rejection. "I need to know, because if it happens again and I can't find you, Paige will come for me. My life will be in danger."

I squeezed my legs, shivering as a cold draft blew across the floor. "I know it won't make sense but those threatening messages were more frightening to me than what happened on Michigan Avenue. When the guy tried to grab me on the street, it was shocking and terrifying, but it was in a public place and part of me still believed it could have been a random grab like the police said. But the messages were different. There was no chance they were meant for someone else." A shiver ran down my spine and I crumpled the page of lyrics in my hand.

"Haley . . . don't . . ." Ace gently pried my hand open and took the page, smoothing it out on the floor.

"He came onto *my* show, *my* happy place, and made me feel unsafe," I said, my voice wavering. "I know the station broadcasts to hundreds of thousands of people, but when I'm on the air, sharing my stories and playlists, and giving people space to share with me, it's an intimate experience, and those messages made me feel violated. Now, I can't pretend anymore. Now, it's in my face and I have to deal with the fact that it's real and it's not going away. Someone wants to hurt me, and I never did anything to them."

"That's why you have me," Ace said firmly. "No one is going to hurt you while I'm around, but like I said before, you have to tell me when stuff like this happens. You have to let me know when you've been threatened, or when you're afraid or feeling so distressed you can't sleep. I'm here for you however you need me."

"Honestly, Ace." I stared at the door, unable to meet his gaze. "I still don't completely trust you. You kissed me all those years ago and made me think certain things, and then you left Tyler's party with Esme Duncan and made me feel like an idiot. And now you've done it again."

"It wasn't my choice," Ace said. "The company has a rule about taking time off when we're doing full-time protection. I'd already broken it. If I hadn't agreed to take a break, Tony would have pulled me out entirely."

I shifted away from him, shivering as the cool air filled up the space between us. "It's just very hard to believe given the timing." And then, the questions I'd always wanted to ask spilled out before I could stop them. "Why did you kiss me at Tyler's party? Was I just there when you felt the need to kiss someone? Did you feel sorry for me? Was it just a friendly kiss that I misinterpreted? Did it mean anything?" My voice rose in agitation. "Or were you just trying to be cruel?" I picked up my pen and clicked the top over and over, trying to find a focus for the pain that was escaping the black box where I'd kept it hidden for years.

Click. Click. Click. It seemed like forever until Ace finally answered.

"I didn't *just* want to kiss you, Haley."

I stopped clicking. Looked up for the first time since he'd sat down beside me. My heart thudded a frantic rhythm in my chest. "What else did you want to do?"

"Everything."

CHAPTER 16

Ace

"Knock knock." Mav thudded on Haley's bedroom door before pushing it open. "Ready to head out, Ace? I called Paige and let her know Haley's okay. She says she might not kill you after all."

Mav wasn't a bad guy, and I appreciated the subtle warning that I'd be in big trouble if Tony found out I was still around when I was on mandatory leave. I also couldn't fault his timing. I'd crossed another damn line telling Haley what I'd been denying for so long, and I needed to get out of there and figure out what the hell I was doing.

"I've got to go." I moved to stand, and Haley grabbed my arm, waiting for Mav to leave before she said, "You can't say that to me and just walk away."

"I don't have a choice. Tony won't just pull me off your detail for good if I don't take time off; he'll fire me."

"I want to come with you." She grabbed a bundle of papers and held them up to me. "This is pain and loss and all the other emotions that I can't let out. If I stay here, I'll get sucked back in. I need to get out of my head." She scooped up more papers, pressing them against her chest. "My head is still here."

"Mav has to go where you go. He'll tell Tony if you come with me."

"Not if he doesn't know I'm gone." She ran over to her window and looked out over the roof. "I'll tell him I'm going to bed and climb out." Her eyes sparkled when she turned back to me. I knew that look. She might have been older but the daredevil side of her was still there.

"Absolutely not."

She pushed open the window and leaned out into the night. "It's not too steep and there's a thick tree branch hanging right beside it. I would just have to jump from the branch to the ground."

My pulse kicked up a notch, and I crossed the room and slid an arm around her waist to pull her back. Big mistake. She fit perfectly against me, her body soft, her ass pressed so tight against my cock, I was hard in an instant.

Haley sucked in a sharp breath and looked at me over her shoulder, her lips parted, eyes dark with sensual promise. "By 'everything,' did you mean *'everything'*?"

I didn't know this new Haley well enough to share all the dark thoughts that were going through my mind. I didn't know what she would do if I spelled out exactly how I wanted to touch her, to taste her, to make her writhe in pleasure and scream my name. I didn't know how to be that open because the two times I'd let my guard down with her, it hadn't gone well.

"I don't . . ." *But I did.*

"Does 'everything' include this?" She covered my hand with hers and slid our joined hands underneath her shirt. Her skin was warm and soft and I couldn't help but caress her, spreading my fingers until the tips brushed along the edge of her bra.

"Is this what you want?" I cupped her breast, squeezing gently, my thumb brushing over her nipple peaked beneath the silken fabric.

Haley shuddered and sank farther into my body. "Yes."

Fuck it. I twisted my free hand through her hair and tugged her head back, baring her neck for the heated slide of my lips.

"And this?" I murmured, breathing in the floral fragrance of her skin.

"Yes." She arched against me, her ass rubbing against my fly, an exquisitely painful pleasure that had me gritting my teeth as I fought for control.

"I want everything, too," she whispered. "Everything you want to give me."

It was an effort to release her, and almost impossible to walk away when she turned to face me, her cheeks flushed with heat. "Stay here. I'll go and talk to Mav to see if we can work something out. I'm not in his good books right now. He wasn't happy when he found out I was in the basement gaming with Chad and Theo."

A maelstrom of emotions crossed Haley's face. "You were downstairs?"

"I was off duty, but I wasn't going to leave officially until I talked to you and explained the situation. I spent the afternoon at the gym with Chad and Theo and then we were gaming until Paige sent me her threatening messages."

Haley leaned up and gave me a peck on the cheek. "You weren't going to leave me."

"No, bug. I wasn't going to leave without talking to you in person. I would have slept on their fucking couch if I had to."

I wasn't aware I'd used her old family nickname until a pained expression crossed her face. "No one has called me 'bug' for a very long time."

"I'm sorry. I wasn't thinking."

"It's okay." She smiled. "It's not a bad memory."

I left Haley to change her clothes, and went downstairs to talk to Mav. I never asked for favors. I handled my own business and never put myself in a position where I had to rely on someone else. I'd also never let myself get close enough to people to ask. But Mav seemed like a good guy, and this was for Haley.

"We could both get in trouble for this," Mav pointed out when I told him Haley was still shaken from the online threat and didn't want to stay at the house.

"She'd still have protection," I said. "She'd be with me."

Mav laughed. "I have a feeling your attention wouldn't be fully on the job."

"How about tickets to the next Bears game? Chad gets comps through the radio station. He offered to take me to the next game and said I could bring a friend. I doubt I'll still be here when they play, but I'm sure he'd be happy to have company." I didn't know

Mav well, but one of the few times I'd met him he'd been wearing a Bears cap.

"Can't say no to the Bears." Mav grinned. "Two games. One night. And I'll come and walk the floor at the hotel. But the Bears better fucking win."

We bumped fists to seal the deal, and something shifted in my chest. Asking favors. Making friends. If I closed my eyes and opened them again, would it still be real?

As I passed the living room window on my way to get Haley, I caught movement in the bushes. My adrenaline spiked and I drew my weapon, crossing back to the kitchen so I could slip out the back door. I made my way around the house and came up behind the intruder. It was only when I saw the brown ponytail that I lowered my gun.

"Christ, Haley. I didn't think you were serious when you said you'd climb out the window."

A grin spread across her face. "I was worried Maverick would say no. It wasn't hard . . ." She trailed off when I scowled.

"I told you I was going to talk to Mav and work something out. What if you got hurt?"

"I didn't get hurt," she said. "You know I'm good at climbing trees, and I used to climb down the roof all the time when I'd sneak out of the house to Ryan Trevino's parties with Paige."

"You did what?" No way would Matt or I have let Haley go to Trevino's parties. He was a local drug dealer who also sold alcohol to minors and was known for wild parties that usually ended with some sort of emergency vehicle attending his property.

"It's like riding a bicycle." She slid her arms around my waist and looked up at me with an expression of pure manipulative innocence. "Don't be grumpy. Did you work things out with Mav, because if you didn't . . ."

"'Grumpy' isn't the word I'd use to describe how I'm feeling right now." I cupped her jaw, running my thumb over her cheek, seeking the simple assurance she was indeed here after jumping off the roof and not a ghost. "And yes, we worked something out. He's coming with us."

Haley's eyes widened. "With us as in *with us*?"

"He'll be in the hallway." I didn't want my mind going down that path, because just the idea of anyone else touching Haley set my teeth on edge. "And I thought I told you to stay in your room. There are consequences for not following the rules."

Her eyes lit up and she licked her lips. "What kind of consequences?"

I'd always known going down this road with Haley would be a wild ride. She had few inhibitions, and an openness to new experiences unmatched by anyone I'd ever met. Jump a creek? Climb a tree? Steal an apple from an orchard guarded by a ferocious dog? Go outside to "see the stars" with a senior who didn't just have notches in his belt, he had a whole damn collection? If I didn't keep control, the two of us together might combust.

"You'll have to wait and see."

CHAPTER 17

Haley

"This is amazing." I walked around Ace's lavish hotel suite at the Four Seasons, taking in the vast, elegant room decorated in soothing shades of beige and gray, while trying to ignore the simmering tension between us. Ace had insisted on driving his SUV with Maverick beside me in the back, and by the time we got to the hotel, my imagination had gone wild. I was all ready for a little spicy action in the elevator, but Ace had other ideas. He ordered room service at the front desk when we checked in and then we had to ride the elevator to the fifteenth floor with Maverick like two civilized adults who didn't want to tear off each other's clothes.

"Look at the view," I said, trying to hide my frustration. I'd imagined spending the night with Ace for years and in detail, and now that it was finally happening, I didn't want to waste any time. I was so wound up, I didn't care if he slept with me and disappeared the next day, breaking my heart into smithereens. I was living in the moment and this moment was supposed to be all about sex.

"I am."

I turned to see Ace leaning against the minibar, arms folded, watching me like a predator about to feast. I wasn't sure what was happening between us. All I knew was that Ace had been there when I needed him, the chemistry between us was insane, he wanted to do everything with me, and now we were alone in a fancy hotel room that was dominated by the biggest bed I'd ever seen, and we weren't in it.

Before I could suggest a little appetizer before the meal, his phone buzzed in his pocket. He checked the screen, then motioned for me to be quiet while he took the call.

"Tony." He pulled out the desk chair and took a seat. "Yeah, I'm at the hotel. Any info from the FBI?" He mouthed the words "I'm sorry" and shrugged.

I smiled, partially relieved for a moment to catch my breath. "It's okay," I mouthed back.

I took a last look out the window at the twinkling skyline and then vaulted onto the bed, landing on the pillowy duvet with a loud flop. I heard a snort behind me and looked over my shoulder to see Ace's amused smile.

"It's all good," he said into the phone. "Haley was fine with Mav. I told her it was just the weekend . . ."

Trapped on the phone. Such a perfect time to tease. I sat up and waved my hand in front of my face. "Hot," I mouthed.

Ace gestured to a control panel by the door. I shook my head and slowly slid my hoodie up and over my head.

"A weekend is all I need, Tony . . ."

I reached for my T-shirt. Ace's eyes widened, and he shook his head.

Maybe I was moving too fast, and I shouldn't have been reading anything into Ace telling me he wanted to do "everything" to me. What did "everything" mean exactly? I had a vivid imagination and over three hundred romance books on my Kindle in various shades of spice. I was pretty much up for anything. Not one of my high school flings or my limited hookups had had more than two chili peppers' worth of moves, but from the way Ace was watching me, I had a feeling he was a five-chili-pepper kind of guy. Maybe six.

Bad imagination. I could feel the heat building down below. I hoped "everything" didn't mean he wanted to take me for a stroll by the lake after dinner with Maverick following behind us. I still couldn't believe I was alone in a hotel room with Ace and my teen fantasy was about to come true.

In an attempt to distract myself, I scooted up the bed and

leaned against the headboard. How long did we have before room service arrived? I'd told Ace when we checked in that I wasn't hungry, but he had insisted that I needed food. I'd agreed only because I wanted to have enough energy to do all the things I'd ever imagined doing . . . and more.

"Tell her I don't do repeat assignments," he said into his phone, turning in his chair so he could watch me. I took that to mean he didn't really want me to stop taking off my clothes, so I pulled my T-shirt over my head and tossed it on the floor.

"Tony, I . . ." A scowl creased his brow and he pointed at the shirt and motioned for me to put it back on. Instead, I undid the button on my jeans and pulled down the zipper. I imagined him telling me to spread my legs and touch myself while he watched. I imagined him fucking me while he talked to Tony. My nipples tightened under my bra. There was no way he couldn't notice.

"Sorry. The phone cut out." He drew a line across his throat. I laughed and I pushed my jeans down over my hips and threw them across the room.

His gaze swept over my body. Carnal. Intent. Something changed in that moment and the air between us crackled with electricity. He beckoned me forward with his free hand. Two fingers. A brusque motion that I felt deep in my core.

"I don't know why she would say that." He leaned back in his chair and patted his lap. Motioned me over again.

I was acutely aware of how he tracked my movements, the lazy way his eyes slid over me, the hitch in his breath when I straddled his lap. I wouldn't have been as bold with anyone else, but this was Ace, and I'd wanted him forever. My body was safe with him, but maybe not my heart.

"She'll be fine with someone else," he said into the phone, his voice thickening. "Tell her we don't know how long this . . ." His breath hitched when I took off my bra and his gaze went feral. ". . . assignment will last."

I rocked against his hard length, threaded my fingers through his soft hair. He hadn't touched me and I was already so wet my panties were soaked.

He closed his eyes, gritting his teeth. "Tony . . ." His Adam's apple bobbed when he swallowed. "Listen. I've got to go. I've got another call."

I licked my lips and then leaned forward to pepper tiny kisses along his jaw. His muscles went rock hard and he grabbed my hair, yanking my head back.

"Be still," he mouthed.

By way of response, I cupped my breasts, squeezing and rubbing my thumbs over my nipples until a soft growl ripped from his throat.

"Bye, Tony." He tossed the phone on the bed.

"Haley." His voice was rough and husky with desire as he brushed his lips against the hollow at the base of my throat.

"Yes?" I was breathless, my heart thudding in my chest, my body caught in a cyclone of need.

"I want you like this. I have fucking dreamed of having you like this." His hand tightened in my hair and I could feel the press of his erection against my core.

"I want you to have me like this," I said. "But you're wearing too many clothes."

"We need to talk first," he gritted out, releasing me. "I can't . . ." His voice caught, broke. "I want to do this right."

I wiggled against him and let out a groan. "This feels pretty right to me."

"If you keep moving like that," he warned, "I won't be slow or gentle."

"I don't want slow or gentle," I said when I took a moment to catch my breath. "I don't want to make love. I don't need you to whisper sweet nothings in my ear. I want you to fuck me, Ace. Hard. I want you to steal my breath away."

It was like a dam broke.

His tongue slid into my mouth, touching, tasting, exploring every inch until my thighs trembled and I collapsed against his chest. I tasted whiskey and fresh mint, drew in his familiar scent of pine and crisp autumn air. I felt nothing but his strong arms. I heard nothing but his groan. My mind stopped whirling and focused only on the rush of sensation and the fact that Ace—my Ace—wanted me in his bed.

His eyes blazed liquid heat. "You're a bad girl."

"You have no idea how bad I can be." I trailed my fingers over the stubble on his jaw, rough with a five-o'clock shadow. "I'm not the Haley you left back home."

"Haley is the last girl I would ever want to be with. She's just a kid playing dress-up."

I pushed away the memory of Ace's words from a night when I was sixteen and crushing on him so hard I didn't care if Matt found out. It was a long time ago, and there was no point dredging up the past humiliation of learning what he really thought of me. That Ace didn't want that Haley. But the hard ridge beneath Ace's fly told me that things had changed. Could I have him for just one night and put everything else behind me? I appreciated his heartfelt apology, but they were just words, and the pain of the broken trust between us was still there, although maybe not quite as sharp.

He groaned and buried his face in my neck, making me even hotter. "Be my bad girl, Haley."

Answer: yes.

"I'm already your bad girl." I slid my hands under his shirt and peeled it off his body. His skin was warm and slightly tanned, ridged with muscle and a six-pack that just begged to be licked. "I jumped out the window, remember? I would have escaped from Maverick to come to your hotel with you."

His hands tightened around me. "That kind of behavior needs to be addressed. It can't happen again."

I was pretty sure I wasn't going to be climbing out my bedroom window again. Aside from the fact that it wasn't as easy as it had been when I was fifteen, I wasn't oblivious to the danger and had been careful to stay in the bushes near the window where I'd be able to get Ace's attention if anyone came by. This was a one-time thing. Ace was an itch I wanted to scratch. I didn't need anything more.

"What are you going to do?" I asked, breathless.

"First, I'm going to fuck you the way I always imagined." He stood, lifting me against him, and walked us over to the desk. He settled me on the cold, hard surface, and stood between my spread legs. "And then I'm going to punish you for putting yourself at risk, and then I'll fuck you again but I'll take my time. Are you good with that? I need to hear you say it."

I couldn't answer fast enough. "Yes. I'm good with that."

Ace opened his buckle and ripped his belt off with a crack that made my eyes glaze over and my mouth water.

"She likes that," he said, his voice dangerously soft.

"She does."

"Do you like this?" His hand moved between my legs, cupping me before he pushed my wet panties aside and slid two fingers inside me.

My back arched at the delicious intrusion. "Very much."

"And this?" He thumbed my clit and my mind went quiet. All the noise disappearing as lust infused my brain.

"S'good." I could barely get the words out as he pumped his fingers and circled my clit in teasing strokes.

"You're so wet," he groaned. "I want to fuck you so deep."

"Please do. We don't have much time. You made a very bad decision and ordered something to eat when there is plenty to eat right here."

"Christ." He groaned, and the desperation in his voice, the slow, steady thrust of his fingers, took me to the edge in a heartbeat. "If you keep talking like that I—"

"What?" I asked, my heart pounding in anticipation. "Tell me."

"I'll lose control."

"I would pay money to see that, but since I'm almost naked

and have no cash hidden on me, I can offer you this." I took his free hand and placed it on my breast.

"I always wondered what you were hiding under your clothes." He withdrew his other hand and squeezed both my breasts, thumbs running roughly over my nipples. "You have beautiful breasts."

"Thank—" My words were lost in a groan as he yanked my hips forward and leaned down to take my nipple in his mouth, sucking so hard white-hot heat shot through my veins.

A delicious shudder ran through my body. I'd never been man-handled before, never been treated with such delectable roughness. The men I'd been with had been gentle and caring. I never realized until that moment that what I really wanted was to be taken, my body devoured out of blazing need.

"Maybe we should wait." His carnal gaze as he looked me up and down made me hot all over. "I should take my time with you, give your sweet pussy the attention it deserves."

"No waiting. Not the first time." Some part of me was struck by the irony of a person who rarely stopped talking being rendered incapable of giving more than two- or three-word answers. "Your turn to strip."

"Someone has to be dressed to answer the door." He ripped off my panties and then unzipped, pulling out his cock, thick and hard and bigger than I'd ever imagined.

Unable to resist, I wrapped my hand around his length, stroking and squeezing until he groaned.

"Is this for me?" I asked as his eyes glazed over and his body shuddered.

"You're going to get that and more if you don't stop." He put a gentle hand over mine and moved me away. "I want to be inside you the first time. I want to feel your hot, wet pussy around me when you come all over my cock."

My breath hitched. "I want that, too."

Ace rolled on a condom from his pocket. "Are you ready for me?"

"So ready." I wrapped my legs around his hips, licking my lips in anticipation. It had been a long time. Too long.

I felt him pushing at my entrance, so big, so wide. For a moment I thought he'd be too much, but when he pushed inside all I felt was pleasure. I let out a shuddering breath at the sensation of being stretched and filled, bracing myself on the desk. Me and Ace. Together at last. He pulled out and thrust again, burying himself to the hilt in one hard stroke.

"You feel so good when you take it deep." He slammed into me, and I let out a moan as the desk banged against the wall.

"Desk," I panted. "People."

"I don't give a fuck. I have wanted you for so long I don't give a damn who hears us." He pounded into me, setting up a rhythm that was matched by the slam of the desk and the thud of my heart. Everything tightened inside me as he quickened his pace, the drag of his cock against my sensitive inner walls winding me tighter and tighter. "I want to hear you come," he gritted out. "I want to hear what I do to you."

"I need it rough." I groaned. "I need you to fuck me so hard we break the desk."

He hissed in pleasure. "I'll give you that and more." Reaching between us, he circled his thumb around my clit as he ground into me, his gentle touch a contrast to the hard thrusts that slammed the desk into the wall over and over. When we were both breathless, our skin slick with exertion, he caught my lips in a scorching kiss and pressed his thumb down firmly, sending me into a whirlpool of ecstasy that swirled through my body until I was nothing but a blaze of sensation. With one last thrust, his cock pulsed with his own release, and a groan ripped from his throat.

"Oh my God." I was sticky with sweat, pulse thudding, chest heaving, physically spent, and all I could think was how I wanted him again. Save for that singular image, my mind was uncharacteristically quiet and still. I could actually hear myself think. I could follow one thought, and it led to the man who had dropped his hands to the desk and rested his forehead against mine. I followed the thread, and realized with hideous certainty that if I let him get too close, he might open that black box of pain inside me and set everything free.

I didn't want to go down that road, didn't need that emotional connection. We were compatible on a physical level. I didn't need any more.

"That was—" A knock on the door cut him off and he quickly zipped up his pants.

"Room service."

I jumped off the desk and made a run for the bathroom while Ace pulled his shirt over his head.

"This reminds me of the night you and Matt came home from a party, and I had sneaked Adrian Yang into the house," I called out. "I ran naked into the washroom then, too."

"You told Matt you were studying."

"I didn't lie." I leaned out the bathroom door. "We were studying anatomy."

We ate. We had more sexy times. Finally, we collapsed on Ace's enormous bed. I'd only had a few hours' sleep the night before, and that was on the floor, so my eyes closed as soon as my head hit the pillow. "No funny stuff," I mumbled.

"There's nothing funny about a naked Haley in my bed." He lay on his back and pulled me across his chest, tucking my head against his shoulder. Not as soft as a pillow, but so much warmer.

"Are you going to sleep, too?"

"I'm too wound up," he said. "Sing me one of your songs. I don't remember hearing any of your originals in your streams."

"I haven't uploaded them," I said. "They're more of a catharsis for me. I don't know if I could open myself up to sharing that kind of pain."

Ace folded his hands behind his head. "So that's what you do instead of cry?"

It took a few moments before I could answer. He saw me. He'd always seen me. He'd always known when "fine" didn't really mean "fine" at all.

"I suppose so." I ran my finger along the rough bristles of his jaw, and then over the mouth that had given me so much pleasure. Ace took my finger and sucked it gently between his lips. I felt the gentle pressure as a throb between my legs and suddenly I wasn't tired anymore.

"Do you enjoy working with A-list celebrities?" I asked, moving away from the uncomfortable subject of my feelings. "What are they like?"

"Mostly they're just lonely people," he said. "They can't go out to a restaurant or a movie without everyone gawking at them or asking for an autograph, so they often just stay in or visit with other celebrities. They can't go out on a date in public without it being front-page news, and even if they book a private room somewhere, they've usually got a bodyguard or two watching over them."

"I can relate," I said, smiling. "Between you and Matt, it was an effort to have a proper date."

Puzzled, he frowned. "What do you mean?"

"Sixth grade. Jay Harris tried to kiss me behind the school, and you showed up and told me my dad needed me at home."

"You were too young to be kissing anyone," he grumbled.

"Seventh grade. Dev Kumar invited me to go for a walk in the woods and you and Matt just happened to show up on your bikes and decided to walk us home."

"He wasn't there to appreciate nature," Ace said. "I overheard him talking to his friends."

"High school," I said, ignoring him. "My first real boyfriend, and yet every time I tried to be alone with him . . ."

"You and Dan Garcia were a disaster waiting to happen," he bit out. "He was you but without any modicum of restraint. If

Matt and I hadn't intervened, you two would likely have wound up in some serious trouble."

Dan Garcia was the most thrilling person I'd ever met. He would do anything, try anything, break any rule. His brain moved faster than mine, jumping from one crazy idea to the next—climb on the school roof at night, sled down a steep hill into a frozen river, light things on fire—he was particularly enamored of fires. Ace was right. We weren't good for each other, but damn he'd been a good time.

"Are you talking about the fact he was my first kiss? Do you know how much maneuvering I had to do to be alone with him? Matt's truck didn't break down by itself the night of the Halloween dance . . ."

Ace looked over, his eyes glittering in the dark. "That was you?"

"You weren't the only one who was good with engines." I shot him a sly look. "Dan was pretty good with his hands."

"Don't tell me things like that. I might have to hunt him down the next time I'm home."

"Well, then I'd better not tell you about the first time we had sex."

"He still lives in Riverstone," Ace muttered, half to himself. "Janice mentioned that he'd worked on her car. He took over his dad's auto body shop. Maybe he has an accident. Car jack fails. Electric shock. Fire . . ."

"I snuck him in my bedroom window," I said smugly. "Matt thought I was all tucked safe in my bed. It made it all the sweeter."

"God, Haley."

"That's what Dan said." A smile tugged at my lips. "I didn't even like him that much, but he was willing to climb up the drainpipe and risk being caught by Matt, which made him worth having." I had been determined not to leave high school a virgin, and since the boy I'd been crushing on since I was old enough to have crushes had dumped me for Esme Duncan, I'd taken what was available and regretted it the next day. I didn't feel anything for

Dan, and he didn't feel anything for me. He loved to experience things, and I'd been a new experience that he didn't need to have again.

"I miss Matt." The words dropped from my lips before I could stop them. I never talked about Matt, especially not the stuff that made my heart hurt, but Ace had given me a safe space to say the words that were always there. "He was a good big brother."

Ace pressed a kiss to my forehead. "He loved you very much, bug. He was always worrying about you."

"I tried to look after myself, so he didn't have to," I said. "After Dad died and Mom got lost in her work, I just—" I drew in a shuddering breath. "I didn't want to lean on him too much. He put so much pressure on himself trying to be the man of the family. I didn't want to add to his burden. I didn't tell him when I was sad or scared or lonely. I let him think everything was fine."

"He would have been there for you if you'd let him," Ace said. "He was there for me. Just like you were there for me that day at the creek after your dad died."

"You cried," I said softly. "I didn't realize how much you cared for my dad until that afternoon. And I didn't know that people like you cried."

"People like me?"

"Strong and steady. So calm and in control. You seemed a lot older than fifteen. Nothing ever seemed to bother you."

Ace laughed. "That's what Matt said about you, when I told him you weren't acting like yourself after the funeral. I realized that afternoon that I'd never seen you cry. No matter what happened you were always cheerful and upbeat. You never stayed angry with anyone. You'd sulk a bit when your parents scolded you, but then minutes later, you'd be laughing and joking again. Matt said you didn't feel things the way other people felt them, and they just bounced off you like water off a duck's back."

"I feel things," I said. "But he was partly right. I keep those strong emotions buried deep inside."

"You could have let them out that day at the creek with me," he said. "I wouldn't have judged you."

"I know." I leaned up to kiss his cheek before closing my eyes as sleep pulled me under. "But the tears wouldn't come."

CHAPTER 18

Haley

EIGHT YEARS AGO

Dad died two years after Ace came into our lives. He was in the kitchen at home doing what he loved to do when his heart finally gave out. His doctor had been warning him for years about his weight and blood pressure and had put him on a strict diet. But Dad loved food. It was his life. And there was no way he would let a dish leave the kitchen if he hadn't tasted it first.

I was the one who found him. I came home from school excited for snack time. Dad had promised me a new type of grilled cheese with three different cheeses and artisan bread, and I was looking forward to being his taste tester and telling him all about my day.

Even when I saw him lying on the kitchen floor, it never occurred to me that he could be gone. Dad was a big man with a loud, hearty voice, and he could fill up a room with his presence alone. At first, I thought he was doing something funny, like hiding or pretending to look for spiders on the ceiling, but then I noticed the silence. No music. No laughter. Not even the huff of Dad's breath—he'd been huffing a lot going up and down the stairs to the cellar. Mom said it was too much exercise, but Dad didn't listen.

"Dad?" Part of me already knew it was bad the second my knees hit the floor. Part of me had already started building the black box I would need to keep the overwhelming feelings contained. Little girls aren't supposed to handle big emotions or try to lift their daddies off the floor. "Dad? Wake up. It's not funny."

I couldn't move him, so I wrapped my arms around him and gave him a hug, waiting for him to jump up and tickle me until my stomach hurt from laughing. "Dad? Wake up. Please wake up. I have to tell you what happened at school." I pressed my ear to his chest and heard the faintest thud of his heart, lighter than butterfly wings.

That's when Ace found me.

Ace called for an ambulance and then he called Mom. After they took Dad away, he took me to the hospital where we met Mom and Matt in the waiting room. Dad was in surgery by then, and all we could do was hope and pray.

Matt couldn't handle the wait. He prowled around the room, flipping switches, rifling through magazines, and thumping on the vending machine when it didn't deliver his soda.

"What the fuck is wrong with this place?" He kicked the machine. "If they can't even fix a soda machine, how can they fix a heart?"

Ace went over to him and put a hand on his shoulder. I couldn't hear what he said, but it seemed to calm Matt down. Ace shook the machine gently from side to side and the soda slid free and dropped into the well.

"Thanks," I whispered when he returned to the seat beside me. "Matt loses it when he's scared."

"I'm not scared," Matt shouted. "It's going to be fine. They can do all sorts of things with hearts. I read it on my phone. Stents, bypasses, quadruple bypasses, pacemakers . . . They'll fix his heart and then he'll come home."

I wasn't so sure. Dad had been in surgery a long time. Mom had gone to get an update and still hadn't come back, and every so often a nurse would come out and look at us with a sorrowful expression on her face.

As if he knew what I was thinking, Ace wrapped my hand in his and gave it a squeeze.

"You don't have to stay," Matt said to Ace. "We've got that big math test tomorrow and I know you need to study."

I tightened my grip on Ace's hand. With Matt about to lose it and Mom gone to find a doctor, he was the only thing keeping me steady.

Ace looked down at me and his eyes softened. "I'm not going anywhere. Fuck the test."

"Fuck the fucking test." Matt laughed, a hollow, bitter sound. "Wonder what Dad will say tomorrow when I tell him we said 'Fuck the test.'"

I saw Ace's throat move as he swallowed, and I knew that he was thinking the same as me. He'd seen Dad on the floor. Dad wasn't going to be there tomorrow. He would never know about the test or the swearing or the dents in the vending machine. He wouldn't take Matt aside for a "talking-to" and then send him out to rake the lawn.

I closed my eyes and leaned against Ace's shoulder. He was so calm, so still, so utterly in control. I tried to absorb his strength, but even with his hand wrapped tight around mine, and his warmth seeping into my body, I couldn't breathe when the news finally came. It was too big. Too overwhelming. Dad was my person, and my person was gone.

I don't remember much about what happened in the days afterward. All I knew was that Ace was always there, helping Mom with the funeral and celebration of life, holding my hand or sitting with me on the back steps, talking to Matt and playing games with him until late into the night. I never thought about who was there for him.

Everyone thought Matt would be the problem after Dad died, but as it turned out, it was me. I became completely untethered, vaping in the restrooms between classes, skipping lessons, hanging out with older kids after school. My marks went from straight As down to Ds and the principal arranged a meeting with Mom because she was worried I was going to fail.

"Have you considered counseling?" she asked Mom as I scrolled through my phone in her pristine modern office and tried to look bored.

"She won't go."

"How about her friends? Could she talk to them?" The principal seemed to have forgotten I was sitting right there.

Mom told her Paige had done everything she could to pull me out of my whirlpool of destruction. Mostly, she was concerned that I was staying out late every night with the wrong kind of kids. She didn't seem to understand that I didn't want to come home and see the empty kitchen and the hear the echo of my dad's "baby girl" ringing in the house.

"She was close to Matt's friend Ace, too," Mom said. "But Ace hasn't come around since the week after the funeral. Dave was like a father to him. He took the death very hard."

"I had his grandmother in here the other day," the principal said. "He hasn't been coming to school either. It's so sad. He'd already been through so much in his life, and he was doing so well."

My head jerked up, shattering the pretense that I hadn't been paying attention. Ace had dropped out? He loved school. Every day he used to come over and tell Dad everything that he'd learned in every class. I'd been so wrapped up in my own pain, I'd forgotten that I wasn't the only one affected by my father's death. And if Ace wasn't in class, I knew exactly where he would be.

After school, I made my way through the forest to the creek where Dad had taught Ace how to fish. Autumn had come and the forest floor was covered in leaves, the air crisp with a hint of the coming frost. I found Ace sitting against a tree on the bank, idly tossing stones into the water. He had to know I was coming from the crackle of leaves and the snapping of sticks under my feet as I approached, but when I sat beside him, he didn't even turn his head.

I was twelve and I'd never lost anyone before. I didn't know what to say—an unusual situation for me because people always thought I talked too much. I wanted to hug him, but I could feel the pain radiating around him, like a porcupine's prickles warning people to stay away. I sat down, careful not to touch him, and for the first time in my life, someone actually needed me to chase the silence away.

"Dad really liked you," I said after a long moment. "He said you were part of the family. When we were going places together, he would always ask if you were coming, and when you weren't there, he liked to tell us about interesting things you guys had talked about. He always put out an extra plate for you at dinner, too, even on days you weren't coming, just in case you changed your mind." Dad was gone but I would always carry his love with me. I had a lifetime of memories of hugs and kisses and laughter and stories. I wanted to give Ace something to carry, too.

Ace froze, his hand curled around a stone by his side. I took that to mean he wanted to hear more. So, I gave him more. Stories about camping trips and testing new recipes, Christmases where Dad dressed up as Santa, and one Easter where he dressed as a rabbit and fell into Paige's blow-up pool. I told him how Dad had read bedtime stories, giving each character a different voice, and about the time he'd taught me to ride a bike, and the minute he let go of the seat I raced down the road and he had to call the neighbors to find me. I told him how one day, after Ace had helped him fix the car, he said he was blessed because he felt like he had three kids, not two.

Ace dropped his forehead to his knees and wrapped his arms around himself. His body shuddered as his tears formed small muddy puddles on the ground.

I'd never seen Ace cry. I'd never seen him be anything but a regular teenage boy, albeit quieter, more reserved, and more polite than Matt and his friends. He laughed at Dad's jokes, played pranks with Matt, and was always around to lend a helping hand, whether it was in the kitchen with Dad, or carrying heavy boxes of files for Mom, or fixing swing sets and bicycle chains for me.

I wanted to cry, too. Everyone had cried. Mom cried at dinnertime when we ate the meals people had prepared for us, somehow knowing we couldn't bear to be in the kitchen. Matt cried in his bedroom at night when he thought we couldn't hear him. But the tears didn't come for me. Something inside me was broken and the black box had swallowed up my feelings. I tried hurting myself—paper cuts, falling off my bike, once I even took a kitchen knife and sliced my thumb. I watched sad movies and listened to sad songs, and one night I broke into Dad's old restaurant, took down the "For Sale" sign, sat on his worn leather stool and imagined he was still alive. But nothing worked. I was frozen inside.

I awkwardly put my arm around Ace, and he leaned against me and sobbed until the light began to fade and the cool air chased the last of the late-summer warmth away.

When he finally looked up, his eyes swollen, face red, he seemed lighter somehow, like the tears had taken away his pain. I wanted that too, but even Ace's tears weren't enough to open up the core of me.

"We'd better get you home." He held out his hand to help me up, and for some reason he didn't let go.

"Mrs. Whitby told Mom you weren't going to class," I said as I kicked the autumn leaves.

"What's the point?"

"I thought you loved learning. Dad said you were super smart, but you'd never been given a chance to shine. He told Matt he would need to work as hard as you if he wanted to become a dentist."

"He was the only person who cared," Ace said. "Now, it doesn't matter."

"I care." And then because I didn't want him to misunderstand, I added, "Mom and Matt care. Your grandmother cares . . ."

"You're only twelve," he said. "You don't even know what you're talking about, and I heard you've been hanging around with some bad people."

"I wanted to feel something," I admitted. "I don't feel anything anymore. I thought they could help me."

"That's not the way to do it, bug." He shook his head. "That's a bad path. Drugs and alcohol will make you feel better for a short time, but then you need more and more, and it gets out of control. You need to let it out. You need to feel the pain."

"I can't." I kicked another pile of leaves and stubbed my toe on a hidden root. "There's nothing inside me but a black box that swallowed up all my feelings." I'd never told anyone about the black box, but Ace had cried in front of me, and I knew he wouldn't judge.

"That's the kind of thing people write in songs," he said. "You should write a song about how you feel. Maybe that will help."

"I stopped writing songs when Dad died."

I didn't know how Ace knew about my songs. I'd been writing lyrics as long as I could remember. Mostly they were attempts to capture feelings that I didn't have the vocabulary to express, or to say things that I was otherwise afraid to share. I didn't have the kind of deeply emotive experiences many singers wrote about. My life until my father's death had been a happy one. But the moment he said it out loud, I wondered if I should try again. Now, I knew death and sorrow. I couldn't cry, but I knew pain.

As we walked the worn trail home, I told Ace about school and all the drama. I talked about shows I'd watched and a story I'd written for English class. I talked the way I used to talk when Dad was around. Ace listened. Really listened. He heard what I was trying to say.

When we finally reached the house, it was almost dark. Mom was still at work and the only light was coming from Matt's bedroom window. Mom was leaving in the morning for another trip to Washington. She said she was trying to raise awareness about the problems with the medical system so people like Dad didn't die when they weren't supposed to.

"Ace?"

"Yeah?"

"Do you need a hug?"

"Yeah, bug. I do." He got down on one knee and I gave him a hug and he hugged me back. I hadn't had many hugs since Dad died. Mom always hugged me good night when she was home, but it wasn't the same. Some nights she held me too tightly and other nights she barely held me at all. Ace hugged me just right.

"Matt cries, too," I said after he pulled away. "But only at night in his room. Don't tell him I told you because he'll be angry. He thinks he has to be the man of the family now, but he doesn't know what to do. He misses you. We all do."

"I can't be in your house," Ace said. "I can't be in the kitchen and not hear your dad's voice."

"I don't like it there either. It's lonely. That's why I wasn't coming home from school." I looked up at him. "You should come in today. Mom isn't getting home until late, and we've run out of community dinners. Matt said he would try to make chicken Parm."

Ace snorted a laugh. "Matt can't cook."

"I know. I need you to be there to call the ambulance when I get food poisoning."

Ace laughed, a reluctant bark that came from his throat like he wasn't expecting it. The sound made me giggle and I felt lighter than I had in months.

"I'd better come and help him," Ace said. "Chicken can be dangerous if you don't know what you're doing. I'll bet he hasn't even defrosted it."

"Maybe we should just have spaghetti."

"I can do spaghetti." He squeezed my hand. "I learned from the best."

CHAPTER 19

Ace

Two days of "vacation" was two days too many. Mav had taken Haley home after our night together, and I spent the rest of the day beating myself up for taking her to the hotel at all.

Was it amazing? Yes. Was it something I'd always fantasized about? Yes. Did I want to do it again? In a heartbeat. I'd had sex with a lot of women, but I'd never had the kind of connection with them that I had with Haley. We had a history, shared experiences, and she understood me in a way no one else did. Haley could make me laugh and draw me out of the darkness like no one else. She was wild and uninhibited and free and could make the most ordinary activity exciting and new. Sex with her had been out of this world.

It had also been wrong on so many levels. I'd pretty much ignored every rule in the bodyguard handbook. I'd also dishonored my fallen best friend and broken my promise to his father. I was supposed to be her protector, and I'd taken advantage of that duty.

The more I thought about it, the worse I felt, and after only half a day alone, I found myself back in the basement with Chad and Theo, trying to assuage my guilt by teaming up with them in their online game. Chad, especially, was easy to get along with, and he and Theo had no issues with me secretly hanging out with them while Mav roamed around upstairs. It was almost like I was back in Riverstone with Matt and Rafael, shooting bad guys and yelling at the screen. It was almost like I had friends.

"I got a lead on that incident on Michigan Avenue," Theo said, his thumbs flying over the controller as he pumped the "boss" full of lead. "I've got a hacker friend who can get into the CCTV database. Everything that happened on that corner of Michigan Avenue from fifteen minutes before the attack until fifteen minutes after is gone."

"What do you mean gone? I thought there were fifty thousand cameras in Chicago. Not only that, the head of our Chicago office said that local businesses can feed their surveillance into the system as well, doubling the coverage area."

Theo brought down the low-level boss without any assistance and pumped a virtual fist. "It's been erased, dude."

"By who? The police? Maybe it was just a glitch." It didn't make any sense. The police would have checked for the footage. Wouldn't they have noticed it was missing?

"Maybe, but it's a specific blackout period, which makes me think it was deliberate and done by someone with serious hacking skills. I almost didn't catch it but the time stamp was off, too."

"What about surveillance footage from nearby businesses?"

Theo shook his head in time to his shooting. "She was on the park side. Business surveillance cameras were too far away to catch anything."

"But people must have videoed it on their phones," Chad protested.

"Haley's mother talked to the detective in charge and he said there weren't many people around and it happened so fast that the ones who did see it didn't have time to film it."

Chad rolled his character down a hill and then leaped over a bridge. "I think something bigger is at play—something political and connected to Haley's mom. I've been looking into her work over the last year and she's spearheading three very controversial bills, but what I think is most interesting is the rumor that she is being considered as a candidate for vice president. If John Ellison wins the nomination and partners with her, they would be a powerful ticket. Maybe someone doesn't want him to have that edge in the next election."

"Or maybe someone wants her place in the Senate," I said. "But why go after Haley and her stepfather?" I shot a legion of bad guys to clear Chad's path. I hadn't played video games much after Matt died, and I'd missed it for both the camaraderie and the catharsis.

"To scare her out of the Senate race." Chad ran to catch up with us and switched out his weapon for something with more power. "Ellison won't appoint her as VP if she's not a senator, and if it's about the bills, they won't go through if she's gone. Threatening her family is much more effective than threatening her directly."

"You know your politics." I took a header off a cliff and waited to respawn.

Chad grinned. "I need to know all this stuff if I want to be a news anchor. I'm not going to be the guy who just reads the news. I'm going to offer commentary, and for that I need to understand what goes on behind closed doors."

"I'll talk to her mother again," I said. "My boss isn't supportive of an investigation. Our job is to protect people; not catch the bad guys."

"Theo and I are still on the case." Chad covered me when I re-entered the game. "I even got approval from my journalism prof to use this as my investigative journalism credit for the year if I dig up some good dirt, so I've got an incentive to keep going. Theo just likes the challenge of getting into systems he's not supposed to see."

Theo was entirely focused on the game but nodded in agreement. "Gonna hack the Chicago PD next. Should be fun."

Aside from an easing of the tension, nothing outwardly changed between Haley and me in the week after our night together. I followed her to class, her clubs, and her work at the coffee shop. She slept in her room, and I slept in mine. We talked about neutral things like the weather or what the professor had said in class, but the bigger issue of what had happened at the hotel was one we didn't touch. We'd crossed a line and there was no going back. But we didn't know how to move ahead.

Friday morning, Haley walked into the kitchen and smiled. "Ace . . ."

I knew that smile and that tone of voice. She wanted something that she knew I wouldn't like.

"No." I scrolled through my phone. "Whatever it is must be dangerous or you wouldn't have waited to tell me until after I'd had breakfast when you think I'll be more amenable to whatever it is you have planned."

"Okay then." She folded her arms and leaned against the counter. "I've been offered a gig at Bin 46 tonight. It's an upscale rooftop bar in the Loop. I have a deal with the owner. When one of his acts cancels at the last minute, I get time on the stage, and in return I work the rest of the evening for tips."

"Definitely no." I sipped my coffee. Theo had an espresso machine the same size as the one at Haley's coffee shop and the coffee was almost as good.

"I have to go," she said. "Music producers sometimes show up. It's a chance for me to get discovered."

"No point in being discovered if you're dead." I didn't even look up from my phone. Not because I was trying to signal that "no" was the end of the matter, but because I knew that if I looked at her, I'd give in.

"No one will know I'm there until I'm actually on stage," she protested. "I'm not on their regular schedule, and I won't advertise on social media."

"What if you're being followed?"

"Then you wouldn't be doing your job," she retorted.

I made the mistake of looking up. She was wearing a low-cut, tight red T-shirt that accentuated her beautiful breasts. Her hair was loose over her shoulders and if I wasn't mistaken her lips looked redder and fuller than usual. "You aren't being followed."

"Then we're good to go." She gave me a happy smile. "I work from six until ten and then I've got the stage from ten to eleven."

I had to tear my gaze away. "Still no."

"I believe I'm the boss, and the boss says we're going." She put a hand on her hip and struck a pose that drew my attention to the curve of her hip and the dip of her waist. *Fuck.* How was I going to keep it professional when all I wanted to do was rip off her clothes?

"You're mistaken. I'm the boss, and rule one is you do what I say."

Her face flushed and she spun around and yanked open the cupboard. I made a mental note to use that tone of voice the next time we were in bed together—if there was a next time, which would be a terrible idea, but maybe not that terrible.

"You work for me," she pointed out.

I leaned back in my chair and folded my arms. "I work for Stellar Security and they work for your mother. She's paying the bills."

"Should I call her and tell her you're interfering with my music career?" She glared at me over her shoulder.

"She'd probably give me a bonus for keeping you from making a terrible mistake."

Her back stiffened. "I'm not missing this gig. Either you come with me or I go alone. You can't stop me."

"I could tie you to the bed," I said casually.

Big mistake. Huge. My mind was instantly flooded with images I shouldn't be having after I'd spent the last week beating myself up for my total and utter lack of professionalism the previous weekend.

She turned away again and gripped the counter. I watched her shoulders rise and fall.

"You like that idea," I said quietly.

"It doesn't matter what I like," she said, taking a mug from the cupboard. "It's not happening again. I never imagined that we'd cross paths, or that you'd wind up being my bodyguard boyfriend, or that I'd be able to get over the past enough to spend the night with you, but I did and it's done, and now that we have that out of our systems, I need to look forward and focus on what's most important to me."

I leaned forward, elbows on the table, relieved that we were finally going to hash this out but also afraid of how it might end. "We can't keep pretending it didn't happen, Haley. Or that we don't have insane chemistry. I never imagined being in this position either. But now that we are, we can't go back. You will never be out of my system. I was hired to protect you, but now it's also so much more and I can't let you take that kind of risk."

She turned back to me, a pained expression on her face. "First, I wouldn't be taking a risk, because you'd be there. Second, it's the only time I feel like *me*. When I'm on stage, it's like everything falls away—the pain, the emptiness. I used to feel whole before everything fell apart. When my dad was alive and my family was a family, they'd come to watch me perform. It didn't matter if it was a school talent show or the winter fair or a pretend concert in the basement. They were always there. I felt seen. Loved. It wasn't just about the music—it was them, all of them, watching me, supporting me. And then . . . I lost that. I lost *them*. And I lost *you*."

"Christ, Haley." My gut twisted in a knot. "I never meant to add to your pain."

Haley sucked in her lips as she drew in a shuddering breath. "When I sing, it's like maybe, for a few minutes, I can have all that back. I can matter again. It's like . . . if I don't take every chance, if I don't try, then what was all that pain for?" Her hands tightened around the mug and her voice rose in a pleading tone. "I need this, Ace. I need to matter. I need to prove that I can do something with my life—that I'm not just stuck in the shadow of everyone I've lost. Maybe if I make it as a singer, maybe if people see me, then I'll feel like I'm worth something again."

I'd always known that I'd hurt Haley when I walked away, but I hadn't really considered that I'd compounded her trauma. She'd lost both her dad and her brother, and I was no better than her mom, who had emotionally abandoned her by throwing herself into her new career when Haley needed her the most. I had come to protect her, but the job also gave me the opportunity to make up for past mistakes and show her that maybe we could move forward together.

"What time do you need to be there?" I'd talk to Jordan about getting some backup. This was important to Haley. I'd make it happen.

Her eyes widened in surprise. "Six o'clock."

"I'll see what I can do."

Bin 46 was an Art Deco–inspired rooftop bar set twenty-five stories above the city with sweeping views of the skyline. According to Jordan, who had sent me the bar and building schematics, the open-air terrace was perfect for hot, sunny afternoons in the summer, but also transitioned into the winter with fire pits, warm drinks, and cozy couches. The nightly programming, including DJ sets, acoustic music series, and live runway shows, made it a prime location for everyone from CEOs to attention-seekers, and anyone who loved watching people.

"How did you get this gig?" I asked as the elevator whisked us up to the top of the hotel. I'd arranged with Jordan for two plainclothes Stellar Security officers to attend the venue, although I hadn't told Haley in case it made her nervous. She was in a good mood because she'd won her battle, but she'd inadvertently given me something more valuable in return—a glimpse into what made her tick and how deep her trauma ran.

"I came for an open mic night in my freshman year," she said. "Ryan, the manager, liked my sound, but he liked how I looked in a low-cut dress even more." She held up her hand. "Don't start. There are some lines I'm willing to cross for a shot at fame."

I already hated Ryan and I hadn't even met the dude.

"He needed a cocktail server who could pick up the odd shift when someone was sick and didn't need pesky things like benefits or official pay slips," she continued. "I needed experience on stage and visibility with the high-profile people who come here. So, we worked out a deal."

I took a quick look around when we reached the open-air venue, noting the limited elevator access, the single fire exit, and the crowded tables. "I don't like it." Even with the backup, I was tempted to enforce rule one and march Haley out of there.

"You don't have to like it." She patted my shoulder. "You just have to keep me safe."

I took up a position outside the locker room while Haley changed. Only a few moments later, a dude in a mauve shirt and tight gray pants with a sheen designed to make small things look bigger pushed past me and walked through the door.

Hand on my weapon, I followed him in, my eyes on Haley to see if she knew him.

"You're late," he said to her.

"I have twenty minutes before my shift starts, Ryan, and you're in the women's changing room." She glanced over his shoulder and shook her head when she saw me reaching for the dude's collar.

Ryan turned and startled when he saw me, as if he hadn't just shoved me aside. "Who the fuck are you?"

"He's my bod—"

"Boyfriend," I interjected. I had a feeling Ryan wouldn't take kindly to the extra security in his bar. I'd asked one of the Stellar guards to stand in the hallway, and the other was nursing a glass of water in the far corner of the bar.

"Just what I need." Ryan sighed. "Tell the boyfriend to get lost, sweetheart. He'll kill the vibe."

Haley frowned. "What vibe?"

"The hot-girl-who-flirts-with-the-customers-so-they'll-buy-more-drinks-thinking-they-might-get-lucky vibe."

"Are you fucking kidding me?" I thought I was being civil, but the words came out in a growl.

"Definitely a vibe-killer," Ryan said. "Tell him to take a hike."

I folded my arms across my chest. "I'm not going anywhere."

"You're not staying here dressed like that." He gestured vaguely to my jeans and Henley. "We have a dress code."

I'd briefly wondered why the officers Jordan had sent were both wearing suits. Clearly, I'd become too used to dressing as a college student. "I've got a suit in my vehicle," I assured him. "We'll be back in five."

"You'd better be back in time for her shift or I'll start docking Haley's pay." His gaze narrowed. "And you'd better be planning to buy some drinks. Our seats are for paying customers."

"I'll make sure you aren't out of pocket."

"And you'd better stay away from Haley," he added. "She has a job to do and it involves getting the customers to like her."

"They can look, but if anyone touches her—"

"Yeah. Yeah." He gave a dismissive wave. "You'll break his arms, tear him a new one, or some other possessive alpha hole shit. I get it. But if you lay one hand on a customer or cause any kind of drama, Haley is done."

Haley followed me back down the elevator to the underground parking garage, unaware that one of the guards was following us. Her dress was silver, sparkly, cut very low in front, and hugged all her curves. She looked fantastic and I wasn't the only person in the bar who'd noticed.

"It's cold in there," I said. "You might want to grab the sweater you left in the SUV."

"I can't wear a sweater. That defeats the purpose of the dress." She looked over at me and struck a sultry pose. "Do you not like it?"

"Everyone in the fucking bar likes your dress," I grumbled. "That's a problem. Too many eyes on you." I gave myself a mental pat for spinning my jealousy into a safety issue, which it was, of course. Safety. Not wanting to punch every guy who had leered at her since she'd walked out of the locker room.

Haley shrugged. "More eyes; more tips."

"I didn't like the way Ryan was looking at you. Has he ever touched you?"

From the set of her jaw, I knew the answer even before she responded. "I had a bad experience with him one time when I was alone in the locker room at the end of my shift. He was drunk. He tried to kiss me. I slapped him and then I kneed him in the groin so he couldn't come after me. Of course, he didn't remember it the next day, or he pretended not to remember. I just made sure I wasn't alone with him after that. I didn't report him because I didn't want to lose the gig, which is what happened to the other women who complained to management. He hasn't touched me since, so I feel like we have an understanding."

"I'll kill him." I grabbed my suit from the vehicle and slammed the door.

Haley sighed. "No, you won't kill him, because then you'd go to jail, and I'd have no one to protect me." She slipped her arm through mine. "Relax, Ace. I can handle guys like Ryan. Matt made sure of that."

We returned to the bar and Haley pointed out the men's changing room. "You can get dressed in there."

"Come with me. I need to be able to see you."

She looked up at me and her face flushed. "And watch you change?"

"Sweetheart, there's nothing you haven't seen before."

CHAPTER 20

Haley

No. No. No. The last thing I wanted was an up close and visual reminder of last weekend. After Ace's heartfelt apology, I'd managed to put aside the past for one night of pleasure, one night to live out my fantasy, and now I needed to move on. Ace was here for the job, and then he'd go back to LA. Even if he stayed, I wasn't ready for more. There was no way I was opening myself up to be abandoned all over again. But for some reason, every time I looked at him, all I could think about was his hands on my body and his lips on every part of my skin.

I heard the zip of the suit bag and the rustle of clothing, realizing as I tried to focus on the bare wall and the closed door that I could see Ace's reflection in a sliver of the mirror. I tried not to look, but the temptation was too great. I just wanted to see if what I remembered was true.

"Why do you keep a suit in your car?" I watched as he reached behind him and pulled his T-shirt off in one fluid, graceful movement. The play of muscles under his skin was mesmerizing, each ripple accentuating his strength and agility. I felt a flush of heat spread across my cheeks and I tried to focus on anything but the image in the mirror.

"Never know where I might end up," he said. "When I worked in LA, I was in a suit more often than I was in jeans. Some celebs consider their bodyguards part of the entourage and think the way we look reflects on them."

"Ah." I swallowed hard when he turned slightly, giving me a view of his sculpted back and the intricate tattoo that curved over his left shoulder blade. His hand went to his belt, and I closed my

eyes and tried to remember all the reasons I'd decided one night
was all I needed to get him out of my system. When I heard his
jeans drop, I willed my eyes to stay closed, but only seconds later
they opened, giving me a full-frontal view of Ace in his boxers.

Damn. I hadn't had much of an opportunity to ogle when we
were having crazy sex all over his hotel room. He was chiseled
like a Greek god, but not pumped and waxed like the guys at my
gym. Ace was all taut, lean muscle, his body almost vibrating with
raw power. My gaze dropped to his sculpted six-pack abs and the
trail of dark hair leading down to the waistband of his briefs and
beyond.

"Any time you're done looking . . ." His voice pulled me out of
my lust-filled haze, and I blushed, willing the ground to swallow
me up. Ace raised an eyebrow, a hint of amusement glinting in
his eyes.

"Sorry. I just . . ." I trailed off, mentally chastising myself for
apologizing. I'd seen men in their boxers before. Hell, I'd seen him
naked. There was no reason why I should be blushing or why I
should feel this desperate need to run away. "I'm worried about
the time."

"I'll be quick." He pulled on his dress pants, and I breathed out
a sigh of relief. Crisis averted. Temptation gone. Barely. From the
bulge beneath his fly, it seemed he liked being looked at as much
as I'd enjoyed looking.

I stared at the floor, counting the tiles by my feet. "I never
asked you about your tattoo."

"Matt and I got them before we deployed," he said. "They
matched—his on the right and mine on the left. Kinda feels un-
balanced now that he's gone." His smile faded and I felt my heart
squeeze the way it did whenever Matt's name came up. I hadn't
really thought through that aspect of having Ace in my life again.
I wanted to offer some words of comfort, but the vulnerability
he'd shown me felt fragile, like a thread that could easily be broken.

When I looked up again, Ace had put on his shirt and jacket

and his expression had shifted, a shadow passing over his face as he fastened the buttons with a sense of finality.

"How do I look?" He struck a pose in front of the lockers.

"You look . . ." Handsome. Gorgeous. Hot. "Fine."

"Just fine?" Ace repeated, a playful glint in his eyes. He knew he looked more than fine; he looked breathtaking. His shirt hugged his toned frame perfectly, emphasizing the definition of his muscles, and his jacket added a touch of sophistication to his rugged appearance. He looked every bit the part of the charming and capable bodyguard boyfriend.

"You know you look impressive," I said. "And that's all you'll get. I don't want to inflate your already giant ego."

I watched him in the mirror as he came up behind me and slid one arm around my waist, his hand pressed firmly against my belly. He brushed my hair back and pressed a kiss to the sensitive dip between my neck and my shoulder blade. "That's not the only giant thing—"

"Ace!" I knew I should push him away. I had less than a minute to get to the bar. But we looked so good together—him in his suit with his arm around my waist, and me in my sparkly dress, my head tipped to the side as he feathered kisses along the column of my throat.

"You're so fucking beautiful. I don't want to share you," he whispered in my ear. "Your hot-girl vibe is definitely working."

"Ace . . . we can't. Not again." My voice came out in a throaty whisper as desire curled through my body and settled between my legs.

"We can." He pulled me tight against him and I could feel the ridge of his erection against my ass. "Last weekend was—"

"It was great," I said, cutting him off. "Really great. We've always had chemistry, and we had a great night, but that doesn't mean everything's okay now. You left me, Ace. Just like everyone leaves me. And I'm not just talking about four years ago . . . I'm talking about high school, when you were so cold with me. I felt like I'd lost my best friend, and it hurt even more because I'd always thought we'd be together. I never realized that you didn't feel the same way or that I was the last person you'd want to be with. And now, here we are still carrying that baggage. I can handle a hookup but I can't risk getting close to you."

I felt him shudder behind me and a maelstrom of emotions ran quickly over his face. "You've got it wrong. That wasn't how I—"

"Haley! Where the fuck are you?" Ryan's shout echoed from the hallway, and I pulled away, grateful for the chance to put some distance between us.

Ace escorted me out of the changing room, pausing at the door to check the hallway before he let me walk through.

"We've got a couple of Cubs here tonight," Ryan said when I tapped in at the bar. "Their drinks should be ready. I expect a little gratitude. I could have given that section to Cheryl before she left, but I saved it for you." He touched his cheek, expecting a kiss, and my mouth soured. After it became clear that management wasn't going to do anything more than give him a slap on the wrist for his bad behavior, he'd become even more bold.

Ace made a warning sound, low in his throat, and I could feel his tension rising as he observed the interaction. Like Matt, his protective instincts had always been close to the surface. Without a word, he stepped slightly closer, subtly positioning himself between Ryan and me.

I could see things going bad very quickly, so I blew Ryan a kiss and turned away, weaving through the colorful chairs and couches to the service bar. Ace took a seat at the end of the bar where he had a good view of the entire rooftop, and for the next hour he watched and sipped his soda while I mingled with customers and served drinks.

By ten o'clock the bar was heaving. Ryan had called in two more servers, one of whom took over for me when I went on stage. I felt the familiar drumroll of my heart, the adrenaline rush that always hit the moment I picked up my guitar. I started with a cover of Radiohead's "Fake Plastic Trees" and then followed it with some of my best upbeat covers, drawing in the energy of the Friday-night crowd. I was hyperaware of Ace watching me from the bar, the smile on his lips, the slight nod of his head. I ended with my cover of Vance Joy's "This Mess Is Mine," a song about the messiness of relationships and what they mean. Ace's eyes never left mine.

"You killed it up there." Ryan put a hand around my waist and kissed my cheek. "Lots of happy, thirsty customers. That's what I like to see."

When I returned to the bar, Ace was deep in conversation with a dark-haired man in his late thirties, dressed in a T-shirt and blazer. He immediately stopped talking and introduced me to Stefan Foucault, an A&R executive with Atlantic Records.

For a long moment, I couldn't breathe. Artists and Repertoire, A&R for short, was the division of a record label responsible for scouting new talent.

"Your cover of 'Fake Plastic Trees' was exceptional," Stefan said. "I felt like I was rediscovering the lyrics as if hearing them for the first time. You've got one hell of a voice and an incredible stage presence. Where can I hear more?"

I couldn't have smiled any wider. "I've uploaded all my tracks online." I handed him one of the cards Aditi had designed for me. She had managed to capture the essence of my musical style with a bold font and a simple elegant colorful design.

"Do you have any original music?" Stefan asked.

"I've written and arranged a few songs, but I never thought they were good enough to upload."

Stefan handed me his card. "If you do get the courage to put them out there, let me know and I'll have a listen. I think you've got real talent, but what's missing from your music is that raw emotion and personal connection that can transform a song into an unforgettable, emotionally charged performance. The difference between a good cover and a great one is the ability to connect with the emotions of the song, and that's not easy to do. I feel like you're holding back, keeping all that emotion contained like a dam holds back water. But if you were to sing your own music, give us *your* story, your raw emotion, let it go and really feel the music, I think the full power of your voice will blow everyone away, and I would sign you in a heartbeat."

I managed to stammer out a thank-you and didn't embarrass myself in the next few minutes as we chatted about music and the state of the industry. I was stunned, shocked, disappointed, and elated at the same time. He liked me but wasn't going to sign me. He saw my potential and wanted more.

"Thanks for coming." Ace stood and shook his hand after Stefan indicated he had to leave.

"Anything for Jessica." Stefan smiled. "Tell her I'll see her at next year's Academy Awards, and this time I expect to see her with a gold statue in her hand. I've heard good things about *Heartfelt*. The early buzz is that she's going to be an Oscar contender."

"I'll pass the message along."

I waited until Stefan was out of earshot before I grabbed Ace's arm. "You know him?"

Ace shrugged. "I know someone who knows him."

"And you asked him to come here? To see me?" My voice rose to a squeak. "And he came?"

"I called in a favor," Ace said. "It's no big deal."

"You got an executive from Atlantic Records to come out to Bin 46 with almost zero notice to listen to me sing, and you think it's no big deal." My eyes were wet. I had to blink to clear them. "Ace . . . That's the nicest thing anyone has ever done for me."

"You're an amazing singer, bug. I want everyone to know it."

I threw my arms around him and gave him a hug. "Thank you. Thank you. Thank you."

"For the love of . . ." Ryan tapped me on the shoulder. "Vibes. Bad. No one wants to see displays of affection from a girl they fantasize about taking home for the night."

"My shift is over," I retorted. "I can hug who I like."

Ryan nodded toward the door. "What did Stefan Foucault want with you? He's never been here before, although he's a

South Side boy, born and bred. If he's scouting for talent, I might change up the entertainment."

I held up Stefan's card. "He liked my music. He wants to hear more."

"Hmmm." Ryan studied the card. "How about we put you on the regular rotation starting next month? Weekdays to start. I'll play with the schedule and send you some dates."

My brain almost couldn't process what was happening. I'd met Stefan Foucault, and he liked my voice. I'd just been offered a regular gig at a high-end Chicago bar. And Ace had made it all happen. "Yes, but only if you're paying me. I'm not working the floor."

"Done." Ryan nodded. "Just you, though. Lose the boyfriend and the suits."

Puzzled, I frowned. "What suits?"

"The dude in the hall and the one in the bar." He gestured to a man in a suit standing near the doorway. "My security guards noticed them hanging around, and they said they'd been hired to keep an eye on you. Not sure if that's because you're in trouble or you're playing at being a big star, but they were killing the vibe."

I glanced over at Ace, and he whispered in my ear, "I had Jordan send them to make sure you were safe."

A warm, squishy feeling spread across my chest, and I clasped Ace's hand. "I could give up the suits," I said to Ryan. "But this one isn't going anywhere."

CHAPTER 21

"Don't go home," I ordered Ace as we left the underground parking garage. "I'm too wired up. I'll just bounce off the walls."

"You're safest at home," he pointed out.

"I'm safe with you," I said. "Let's drive somewhere."

"Where do you want to go?"

"Lakeshore Drive. I want to see the water."

"It's dark," he turned onto West Jackson Boulevard. "There's not much to see."

"You can still see the water at night, and it's pretty with all the lights on the piers, the moored boats, and the cities on the other side of the lake. I want to roll down the window and feel the breeze."

"Are you going to hang your head out and stick out your tongue?" he asked, amused.

"Funny." I gave him my best side-eye. "Paige and I bike along the lake all the time. We're there for the beaches in summer and hiking in the forests in spring and fall. Sometimes when we're in the woods, I close my eyes and imagine I'm back in Riverstone."

Ace's hands tightened on the steering wheel. "How far do you want to go?"

"Montrose Beach. I can direct you. There's a relatively unknown section over a fence where they've made hiking trails through the grass, and there's a cute little bridge—"

"You want to go into the woods at night?" Ace's voice rose in pitch. "Are you serious?"

"It'll be fun."

"Carnival rides are fun," Ace said. "Bears games are fun. Naked Haleys in hotel rooms are very fun. If you want fun—"

"Are you not confident in your ability to protect me?" I wasn't above using his work against him. Ace needed to loosen up. Under that stiff exterior was a boy who loved a thrill just like me.

"I don't see the point in putting you in danger."

"That's exactly why we need to go. I'm totally pumped after the gig and meeting Stefan. I need some excitement, Ace. I want to feel alive."

"I could speed," he offered. "Is five miles per hour over the speed limit enough to burn off that adrenaline?"

"Do you even know me?" I laughed. "Every time I rent a car I get pulled over by the police for speeding. Usually, I can talk my way out of it."

"Don't tell me these things," he said. "It's stressful enough knowing you spend your nights running around in dark forests."

I laughed, relaxing into the easy banter that had marked our early friendship. "I try to limit it to a few times a month. Too much and the thrill wears off, and only between June and September, when it's warm enough to take off my clothes."

"What's terrifying is that I don't actually know if you're joking," he said, his voice tight.

"And you never will."

I talked without stopping for the duration of the drive to Montrose Beach. My brain wouldn't shut off, so I told him about my classes and how hard it had been to pick a major, and about last year's adventures with Skye, and how she'd exposed a major cover-up at the university.

Usually when I was wired I made a conscious effort to be quiet, because I talked too much at the best of times and the adrenaline made it ten times worse. But I could just be myself with Ace. I didn't have to worry about the filter. I could say anything, and he didn't judge me. He was a patient and active listener, making me feel like he was interested in everything I had to say. Only my dad had ever made me feel so accepted for being me.

"Dangerous woods, as requested," he said, pulling into the

parking lot at Montrose Beach. "Should I put up a sign to let the criminals know which way we've gone?"

"Don't be silly," I said, laughing. "They're already out there."

Despite the late hour, there were several cars in the parking lot and at least six couples on the beach in various stages of undress. The air was cool and crisp, and I drew in a deep calming breath.

"Not a place to go if you want to be alone," Ace said, pointing to a couple going at it under a blanket near the water's edge.

"I don't like beach sex," I said. "The sand gets into places sand isn't supposed to go. It took me forever—"

"I don't need to know." Ace pulled a backpack from the back seat.

"What's in there?"

"Survival supplies," he said. "Flashlight, blanket, water, compass, matches . . . I packed it after Jordan called to tell me you'd changed your mind about Maverick. I knew protecting you wasn't going to be like a regular gig. I would have to be prepared for any eventuality. You never know when you might meet a bear."

I smiled at what should have been a traumatic memory, but with Ace it was something warm and sweet. "I have your stone in my bag," I said. "You'll be safe with me."

I led him to the right, past the people and over a fence, to my favorite hiking trail. Leaves crunched under our feet as we followed the path into the forest. Even with the canopy of trees blocking the sky, the twinkle of lights from the city and nearby pier and the glimmer of the moon overhead were enough to light our path.

I stopped in the middle of a small bridge and leaned against the wooden railing, drinking in the stillness. "Can you believe we're here?" I said, wishing for the night sky of Riverstone, where we could see countless stars. "A few weeks ago, I was busking on a street corner, and now I have a producer's card in my pocket. I hadn't seen you since Matt's funeral and now you're my bodyguard boyfriend. I would never have imagined this in a thousand years."

"Neither could I," he said. "I can't imagine ever going back to a time where we aren't in touch." His voice was a quiet rumble in the darkness. "I've missed you."

I wanted to tell him I'd missed him, too, but my chest tightened, squeezing my lungs. *Breathe. Breathe. You're fine. Lock it away.* I closed my eyes and pushed the feelings away into the dark corner where all the scary things lived.

Back into the box where Stefan had suggested my real voice was hiding.

"Do you think Stefan was right? That I'm holding back?"

Ace wrapped his arms around me and drew me close. I should have pushed him away, insisted that we had to keep things professional, reminded him that our night together had just been one night, but my emotions were all over the place and he was warm and strong and so, so steady. I'd said some harsh words in the kitchen before we'd left, and yet he'd still called in a favor to get Stefan down to the bar to hear me and brought backup to keep me safe. I'd been even harsher in the changing room, and yet the look on his face when he watched me on stage had made me feel like the best singer in the world. And now he was tramping around the forest in the dark because I was too wired to go home. He wasn't the Ace who had kissed me and walked away. He was the Ace I knew before. Maybe I did know him, after all.

"I think you've had a lot to deal with in your life, and you handle things in a way that works for you," he said.

"That's not an answer."

He brushed his lips over my forehead. "I think the best person to answer that question is you."

"I feel things, Ace. Just like everyone else. I felt sick for Paige when her mother was diagnosed with cancer. I get all warm and squishy inside when we go to Puppy Day at the student center. I was happy when Skye and Dante got together. I felt unbearably sad when Dad and Matt died. I just don't dwell on things. I don't let them drag me down. It's better to move on and be happy.

That's who I am. I'm the person who cheers everyone up or lightens the mood or comes up with fun things to do."

Ace rubbed his hand up and down my back in a soothing motion. "You don't have to justify yourself to me, and you don't need to be anyone other than yourself when we're together. I know you, bug."

"Not everyone cries," I insisted.

"I'm not judging you."

I still felt the need to explain, maybe not to him, but to myself. "Some things just hurt too much to feel."

"I get that, but sometimes it's better to rip off the bandage and let it out. After your dad died, that worked for me."

I didn't take the opening to pursue the topic any further. I didn't want to think about fifteen-year-old Ace crying in the forest and how I'd felt horrified and sad and sick and jealous all at the same time. It was *my* dad who had died. Why was Ace the one crying and not me?

Because he cared. Ace may have been quiet and reserved, but he'd cared deeply about our family. He'd cared about me, and judging by his actions, maybe he still did.

"Do you know what I like best about the forest?" I drew his hand down over my hip to the edge of my sparkly dress and curled his fingers under the edge, feeling raw and vulnerable and desperate for a distraction from the unsettling conversation and the pain that went along with it.

Ace let out a low growl of appreciation. "What do you like best?"

"No sand."

His fingers tightened, knuckles digging into my thigh. "I thought you said you didn't want more than one time."

"I want to thank you for what you did tonight."

Ace froze, his hand dropping from my hip. "I didn't do it for sex. I did it for you, because I believe in you. I've always thought you were an incredible singer, and I was in a position to be able to help you. I don't need anything in return. I made mistakes, and I hurt you, but I'm going to do everything I can to make it up to you. I don't want you to ever feel like you owe me anything."

Damn Ace. Always so honorable. "I don't feel like I owe you anything, but I do feel . . ." Feelings were hard to handle, harder to express. "I missed you," I blurted out. "I missed our friendship." I listened to the slow, steady beat of his heart, warm in the circle of his arms. "I'd decided long ago you were a certain kind of person, but now you don't seem like that person at all."

Ace chuckled. "I hope not. I like to think after all the shit I've gone through over the years, I've changed. I've done a lot of running away, but I don't feel like running now."

"I don't feel like running either." I took one of his hands and dropped it back down to my thigh.

His hand tightened, fingers digging into my skin through the thin fabric of my dress. "What do you want? Tell me."

"I've never had sex in the forest," I said softly. "And the idea that someone could come around the corner at any moment and see us is very—"

"Very what?" His voice dropped low as he pushed up the hem of my dress, backing me against the railing of the small wooden bridge.

"It turns me on," I whispered, even though there was no one to hear us.

Ace crushed me against him and kissed me hard and deep. I breathed in his scent, woodsy and more intoxicating than the crisp, earthy scent of fallen leaves mingled with the sharp tang of evergreen needles. In that moment, I let go of my doubts and surrendered to the pull between us.

"You are impossible to resist, especially in this dress." Ace's hands moved with purpose, roaming down my back as he pressed my hips against his, letting me feel just how much he wanted me.

I arched into him as he slid the dress up and over my hips.

"You were so fucking sexy on that stage. Every man in that bar wanted you. I thought I'd have to fight them all off."

"You say the nicest things."

"I wasn't thinking the nicest thoughts." He pushed down the straps of my dress and undid the catch of my bra, pulling it away to bare my breasts to the cool night air. His lips trailed a path from my neck to my collarbone, his tongue darting out to taste my skin as he kissed his way down. "These are for me to see." He bent down and took my nipple between his lips. "These are for me to taste."

The sensation of his touch sent shivers through my body. I ran my hands through his thick, soft hair as his tongue rolled over the sensitive peak of my nipple, then he sucked hard.

My fingers contracted against his scalp, my nails scraping against his skin as pleasure fuzzed my brain. He turned his attention to my other nipple, rolling it between his teeth. I arched into him, feeling his erection press against my hips as he inhaled a stiff breath.

He palmed my breasts with cool hands, but his kisses were hot. "Is this what you want? Or do you need more danger?"

Before I could respond, he yanked on my panties, shoving them down to my knees and exposing me completely to the night. My heart pounded, and we worked together to get them off until I was completely exposed, raw and open to whatever he wanted to do to me.

"Spread your legs."

I did as he commanded, aching, waiting, bracing for his touch. Ace dropped to one knee in front of me. The moment his fingers slid between my thighs, we both groaned.

"Touch your breasts," he said. "Imagine my mouth on them, my hands."

I cupped my breasts, squeezed them gently, imagined his rough palms on my skin, his lips on my nipples. He watched me, chest heaving, his dark eyes heated, intense.

"You're beautiful."

"And you're not moving," I groaned, impatient. "I'm doing all the work."

He smirked and slid his hands slowly up my legs from my ankles, then along my calves to my thighs. His fingers moved inward, his thumbs massaging the sensitive skin, closer and closer to where I wanted him to go.

"Touch yourself." His voice was low, raw and husky with desire. "Show me how you like it." He lifted my left leg over his shoulder, spreading me wide.

I was so wet, so close, so needy, I did as he asked, first circling my clit and then slipping two fingers inside. His eyes never left mine, and the intimacy of being watched so intently sent my desire sky-high.

"Stop," he ordered, grabbing my wrist. "I didn't say you could come. That's my job."

I didn't know this side of Ace. Dominant and demanding. Utterly in control. But maybe it had always been there, and maybe that's why he always made me feel so calm. Part of me knew that no matter how wildly I spun out of control, he would always be there to ground me.

"Maybe you should get to work then," I gritted out, my voice tight with unmet need. "Or I might have to file a complaint with your manager."

"You won't have anything to complain about when I'm done with you." He pushed two fingers inside me and moved in to tease my clit with his tongue. My hands weaved into his hair, holding him in place as he teased and tormented me, the sensation of his hot wet mouth driving me wild.

"I got you." Ace curved his fingers, pressing against my inner walls as he circled my clit, drawing out my pleasure until finally the world exploded in a shower of sensation. I collapsed back against the railing, utterly spent.

"I love watching you fall apart." He lowered my leg and stood to kiss me, his hands cupping my face as gently as he'd once held a butterfly that had been trapped in our garden shed back home. "That was almost worth a walk through a dark, dangerous forest."

"Almost?"

"I've put you at risk." He tugged my dress down over my hips.

"Wait." I grabbed his wrist. "What about you?"

"I think we should get you home."

"But . . ." He wanted me. I could see the bulge beneath his fly, feel his desire in the lightness of his touch. There was more to this than a concern for my safety, more than the risk of being caught, more than the ambivalence he had shown me so long ago. I didn't know why he was backing off, but I wasn't letting him go.

I pressed my body up against his and kissed him, hands in his hair tugging him down. He tensed, resisting, but then he shuddered, groaned, and suddenly I was crushed against his body. He threaded his hand through my hair, tugging my head back as he took my mouth in a mind-bending kiss.

"You want me," I murmured, pulling away.

"You know I do."

"Then it's my turn to watch you fall apart." I didn't give him a chance to respond. I unbuttoned his jeans and reached beneath his boxers to free his hardened length. His body tensed, and I met his gaze as I dropped my sweater on the ground and knelt to take him into my mouth.

"Haley . . ." His voice caught, broke. "You don't have to do this."

"I want to make you feel good." I licked the velvet head of his shaft, tasting the salt on his skin. The moon filtered through the trees, lighting him from behind, his hard body taut against the deep grays and blacks of the forest.

"Fuck. You have the sweetest mouth." He groaned and fisted his hands in my hair as I sucked him deeper, running my tongue down the hard ridges and over hot skin.

Wrapping my hand around the base of his erection, I worked him in time to every stroke of my tongue until his body tensed, and his thighs trembled. There was power in taking a man to the edge, and feeling his need in the quiver of his muscles made me hot all over again.

"I need to be inside you." His hands tightened in my hair, holding me still.

"I want to finish you." I swirled my tongue over the head of his cock, and he cursed.

"Not here. Not like this." With a pained groan, he pulled me to my feet and kissed me full on the mouth. "Turn around. Lean over the railing. Lift your dress and show me that ass."

My head reeling from his sudden change in demeanor, I did as he asked. I heard the crinkle of a condom wrapper, the gentle pressure of his hands on my hips, the press of his tip at my entrance, and then with a hard push, he was inside me.

"Fuck, you're so wet for me." He pulled out and thrust in again, enough to tease but not enough to give me what I wanted.

"Harder."

He withdrew and gave me just an inch, holding me in place with a firm hand on my hip. "Bossy."

I hissed out a breath. "I'll be anything you like if you keep going."

"Be mine." He pushed all the way inside me. And then he leaned over and pressed a kiss to my nape. "Tell me you'll be mine."

"Ace . . ."

His free hand slid over my hip to my clit, and he circled it slowly, moving closer and closer to the center. Pleasure built with every breath. His body was hard and heavy against me, his shaft filling me completely. He pulled out the tiniest bit and thrust in again, spiraling my pleasure.

I was so close, and he was so deep. I was him and he was me and we were together in a way that felt like it was always meant to be.

I came before I had to answer, my body tightening around him, hands gripping the cold wooden rail so hard my knuckles turned white. He followed me quickly into oblivion, my name on his lips as he fell apart.

He hugged me close after we dressed, kissing me softly, his eyes lingering on mine. We held hands in the car on the way home and then we spent the night together. But he never asked me for my answer. And I was glad. Because I didn't know what to say.

CHAPTER 22

Haley

FIVE YEARS AGO

"That was totally humiliating." I stormed into the house, wobbling on a pair of heels that I'd taken from my mother's closet. I didn't know how Matt had found me, but he'd not only shown up with Ace at my high school, he'd also dragged me and Paige home. I'd been crushing hard on Ace for the past two years and to be shouted at and ordered home in front of him was just too much.

"What's humiliating is finding your fifteen-year-old sister and her friend dressed like hookers and drinking in the field behind the high school with a couple of seniors, when they're supposed to be inside at the dance where it's safe," Matt snapped, looking to Ace for support. Ace gave him a curt nod before following him in and closing the door behind us.

My cheeks burned, and I smoothed down the white tube dress that I'd bought at the mall on the weekend. Plunging, sleeveless and with side cutouts, it was the first piece of clothing I'd owned that made me feel like a woman. Paige had styled my hair in long soft curls, and we'd done each other's makeup using a YouTube video as a guide. We'd taken dozens of pictures of ourselves in various sexy poses before we left. In our eyes, we'd never looked so good.

"If you hadn't noticed, I'm not a child," I spat out. "I don't wear children's clothing anymore. The dance was boring. The DJ sucked. Tom had stashed some wine coolers outside and offered to let us have some. You drank when you were my age, so why shouldn't I?"

"Because I'm a guy," he snapped. "And, as a guy, I can tell you those dudes didn't take you and Paige out there to look at the fucking stars or out of the kindness of their hearts. They wanted to get you drunk and . . ." He made a strangled sound, and his face turned red. Ace, who had been silent the whole way home, put a hand on his shoulder.

"I'm not stupid," I bit out. "No one will be taking advantage of me, because I'm saving myself for someone special . . ." My voice trailed off when I noticed that the someone special was staring at me. I didn't know why Ace was at our house instead of out with one of the multitudes of girls who were desperate for his attention. His dark, dangerous vibe and breathtaking good looks had made him one of the most highly desirable seniors in the school. He had a different girl under his arm every time I saw him, and he and Matt were always going out on double dates together. I also didn't know why he was looking at me like he'd never seen me before. He'd had that look on his face since he and Matt found us in the field.

Matt looked from me to Ace and back to me. His jaw tightened and he pointed to the stairs. "Go to bed."

"I'll load up the game." Ace turned on the television and plonked himself down on the couch.

Emboldened by the attention I'd had from the seniors, I put my hands on my hips. "I don't take orders from you. Maybe I want to stay up and game with you and Ace and have a few more drinks. You can't stop me."

Matt was apoplectic at my show of defiance. "You've got to be fucking kidding me," he yelled. "You're fifteen, and Mom's never around. Someone has to protect you. Someone has to keep you safe."

At the word "safe," Ace looked up. My body burned beneath his scrutiny. Was it my imagination or was he looking at me the way the seniors had looked at me when they invited me and Paige outside? Was he finally seeing me as a woman and not as a little kid?

"It's not just up to you," I said, my gaze locked on Ace. "We have a guest. Let's ask him what he wants." I teetered my way over to the couch and sat beside Ace, so close our bodies touched. He was all rock-hard muscle and blistering heat, and my blood pumped furiously through my veins, every sensation new and raw. I turned ever so slightly to glare at Matt, and my breast brushed against Ace's thick bicep, sending a bolt of white-hot heat through my veins that made me tingle all over.

Ace stiffened and shifted in his seat, putting a few inches between us. His hands tightened on the controller; his fingers going rigid. I didn't know much about boys, but I imagined he wanted me. Finally, in my grown-up clothes, I was worthy of his attention. Monday morning it would be me hanging off his arm in the hallway. Me kissing him behind the school during lunch break.

Empowered by what I took as interest, and the knowledge that I was no longer the child Matt thought I was, I leaned closer and whispered in his ear. "What do you want, Ace? Do you want me to stay?"

Ace stood so quickly, I almost fell over. "I'm gonna get a beer."

"What the fuck?" Matt glared at me and then followed Ace into the kitchen. Curious, I slipped off my shoes and tiptoed into the dining room where I could hide behind the door and listen.

"What the hell?" Matt's low, furious whisper was audible through the closed door. "She's my little sister."

"Don't be stupid," Ace growled. "I'm not interested in skinny little kids playing dress-up in big-girl clothes. Hell, she couldn't even fill out that dress or walk in those shoes. To be honest, I felt embarrassed for her when we caught her and Paige outside, and even more embarrassed for her when she sat beside me on the couch. I don't see Haley that way. She's like my little sister, and she's not even my type. She is the last girl I would ever want to be with. Now Esme . . ." He said something I couldn't hear, and Matt laughed out loud.

Bile rose in my throat, and I almost choked on my humiliation. All those years. All those fantasies. I thought it was just a matter of time before Ace finally realized we were meant to be together. It had never occurred to me that the time would never come, that he didn't share my feelings, and worse, that he didn't even find me attractive. I wasn't good enough for him, and I never would be. Not only that, I'd never be able to look at him again without thinking about how utterly sick and devastated I felt in that moment.

A sob erupted from my throat, and I slapped my hand over my mouth, just as Ace walked into the living room. He didn't look surprised to see me standing by the door, and I wondered if he'd known I was there all along.

"Did you get the beer . . . ?" Matt trailed off when he saw me beside the door. "Shit. Haley. Did you hear us?"

My face flamed and I willed the ground to swallow me up. When that didn't happen, I raced past them and ran upstairs to my room, turning the lock behind me after I slammed the door.

"Haley." Matt came up behind me and thudded on the door. "Let me in. It's not like that . . . He didn't mean—"

But he did.

And it would be three long years before I was able to put him out of mind, only to have him come back and humiliate me all over again.

CHAPTER 23

Ace

I knew myself well enough that I should have predicted what would happen if I let down my guard with Haley. I hadn't had much to call my own growing up, and in the air force I had only what they gave me. But now I had her, the only person I had truly ever wanted, and my protective instincts were out of control. We'd been together every night since our hike in the forest, and five days later I still got annoyed when we had to leave the house to take her to class.

"Why do we always have to sleep in your room?" Haley asked, stretching out naked on my bed. I'd just come back from washing up after a night of furniture-breaking sex, and seeing her lying languid with the sunshine turning her body into gold, I wanted her all over again.

"Because your room is a disaster. I can't even see the floor."

"I've been writing songs," she said. "Stefan was wrong that I don't let my emotions out. I feel things, Ace. Deeply. I'm going to put an album together that will blow Stefan's mind."

Some people would have taken Stefan's comments as a criticism or would have let him shake their confidence, but not my girl. She took it as a challenge. She'd been spending all her free time on her bedroom floor with her guitar and her notepad, trying to write the perfect song.

I climbed on the bed and pinned her hands over her head, bracketing her wrists with one hand as I shoved her thighs apart with my knee. Only my sweatpants stopped me from going too far and taking her all over again. "I know something else you can blow that's more readily available."

"Ace Murphy. I'm shocked," she teased. "Absolutely shocked. Do you really think I'm that kind of girl?"

"I know you're that kind of girl." I buried my head in her neck and licked the love bite I'd given her last night. I'd had a sudden urge to mark her, to let the world know she was mine. "And I'll give you a chance to prove it tonight."

She wrapped her legs around my hips, holding me fast. "Why not now?"

"Because you've got class in an hour." *Fuck me.* I was rock hard and there was no way she didn't notice. "And I believe you have a test." I released her hands, although it was the last thing I wanted to do.

Haley's eyes widened and she sat up in the bed. "Oh my God. I totally forgot. I'll have to study on the way to school." She jumped up and quickly pulled on her clothes. "I'll see you downstairs."

It was a few long minutes before I was in a state to get dressed, and a few more minutes before I had calmed myself down. I couldn't imagine forgetting about a test and cramming for it at the last minute. I had been a diligent high school student, preparing for assignments well in advance. I'd carried that discipline into the military and left with a perfectly clean record when I was discharged.

Haley processed information in a different way. She absorbed lectures without having to take many notes and could retain entire chapters of a textbook after only a quick skim. When she studied, she would stream a show on her tablet, while texting friends on her phone, and working on her laptop with the screen split in two. If I hadn't known that her unique study technique had put her at the top of her high school classes, I might have said something about her chaotic approach to learning, solely because it was the stuff of nightmares for a rule-follower like me.

A scream pulled me back to reality and I raced out of the room only to see Haley hugging Paige in the hallway. Paige had been away for the last ten days while her mother went through testing to see if she was a good candidate for a clinical trial at the hospital in Riverstone. Now she was back, and from the way she glared at me over Haley's shoulder, I could tell there was a reckoning coming.

I didn't have to wait long.

"Are you insane?" Paige accosted me by the front door twenty minutes later, after I'd changed and walked downstairs to wait for Haley. "You're supposed to be her bodyguard."

"I am her bodyguard," I pointed out.

"Well, you forgot to guard her body . . . from you." She shoved my chest. "I told you that if you hurt her again—"

"I'm not going to hurt her, Paige."

"Yes, you will. What happens when this whole thing is over, and you go back to your celebrity clients and fancy LA life? What happens then?"

I glanced up the stairs, hoping Haley would come down to save me. "I don't know. I haven't thought that far ahead. Right now I'm focused on keeping her safe."

"Big surprise," she said. "I know what happens because I saw what happened with all the girls you slept with in high school. You moved on. Fast. And you didn't look back."

"That was years ago. I'm a different man now."

"Are you though?" She held up her phone and flashed a picture of me and Jessica outside Jessica's mansion after the *Vanity Fair* party. Jessica had had way too much to drink and that, coupled with her emotional despair after losing the award to her greatest rival, had left her barely able to walk. I'd had to pick her up and carry her inside. "Do you know what all the gossip columns are saying?" She showed me another picture. "That you're together. Not only that, someone did some digging and found out you've been very, very close to all the female celebrities you've guarded."

I didn't bother looking at the screen. I knew about the rumors.

"Gossip sells. It doesn't mean any of it is true."

"That's hard to believe when I know your history," she spat out. "I'm sure you know how Haley felt about you when we were growing up. You took advantage of her before you deployed, and you're doing it now, and I won't stand for it. She's been through enough, Ace. She's lost enough. She has so much pain buried inside her that I'm terrified one day she's going to break."

Paige had always been viciously protective of Haley. There was nothing I could say that would change her mind about me, but I tried.

"I care about her."

"If you cared about her, you would have left her alone," Paige spat out. "As soon as this job is over, you'll walk away just like you did before, and she'll never hear from you again. And it will kill her, because she's not like all your other girls. For some reason I have yet to understand, she thinks she has a connection with you. She likes you, and now you've already hurt her because you slept with her knowing exactly how this is going to end."

"Paige! Do you have a class, too?" Haley called out from the stairs. "Are you going to walk with us?"

"No, I've got some work to catch up on," Paige replied. "Good luck on the test." She shot me one last glare before she stormed away. I made a mental note to lock my bedroom door at night.

"What were you and Paige talking about?" Haley asked after I'd checked the street to make sure she was safe to walk outside. "She didn't seem happy."

"She's not happy we slept together," I said honestly. "I'm not her favorite person."

Haley shrugged. "She'll get over it when I tell her it's not serious. You'll probably be leaving for your next assignment soon. It's been weeks and nothing else has happened. No threats. No attempted kidnappings. The whole thing has probably blown over."

Her words felt like a knife in my heart. I hadn't really thought through what we were doing except for feeling guilty that we were doing it at all, but until that moment I hadn't realized it wasn't just casual to me. I had wanted Haley for what seemed like forever. From the first day we met, I'd felt a connection to her that I hadn't felt with anyone else before. She'd seen me—the real me. And I'd seen her. We'd been friends, shared the tragedy of her father's death, and we'd always been there for each other. Even when I made the mistake of kissing her before I deployed, I thought the best thing I could do for her was leave her alone. I'd never imagined that it would be four years before I'd speak to her again—four years of running from my feelings. But I wasn't that man anymore. I'd gained perspective in the air force and now I had a chance to be physically present for her in ways that I wasn't before. I'd never stopped caring for her, and this time I wasn't going to run away.

Paige was worried that Haley would be hurt, but I had a feeling the person who was going to wind up being hurt was me.

Chad came to meet me at the coffee shop later that afternoon. I was at my usual table in the corner where I had a good view of the door and the counter where Haley was busy serving customers.

"What the hell, dude?" Chad sat beside me. "You look like you want to kill someone."

"That ball player has stopped by every time Haley is on shift." I nodded at the tall, lanky blond wearing a Havencrest Warriors jersey. "And he's not here for the coffee."

"Is he a threat?" Chad chuckled as he sipped his energy drink. "Should I call the police?"

"Only if he touches her." My hand clenched on the table. "And in that case, he'll be needing an ambulance."

"I don't think she needs that level of protection. Haley can take care of herself." Chad, always so chill and relaxed, tried to reassure me. "We all went dancing on the stage at a club one night. Some dude kept getting in Haley's space, trying to dance right up against her. She put two hands on his chest and shoved him off the stage without missing a beat."

I didn't doubt his story. I'd seen Haley wrestle Matt in their backyard, and it wasn't until he was well into puberty that he'd

been able to beat her. Even then, he would be packing a few spec-
tacular bruises.

I folded my arms and tried to glare the baller out of existence.
"He's too tall for her," I grumbled. "He's got to be at least six foot
seven. Why doesn't he find a woman his own size?"

"Probably because there aren't any." Chad pulled out his phone
and flipped through the screen. "You've got it bad, dude."

"I'm just doing my job."

Chad wasn't buying it. "Things were bound to get complicated
when you two decided to hook up."

I raised an eyebrow in query, and he shrugged. "The house
isn't that big, and we're all pretty tight."

All my fears and regrets surfaced in an instant and I was
tempted, so tempted, to share. I hadn't had a close friend since
Matt died, but I couldn't trust myself not to lead someone astray.
I couldn't put myself through the pain of losing another friend.
I'd opened up to Chad about the attack on Haley, but this was
personal, and I didn't do personal anymore.

Before I could say anything, Chad lifted a dismissive hand.
"I'm not judging you. But I'm not surprised. You guys have a history. I just want to make sure you can still do what you need to do
if you're that close. I was dating this girl on the women's wrestling
team. Arms like pythons. Powerful thighs. She could bench one
eighty without breaking a sweat. Everyone said she was just using
me for my looks and squeaky-clean image, but I didn't see it. I
was too close. It was only when her parole officer called me to ask
where she'd been the night a grocery store clerk got stabbed that
I clued in. It was heartbreaking. I'll never find another woman
with thighs like that. The things she could do . . ."

I snorted a laugh. Chad always knew what to say to lighten my
mood. "I appreciate the advice, but I'm more interested in what
you and Theo found out about Haley's attacker or the people who
erased the camera footage."

"Theo's still working on the cameras," he said. "But I've been
looking at the recent trend of protesting at public officials' homes,

and I think this isn't about the bills Senator Chapman is spearheading. Those people want media attention. They want videos of their protests to go viral. Because the footage of Haley's attack was erased, I think this has to do with the senator's reelection campaign. I suspect someone—either one of the senator's opponents or someone within her own party—doesn't want her to win and is trying to intimidate her into stepping down, without drawing the kind of press attention that would happen with an outright attack."

I tucked that information away to process later. Politics was big business and that meant the people behind the kidnapping attempt might be well funded, giving them access to the kind of resources that made them a serious threat. "Do you think they would actually harm Haley or her family, or is this just a scare tactic?"

"It depends on how badly they want the senator replaced, but I think it's good that you're around."

"Haley is safe with me," I assured him. "I won't let our personal relationship interfere with my work."

"I'll see what else I can find out." Chad tossed his empty bottle in the nearby recycling bin. "Making contacts, working my connections. It's what I do best."

"You're not just a pretty face."

Chad clapped my shoulder as he left. "Tell that to my ex."

CHAPTER 24

Haley

"Bars are bad," Ace grumbled. "Very unsafe. I wish you'd reconsider." He pulled open the door to Shakers Bar and stood aside for me to enter.

"It's been a long time since I got together with my girls." I paused out of habit for him to do a quick security check. "I wasn't about to turn down a fun night out."

"You could have had fun in the kitchen or the living room. I could have brought chairs up to your bedroom—"

"And what? We all sit in a circle and knit?" I breathed in the familiar scents of beer and fried food and my pulse kicked up a notch. I'd missed going out drinking with my friends, and the only reason Ace had agreed to our night out was because the bar had an alcove near the back entrance that was easy for him to protect. The air hummed with the buzz of conversations and clinking glasses, the raucous atmosphere creating the perfect soundtrack for a night out.

"There's nothing wrong with knitting," he said, bristling. "My grandmother used to knit. I still have the sweater she made for me the second Christmas I was in Riverstone."

I looked over my shoulder and laughed. "The one with the squished snowmen and the reindeer with three legs?"

"It was made out of love."

"And you wore it out of love." I patted his arm. "That's when I knew you were the real deal."

"Is that why you laughed so much you got a stomachache, and kept hiding around corners to take pictures of me to send to

Paige?" His hand found my back and he guided me past a particularly raucous table.

"I took pictures because you looked so sexy in your three-legged-reindeer sweater. You should wear it next time we're in bed. Who knows what it might do to me?"

Ace froze, his hand tightening on my back. "Don't say things that are going to make me have to take you home."

"Since you've been such a good bodyguard and let me come out, I might just imagine you're wearing it tonight and see where that takes us."

I heard a soft growl of approval, and my mouth went dry. I'd never been with someone who shared my love of sexual adventure. Ace was willing to try anything and everything. The only way we hadn't had sex was missionary style on his bed.

We found Paige with Skye, Isla, and Aditi in a booth at the back of the bar. They'd also grabbed a small table nearby so Ace would keep watch but still give us some privacy.

"Dante's finally getting ready to go on the road," Skye said after we'd had our first round of drinks and some snacks. "He still feels terrible about breaking up the band. I told him I'd tell you that when I saw you tonight."

I felt a familiar ache in my chest. I still missed the band. I loved the vibe and the freedom of knowing that if I made a mistake there were four other musicians who would carry me. I could draw on their emotional energy and feel the lyrics in a way I never could when I was playing alone.

"Are you kidding me?" I adored Skye and didn't want her to feel bad about Dante following his dreams. "I would kill to have that kind of opportunity. I hope he remembers us when he hits the big time."

"He's still trying to find a producer to come out and hear you," she said. "He hasn't given up."

"Actually, Ace called in a favor and an executive from Atlantic Records came to see me at Bin 46." I told them about the meeting and how I'd been writing new songs, trying to draw out the emotion Stefan thought I'd somehow repressed.

"That's very boyfriend of your bodyguard." Skye shared a look with Paige. "It's one of the reasons we wanted to get together tonight. We think what you've got going on together isn't a good idea."

I glared at Paige over my second Long Island iced tea. We'd already had this conversation. I'd assured her I knew what I was doing. Clearly she didn't believe me, and now she'd brought backup.

"I've wanted him forever. I don't see a problem with fulfilling my teen fantasy of sleeping with my brother's best friend."

"What about the night he told Matt he would never in a million years want to go out with you?" Paige asked. "When he said he just saw you as a little kid playing dress-up? You climbed out the window and came to my house and cried all night. What did he say about that?"

I took a sip of my drink and stared at the table. There was no point mentioning I'd briefly touched on that night in the changing room at the bar because we hadn't had a chance to get into it. "It didn't come up."

"What do you mean it didn't come up?" Her voice rose in pitch. "You were utterly devastated. And then there was the night before he deployed. And four years of being ghosted. You have unresolved issues with him, Haley. You are supposed to deal with those first, before you jump into bed."

"We haven't really used the bed." My cheeks heated even though it was Paige and my girls and they knew everything about me.

"Babe . . ."

"It's just sex," I assured them. "The hottest, wildest, most exciting sex I've ever had. It's been fun and I wasn't going to slow things down to ask him why he suddenly had a change of heart. I'm not looking for a relationship and neither is he. We're two consenting adults having a crazy good time, and when he's done with the bodyguarding, it will be over."

"Crazy is right," Skye said. "He's here as your bodyguard, babe. What if things go south? It's not like you can ghost him or say thanks for the hookup but now we're done. How is he going to protect you if the two of you have a fight? It's not just about what happened in the past; it's about right now. We want you to be safe, and if he's emotionally compromised—"

"He's a professional," I said, bristling. "If he felt he couldn't protect me because we slept together a few times, he'd let me know."

"Maybe you shouldn't have put yourselves in that position in the first place," Paige suggested.

"I didn't think that far," I said honestly. "He touches me and my brain fuzzes with lust. It's like I'm caught in a whirlwind, and I lose all control."

Paige took a long sip of her drink. "I go away and look what happens."

"I had sex," I said. "People have sex. I've had lots of sex with lots of men. You guys never had an issue before. Maybe you should stop judging me and start feeling happy that I'm with someone who totally gets me."

"That's because he's known you since you were ten years old, and then he didn't want to know you that way until he was leaving and took advantage of your feelings to get a kiss before he went home with Esme Duncan." Paige couldn't hide the bitterness in her tone. "Did it occur to you he might be doing the same thing now?"

"I don't know why you can't just be happy for me," I snapped, shocked and disappointed that Paige of all people didn't support me. "It's not serious."

"Haley!" Paige's voice rose so high that Ace looked over, forcing her to drop to a harsh whisper. "He hurt you. Twice. More than anyone else has ever hurt you before, and I know, because I'm the one who picked up the pieces. You can't just pretend those things didn't happen. He can't just say 'sorry' and wipe the slate clean. You can't get involved with him without really talking things through, otherwise you're sleeping with a dick who's taking advantage of the fact that you crushed on him when you were a kid and now you're together all the time so he figures why not have a little fun at your emotional expense."

"It's not like that." I stared at her aghast. "He's not like that. I don't know how to explain it but he's not that kind of guy."

"I know exactly what kind of guy he is." Paige crossed her arms. "And if you shed even one tear because of him, the kind of guy he will be is dead."

"You're reading too much into it."

"And you're not reading into it enough. You're in denial. It's not like you're having a hookup with someone you just met or a casual acquaintance and there is no risk of an emotional attachment. You two have a history together. A long history. You had a connection, a friendship, and then you caught feelings and he brutally ripped out your heart. You loved him before you knew what love was. You can't just have sex with a guy like that. You say it's not serious, but you're already emotionally involved, and I know this because we're still talking about it. You couldn't even remember the name of your last hookup. Where's your self-respect? He treated you like—"

"Paige. Slow down." Skye put a hand on her arm. "I know you're worried about Haley but maybe she needs time to process. Why don't we put it aside for now?"

I shot Skye a look of gratitude, but I was done with the conversation and done with what I'd thought was supposed to be a fun evening out. As usual, Paige had drawn out all the things I had been trying not to think about, all the unsettling feelings and misgivings I had blithely ignored. It was no coincidence that things had heated up between Ace and me when she was away. Paige was my conscience, and at the back of my mind, I'd always known what she was going to say. "I thought you, of all people, would be happy for me," I said to Paige. "I always wanted to sleep with him, and I did, and it was great, and that's all there is to it.

Sometimes it's okay to just be in the moment. Sometimes you just go with the flow and deal with everything else later."

"You can't keep burying your feelings and putting everything off until later," she retorted. "That's all you ever do. It's better to get everything out in the open and feel it, deal with it, and then you can move on."

"I feel like you're holding back, keeping all that emotion contained like a dam holds back water."

First Stefan, and now Paige. Why did people think I was repressing my emotions? I was out there, laying everything on the table. I was the most talkative person in class, with my friends, even on the air. I grabbed my bag and slid out of the seat. Paige and I had had many heart-to-heart talks over the years, and she'd never held back when she thought I was making a mistake, but for some reason this time I didn't want to hear what she had to say.

Breathe. Breathe. You're fine. Lock it away.

"You may not like Ace," I said. "But at least he accepts me for who I am."

"I hope so," she shot back. "Because from where I'm sitting, he doesn't really know you at all."

CHAPTER 25

Haley

Good morning, Chicago. This is Hidden Tracks *on WJPK, broadcasting from the heart of Havencrest University. I'm Haley Chapman, and tonight we're exploring songs about hidden truths and the emotional barriers we put in place to protect ourselves. Do you ever feel like you have stories you struggle to tell, or feelings you can't quite express? Today's playlist is for anyone trying to find the courage to confront the past, to have those difficult conversations, and those of us questioning whether our hearts and our heads are in alignment. Our first track is from an emerging artist who sings about trust and vulnerability in complicated relationships. Stay tuned, and remember—in music, as in life, sometimes the most powerful messages are hidden between the lines.*

I pressed the button and put on a song from the playlist I'd put together last night after Ace and I returned home from the bar. When he'd asked what was wrong, I'd told him I had a headache and needed some time alone. Paige and I had had many disagreements over the years, but we'd never had a fight like that. I'd never had to walk away. I'd never felt like a hole had been ripped through my heart.

Guarded heart, crumbling in the dark.

I grabbed my phone and pulled up the lyrics to the song I'd written last night after Ace had gone to bed and I was finally alone. The tune was fluid, melancholic, and lyrical, very different from the upbeat songs I usually wrote. It had come to me in a frenzied burst of inspiration, and I couldn't sleep until it was done—the chords set, the notes written, the lyrics finalized over dozens of sheets of paper. Maybe someday I'd share "Guarded Heart" with the world.

I felt, rather than heard, the studio shake, my microphone gently bouncing on its metal arm. Puzzled, I looked up and saw Ace's frantic face in the window, his fist pounding on the glass.

"Open the door," he mouthed. "Now."

Studio policy was to keep the door locked during a show so that there would be no unexpected interruptions during a broadcast. But this was Ace and he wouldn't have interrupted if it wasn't important. I quickly cued up another song and ran to unlock the door.

"Someone's here. I think he's after you." Ace grabbed my arm and yanked me out of the sound room. "Chad saw a stranger wandering around the hallway. Some fucking idiot had let him in. The dude said he was here to interview with Dante for the station manager position and wanted to take a look around, but Dante's out of town. He wouldn't have set up an interview for today. It may be the guy who tried to grab you on Michigan Avenue. I called campus security and Chad is trying to distract him until I can get you hidden. Someone blocked the fire exit and there's no other way out."

Goose bumps sheeted across my skin, but my brain couldn't fully process what he was saying. "But my show . . . There will be dead air when the song ends. Noah used to say there was nothing worse than dead—"

Ace cut me off by grabbing me around the waist and hoisting me over his shoulder like a sack of potatoes.

"Put me down." I wriggled in his grasp. "I'm not a fucking child."

"You're a target," he gritted out. "And I'll do what I have to do to keep you safe."

"You don't even know if he's the same guy," I protested.

Ace gave no sign that he'd heard me. Instead, he made his way to the music library, opened the storage closet and dumped me inside. "Stay there until I come back."

"You're overreacting," I snapped. "I'm not hiding in a closet and compromising the show unless I know the threat is real."

Ace's face darkened. "Threat assessment is my job."

"And the station is my place," I retorted. "My odds of survival are much higher in the studio, where I have a locked door and access to a fire extinguisher, tools, and all sorts of wires that can be used to electrocute someone. I'm a sitting duck in here, and all I'll have to defend myself are dusty magazines and warped LPs. I'm also the only person who may be able to identify him."

Ace stared at me for so long I began to worry that I'd pushed him too far. He'd always been protective, and when I was younger, I did what he said without question. I'd climbed down from trees, left parties, and given up kissing opportunities with guys way too old for me when Ace would appear out of nowhere and tell me it was time to go. But I wasn't a little girl anymore. And I wasn't about to have my agency taken away.

"This is the only time," he said abruptly. "When we leave here, you do what I say. If I say run, you get into that studio and lock the door. If I say down, you hit the ground."

"I promise."

We made our way down the hallway, Ace in the lead. Fortunately, the permanent staff had gone home for the day and no one else was around. I heard voices coming around the corner from the entrance. Ace motioned for me to stop, pushing me behind him against the wall.

"I think there must have been some kind of miscommunication," Chad said firmly. "Dante is out of town. If you give me your name and details, I'll let him know you were here, and you can reschedule the interview."

"I came all this way. I won't disturb anyone. I just want to wander around and check the place out." Something about the man's tone, firm and unyielding, sent a shiver down my spine. Ace must have felt it, too, because he stepped out into the hallway, one hand behind his back wrapped around the gun tucked under his belt.

"I'm afraid we can't let you do that," Ace said. "All our visitors need to be accompanied by station personnel, and we don't have anyone free to give you a tour."

"C'mon, man. I'll be five minutes." The dude's sudden shift in demeanor and irritated tone just served to increase my sense of unease.

I heard a soft click from what sounded like Ace's gun. Heart pounding, I squeezed between Ace and the wall and took a quick peek around the corner. I didn't recognize the man in the hallway. He was middle-aged with slumped shoulders and a soft belly, mousy brown hair, and a nondescript face. Dressed in jeans and a plain T-shirt beneath a brown jacket, he looked like somebody's dad, and yet he spoke with the confidence of someone used to being obeyed.

The man caught my gaze. His eyes widened, and I jerked back, but it was too late. Ace caught me on the retreat and his warning look made me shudder.

I heard the beep of buttons from the lock. Moments later the door opened, and two campus police officers walked in.

"Did someone report a security issue?"

"I did," Chad said. "This gentleman says he had an interview when in fact, Dante is out of town. He insists on walking around the station and refuses to leave."

"My bad." The visitor held up his hands, reverting back to his softer "dad" persona. "I must have got the wrong date, and I thought since I was here, I'd check the place out."

"You knew he wasn't around." Ace's voice dripped menace. "You knew the staff weren't in yet and no one would be here."

The dude shook his head. "It was an honest mistake."

After a brief conversation, the campus police let the man leave without even looking at his identification. Chad headed for the studio to fill the last five minutes of dead air before his show, leaving me alone with Ace.

"What the fuck were you thinking?" he shouted, backing me up against the wall. "Why didn't you stay behind me? He saw you. That could have gone so wrong."

"I needed to know what was going on. I wanted to see if he was the guy who grabbed me and if he had a gun." My voice shook from the adrenaline still coursing through my veins. "I didn't want anyone getting hurt because of me. I've lost too many people, Ace. I couldn't lose you, too."

"I'm here because of you." His hands clenched by his sides. "Getting hurt to keep you safe is part of the fucking job. You were right in his line of sight. If he'd had any kind of weapon—"

"But he didn't."

"You still don't trust me." A statement. Not a question.

I took a deep breath and tried to slow my pounding heart. Were we still talking about what had just happened, or were we talking about what was going on between us?

"Maybe he really was here for an interview and got the wrong date," I suggested, dissembling my true feelings. "It didn't make sense that someone would come here and try to kill me. I'm an easier target outside."

Wrong thing to say.

Ace planted his forearm on the wall above my head and his face turned two shades of purple. "You are not a target anywhere because I *will not* let anyone hurt you."

In all the years I'd known Ace, I'd never seen even the barest hint of anger. Even when he'd rescued me from difficult or dangerous situations, I'd never seen him lose his cool.

"Ace . . ." I put my hand on his chest, eliciting a low warning grumble. I thought to soothe him. Instead, he pushed my hand away.

"We're going home. You almost died today."

Overbearing. Bossy. Intransigent. Paranoid. "I did not almost die, and I'm not going home, because I need to go to work," I said, sliding out from under his arm. "I have to pay my rent, and I can't just miss my shift without giving my boss notice because then Skye would be on her—"

"Rule one." He cut me off as he followed me down the hallway. "I say we go home."

Something snapped inside me. It wasn't just about the stranger in the station. It was about Paige making me second-guess my relationship with Ace. It was about the way he'd taken away my agency and thrown me over his shoulder. It was about all the times that Matt and Ace had swooped in on my life, ostensibly to protect me instead of letting me make my own decisions, my own mistakes. I had wanted those experiences. I wanted the thrill of holding a boy's hand. I wanted my first kiss. I wanted to get down and dirty with one of the "bad boys" at school. I wanted to get drunk and throw up in the bushes or be so hungover that I couldn't go to school.

I wasn't oblivious to the danger that had brought Ace back into my life. I needed protection, but I didn't need overprotection. I respected his experience, but I needed respect in return. I also needed Ace to realize that I wasn't a little girl anymore, and getting involved with him when he'd been hired to protect me had complicated the situation. I wasn't just his job, and I wasn't a damsel in distress. I was a woman trying to live my life, make my own choices, and learn from them. But now, every time Ace overreacted or tried to shield me from the smallest threat, it felt like I was losing a part of myself. And in that moment, I realized I was suffocating under the weight of his protection, and what I really wanted was to breathe on my own.

"I'm going to work," I said firmly. "You can come and keep an eye out for strangers, or you can call Maverick to take over, because I'm not changing my mind."

"He could still be out there." Ace stood in front of the doorway, blocking my exit.

"Then make sure he isn't. That's supposed to be your job. I think you're being overly cautious because it's me, and given our history, we shouldn't have gone as far as we did. How many of your clients have you thrown over your shoulder and tried to hide in a closet? I'm guessing none. I don't run away from my problems. Not like . . ." I caught myself before I said something I'd regret, but it was too late. From the look on Ace's face, I'd already said too much, and part of me wished I could take everything back.

"You're right; you don't run away from your problems," he said, his voice tight. "Instead, you pretend they don't exist, which is what you're doing now. You put the blinders on and lock everything up inside you, just like Stefan said."

I felt his words like a physical blow. It was one thing to talk through our issues; another entirely to bring my music into the mix. "Get out of my way."

Ace didn't get out of my way. Instead, he opened the door and led the way up the stairs to the student center. I waited patiently for him to make sure the coast was clear before we left the basement stairs. For the first time since he'd started coming to the station with me, he didn't put his hand on my back to guide me through the crowds, and although I would have pushed his hand away, I still felt the absence of his touch like an ache in my chest.

Ace maintained a discreet distance behind me as we walked toward the library. First Paige, then him. I felt like my world was spinning out of control. I was so lost in my thoughts that I didn't see Ben until I'd run right into him—not an easy thing to do with a baller who was six foot seven.

"Ooof." I wheezed out a breath when I recognized him. "Sorry, I wasn't paying attention."

"No worries. I was hoping to catch you before you started your shift."

Ben had been coming by the coffee shop a few times a week, and I'd been expecting him to eventually gather up the courage to do more than ask me about the weather and comment about how busy it was while he waited for his matcha green tea latte.

Maybe that's what I needed. I could go out on a date with Ben and show Paige and Ace, and even myself, that what Ace and I had was casual. I wasn't emotionally involved and therefore not at risk of getting hurt. The only problem was my total lack of attraction to Ben, and my overwhelming attraction to the scowling man behind me.

Ben stammered through a conversation about the weather as he walked with me to the library. I was hyperaware of Ace behind us, his disapproval almost palpable as he gave us space to talk.

"Tin Griffin is giving a concert at the Salt Shed." Ben ducked his head to walk through the library door. "I'm going with a couple of friends. I was wondering if you wanted to come. They're not as good as your band, but you've played their songs on your show before and I figured you must like them."

I could feel the weight of Ace's gaze on me, but I couldn't bring myself to look back. What if Paige was wrong? What if he'd changed and he felt something real for me? Not the casual intimacy of a hookup, or the need to look out for his best friend's little sister, or even the warmth of a friendship, but something more, deeper, the kind of feelings I didn't want but still seemed to have for him despite his behavior at the station. But then again, what if she was right?

"I . . . um . . ." I looked over my shoulder at Ace. His face smoothed to an expressionless mask, and I couldn't even guess what he was thinking. I willed him to say something, to put his arm around my shoulder and tell Ben he was my fake boyfriend, but he didn't move.

"Are you guys together?" Ben asked, following my gaze.

I thought about the concern on Ace's face when he lifted me off the bedroom floor, the gentle way he'd brushed my hair off my cheek, the care with which he'd held me until I'd come fully awake. I thought about the way he'd kissed me at the bar in Riverstone, holding my face like I was the most precious thing in the world. I thought about the way he'd hoisted me over his shoulder and carried me to the library, and his anger when he thought

I'd put myself in danger. It wasn't nothing. There was something between us, and it had been there since the day we met. "Ace is my boyfriend."

Ben's face fell but he rallied quickly and shook hands with Ace before he "just noticed the time" and "had to run."

"You didn't have to do that," Ace said after he'd gone. "If you wanted to go out with him—"

"Seriously?" I turned on him, needing an outlet for the maelstrom of unsettling feelings that were becoming difficult to contain. "You would have been okay if I hooked up with Ben right next door to where you sleep?"

His corded throat tightened when he swallowed. "Your mom hired me to be your bodyguard. I'm not here to interfere with your life."

I pulled him away from the main door and over to a small winter garden full of evergreens. "So, you're here out of a sense of duty?" My hands found my hips. "And nothing else?"

"It can't be anything else," he snapped. "I'm supposed to be your protector. I'm supposed to keep you safe, but I can't seem to be objective anymore. I can't rely on my instincts the way I usually do. Everybody seems like a threat. You were right back at the station when you said we'd made a mistake. We should have kept this professional. I made promises to your family. I can't let them down."

Puzzled, I frowned. "Them? You mean my mom."

A pained expression crossed his face. "And your dad. I was with him in the kitchen one afternoon waiting for Matt to get back from baseball practice. You and Matt were fighting all the time, and it was hard to be around you guys without picking sides. It was only a few weeks before your dad's heart attack. I don't know if he somehow knew it was coming, or if he was just worried you guys would never work out your issues. He asked me to look out for you, to keep his baby girl safe if Matt wasn't around."

Baby girl.

My stomach clenched, so fast and sharp I doubled over. Those words were my everything. Love. Safety. Warmth. Home. I had videos on my phone of Dad calling me his baby girl, but in the years since he'd died, I hadn't been able to watch them.

"Fuck. I'm sorry." Ace put his hand on my shoulder. "Are you okay?"

"Don't touch me." I dropped my hands to my knees and forced my lungs to move. *Breathe. Breathe. You're fine. Lock it away.* Ever since Ace had come into my life, it had become harder and harder to push all the uncomfortable feelings back into my mental black box. It had taken all night to process my fight with Paige, and then the dude in the station, the encounter with Ben, Ace having regrets, and now this . . . *baby girl.* A want—no, a need—so deep and fierce and desperate welled up inside me it took my breath away. I wanted to feel that love again. Just for a moment. I wanted him back. I wanted to be my daddy's baby girl.

Gritting my teeth, I stood, blinking away the wetness in my eyes. Ace was a watery shadow, his blurry face creased with concern.

"I shouldn't have told you."

"Yes, you should have told me. You should have told me a long time ago." I hesitated, letting anger wash away the pain. "And Matt? Did he ask that of you, too?"

"No, but he was my best friend, and you were his little sister. I would have protected you for that reason alone, even if your dad hadn't asked."

Bitterness coated my tongue. "So that's all this really is. A promise to my dad. A duty to my family. Some bro code with my brother. Paige was right, and I almost destroyed my friendship with her because I couldn't see what was staring me in the face."

"What did Paige say?" he asked.

"She said you were taking advantage of the situation and my feelings like you did before. She said I mean nothing to you and as soon as your job is done, you'll go back to your celebrity

clients, and I'll never hear from you again. She said I'd get hurt."
I checked my phone and realized I was about to be late for my
shift. "I need to go."

Ace moved past me to pull open the library door. "I care about
you, Haley. More than anyone else in my life. But you deserve
more than I could ever give. You deserve someone better."

I'd never imagined hearing those words on Ace's lips. Never
considered that he might think of himself as less than worthy
in any respect. He'd pulled himself up from nothing to become
one of the top graduates of his high school class and a decorated
air force veteran. My family had adored him. He'd been well
respected in town, and everyone he'd worked for had spoken
highly of him. He'd been my friend and my anchor in the storm
of chaos that had followed my dad's death. He'd been my everything. "What if I don't want better? What if you're enough? What
if you're all I ever wanted?"

I didn't wait for him to answer. I couldn't handle any more. It
was too messy, too complicated, too confusing. I was caught in a
whirlwind of thoughts and emotions, and I couldn't see my way
through. So, I did what I always did. I shoved it all in the black
box, went to work, and hoped it would all go away.

CHAPTER 26

Haley

THREE YEARS AGO

The problem with living in a small town is that everyone knows exactly how old you are. That means no fake IDs, no sneaking into bars, and no ordering alcohol at the Roadhouse Bar & Restaurant.

Not that it ever stopped me from trying.

"I'll have a double burger with home fries and a gin and tonic." I handed my menu to Colette. She'd been in the same grade as my brother Matt before they graduated, but I was hoping she didn't remember me. Paige and I had boldly walked into the "over 21" section and were still high on the fact that no had stopped us.

"We don't serve alcohol to minors," Colette said, sweeping her thick auburn hair back behind her shoulder.

"I have ID." I pulled out the fake ID Paige and I had made using an illegal software program and the laminating machine at her mother's office.

Colette studied the card. "Maria Gomez. Is that you?"

"Sí." I kept my eyes on Colette because I knew that if I looked at Paige across the table, I'd start to laugh. I could already hear her snicker.

"You look exactly like Haley Chapman, who just had her seventeenth birthday party at Pinz Bowling Alley eight months ago," Colette said. "I remember because I was there with my cousin. It was his birthday, too."

Busted. I'd never liked Colette. She'd gone on a few dates with Matt and then dumped him for the captain of the football team. Karma had caught up with her though. Her new boyfriend had gone to Northwestern on a football scholarship and never looked back.

"C'mon, Colette," I wheedled. "Just one drink. Seventeen is practically nineteen and nineteen is the new twenty-one."

Colette tossed the fake card on the table. "We've got soda, water, and juice, and if you hurry you can get the last table near the window in the family section of the restaurant."

"Her brother is about to deploy," Paige said. "Doesn't that count for something? Have a heart."

"I'll have no job if I serve you alcohol, but I do know about a big house party happening tonight . . ."

Paige and I leaned forward. A party would be even better than the bar. We could drink as much alcohol as we wanted, and no one would be there to stop us.

"Where is it?" Paige asked.

Colette lifted an eyebrow. "I don't see a tip on the table."

"We didn't order anything," Paige protested.

"I believe you just ordered an address."

"Two hamburgers and two Cokes that we'll enjoy in the family section." I put some money on the table. "I hope that's enough to cover *all* the costs."

"Nope."

Paige added a few more dollars and Colette smiled. "Tyler Richards's house. His parents are away for the weekend. He's invited a ton of people. I'm heading there after my shift. Should be fun." She scooped up the money and we went back to the restaurant and grabbed a table beside a family with two screaming kids.

"Why don't we just forget the food and go there now?" Paige grimaced when a french fry flew over her head and landed on the table.

"We need to eat before we drink. I heard Matt and Ace talking about it one time. You're supposed to coat your stomach so you can drink more."

"What if they show up?"

"They won't," I said. "They decided to spend their last night at home gaming. I told Matt we were coming here for a meal and then going back to your place. He won't suspect a thing."

Two hours later, Paige and I were blitzed, and Tyler's party was going strong. We were taking a breather at the edge of the outdoor patio overlooking the beach after a crazy hour of dancing.

"Some of Matt's friends from high school are here." Paige sipped her piña colada. With over one hundred people scattered throughout the house and on the beach, no one was keeping track of who was seventeen and who was over twenty-one. "His baseball buddy Lucas is checking me out."

"If I was into girls, I'd check you out in that dress, too." She was wearing a sleeveless lime-green dress with a plunging neckline that would have put me at risk of indecent exposure. I'd chosen a tight black dress with a sweetheart neckline that could keep my girls in check.

"He's waving me over. He wants me to dance with him." She stumbled back on her heels, saved from a fall by the massive potted plant behind her.

"I'll come with you." I was about to follow her to make sure Lucas did, in fact, just want to dance, when the crowds parted, and Ace walked through the patio door.

Damn. If Ace was at the party, then so was Matt, which meant I wouldn't be there for long.

I moved into the shadows at the edge of the patio and took the opportunity to drink my fill of Ace. He'd stopped coming by the house as often after the night I sat beside him on the couch, and when he did, he rarely spoke to me. Then he'd joined the air force, and the few times he'd been home, he'd stayed at his grandmother's place and Matt had gone to see him there.

But it was a night for indulgence. He was deploying in the morning, and I didn't know if I'd ever see him again, so I took my time, studying every inch of him, committing him to memory.

Dark hair, cut military short. Dark eyes. Tanned skin. He'd

mentioned once that his mom was Italian, and it showed in his sensual mouth and the sweep of his thick lashes. He was bigger than I remembered—more muscular. He'd definitely been working out. He wore a pair of jeans low on his hips, and a black T-shirt that clung to the ridges of his broad chest and rippled abs. He wasn't classically handsome, but something about the way he looked always took my breath away.

Our gazes met. Locked. His eyes swept down my body and then up again. Slow and sensual, his visual caress sent tingles through my body.

My cheeks flamed, and my stomach flipped. Even if this was all I got, I would always remember the way he looked at me that night.

And then he was there, standing in front of me, his body a breath away from mine.

In the few moments we'd stared at each other, I'd imagined a dozen different things he might say: *You're beautiful. I want you. I've been waiting for you all my life.*

"Paige is wasted," he said. "You need to get her away from Lucas."

I bit back my disappointment. "I'm keeping an eye on her." I glanced over at Paige flailing in front of Lucas, lost to the music. "She'll be fine."

His head bent, his dark hair tickling my cheek. I inhaled deeply and the scent of his cologne sent a wave of heat between my legs. Powerful. Primal. Utterly masculine. If I were writing a song about it, I'd have called it "Killer Instinct."

"Are you fine, too?" he murmured in my ear, the deep, rich sound of his voice curling around me like a warm blanket on a cold winter night.

I wasn't fine. Not with Ace standing so close. Looking at me. Speaking to me. Treating me like I was a normal girl, and not his off-limits, uninteresting, last-person-he'd-ever-want-to-be-with best friend's little sister.

"I'm good. I can hold my liquor." I immediately regretted my words, but instead of chastising me, Ace just smiled. "I know."

Did he know I could hold my liquor, or did he know I was good? And if the former, how did he know I could drink like a champ and still walk a straight line home? He'd only ever seen me drunk that one time at the high school dance, and even then, I was sober enough to understand just what was going on.

"Where's Matt?" I figured that was why he was here, and since there was no way Matt would let me stay, I might as well get the lecture over with.

"Your mom's dishwasher broke after dinner. He's trying to get it fixed before he leaves."

Of course he was. Matt didn't care that this was his last night before his first deployment, or that he might not see his friends for a very long time. He didn't think about how he needed to kick back and relax or mentally prepare himself for what lay ahead. Mom needed him. He was there. Just like he was always there for me, even when I didn't want him.

"I thought dishwasher repair was your jam." Ace was always fixing things around our house. He loved to take machines apart and put them together again, much more so than Matt, who was more academically inclined. Usually, they'd work together, with Matt reading through instruction manuals and Ace putting the information into practice.

"When Matt got a message about the party, I knew you'd be here," he said. "You seem to have a knack for finding your way into places you shouldn't be."

"You and Matt went to parties when you were my age," I countered. "No one showed up to drag you away."

"We had more self-control."

I snorted a laugh. "Is that what you call Matt throwing up in the bushes outside the house or being so hungover he couldn't go to school?"

"One of us had self-control." He glanced over at Paige. "In

your case, it's usually Paige, but tonight it looks like the roles are reversed."

"I didn't want to be hungover when Matt leaves tomorrow," I admitted. "It's been so great to have him home. He's different now. Nicer and not so bossy. We didn't fight once. I'm really going to miss him." I hesitated, biting my lower lip. "What if he doesn't come back?"

"You don't need to worry," he assured me. "We'll be deployed together. I'll watch out for him."

"Promise me you'll keep him safe," I begged him. "You know what he's like. He'll forget about his own safety if someone is in trouble. I need him home, Ace. I need you to protect him."

"I promise I will keep him safe, bug. He'll come home to you." Ace's eyes softened and he gently tucked a piece of hair behind my ear. His hand lingered for a moment, fingers brushing the curve of my neck.

My breath hitched, and I shot a look at Paige, mentally screaming, "Ace touched me," but she was still lost in her own world of alcohol-inspired interpretive dance.

"Do you want to go for a walk on the beach?" Ace asked.

A tremor ripped through my body. I don't know if it was his tone, or his words, or the fact that this was D-night, but after years of crushing on him despite knowing he didn't want me, my dreams were suddenly coming true.

"I should keep an eye on Paige." I wanted to go with him. So desperately that I could taste it. But I got bad vibes from Lucas, and I couldn't leave her alone.

"Then I guess we're dancing." He dropped his hands to my hips and pulled me close.

"We're dancing." I repeated the words so that I would remember them, remember how he pulled my body against his, how his hands felt on my hips, how I could feel his heat as he moved against me.

It was heaven. It was hell. It was everything in between. I closed my eyes and let the rhythm find me, dancing in time to the pulse of arousal between my legs in a magically reversed night when anything was possible.

Stay cool. Ace is dancing with you. He probably felt sorry for you because Matt's leaving again, and you were standing here alone while Paige is having fun with Lucas.

Ace's arms tightened around my waist, and he drew me closer. I could feel the hard muscles of his chest, the ridges of his six-pack, and the unmistakable press of his erection against my hips. I slid my arms over his shoulders and rocked gently against him.

Ace groaned so softly I almost wondered if I'd heard it. He liked the feel of me against him. He liked it enough to risk Matt's wrath.

"Haley." My name was a whisper on his lips, a deep rumble in his chest. The air around us was charged, liquid, like an invisible river of desire flowing between us.

"Ace?" My words fell away abruptly when his lips grazed my neck, sending electricity skittering across my skin. I didn't understand what was going on. After all these years, when he'd barely spoken to me, when he'd explicitly told Matt I was the last girl he'd ever be with, why did he want me now?

"Could I kiss you goodbye?" he whispered.

My heart pounded so hard I thought I'd break a rib. Ace wanted to kiss me, or had I misunderstood? "As friends?"

"I don't think I could be your friend." His voice dropped, husky and low. "I want you too much. I've wanted you for a very long time." His hand fisted in my hair and he gently tugged my head to the side, baring my neck to the heated slide of his lips.

There was only one answer. There had only ever been one answer. I didn't care that he'd told Matt he didn't want me, because I wanted him. "Yes, Ace. Kiss me goodbye."

Without waiting, without warning, he cupped my nape and crushed his mouth against mine. His lips were soft, his breath sweet with whiskey, and my arms tightened around his neck, dragging him closer until we were one person, not two.

It wasn't just a kiss. It was a joining of bodies, a melding of souls. Deep down I knew it was a mistake, but I couldn't stop, wouldn't stop, and when he groaned, something snapped inside me.

"Fuck." He groaned into my mouth. "Haley. Jesus. Fuck."

I whimpered in response, fisting his hair, my body taut with an urgency that wiped away every rational thought in my brain. He lifted me against him and pushed me up against the brick wall deep in the shadows, kissing me with a ferocity that had me panting his name before we were lost again in the heat of desire.

We clung to each other, my legs around his waist, his arms around my shoulders, lips on lips and tongues tangled, kissing and kissing and kissing like we would never get another chance and once we stopped the world would stop, too.

"Matt," someone shouted in the distance. "Glad you could make it."

We froze mid-kiss, and Ace dropped me so quickly, I almost lost my footing. He gave me a cursory once-over and adjusted my dress, pulling it down over my hips with a firm yank. A chill replaced the heat that had burned between us, hitting me like a cold wave and washing away the haze of lust that had clouded my senses.

"Goodbye, bug." He pressed a kiss to my forehead.

And then he walked away.

CHAPTER 27

Haley

Two days after the incident at the radio station, I still couldn't bring myself to talk to Ace about anything other than the most mundane topics—weather, traffic, dates and times and places I had to be. We walked to school and ate in relative silence. After dinner, I would go up to my room to study and he would go downstairs to game with Chad and Theo. I wouldn't see him again until morning, although I would hear him pause at my door on his way to bed, as if he were checking to make sure I was still breathing. I would drop a pen or turn up my music to let him know I was still alive, and then the floor would creak, and his door would rattle, and I'd spend the next hour mentally kicking myself for being a coward when there was so much we needed to say. The tension between us was so thick, even my housemates avoided us, so it was a pleasant surprise to see Aditi in the kitchen when we got home from my Sunday-afternoon shift at the Buttercup Café.

"I'm making spaghetti," she said when she saw me. "Do you want to share a meal?"

"Can we make it for three?" I glanced over at Ace, who was staring intently into the pot. "Someone is grumpy because he hasn't been fed."

"That someone is her boyfriend." He smiled at Aditi. "She told Ben I was her boyfriend."

"You're my fake boyfriend," I snapped. "And wipe that smug smile off your face. I didn't want to hurt Ben's feelings by turning him down without a good reason. And I'm still not talking to you."

"I didn't realize we weren't talking when you were complaining about the customers after your shift," he said casually. "Or when you told me you had a meeting with a prof but not what it was about. Or when you were telling me about what you were going to eat when we got home, how much laundry you had to do, and how many tests and assignments are due next week."

Had I said all those things? There was so much more going on in my head, I thought I'd barely spoken to him, and I was even more irritated that I hadn't been able to keep my mouth closed enough to make him suffer my silence for manhandling me at the station when it wasn't even necessary.

"Did you salt the water?" Ace asked Aditi as he peered into the pot.

"Is that a thing?"

"Yes." He pulled out the salt shaker. "Have you started the sauce?"

"Do you mean have I opened the jars?"

Ace looked over at the jars of spaghetti sauce lined up on the counter and grimaced. "How about I make something that has taste and isn't full of sugar?"

Aditi held up her hands and took a step back. "Be my guest. I have no complaints if you want to cook."

"I'm happy to help. You can both sit down and relax and talk to each other, because Haley isn't talking to me."

"That's because you were bossy and overprotective."

Ace snorted a laugh. "That is the literal description of a bodyguard."

"I liked fake boyfriend Ace better," I muttered under my breath.

"Boyfriend Ace isn't being paid a lot of money to keep you safe. Boyfriend Ace didn't spend four years in the military, six months of security training, and two years in the field to get the experience to make the call about whether someone is a threat or not. Boyfriend Ace was forced to take drastic action because he knew you wouldn't follow the rules and he needed to get you to a safe place." Ace gathered up some tomatoes, tomato paste, onions, and spices and then shot me a smug look. "Feel free to thank me anytime."

"Oh my God. Did something happen?" Aditi looked from me to Ace and back to me.

"It wasn't a big deal," I said. "Some guy got into the station and was wandering around. He said he had an interview, but Dante was out of town. Ace thought it was suspicious and tried to lock me in a closet."

Aditi laughed. "I hate to say this, but I feel for Ace in that situation. I would never try to lock you in a closet."

"And that's why I'm talking to you," I said. "You understand me."

"I just have a strong sense of self-preservation." Aditi took out some plates and cutlery and set the table. "So, did it turn out okay? Was the guy legit?"

"We still don't know." Ace chopped the onions with a light, quick touch, Master Chef style. "Dante has been going through the applications but without a name or even a photo, he said it's hard to tell who it might have been. If it turns out the guy wasn't legit, someone is going to owe me a big apology. Huge." He held his arms wide. "I'm talking meals, laundry, shining my shoes, making my bed every morning, maybe a little begging for forgiveness . . ."

"Never going to happen," I said. "If an apology is warranted, I might nod my head, but that's all you'll get out of me."

"What do I get if I make you an amazing meal?" he asked, gently teasing. "No one makes spaghetti sauce the way I do."

"You might get a few words of appreciation." I knew what he was asking, but I still didn't feel like myself, and for the last two nights I'd wanted to sleep alone. It made no sense. I was positive the guy who had come into the station had made a genuine mistake about the interview date and Ace had overreacted to the threat, but I couldn't put it behind me like I usually did. I kept having flashbacks to Ace pounding on the station window,

scooping me up and dumping me in the closet. I kept hearing
him agree that we'd made a mistake. I kept seeing his face when
he said he thought I could do better. I kept waking up at night
with my heart pounding and my body drenched in sweat.

"Where did you learn to cook?" Aditi asked him.

"From Haley's dad. He was a chef. They had gourmet meals
for breakfast, lunch, and dinner. Her family very kindly let me
hang out after school when my grandmother was at work, and I
spent a lot of time there because I was friends with her brother
Matt. Haley and I would be her dad's sous-chefs in the kitchen.
He taught me everything I know about cooking, and this sauce
was his specialty."

Dad. I didn't talk about him. I tried not to think about him,
but Ace had brought him back into my life, and the last thing I
needed right now was a taste of his special marinara. My stomach tightened and my appetite disappeared in an instant. It was
all I could do to stay at the table.

"I didn't know your dad was a chef," Aditi said. "And why
didn't I know you had a brother?"

"They've both passed," I said, my voice tight. "I don't talk
about them."

"I'm so sorry." Aditi squeezed my hand. "Is that why you don't
like to cook?"

"She was too busy singing, dancing, and getting into trouble
to spend time in the kitchen when her father wasn't around," Ace
interjected, coming in for the save. "Biking on dangerous trails,
climbing tall trees, playing with her brother's toys, dressing up
in her mom's clothes, stealing cookies from the pantry, dropping water balloons on Matt and me when we came home from
school . . ."

"I like to think of it as a curiosity about the world." I shot him
a grateful look as the moment of darkness passed, but that unsettled feeling I'd had all weekend just got worse.

"I like to think about all the times I saved you from imminent disaster." Ace added the chopped onions to the frying pan

and then looked over at Aditi. "Once I even caught her when she rolled off the roof."

I smiled at the memory and my tension eased. "I thought you just happened to be standing there."

"In your mother's azaleas?" He chuckled. "I liked flowers but not enough to want to become one with the bush. I knew you'd been in Matt's room setting a trap to get him back for painting stripes on your stuffed pig. After saving your life, I went upstairs and dismantled the trap to save him from getting a face full of paint and you from being grounded, which you would have been when you destroyed his room."

I folded my arms and glared. "I thought it had just misfired. You ruined a perfectly good prank."

"You're welcome." Ace grinned. "And to think I did all those protective services for free when I could have been paid like I am now."

I sent out a group text to see if anyone was around and wanted to share the meal, and then feigned exhaustion so I didn't have to explain why I didn't stay at the table. By the time Ace knocked on my door, I'd slipped on my pj's to get comfy and was trying to play away the memories with my guitar.

"I brought you a sandwich." Ace put the plate on my desk.

"Thank you. I'm sure what you made was delicious, but I just—"

"I know. I didn't realize you hadn't told your friends." He leaned against the doorframe, arms folded across his broad chest.

"Some things are just too painful to talk about," I said. "It's easier not to bring them up."

"Eight years is a long time not to talk about your dad. I think about him all the time. I've tried to re-create a lot of his recipes—"

I held up my hand, cutting him off. "I can't, Ace. Just like I couldn't eat your dinner, although I appreciate you cooking for all my roommates."

"I was actually cooking for you, because you've hardly eaten anything since Thursday."

Damn Ace for noticing, and for trying to make me something nice, and for knowing why I couldn't eat it, and for making me a sandwich. How was I supposed to stay angry with him when he was being so sweet? "I had Doritos and a cup of coffee for lunch. I'm not going to starve."

He lifted an eyebrow in censure. "How's that working for you eight hours later?"

"I forgot the packet of Skittles."

Ace moved to the door. "We need to talk, but I don't want to stress you out any more than I already have. Maybe tomorrow."

"I won't be able to sleep now," I protested. "I've just added 'What did Ace want to talk about?' to my list of things to try and not think about while I lie in the darkness listening to waves and rainstorms to help me fall asleep."

Ace came in and closed the door behind him. "What else is on your list?"

"School, work, too many extracurriculars, not enough gigs. I haven't done an open mic in weeks. I don't remember the last time I was in a recording studio. I can't go busking. Stefan opened a door, but I can't walk through. I write songs but I don't feel them. And then there's Paige. We've never had a fight that lasted this long. She didn't even show up for dinner. I don't know where she is or if she still wants to be my friend after the way I treated her. She was trying to help me, and I threw it in her face. And then there was the dude at the station . . ." I drew in a ragged breath, trying to give voice to my feelings.

"You were scared," Ace said quietly. "You don't do scared."

"You scared me when you banged on the studio window, told me that I was in danger, and then picked me up and ran with me down the hallway." The words came tumbling out in a rush, tripping over my tongue. "And then you were shouting, and I was shouting, and then Ben, who is a perfectly nice, decent guy asked me out and I wanted to say yes because you'd pissed me off, but I couldn't. I couldn't say yes because I hated you at that moment and didn't hate you at the same time. It was like that night after the school dance when you told Matt I was a silly girl playing dress-up and that I was the last person in the world you'd ever be interested in. I'd never felt so hurt and humiliated, and I wanted to hate you and I couldn't."

A pained expression crossed his face, and it took me a minute to realize I'd been expecting surprise or words to the effect of "You heard that?" but those words didn't come.

"I had to say it," he said. "Matt was my best friend. You were his little sister. It didn't matter how much I wanted you—and I did, Haley. I wanted you in ways I shouldn't have wanted you at only fifteen. You don't know what it did to me when I saw you in that dress and realized you weren't a little kid anymore, and worse that other guys were seeing you that way. We've always had a connection, but that night I realized that connection could be deeper, and it scared me. I didn't want to lose you or Matt. So, I said what I had to say even though it killed me."

Five years of pain and heartache and anger and longing swept through me in a heartbeat. Ace did want me. He'd felt what I felt. He'd denied us to save us, and to make sure Matt wouldn't be alone.

"Say something," he said into the silence.

"Is that the same reason you ghosted me after kissing me before you deployed?"

He let out a shuddering breath. "Yes and no. I was being selfish. I thought I might never see you again, and I didn't want to die without knowing how it felt to kiss you. And then you said yes and it was everything. More than I'd ever imagined. But it just made me realize that I had to stay away from you, because if I kissed you again, I'd never want to let you go, and I just couldn't do that to you because what if I didn't come back? I didn't want you to lose someone else. I didn't want to betray Matt. And I didn't want to keep you from meeting someone better than me."

I wasn't sure why Ace would think I could meet someone better than him when things had always been so easy between us, but it didn't ease my pain. "I felt that kiss in my bones. It felt right. We felt right. I'd wanted you for so long, and then you ripped us apart. You hurt me, Ace. So much."

"If I could take that moment back . . ." He trailed off, shaking his head. "I can't say I would. That kiss got me through some terrible times. The pictures I had of you, the memories we made . . . they carried me forward when nothing else did."

I strummed a few chords on my guitar, filling the empty space between us with sound. "What's going to happen now?"

"I don't know," he admitted. "Things have become messy. That's what I wanted to talk to you about."

"Messy is where I live."

Ace picked his way across my paper-strewn floor to sit beside me. "I came here to protect you, but I don't know if I can do that anymore. It might be better if I leave and let Maverick take over. I can't be objective."

No no no. It was one thing to be annoyed and unsettled, another thing entirely to be alone. I tried to play it cool when inside I was bracing for the worst. "You seemed pretty objective when you tossed me in the closet."

"But you didn't stay there, bug. This doesn't work if you don't trust me."

"I trust you to keep me safe." It wasn't the trust I suspected he wanted, but even though he'd explained why he'd hurt me, and he'd shown me that he was committed to making up for the past, it was a long road back to the kind of trust we used to share.

Ace dropped his elbows to his knees. "It's a start."

"I also need you to trust me," I continued. "I'm not that little girl you told Aditi about who was always getting into trouble. You don't need to protect me from myself. I'm not going to unnecessarily put myself at risk, but I need to be part of the conversation, so I can make an informed decision."

"I'll do my best," he said. "But if danger is imminent, I need to act, and there won't always be time for a discussion."

My heart leaped into my throat. "Does that mean you aren't going to leave?"

"Not unless you want me to." He took my guitar and placed it on the nearby stand. "But I would like to work on earning back your trust."

I leaned against his shoulder, soaking in his aura of calm. "How?"

"I have an idea."

I looked up and grinned. "Is sex involved?"

"Possibly." He pulled me into a straddle over his lap. "Would you be good with that?"

"I suppose so." I gave a noncommittal shrug. "I do like sex with you."

He slid his hands under my nightshirt and cupped my bare breasts. "I do like this easy access."

"Then you'll love what I don't have on under my shorts." I ground against the bulge in his jeans. Never in my life had I reacted to a man the way I reacted to Ace. Somehow, we'd turned a serious talk into sexy times and I was pretty sure I wouldn't be spending another sleepless night writing songs on my cold, hard floor.

Ace slid my shirt over my head and tossed it on the bed. "This is one of my favorite sights," he said, cupping my breast and gently running his thumb over my nipple. "You without clothes."

"I'm still wearing some clothes." I wiggled on his lap again and he let out a groan.

"Not for long." Lifting me from his lap, he helped me to the bed. "Lie down. Hands above your head. Hold on to the bars."

"This sounds like it's going to be serious sex and not shake-the-furniture sex." I wrapped my hands around the cool bars of the headboard. I wasn't a fan of the wrought iron design—too harsh and austere for my taste—but in that moment I could appreciate the functionality.

"It's very serious," he agreed as he slid my shorts over my hips. "I'm going to make you come so many times you lose count."

"I can count pretty high."

Ace's dark eyes gleamed and his nostrils flared like a predator on the hunt. "Don't tempt me."

"I am tempting you. Maybe you should finish taking off my shorts and get started."

"I think you're getting confused about who's in control here." He removed my shorts and tossed them on the floor. "Spread your legs."

His commanding tone sent shivers down my spine, but I did as he asked, curious to see how far he would go and how much I could take. My nipples were already tight with desire, the ache for his touch almost unbearable.

"Don't move." Ace sat beside me and leaned over to give me a kiss, overwhelming me with his powerful body, and yet his hand was gentle as it smoothed over my curves, his fingers soft as they feathered up my inner thigh toward my throbbing center. The constant motion focused my senses completely on him and the heat that followed his touch.

"Do you like this position?"

"It feels very naughty," I admitted. "I'm not used to being still."

"I want you still, Haley. I want you restrained with your legs wide so I can see how much you enjoy what I do to you. I want to touch you, taste you, and drive you so wild you can't think of anything but the pleasure I give you."

My mouth went dry and my words, when they came, were barely a whisper. "I want that, too."

"This is about trust. Do you trust me to give that to you, to take care of you tonight?"

The idea of being restrained was both terrifying and thrilling, but this was Ace, and I did trust him. I knew he wouldn't physically hurt me. I'd never done anything truly adventurous in the bedroom until Ace came back into my life, and I was willing to go wherever he led. "Yes, I trust you."

Ace climbed off the bed, leaving me bereft. "Do you have anything I can use to tie you up?"

"Scarves." I lifted my head in the direction of the dresser. "Top drawer. Janice Welling used to knit us scarves every Christmas. I used to hate them, but when I moved to Chicago, they became my favorite piece of clothing."

"I don't know if I can do this using Janice's scarves." He pulled out four long wool scarves in various colors. "I mean . . . It's Janice."

"I promise never to tell her."

Gently, he lifted my left leg and slid it toward the edge of the bed before he wrapped the scarf around it. "You'll be open to me." He quickly did the other, leaving me spread wide. "Completely."

I pulled on the scarves and silently thanked Janice for using a stitch with enough give that I could move my legs but not close them.

"How does that feel?" Ace asked.

"I'm glad I brought her more recent scarves," I said, trying to hide the tremble in my voice. "She used scratchy wool in her earlier scarf iterations." I opened my eyes to look at him and was overwhelmed with the intensity with which he was watching me.

"Haley?"

"Yes?"

"Let's not mention Janice again." His lips quivered at the corners. "She's killing the vibe." He caught me trying to move my legs again and lifted an eyebrow.

"Is anything too tight?"

"No."

"Then, relax." He leaned in and brushed a kiss over my forehead. "Your hands are clenched so tight around those bars I'm worried you might actually break them. I don't want to have to buy you a new headboard."

"Are you going to tie my hands too?"

"I trust you to hold on and not let go." His hands moved up my legs, sending goose bumps racing across my skin.

"I won't be able to touch you," I complained, watching him climb onto the bed between my spread legs.

"Tonight isn't about me," he said. "It's about you. I want to make you feel good tonight. I want to show you I'm worthy of your trust."

His lips met mine, and I melted into his kiss, my body softening and sinking into the bed. And then he took advantage of my willing restraint by trailing more kisses down my throat and collarbone to the crescents of my breasts.

I was hot everywhere, wet between my legs, my breasts aching, my body desperate to move and take what he had teasingly offered. "Please . . ."

"Please what?"

"Touch me. Kiss me. Lick me. Do anything. Everything."

He blew a warm breath over my aching nipple before he closed his mouth and drew me in. He sucked and licked, then bit down gently while his fingers traced teasing circles over my other breast. The sharp sizzle of pain mixed with pleasure had me arching into him, trying to get more of his mouth, more of his fingers, more to soothe the ache between my legs.

Ace turned his attention to my other nipple, alternating between sucking and nipping until I couldn't tell the difference between pleasure and pain. His every touch seemed magnified, flooding me with sensation and heightening my awareness. My duvet felt softer, the scarves scratchier, the air heavier and laced with sensual promise. I could taste him on my lips, the lingering tang of tomato sauce and the bite of whiskey he must have had before he came upstairs. I inhaled, and the fresh soapy scent of his hair flooded my senses.

"When do we get to the part when you're inside me?" I arched again, trying to draw his attention back to my other breast.

"When you stop thinking and just feel." He moved down my body, brushing light kisses over my hip and stomach until they reached my mound. I twisted in frustration, struggling against the scarves, my hands aching from my tight grip on the bars.

"Keep going."

"Do I need to tighten the scarves?" he murmured against my

skin. "Or will you be still?" His breath was hot, his mouth hovering over my aching center. I felt him all over even though his lips were the only part of his body that had touched me.

I closed my eyes and forced myself to stop moving, trying to focus on just processing the sensations. His lips grazed the top of my pubic bone, his breath hot on my skin as he whispered, "Very good."

A wave of pleasure flushed through my body, and I trembled in anticipation as he moved lower. I'd never been so wet, never felt the pulse of blood pound so hard between my thighs. My entire being focused on his heat, his body, his lips working their way down to where I needed him the most.

"Ace," I moaned. "Please." I'd never begged for anything in bed, but I didn't feel embarrassed with Ace. I trusted him to give me what I wanted—what I needed.

"Not yet." He pushed down the bed and pressed a kiss to my inner thigh, and for some reason, the denial of the pleasure I'd been expecting made me even wetter.

"How about a rough timeline?" I suggested, my voice hoarse. "Just so I can plan ahead."

Ace looked up and smiled. "Still not there."

"I am there," I pleaded. "All I want is for you to be inside me."

"I don't think you want it enough." He licked lazy circles along the sensitive skin of my inner thigh, stopping only when he reached the crease of my hip. His hair brushed gently over my clit, the barest whisper of a touch, and my entire body jerked as if electrified.

"Oh, God." I writhed in my bonds.

"I prefer 'Ace,'" he said, amused as he turned his attention to my other thigh. "I want to hear my name when you come."

His smooth, sensual voice licked along my skin. This was Ace—Ace, who had always been there when I needed him; Ace, who had saved me countless times when I'd let impulse take control; Ace, who was here to protect me. Ace, who I trusted.

I closed my eyes again, pushed everything away and focused

on wholly experiencing the sensations in my body, the brush of
Ace's lips on my skin, the heat of his breath, the tickle of his soft
hair.

"That's it." He trailed a finger through my folds, a slow caress
that had me tilting my hips into his touch.

"More." I slid down the bed, bending my knees as far as the
scarves would allow, bringing myself closer.

Ace responded to my invitation, by repeating the stroke of his
finger and following the path with the hot, wet tip of his tongue.
Pleasure coursed through my body in a wave of white-hot heat,
ripping a moan from my throat.

This time he didn't stop. He licked me again, flicking his tongue
over my clit as he pushed a finger deep inside me. I cried out then
turned my mouth into my arm to muffle the sound.

Another finger pushed inside me, and I rocked my hips to
meet his steady rhythm and the hot warmth of his mouth as he
teasingly circled my clit. I gave myself over to the moment, muscles tensing, fingers clinging to the bar, lungs heaving for breath,
my mind shattering until there was nothing but touch and sensation coalescing into waves of pleasure that built faster and higher
until finally, I soared.

Ace slid up my body and kissed me, his hand cupped between
my legs, his finger idly stroking between my folds, keeping me
on edge.

"What are you doing?"

"Whatever I want." He rolled to one side and pushed his finger
firmly inside me. Pleasure zipped through my body, setting my
already sensitized nerves on fire. He thrust in and out, the slow,
steady movements ratcheting my tension up again. "You're so wet.
I think you like being tied up and at my mercy." He added a third
finger, and I squirmed at the erotic sensation of being almost un-
comfortably full.

"I've never done anything like this before."

"I'm your first." A self-satisfied smile spread across his face.

"You're a first for a lot of things." I wriggled on the bed, trying to release some of the erotic tension that was building up inside me. His fingers withdrew, and the pulse of desire eased to a low throb that left me feeling empty. Ace licked his fingers, his gaze never leaving mine. "Are you ready for me?"

"So ready."

Without taking his gaze from mine, he pulled a condom from his pocket and unzipped his jeans. His cock sprang out, hard and thick, and my mouth watered as he covered himself.

"I want you."

He leaned over and kissed me slowly, his mouth moving over mine, tongue sliding between my lips in a gentle caress. "You have me, Haley. Every damn inch of me."

With a groan, he reached over me and grabbed the top rail of the bedframe with a powerful arm. His bicep bulged as he shifted his weight and pushed inside me inch by slow inch, as if he had all the time in the world. I tilted my hips, trying to hurry him, almost desperate to feel his hardness filling me completely. He kept advancing at the same pace, his gaze on my eyes, my mouth, the rise and fall of my breasts, as the tortuously slow slide of his length inside me sent white-hot pleasure through my veins.

When he was fully seated, he brushed his fingers over my cheek. "I like you all pink and flushed," he murmured, holding my gaze with the sheer power of his. "I like you beneath me, trusting me to give you what you need. But I like knowing that the second I release you, I'll have my Haley back again."

He leaned forward, his weight on one arm, and started thrusting in a hard, driving rhythm, pausing only to take my mouth in a slow, sweet kiss. How had I ever thought I'd had sex before? When I was with Ace, it wasn't just a physical act. I felt him in my body and my soul.

"I feel you, Haley," he said, as if he could read my thoughts. He reached between us and slid his fingers over and around my clit.

Arousal turned to clawing need in a heartbeat. He thrusted

harder and deeper, while his fingers teased and stroked until the
world shifted sideways, and I surrendered to the feeling of being
totally and utterly possessed.

Ace groaned and moved faster. I hadn't realized how much
he'd been holding back until the bed started squeaking, the headboard tapping against the wall. My hands clenched around the
bars as Ace rocked his hips, changing the angle of his thrusts. My
vision blurred. The room disappeared. Through the pounding of
my pulse in my ears, I heard him make a rough, guttural sound
that was almost a growl.

With a choked cry, he slammed into me one last time. His cock
thickened and pulsed inside me, and I went over the edge with
him, the unexpected surge of pleasure intense enough to make
me gasp.

Ace dropped over me, taking his weight with his arms. My
mind felt hazy, my thoughts tumbling through a surf of sensation until there was nothing but a serene stillness like nothing
I'd ever felt before. He kissed me gently, bringing me back, when
his fingers tilted my chin, forcing me to look into his intense dark
eyes.

"You're so quiet. Are you okay?"

"I feel calm. It's a strange feeling. Good, but strange."

He stared at me for a long moment, but I wasn't sure if he was
seeing me. He seemed far away, lost in thought. "You don't know
what you do to me," he said quietly.

"Hopefully the same thing you do to me." I unclenched my
fingers from the bars and wrapped my arms around his neck. His
breath was warm against my cheek, and he smelled of sweat and
soap and sex.

"Thank you for trusting me." His fingers combed through my
hair, brushing the loose strands from my face. "I know it's not
easy to give up control."

"It was and it wasn't." I let my hand run up his chest and over
the planes and angles of his pecs. "I never imagined it would be
something I'd enjoy. I like to move. I like action. I've never been

someone who could just be still—at least I haven't until tonight. But I never thought for a moment you'd hurt me or even that you'd push me too far. You know me in a way not many people do. I knew I could let go and you'd keep me safe."

Ace sucked in his lips and his gaze softened. "You trust me with your body, but not your heart."

I knew what he wanted to hear, but I wasn't there—not yet. "It's not easy to go from trusting someone not to hurt you physically, to being emotionally vulnerable and open with them." And then, because he looked disheartened, I kissed him and said, "Although I was pretty open and vulnerable when you tied me to the bed."

His expression cleared and he smiled. "Does that mean that from now on you'll do what I say?"

"Of course not." I twisted my ankles and slipped the knots on the scarves before wrapping my arms around him. My outdoors-loving dad had taught us knots from an early age, something I was surprised Ace had forgotten. "But I do promise to try."

CHAPTER 28

Ace

I knew something was up the next Friday when Haley bolted down her dinner and disappeared the moment we finished drying the dishes. No lingering in the kitchen to gossip. No reflections on what she'd learned in class that day. No suggestions for alternate uses for the scarves that she now kept under her bed for late-night activities.

My worst fears were realized when she hunted me down an hour later while I was fixing one of the window sensors. She was dressed in a tight, backless dress and a pair of heels that gave her an extra three inches of height. Her hair fell in loose waves over her shoulders, and she'd glammed herself up with makeup. She was hot as hell, and the idea of other men looking at her, thinking the kind of thoughts I was thinking, put me in an instant bad mood.

"Are you trying on new outfits or are you planning to go somewhere that you didn't clear first with me?"

"Chad organizes a monthly karaoke night for the volunteers at the radio station and tonight—"

"No."

She moved closer, placed her hand on my chest and licked her lips. Her eyes sparkled, despite my refusal. Only then did I notice she was trembling. "Everyone is going to be there—"

"Still no."

"Including Mark Hansell, Vice President of A&R at EMI Records!" Her voice vibrated with excitement. "He was in town a few weeks ago and heard me singing on Michigan Avenue. He found me online and listened to my music. Now he's back in Chicago, and he wants to hear me live!"

I couldn't fully share in her excitement because I was still try-ing to process her outfit and what it might mean. "That's fantas-tic. I can call Jordan and arrange for backup the next time you have a gig at Bin 46—"

Haley shook her head, cutting me off. "Tonight."

And suddenly the outfit made sense, and so did her decision not to tell me until the last minute. "He wants to hear you to-night?"

"He's on a flight first thing tomorrow morning and he wanted my performance schedule so he could arrange to see me on his next trip. I hadn't planned to go to karaoke night because I knew you wouldn't approve, but I couldn't turn down this opportunity. I told Mark that I'd be singing tonight, and he said he'd drop by if he has time." She threw her arms around me in a hug. "Can you believe it?"

"What I can't believe is that you wouldn't discuss it with me first." I pulled out of her arms. "It's too risky. You'll be too ex-posed on stage."

"No one knows I'll be there," she said. "I haven't even told Chad I'm coming. The Uber will be here in twenty minutes. That should be enough time for you to check the street and make sure we aren't going to be followed and ask Jordan for backup if you think we need it."

I picked up my screwdriver and turned back to my work, pry-ing the sensor from the ledge. "Were you not just the target of an attack at the station last week?"

"Dante said he had set up interviews," she reminded me. "He just couldn't say if the guy who showed up was one of the people he was planning to meet."

"Until he's met the candidates and checked their images against the video from that day, we have to assume the guy was after you," I said. "In my professional opinion, it would be better to wait until he can confirm the guy was legit before putting yourself at risk."

"Seriously?" Her sweet smile faded. "This could be the break I've always dreamed about. He heard me on the street. He's listened to everything I've posted online . . . The contract is practically signed. There's no way he's going to change his mind after tonight. I kick ass at karaoke and I'm singing one of my favorite songs: Taylor Swift's 'Shake It Off.' It shows off my entire vocal range."

"What about Stefan?" I scrambled to find reasons to change her mind. "He said you were holding back emotionally with your covers. He said your true talent would come out with your original music. He's the real deal. What do you even know about this guy Mark? Why didn't he see the same problem? Did you even look him up?"

"Ace." She slipped between me and the window and slid her arms around my neck, pressing her soft body against me. "He's from EMI. They are one of the top five record labels in the world. This is a huge opportunity, bigger than Stefan, bigger anything I ever imagined. My dad . . ." Her voice caught, broke. "He would have been so proud. He would have shouted 'That's my baby girl.' He would have been dancing around the kitchen . . . I'll bet he would even have jumped in his car and tried to get here to watch me tonight. He always wanted this for me. We dreamed about it together."

Fuck. Even if I could have stopped her, there was no way I could say no. Not now, with the image of her dad in my head, and knowing how much it meant to her to find success in something that was so deeply connected with him. Music was her way of keeping his memory alive, a symbol of the love and connection they shared. This wasn't just about a career for her, it was a way she could honor his memory.

"Would it change your mind if I *asked* you not to do this?"

"You've been grumpy all week," she said. "It will be good for you to get out, too. It must be boring to be stuck in a college town when you're used to going to the best clubs and restaurants in LA with all your celebrity clients."

I would have traded every minute I'd spent in every Michelin-starred restaurant for one night with Haley. "I don't get bored, and especially not with you, but I'm concerned about my ability to keep you safe in a venue that Jordan's team hasn't had a chance to check out."

"I promise to do everything you say." She nuzzled my neck. "I'm wearing my special locator necklace. I'll sit where you tell me to sit, and after I'm done, I'll leave when you tell me to leave. I won't even have a drink if you think that's a bad idea." She pulled me closer, rocking her hips against mine. "You can even punish me when we get home. I can't get free when you use that new knot I showed you."

I could feel my resolve weakening. "I'm supposed to make you feel safe by ensuring there are no outside threats, discouraging you from going into dangerous situations, and protecting you if someone tries to hurt you. Not tying you to the bed."

"I love being tied to the bed," she whispered, even though there was no one else around. "Maybe this time you could also tie my hands . . ."

Fuck. "How about we go straight to punishment time instead of karaoke?"

"One song," she said, brushing her lips over mine. "I just want to sing one song for Mark and I'll leave right away. Then you can do anything you want with me."

"Haley . . ." I groaned when she feathered kisses along my jaw. She was impossible to resist at the best of times, but this sweet seduction was too much. Her soft kisses and the floral scent of her perfume clouded my senses, and the press of her body against mine was like a fist around my cock. "I can't agree to this."

"In the end, it is my decision," she said. "I could just go and stay all night and you wouldn't be able to stop me. I'm trying to be sensible and respect your concerns while also making sure I don't miss out on what could be the biggest opportunity of my life."

She was right that I couldn't stop her. My job was to protect my clients wherever they decided to go. I could advise about the risks and recommend against attending an event or venue, but

I had no enforcement power. If I had my way, my clients would stay safely at home and out of danger, but the celebrities I'd worked for needed to be out and about, posing for the paparazzi and meeting their fans. Jessica had gone against my recommendations many times and I'd managed to keep her safe. Haley wasn't a celebrity—not yet—but I couldn't keep her wrapped in bubble wrap, especially after she'd tried to take my concerns into consideration instead of escaping out a window. And then there were the benefits.

"One song?"

"One song."

"And afterwards," I said. "Anything?"

"Anything."

Isla, Nick, and Derek were waiting for us at the B Street bar in Chicago's South Side. They'd pushed together a few tables, and a short while later Chad and Paige joined the party. Paige and Haley still weren't talking, and I could see how much it hurt Haley when Paige wouldn't even look in her direction.

"Do you want a drink?" Haley asked after she'd ordered a tray of shooters to share with her friends.

"No." I could barely look at her, my full attention on the dubious characters lurking in the shadows. It hadn't even been half an hour and I was already counting down the minutes until I could get her safely home.

"How about a snack?"

"How about we get out of here?" I countered. "Jordan said this bar has a reputation for attracting crime. The residents have been collecting signatures to demand the city close it down. He's sending backup but he's short-staffed right now, so try not to get into trouble until he can get someone out here."

"But that's what makes it so interesting," she said. "It's got a different vibe, a little edgy and dangerous, and the DJ is awesome."

"Several illegal acts have occurred here or nearby," I informed her, "including public indecency, vandalism, and two shootings. How did your friends manage to pick the most dangerous karaoke bar in the city?"

"Just lucky, I guess."

I lifted an eyebrow in disbelief, and she sighed. "Chad forgot to call ahead to our usual karaoke bar and there were no tables left. He did a quick internet search and found this place. It had good reviews . . ."

"Best place for a shootout? Most crimes committed in one week? Number one for bar fights?" My voice rose in agitation. "Top ten places to die? Do you really think a top-level music executive is going to come to a place like this?"

"I think you're overreacting," she said. "I sent Mark the name and address, and he didn't have a problem with it. This isn't a bad area, and the place looks clean . . ."

"The bar is already on the floor, and you just brought an excavator," I said dryly.

"All the tables are full—"

"Of criminals."

"People are just chilling," she complained. "Maybe you should just try to relax and have a good time."

"I should never have allowed you to come," I grumbled. "If you hadn't distracted me dressed the way you're dressed and looking how you look and doing the things you do, I would have tied you to the bed and made you forget all about karaoke." I raked my fingers through my hair, cursing under my breath at clients who insisted on living their lives despite the risk. But that was Haley.

"You like my dress?" She smiled and spun around to torment me further.

"Like" didn't even begin to describe the effect that dress was having on me, with its naughty slit and low-cut neckline and the damn back that showed way too much skin. I wanted to fuck her in that dress and then I wanted to tear it off her and tie her up and make her promise never to wear it again where any other man could see her.

"I'd like it better with a thick parka around it, and instead of those stilettos, maybe a pair of winter boots." I glared at a dude who was looking in Haley's direction. "How about a balaclava and a few of Janice's scarves? That would be a better look for a place like this."

"Stop grumbling." She leaned up and kissed my cheek. "You did your job and said no. You pointed out the risks. Unfortunately, you were overruled, as you knew you would be. Risk is my middle name."

"I was seduced, not overruled." I was saved from letting loose all the thoughts in my head when Skye arrived with Dante. I'd met Skye at the coffee shop, but not Dante and I'd been curious to meet the bass player who'd finally made it big. He was around my height, muscular and solidly built. But there was a darkness around him, the barest hint of violence pulsing beneath his skin. He was a man you would only want on your side of a fight.

"I see I'm not the only one who lost the battle when he said no to this bar tonight," Dante said after Haley introduced us. "It's a disaster waiting to happen."

"I didn't get the benefit of knowing where we were going in advance." I glared at Haley. "If I had, I would have tried even harder to shut it down. I wasn't happy about going out at all. I played all my cards—"

Dante glanced over at Skye and his face softened. "But then she got all dressed up and walked up to you with her sweet talk and sexy smile and suddenly you're in a fucking South Side karaoke bar with a bunch of crime lords and you're damn glad you came."

"Pretty much sums it up." Every instinct in my body was screaming at me to take Haley home, but every time I even thought about suggesting it was time to go, she would look over at me and smile and my brain would fuzz all over again.

"Twenty bucks says someone gets beat up before eleven," Dante said, pulling me out of my train of thought. "Thirty says someone pulls a gun and we all get to go home early."

"Forty says the undercover cop in the corner arrests someone for dealing." I'd spotted him five minutes after we arrived. He was too stiff, too aware, and too underdressed in his jeans and polo shirt, despite the rough vibe around us.

Dante laughed and we spent a few minutes trying to spot the most likely criminal elements in the bar.

"Are you packing?" Dante asked. "I want to know what kind of backup I'm going to have if we have to make a quick exit."

I moved my jacket aside to show him my gun. "I try to identify the threats in advance, so I don't have to use it."

"They're all threats," he said. "I know one of the guys at the bar. He's big in organized crime."

"I can't figure this place out. On the surface it looks like a decent bar—nice decor, great vibe, good DJ, no one has food poisoning yet. And then you take a closer look—"

"And you want to get your woman the hell out of here," Dante said.

My woman. I liked the sound of it too much.

"I'm just her bodyguard."

Dante chuckled and lifted an eyebrow. "Been there, my friend. I told myself I was just Skye's internship supervisor, but she was mine from the moment we met."

Had Haley been mine since we first met in her kitchen ten years ago? Not in the way Dante was talking about. We'd been too young, and I'd just been ripped away from the only family I'd ever known. But she had touched my soul and lit up my life with her joy and her laughter as she danced around the kitchen with Paige and her father. I'd never seen that kind of spirit, the utter abandon with which Haley and her dad spun each other around, singing at the top of their lungs. I could have watched them for hours. We'd been friends until the longing came, and then I'd had to make a terrible choice between honor and following my heart.

After two torturous hours, and a no-show from the music executive, the DJ called Haley's name and she walked up to the stage with all the poise and elegance of the celebrities I'd spent two years protecting. I moved closer, positioning myself so that anyone who wanted to get at her would have to go through me.

Her first notes came out loud and clear and the crowd cheered when they recognized Taylor Swift's "Shake It Off." She gave an incredible performance, filling the bar with same light and energy she'd had that first day we met. At one point, she caught my gaze and the distance between us vibrated, humming deep in my bones. Space became music, a beautiful sound.

After the applause died down, I moved to intercept her as she stepped off the stage. "You were amazing," I said, keeping one hand on her waist and using the other to make a path through the crowd. "You've always sparkled on stage."

"I just wish Mark had been there to see me." She gave a wistful sigh. "One day I'm going to be on a real stage. Not in a bar or in a community hall, but in a stadium or arena, and thousands of people are going to be watching me."

"I'll be right there cheering you on."

"Haley . . ." A tall dude in a blue collared shirt, his body lean with muscle, black hair slicked to his head, stepped into our path. My body tensed and I pulled Haley to the side, putting myself between them.

The smallest frown creased his brow so quickly I wondered if I'd seen it. "Mark Hansell from EMI. We talked on the phone." He handed Haley a business card. "You were great up there. I liked what I saw."

Haley's eyes widened and her smile spread from ear to ear. "Thank you. I was hoping you'd make it tonight."

"Can we go somewhere quiet and talk?" Mark asked, looking around. "I love a bar with character, but they've gone pretty heavy with the bass tonight. I saw an all-night coffee shop around the corner . . ."

Haley looked over at me and I nodded. A coffee shop would

be safer than the bar. Even more so once Jordan's backup arrived.

"I'll just tell my friends I'm leaving and grab my coat," she said. "And this is my boyfriend, Ace. He'll be coming with us."

Mark shook my hand. "No offense, Ace, but I need to talk to Haley alone. I have to get confidentiality forms signed just to have a conversation. It's just easier when fewer people are involved."

Safety or her dream career. I thought I knew what choice she would make, and I was trying to figure out a way to protect her without being seen when she said, "I'm sure Ace won't mind grabbing a different table so we can talk privately. This isn't a great area, and I'd feel more comfortable with him there. He's ex-military so he can handle any kind of trouble."

Mark's face tightened and I got a strange feeling in my gut that had me putting my arm around Haley's shoulders. "No problem, babe. I'll find a table in the corner and stay out of earshot."

After a moment of hesitation, Mark nodded, and his smooth voice took on an edge that made the hair on the back of my neck stand on end. "Of course. I want you to feel comfortable."

Haley led Mark through the bar to our table asking questions about his work in the music industry. I followed behind them, scanning the crowd, my skin pricking with a growing sense of unease. Outwardly, nothing in the bar seemed to have changed. The DJ had just announced the next singer and was pulling the lyrics up on the screen, people were laughing and chatting, the serving staff were weaving their way through the tables with trays full of drinks, and yet something felt wrong. Instinct had kept me alive in the field, and I knew better than to second-guess myself. I grabbed Haley's arm and pulled her to my side. "Apologies. I need a quick word with Haley."

I didn't wait for Mark's response. Instead, I led Haley far enough away that we could talk without being overheard.

"What's wrong?" Haley studied my face, frowning.

"I don't know, but we need to get you out of here. Now." I scanned the bar, trying to find the source of my unease. A couple fighting. A drug deal gone bad. Maybe the undercover cop had nabbed his man. Or was it something more sinister?

Something in my face must have made her realize this was serious. "We need to warn everyone."

"I don't want to cause a panic. Tell Mark you've got to settle the bill or use the restroom and that we'll meet him out front. We'll take your friends out the back."

Her forehead creased in a frown. "Why doesn't he just come with us?"

"He's already annoyed that I'm tagging along," I told her. "I don't want to further agitate him by hustling him out the back door for nothing if I'm wrong. We could go with him but—"

"We have to make sure my friends are safe first. I'll talk to him."

Haley arranged to meet Mark outside and we made our way to the table. Dante was already out of his seat and when our gazes met, I knew right away he'd felt it, too. "Something's off," he said, grabbing his jacket.

"We need to get everyone out of here. There's a back entrance beside the bar. If something does happen, everyone else is going to run for the front door."

Dante grabbed Skye's hand. "Skye and I will get everyone together."

"Where's Paige?" Haley asked, looking around.

"Restroom," Skye called over her shoulder. "She left about five minutes ago."

"I'll go and get her." Haley dashed away before I could stop her.

"Damnit, Haley." I followed her through the bar and had almost caught up when I heard a shout, the scrape of a chair, the shatter of glass on the hard wooden floor.

"Haley." I pushed my way through the crowd, trying to catch up. Behind me, I heard a scream, and then someone yelled, "He's got a gun."

A gunshot ripped through the bar with a sickening crack.

Chaos ensued. People dropped to the floor. Others panicked and stampeded toward the front door. I pulled out my gun and dropped to a crouch, looking for Haley. She was only five feet away crouched under a table.

"Ace?" She looked up, and her panicked expression twisted my heart.

"Stay down." I lifted my head and took a quick look around. I couldn't see the shooter, but the overturned tables and chairs and the broken glass on the floor near the front door gave me a good idea where he might be. Keeping low, I made my way over to Haley and threw my arm over her, shielding her with my body. I'd never felt such relief.

She grabbed my arm, fingers digging into my skin. "What's happening?"

"I don't know. Could be a drug deal gone bad." I gave her a quick once-over. "Are you hurt?"

"No. But Paige and the others . . ."

"Dante and Skye are getting everyone out," I said. "I'll take you out the back entrance and we'll meet them outside."

"Paige must still be in the restroom. We can't leave without her."

Fuck. The restroom was on the other side of the bar. All I wanted to do was get Haley out safely, but I knew there was no way she would leave without Paige.

Another gunshot echoed through the bar. Sirens wailed in the distance. The police were on their way and the last thing I needed was for Haley to be trapped in the bar with the shooter.

"You know she'd want you to be safe," I pleaded. "I'll take you out and then come back for her. I promise I'll bring her out safely."

I promise I'll bring Matt home. I'd broken that promise. I wouldn't break another.

She hesitated for a few long moments, and then she nodded. "Okay. I'll go. But Ace . . ." Her voice cracked, broke. "Please. I can't lose anyone else."

It took everything I had to fight the instinct to just pick Haley up and carry her to safety, but I knew she'd never forgive me a second time. Keeping low and covering her with my body, I moved with her down the back hallway until she was safely at the door.

"Text Paige as soon as you're outside and tell her to get behind the restroom door. She needs to stay low and only move when I knock. As soon as we're clear, I'll bring her outside."

I watched her walk out into the alley, waiting for the door to close behind her before making my way to the restroom. The bar was eerily still. Except for the odd stifled sob and rasped breath there was no sound. I knocked and pushed the restroom door open just enough for Paige to crawl out.

"Is Haley safe?" Paige mouthed, looking around as I covered her for the short journey to the safety of the bar.

"Yes. She's waiting outside."

Paige gave me a thumbs-up and I took her down the back hallway, checking the rooms on either side as I followed behind her, making sure we hadn't left anyone behind.

We joined Haley's friends outside, along with most of the bar staff and a few other patrons. The police had cordoned off the alley on both sides with yellow tape to make sure nobody left until it was safe. Paige looked around and her forehead creased. "Where's Haley?"

"She should be here somewhere. I brought her right to the door." We split up to look for her and Paige caught up to me a few minutes later with Chad in tow.

"Chad saw her about ten minutes ago. She was with the record executive she'd told us about—the one who said he might come out to hear her tonight."

"She introduced us," Chad said. "His name is Mark and he's from EMI Records. They were going to a coffee shop to talk signing. She asked me to tell you not to worry. The cops at the end of the alley let them through. I guess because he's a big deal or something. No one else has been allowed out." His smile faded when I frowned. "Is something wrong?"

Yes, something was wrong. Haley would never have left without making sure Paige got out safely, not even when they were fighting, not for the chance of a lifetime. And she would never tell me not to worry when worrying about her was my job.

"Did she look okay?"

Chad shrugged. "She looked scared, but everyone is scared so I didn't think anything of it."

The bad feeling I'd had all night morphed into sickening fear, and the fear became a reality when my phone beeped with an emergency text from Haley's necklace. I checked the coordinates on the security app. She was five blocks away. Not a distance she could have gone on foot in the short amount of time we'd been separated, and that meant only one thing. My worst nightmare had come true.

CHAPTER 29

Haley

Breathe. Breathe. You're fine. Lock it away.

I should have been scared.

After all, I'd just been kidnapped by a man pretending to be a record executive. He'd shoved a gun into my side in the alley, and quietly threatened to shoot Chad if I didn't lie about where we were going. He had two buddies dressed as police officers who had ushered us out of the alley, and a very thick hand that he'd placed over my nose and mouth when we were out of sight, making it difficult to breathe, much less scream. He and another dude had forced me into an SUV parked on the street, and we'd been quickly joined by the last member of his team, the guy who had fired his gun in the bar to cause a commotion to separate me from Ace.

But fear wasn't the emotion that was making my body tremble or my heart pound. Instead, it was fury—at myself for being so stupid and naive, at these idiots for messing with my life, and at a music industry that had made it plausible that a record executive would come to a run-down karaoke bar to hear me sing, throwing me off guard just long enough to get me away from Ace and my friends. Or maybe that was my ego.

I raised my bound hands to my necklace again and pressed it against my chest two times just in case it hadn't worked the first time. Of course, they'd taken my phone and tossed it out the window. Mark—if that was even his real name—had shoved me into the back seat of the vehicle, and the driver had tied my hands while they waited for their fake police buddies—Tom and Luis they'd called each other—to join them. For some reason, I wasn't surprised when Tom took off his wig and turned out to be the man who had come to the station pretending to be early for an interview.

"Ace was right," I said bitterly as Tom climbed into the seat beside me. "I'm never going to live this down."

Tom ran his hand through his hair. "You've got one hell of an overprotective boyfriend, honey. It was a challenge to get him away from you. You might want to rethink that relationship if this works out the way we hope it will."

I allowed myself a moment to process the fact that there was a slim possibility I might get out of this alive. "Don't underestimate him."

"Is that why you're so calm?" Tom laughed. "You think he's going to save you? He's probably still looking for you around the bar."

I wasn't calm in any sense of the word, but I was an expert at dealing with negative emotions. I'd already put fear away in its black box and my brain was in fifty places at once, considering options, noting landmarks, watching the time and the direction notification on the dashboard screen, praying that the GPS necklace was working its magic, and making a plan in the very unlikely case that it wasn't. I couldn't physically take on four men, but I was resourceful, an expert escape artist, and after years of being chased around the house by Matt, I could run at a respectable speed.

"He knows me," I said. "He knows I wouldn't leave Paige."

"You know what I know?" Tom asked, his voice thick with menace. "If he gets in our way, he's dead."

"Why are you doing this? What do you want with me?" I buried my hands deeper in my lap as I worked the knots on the ropes they'd used to tie me up.

"The why is not our business."

"Shut it," Mark said from the front. "No chatter."

I checked for landmarks out the window again. We'd turned north up the 90 and then west on the 290, passing a high school and hospital and then a small park. Mark called someone en route to report that they'd made a clean exit from the bar.

"We've got an address," he told the driver. "Warehouse on West Arthington. Turn off on Cicero Avenue. I've got the gate code."

By the time the driver turned off the 290, I had fully loosened the ropes and my heart was pounding so hard I was sure they could hear it. We drove through the industrial stretch of a rough neighborhood and pulled up in front of a redbrick single-story warehouse with a tall barbed-wire fence. It was the kind of place police found dead bodies, and the fear I'd managed to contain started to spill out. Even if I escaped the vehicle, how would I get over the fence? And if I did, where would I go? There were no houses, no stores, no police stations, and the people I'd seen lurking about looked to be just as dangerous as the men in the car.

Mark opened the gate and we drove through. I held on to the ropes so they didn't slip as they pulled me out of the car and marched me into the dark, vacant building.

"No fucking electricity." Tom flicked the light switch. "We're going to freeze our asses off."

"They left a portable light in the office and some generators out back," Mark said. "We don't want to draw unnecessary attention. Take her to the office. The car needs to be parked out back so it isn't visible. Luis can get the generators."

Tom grabbed my arm and marched me into the office. My stomach heaved at the overpowering smell of rot, and my nausea worsened when Tom turned on the light to reveal soggy, molding carpeting, crumbling ceiling tiles, two scurrying rats, and a broken sofa with a large, dark stain that looked suspiciously like blood.

The bitter taste of bile coated my tongue and I forced myself to swallow it back down. I didn't want to show them any more weakness than I had already.

"You want her on the couch?" Tom asked.

"She needs to be roughed up for the pictures," Mark said. "Hold her while I put some bruises on that pretty face."

"No!" A wave of terror overwhelmed me, crashing through

my body. I dropped the ropes and used Tom's momentary surprise to twist away. Adrenaline pumped through my veins as I raced for the door, navigating the darkness with the thin strands of light spilling from the office.

As if on cue, the door opened. For a second, I thought it was Ace outlined in the darkness and hope swelled inside me. Only when I was too close to turn away did I recognize Luis. I veered to the right but he grabbed my left hand and twisted it, using my momentum against me. I jerked to a stop, my wrist bending in ways wrists shouldn't bend, and the sharp, intense pain almost dropped me to my knees.

Mark grabbed my hair from behind and pulled me up. "Well, that's a good start."

I don't know how long I'd been tied to the office chair when Mark and Tom finally returned. I'd lost track of time when they started beating me in places they decided would quickly show bruises. One of my eyes was swollen shut and I could barely see out of the other. My ribs ached and my throat burned every time I swallowed. I was so desperately thirsty my tongue felt like sandpaper. I tasted blood on my lips from the slow trickle coming from my nose but at least I could no longer smell the rot in the room.

They'd tied my arms to the back of the chair and my wrist throbbed every time I took a breath. I still couldn't believe this was really happening, and part of my mind kept insisting it was a dream. Except for play fights with Matt, no one had ever hit me before. Despite all my misadventures, I'd never broken a bone.

Mark shone a flashlight in my face, making me squint. "I think we did our job too well. You bruised up almost too much." He gestured behind him. "Tom's got a whiteboard. You're going to read what's written on it while I record you. If you go off script, we'll add another few bruises and start again."

"Water. Please." Hoarse and scratchy, my voice was unrecognizable even to me.

"Say your lines and I'll give you a sip." He held up a bottle of water. "Make a mistake and it goes on the ground."

He walked behind me to adjust the light and then came back to hold up the camera. I silently read the words on Tom's whiteboard and my stomach twisted in a knot. They wanted my mother to resign her Senate seat, publicly announce her withdrawal from politics, and affirm her support for another candidate from her party in the next twenty-four hours or they were going to kill me. If she involved the police or FBI or tried to find me, they also would kill me.

The hope that had sustained me through the kidnapping and the beating flickered and died. I'd seen their faces. I knew their names. Once they got what they wanted, I would be a liability. There was no chance they would let me leave the warehouse alive. I'd never see my mom again. I'd never get to tell Paige I was sorry. I was never going to hear Ace say "I told you so" or tell him I forgave him and trusted him with my heart.

"You're going to kill me anyway so I'm not going to say that on camera," I spat out through swollen lips.

Mark slapped me so hard my head jerked to the side and the burst of pain speared through my already throbbing jaw. "Try again."

"No." They couldn't kill me until they got the video. I just hoped they knocked me unconscious, so I didn't have to feel any more pain.

Another slap. A punch that made my jaw crack and my ears ring. Mark walked behind me, grabbed my hair, and yanked my head back. "How about a different kind of necklace?" He ripped off my locator and tossed it on the ground, then slowly dragged the tip of his knife across my neck.

The searing pain ripped a scream from my throat and the sharp smell of blood filled the air. My vision blurred. I gritted my teeth, trying to keep my fear at bay, but it was too much, too great, even for the black box that had kept me safe, a tidal wave of terror crashing over me, sucking the air from lungs.

Mark's phone buzzed with a message. He released me and pulled out his phone as my betraying body forced me to draw in a breath. "*Fuck.* Luis said someone's coming down the road. Go check it out."

Tom tossed the whiteboard on the couch and pulled out his gun before disappearing into the dark warehouse. Moments later I heard a thud, and then a gunshot rang through the silence.

"Tom?" Mark pulled out his weapon and stepped out of the office. I heard the crack of another gunshot and he flew backward, crumpling on the ground.

"Haley?"

I knew that voice. So deep. Smooth like whiskey. So familiar. Emotion welled up in my throat and his name, when it came from my lips, was barely a whisper. "Ace." I drew in a deep breath and put all my effort into a shout. "Ace. I'm here."

A figure darkened the doorway and then Ace stepped into the light. Beautiful Ace. But he wasn't smiling. Instead, his face was a mask of horror. Was he not happy to see me? A wave of dizziness hit me, and I wondered if he was real.

"Oh God. Haley. Fuck." He turned away and the last words I heard before the darkness took me were "Bring them to me."

Paige arrived at the hospital shortly after the ambulance brought me in, and then all hell broke loose. She shouted, wrangled, cajoled, and threatened until she was satisfied I was being properly looked after.

"I was an idiot," she said, holding a cup of water for me to drink. "Feel free to beat me up when you're better. I was wrong about Ace, and I'll regret doubting him for the rest of my life."

"I think there's been enough beating people up for one day." My voice was hoarse from screaming and my lips and tongue swollen from all the blows. "I'm sorry, too. I don't know why I went off on you."

"Because he's Ace," she said. "Your feelings run deep. I just can't help hating on someone who hurt you. I wish those dudes who kidnapped you hadn't been shot, because I would have liked to do it myself."

"Stand in line." I tried to laugh but my ribs hurt too much. "They beat me just to intimidate my mom. But the worst part was, I believed the guy was a record exec. He knew the industry. He dropped names. He knew my back catalog. When he called me, our conversation didn't ring any alarm bells. And when we met up, his business card looked legit. He came up to me in the alley and we talked about how scary the whole thing had been, and then he suggested we go to the coffee shop to discuss my career. And I said no. I said no, Paige, even though I thought it was my big chance. I wasn't stupid. I told him I couldn't leave until I knew you were safe and Ace was with me, and that's when he pulled out the gun. I'd been so excited at the thought that I was finally going to break into the music business, I didn't realize I was in danger until it was too late. I feel like an idiot."

"You were an idiot for sending Ace to get me," she said. "You should have let him stay with you."

"I couldn't leave you in there when someone was shooting up the bar." My throat thickened and I sipped the water to try and make the sensation go away. "It wasn't an option."

Paige kept me company through the check-ups, X-rays, and splinting of my sprained wrist. She finally agreed to go home to get some sleep when Mom arrived with Steve.

"I am so sorry, darling." Mom pressed a gentle kiss to my temple after I filled her in on what had happened. "When Ace called—"

"Where is Ace?" He had insisted on riding in the ambulance with me, but I hadn't seen him since I'd arrived at the hospital. "Is he okay?"

"He's fine." She sat in the chair beside my bed. "His team went through the warehouse and pieced together the kidnappers' plan to use you to force me out of the Senate race."

"They beat me up so the video would be more effective."

"They didn't need to go that far." She gently stroked my swollen cheek. "Even if they hadn't touched you, I would have done what they asked to get you back. I know I wasn't the best mother after your dad died, but you are everything to me. There is nothing more important in my life than you."

Mom had never made me feel like I mattered before, and it melted me inside. "I wouldn't read it, Mom. I figured they were going to kill me anyway and I didn't want to be the reason you stepped down. I believe in what you've been fighting for. You actually want to make things better, and if you can get even one of your bills through, it will change a lot of lives."

"That means so much to me," she said. "But if I had to give it all up to keep you safe, I would have."

"You did keep me safe. You hired Ace, and he saved me."

Mom smiled. "I knew he wouldn't let us down."

"Did he catch the kidnappers? Do you know who's behind it?"

"Two of them didn't make it," she said. "The FBI is questioning the others, but they believe the conspirators are all accounted for. I also spoke to party leadership. They want to keep this quiet and out of the press for now. They're worried that if word gets out, it might lead to more threats or violence. They also want to get to the bottom of it so when it does inevitably go public, they have things under control."

"Will I still need Ace?" I wasn't ready for him to leave me just yet.

Her voice softened and sympathy laced her tone. "Ace gave me his resignation after we spoke. He's heading back to LA tomorrow."

Ace leaving? Tomorrow? Without saying goodbye? I couldn't even process what she'd said. "But what if someone else is involved? One of them was talking to someone on the phone. I think he should stay, at least until the election is over."

"I thought the same thing," she said. "But Ace said his primary concern is for your safety and he felt that someone else—someone who wasn't close to you—would be better suited for the job."

Her words felt like a punch in the gut. "I don't want anyone else."

"It was his choice, darling. I couldn't force him to stay. He suggested Maverick take his place."

Breathe. Breathe. You're fine. Lock it away. But every breath was a struggle, and it hurt less not to breathe at all. "It wasn't his fault. He told me it was a bad idea, but I made him come with me anyway."

"But this is Ace," she said, squeezing my hand. "Did you know he never reported his parents to the authorities, despite all the abuse and neglect, or that he used to patrol our campsite at night when we were all asleep to make sure we were safe? He was there for all of us after your dad died, mowing the lawn, doing chores, spending time with you and Matt. His loyalty and protectiveness are why I hired him. But when the worst happened, when you got kidnapped on his watch, he felt like he'd failed you. It was more than he could bear."

At first I thought I was dreaming when I awoke the next morning to see Ace standing at the foot of my hospital bed. The nurse had given me something to help me sleep that fuzzed my brain, and my vision was blurry from all the swelling. But when he touched me—a gentle stroke of his hand on my foot—I knew it was really him.

"I thought you'd gone," I said through cracked lips.

"I wouldn't leave without saying goodbye." A pained expression crossed his face as he took in my splint and bandages, and the monitor hooked up to my chest. "This is my fault."

"It's not your fault. You did everything you could to stop me from going. You got me out of the bar. You saved Paige. You saved me."

His voice caught, broke. "Look what they did to you."

I briefly wondered if tears would change his mind, but I was so drugged up and so utterly drained I couldn't feel anything. I didn't even have to try to keep my emotions contained in the black box. I was the box, a cold dark void of nothing.

"What about us?" I tried to sit, but pain sheeted across my chest and I fell back on the pillow.

"There shouldn't have been an 'us,'" he said. "I crossed a professional line and that put you in danger. I'll never forgive myself. Just like I can't forgive myself for Matt."

My forehead wrinkled in confusion. "You're not responsible for Matt's death. You weren't flying that airplane. You didn't have anything to do with the mechanics that failed."

Ace gripped the metal rail on my bed. "He enlisted because of me. He was supposed to go to college. He was supposed to become a dentist. If I hadn't encouraged him to join the air force, he wouldn't have been on that plane. I wouldn't have had to stand there and watch him die and not be able to help him."

I could feel his pain slice through me like a blade, and my heart ached. I wanted to hold him, hug him, but I was trapped on the bed by my own pain, and couldn't move. "Matt didn't want to be a dentist." I forced a laugh, trying to pull him out of the darkness that seemed to be consuming him before my very eyes. "Mom and Dad wanted him to be a dentist. Matt always wanted to fly. He loved planes and helicopters from when he was little. The air force was his chance to do what he loved to do, and having you there, sharing his passion, made it even better for him. He made his choices and so did I. That's not on you."

His gaze was dark and far away, his face creased in agony. I didn't know if he'd even heard me. "I promised you I'd bring him back. I promised your mom I'd keep you safe. I didn't keep those promises. I'm not worthy of the trust you've given me."

My stomach clenched at his defeated tone, the self-loathing in his voice.

He released the bar and turned away. "I have to leave, Haley. I can't give you what you need. You'll be safer with someone else."

"Ace!" I called out as he pushed open the door, terrified that I would lose him to the darkness or worse, that I would lose him forever. "Ace. Please don't go."

I wanted to tell him I loved him, that I'd always loved him, that he had my heart, but the words didn't come, and then I was alone in the dark, with a black hole in my chest that went through to my very soul.

CHAPTER 30

Haley

Good morning, Chicago. This is Hidden Tracks *on WJPK, coming to you from Havencrest University. I'm Haley Chapman, and I'm back after a week that turned my life upside down. Today's show is about songs that speak to the silence after the storm, when the echoes of what could have been are almost deafening. We're exploring music that gives voice to those moments when words fail us and we are struggling under the weight of everything left unsaid. Whether you're hurting or you're healing, you are not alone. Our playlist is for anyone who's ever found themselves at a crossroads, afraid to move forward, but unable to go back. Usually, I like to highlight lesser-known artists, but today we're kicking off with an artist who truly understands the power of silence. Stay with us, and remember—even in the darkest moments, music has the power to tell the story of our hearts. Here's Coldplay with "The Scientist."*

Three notes into the song, I knew I'd made a mistake. The lyrics resonated too deeply with the emotions I'd been trying to hold back. No one could get into my heart like Coldplay.

Breathe. Breathe. You're fine. Lock it away.

But I wasn't fine. I hadn't really been okay since my father died.

I took off my headphones to block out the music and tried to ground myself in the familiarity of the studio—the tile floor, the glass window, the mic and the soundboard. I glanced at the door, half expecting to see Ace standing outside, but the hallway was empty. I'd gotten so used to having him around, I had to keep reminding myself that he was gone. Unlike with Matt and my dad, I couldn't contain the memories in my mental black box. Ace was everywhere. In the studio. Sitting at the kitchen table. Standing at the back of my class. In my bed. And in my heart.

Maybe it was just too soon. Or maybe that black box inside me was finally full.

I managed to get through the show, focusing on some new bands I'd discovered. Still unsettled by the threats I'd received over the station email, I didn't take any call-ins or requests, and by the time the show was done, I was totally drained.

Dante called me into his office as I made my way out of the studio. His new gig had been delayed because of technical issues, and he was back in town. "Good show. I was surprised you made it in."

"I was going crazy at home. I'm not a rest-and-relax kind of person."

"No one would blame you after what happened," he said. "Skye filled me in on all the details, and her thoughts about the details, and what I should think about the details, and then she allowed me a few hours' sleep before she wanted to discuss it all over again. I'd be pretty coldhearted not to give you a break."

"It was nice to be back," I said. "I missed being here."

"How's the wrist?"

"Healing quickly. Almost done with the splint. It was just a sprain so I don't have a cast for you to sign. It's a shame because in twenty years, your signature might buy me a house."

Dante laughed. "Maybe you'll be buying your own house. Skye told me about the record executive you met at Bin 46."

"I don't think that's going to work out," I said. "He thinks I'm full of repressed emotion, and I need to let it out to become a truly good singer."

"How about testing out that theory?" Dante leaned back in his chair and folded his arms behind his head. "A buddy of mine is looking for a last-minute band this weekend and he asked about Dante's Inferno. I wouldn't mind doing one last gig before I have to leave again. Are you interested? We need a singer, but I totally understand if you—"

"Are you kidding me?" I interjected, feeling lighter in that moment than I had been since Ace left. "I'm in. I haven't had a gig in what feels like forever. It's too cold to go back to busking, and I can't do any open mics until my arm is healed enough to play my guitar. It would be perfect."

"I'll check with the others and send you the set list if I get the green light." His lips quivered at the corners. "Coldplay was a bold choice for your show. Was it for Ace?"

"He doesn't really listen to music," I said. "Even if it was for him, I doubt he'd be listening, and if he was, he wouldn't understand."

"I've only met him briefly, but I think he understands you pretty well."

I wasn't so sure. He'd left me. Just like my dad and my brother. Just like my mom. Just like he did before. If he truly understood me, he wouldn't have done the one thing he knew would hurt me the most.

Skye wasn't happy to see me when I showed up for my shift at Buttercup. She glared at me and told me I was supposed to be home resting, and what was I thinking coming to work with a broken arm.

"I couldn't sit around the house anymore," I told her. "I can't write music. I can't take notes. I can't type. I just sit there and scroll through social media until my brain goes numb."

"Why don't you review your psych course material, analyze yourself, and tell yourself what to do." She poured me a double espresso and added a thin layer of foam.

"I'm not the best person to give myself advice. I can't be objective. I'm too close."

"Isn't that why Ace left?" she asked gently, handing me the cup. "He thought he was too close?"

I sipped the hot liquid, letting the foam smooth out the bitterness. "Now who's playing amateur psychologist?"

"Not me, who thinks you should go to the student counseling center and speak to an actual professional. You were kidnapped and beaten up. You can't brush it under the carpet."

"I'm an expert at brushing traumatic events under the carpet," I assured her. "I don't need a counselor to help me with a problem I've already solved. I'm perfectly fine."

She gave me a look that suggested she didn't think I was fine at all. "Dante just messaged me to let me know you were there to do your show and you weren't yourself. He said you opened with 'The Scientist.'"

"Could you two be any cuter?" I tried to divert the conversation with a shift in focus. "How about you don't tell each other everything? Maybe a girl needs her privacy."

"You were on the air," Skye pointed out. "How private is it when you tell hundreds of thousands of people what you're feeling in words only people like us understand?"

"I should have played something upbeat and cheerful, because that's me," I lied. "I'm the most upbeat, cheerful, happy person on campus."

"Sometimes the music just happens." Skye knew more about music than anyone I knew. She had hundreds of playlists and could rattle off songs for any kind of vibe. I loved music, too, but I was more interested in creating it than knowing every song that ever existed.

"My music isn't happening," I admitted. "I tried to write some songs in my head, and all I got was a headache."

A shadow darkened the counter. My pulse kicked up a notch before I recognized Ben's smiling face. Maybe I hadn't finished processing what had happened. I mentally searched for the black box and shoved any lingering fears deep inside.

"I just came by to see if you were okay," he said. "Skye said you'd been in an accident . . ." He trailed off, his eyes widening as he took in my healing cuts, fading bruises, and the splint on my arm. "I didn't realize it was so bad. Are you okay?"

"All good. Thanks for checking up on me." I turned to Skye, muttering under my breath, "Do you tell everyone everything?"

"Only the people who might be interested." She gave me a nudge and dropped her voice low. "Ace is gone. I thought you might need some cheering up."

"You don't look okay," Ben said. "Your whole face is bruised."

I'd tried to hide the bruises with makeup. Clearly, I'd done a poor job. "I was running and not paying attention and collided with someone. It's no big deal."

Ben wasn't convinced by my lie. "Did someone hurt you?" He looked over his shoulder at the empty chair where Ace used to sit. "Was it your boyfriend? Is that why he's gone?"

"No, it wasn't him. It was just an accident."

"Is there anything I can do?" he asked. "Do you want to go for a drink? Or a walk? Can I carry your stuff to class?"

Nice Ben. Sweet Ben. He was good-looking, athletic, kind, and a perfectly decent guy. There was no reason why I shouldn't take him up on his offer. No reason why I shouldn't go out with him or even hook up. Except I wanted Ace. Even after he'd kissed me and left me, and kissed me and left me again. I wanted to be forced out of bed on cold mornings to walk to class instead of taking the bus listening to his irritatingly cheerful lecture about the health benefits of an early-morning stroll. I wanted his grumpy frown when I wasn't following his rules. I wanted to hear him curse under his breath when Aditi overcooked the pasta. I wanted to fall asleep in his arms.

I gave Ben an apologetic smile. "I missed a few classes so I'm going home after this to catch up. Maybe another time."

I gave Ben a free coffee and a lemon square and forced myself to finish the shift even though I felt so exhausted it was an effort to breathe.

"You are very clearly not okay." Skye helped me put on

my jacket and briefed our replacements about what had to be done.

"I miss Ace," I admitted. "I can't stop thinking about him. He was hurting so much, and I didn't do anything to help."

"You weren't really in a position to do anything with your body all beaten up," she said. "And now you have some emotional healing to do. Also, I haven't forgiven him for the way he left you, so don't even think about inviting him back to Chicago, because the moment I see him, he's going down."

Laughter bubbled up in my throat for the first time since I'd left the hospital. "Paige said something similar. He's probably afraid to come back because of what you guys will do to him."

"If he loves you, he'll come back." She smacked her fist into her palm. "No matter how painful it's going to be."

There is no question that a live band brings a level of energy and excitement to a performance that solo singers can't match. On stage with Dante's Inferno, I didn't have to worry about the emotional intensity of my performance, because I could draw on the energy of the band. I didn't have to worry about bookings, staging, set lists, or even equipment. I just had to show up and sing. It should have been perfect. I knew the band. We'd done at least half a dozen gigs together. But as the night went on, I realized something had changed.

Had Nick always turned up his amp to compete with Jules's drum solos, leading everyone to do the same until my eardrums felt like they were bleeding and everything was so out of whack it sounded like a terrible, incoherent mess? Had Jules always gotten mad when she thought she wasn't loud enough and started arguing with Derek and Nick? How many rehearsals had we had when everyone actually showed up? Did the guys always argue about who got to do the vocals for some of the lower-range songs? And since when had Derek forgotten the chorus of tracks we'd played dozens of times?

I kept looking to Dante to sort out the mess, but it was clear he was just there to play his bass and wasn't interested in anything else. Had it always been this way? Why hadn't I noticed that each of us was so focused on our own performance that we lacked true cohesion—the give and take and fundamental trust that were the core of any good relationship.

"You were great," Chad said in the cab on the way home. He'd come with Paige, Theo, and Aditi to support us and we'd decided to split a cab because the temperature had dropped below freezing and no one was excited about taking the late bus home. "I don't know what was going on with Nick and Derek, but I don't think anyone else really noticed."

"I used to think it would be so much better to be part of a band, but it was like herding cats," I said. "I wanted to try out a new song, but Dante couldn't even get them to agree on a set list of songs we'd played before, much less try something new. It was something very personal. I was hoping to try and draw out the kind of emotion Stefan thought I was lacking on stage."

Chad gave an indignant huff from the front seat. "You are an amazing singer. What else did the dude want? For you to rip out your soul?"

"I do keep a lot inside." And then, because nothing else was working to keep my feelings contained, and because trying to draw on the emotional energy of a discordant band had left me feeling curiously unfulfilled, I forced myself to share with people I knew would never judge me. "It started after my dad died. I was only twelve and I was the one who found him after he'd had his heart attack. Every night after that I had nightmares about finding him—he'd been hit by a train, or fell out of a tree, or was in a car crash. He'd say, 'I love you, baby girl,' which is what he used to call me, and then he'd die all over again. It was too much. I couldn't feel those feelings over and over, so I found a way to block them out."

Paige took my hand and gave it a squeeze. She was the only person who knew how I'd coped and what I had to do to get through each day.

"That's a lot for a kid to deal with." Aditi's eyes warmed with sympathy. "I hope your mom got you some help."

"She didn't know. She was very deep into her own grief, and my brother was, too. But Ace knew. I don't know how. I never told him. But he knew, and sometimes he'd just be there, walking me home from school on Father's Day, or sitting with me on the porch on what used to be our first camping weekend of the summer, or bringing me something to eat because I couldn't bear to go into the kitchen. That's where I found my dad. He was a chef, and it was his happy place. He'd been making grilled cheese sandwiches for our after-school snack."

"Jesus, Haley." Chad dabbed at his eyes. "I can't believe you never told us about this stuff before and we've been friends for almost three years. You know we're always here for you."

"I never cried," I admitted as the words continued to spill out. "Not for him. Not when my mom basically abandoned us to deal with her own grief. Not for my brother Matt when he died on deployment. Not for Ace when he left . . ."

Chad gave me a calculated look. "That was never a good idea."

"It doesn't matter now. He's gone. Just like everyone else."

"They don't have to be gone," Chad said. "That's your choice. I did a lot of therapy when my brother died, and what helped me the most was bringing him back into my life. I went through my phone every day and looked at the pictures and videos of him and remembered all the good times we had together. It was hard, but it was healing, and it was good to have those memories back. You should try it. Just one picture or one memory at a time."

Nothing else had worked, so I gave it a try. I mentally opened the black box and a memory slipped free. It wasn't one I would have chosen, but it was the high school freshman talent show. I was terrified, and for a few painful moments after I stepped up to the microphone nothing came out. And then I heard a whoop and a holler and cheering from the back of the gym. Seniors never showed up at freshman events. They were too cool, too classy, too busy. But there they were. Matt and Ace. Making idiots of themselves to support me. I'd felt so loved.

It was the day I realized that I'd found my path and the moment I knew who I wanted to walk beside me.

CHAPTER 31

Ace

Tony wasn't happy to see me back in LA. He drummed his fingers on the desk and stared at me until only military discipline kept me in my seat.

"What are you doing here? I thought you were in Chicago."

"The job was done so I came back here to get my affairs in order and consider my options for the future."

Tony's eyes narrowed. "Are you leaving us?"

"I failed to protect my client, and as a result she was seriously injured," I said. "I'm here to face the repercussions, both professional and legal. There may be lawsuits for negligence or breach of contract. You'll need to fire me because my reputation in the industry will be shot, and you need to protect the company. I'll understand if you blacklist me from working in the security industry altogether. I'm clearly not fit for the job, and I'll likely lose my certification anyway."

I wasn't expecting his snort of laughter. "Is that it?"

"You'll want these." I put my security license, weapon, and my Stellar Security ID on his desk.

"I think you've watched too many cop shows," Tony said. "You're supposed to wait for me to say, 'Give me your badge and your gun' and then you give a half-hearted protest, hand over the goods, march away, and then secretly continue to work on whatever case it was that got you suspended in the first place. Although, those guys don't usually beat themselves up."

I wasn't in the mood for Tony's playful attitude. My failure to protect Haley weighed so heavily on me that I couldn't sleep or eat. I was barely able to function, but this was something I could do, a form of restitution that would ease the guilt that was gnawing at my stomach. "There is no case to return to," I said. "The threat was neutralized, and the client is safe."

Tony sighed. "Do you know what happens in the cop shows after the rogue officer solves the case and the bad guys are put in jail?" He pushed the license and gun toward me. "The chief commends him and welcomes him back."

"This isn't a police show."

"And you didn't fail your client," he said. "I talked to Haley. She was emphatic that you did nothing wrong. She said she insisted on going to the karaoke bar despite your vociferous protestations, and when things became serious, she followed your advice to leave. She also said that she begged you to save her friend and if you'd refused, she would have gone back herself. Nothing was more important to her; not even her own life, so in a way, by going back, you saved her all over again."

"That's sugar-coating it to the extreme." I'd broken the rule about leaving a client unprotected and she'd paid a high price.

"I also talked to Senator Chapman," Tony continued. "She expressed her gratitude for your actions in saving her daughter. She said she knew Haley, and there was no way you would have been able to change her mind about going to the bar, or saving her friend."

I had been so certain that this was the end of my career in security that I almost couldn't process what I was hearing. "So, no lawsuit?"

"No lawsuit. No termination. No loss of reputation. No blacklisting and no loss of your license." Tony folded his arms behind his head. "But there have to be some consequences."

Resigned, I nodded. "Of course."

"You go see one of our psychologists. And for as many sessions as they think you need to deal with your issues. You can't keep blaming yourself for things you didn't do or had no control over. It gives you the illusion of control but really it just allows you to avoid your pain and difficult emotions. I get that you have a strong sense of responsibility and even stronger sense of protectiveness, but you need to find a different coping mechanism."

Puzzled, I frowned. Tony thought I repressed my emotions? That was Haley's coping mechanism. I was the one who'd shed tears for Matt and her father. I was able to step up and take responsibility when things went wrong. I blamed myself because I was, in fact, to blame. I knew I wasn't worthy because my parents had told me time and again that I was a burden, and if not for the money, they would have given me away.

"I know about that way of coping because I've been there." Tony's leather chair creaked when he leaned back and put his feet up on the desk. "I had a rough childhood—foster care, adoption, all that shit. I went into the army to make something of myself and lost my entire unit on deployment. I fell into that pattern of self-blame as a survival response. I never thought I was good enough. I didn't think I could be loved. And then I met Maria, who loved me despite my flaws. I went to therapy. I got my act together and started this business to help other vets. And that's what I'm doing now. This knocked you down, but I'm telling you to get back up, and that starts with talking to a professional. I'll set up the appointment today. Where are you going to be based? If you want to stay in Chicago, we have an excellent psychologist on staff and Jordan's got more than enough work to take you on."

"I'm going to stay in LA," I said. "It's home now. I've lived here for the last two years."

"You've lived in clients' houses and hotels," he pointed out. "Whereas in Chicago, we're still paying rent to Haley's landlord for your room, and in Virginia, you own an actual house."

"I'm putting that up for sale. There's nothing for me there and no reason ever to go back."

He drummed his fingers on the desk again. "If that's what you want, but you take whatever assignment I give you without complaint."

What I wanted was to be in Chicago with Haley. What I wanted was to be the kind of man who could give her the life she deserved—a life of security and stability, a life where one day she would sing and dance around the kitchen in joyful and utter abandon.

"That's what I want."

"I'll set up that appointment today and you can head back over to Jessica's place." He gave me a wicked grin. "She just fired the third bodyguard I sent over. You're the only person she's been able to tolerate."

Jessica was thrilled to have me back on her service.

"You've been down here a long time. I was worried you got lost," she said from the doorway of one of the four suites she kept available for staff and guests. I'd been unpacking my bag when my phone buzzed with a message from Chad, and I'd been distracted by the videos he'd sent of Dante's Inferno playing the Backstop Bar.

"Sorry, Jess. I'll be right up. Is the car here already?"

"No, we've got another ten minutes." She walked in and leaned against the dresser. Every room in her ultra-modern house was impeccably decorated in cool white and gray tones, including the spacious guest suites. "I was delighted when Tony said you were coming back. I thought you never worked for the same client twice."

"Circumstances changed." I paused the video of Haley dancing on stage and singing "Born to Be Wild" to an enthusiastic crowd.

"Or maybe you've changed," she said. "You seem different. Less hollow."

"I don't know what that means, but I'm the same guy I was the last time I was here." I grabbed a handful of shirts, and she moved from the dresser so I could put them in the drawer.

"What were you watching?" she asked, studying my phone.

"A video of a gig at a college bar. A friend sent it to me. We have mutual friends in the band."

"I love new bands." She sat on my bed and patted the comforter beside her. "Let me see."

I wanted to enjoy the videos of Haley singing with Dante's Inferno in private, but I was in Jessica's house, and she was paying the bills. She was also a people person and genuinely interested in others, which was why she was so well-liked in the industry. I didn't know why her personable nature didn't translate when it came to the bodyguards she'd fired, but I wasn't about to start the job off on the wrong foot, so I scrolled to my favorite of the songs I'd heard. Haley was center stage and she'd blown me away with the power of her voice.

"My friend Chad recorded their entire set. I haven't seen it all, but this one stood out." I handed her the phone and she watched, entranced, for the entire song.

"Their vocalist is amazing." Jessica studied me intently. "Is she why you asked me to put you in touch with Stefan?"

"Yes, and thank you again for that. I couldn't believe he took the time. She doesn't even have an agent."

"Stefan is a darling and he owed me." Jessica smiled. "What did he think?"

"He told her she had an incredible voice and stage presence, but there were some things she needed to work on. He gave her his card and told her to call him when she was ready, and he'd come and hear her again."

"Stefan doesn't waste his time," she said warmly. "He must really have thought she had something. I hope she follows through."

"So do I."

Jessica tipped her head to the side. "You like this girl, don't you?"

"She's a friend." I wasn't ready to talk about Haley with anyone. The guilt of having failed her and then leaving her again coupled with Tony's pseudo-psychological analysis was eating me up inside. But Jessica was easily distracted. Aside from gossip, there was nothing she liked to talk more about than herself. "Stefan said there were Oscar rumblings about your new role."

Her face brightened. "I know, and we haven't even finished

shooting. We're on set for the next few weeks so you'll be able to see for yourself. I've really gotten into the role. Single mom. Trying to make a living as a waitress. Daughter in the hospital with a mysterious disease. No one can help her so I investigate on my own and discover it has something to do with the water, but of course no one will listen to me because they think I'm just a pretty face."

"Sounds like it's right up your alley." I finished unpacking my bag and then hung my suit up in the closet. I hadn't worn it since Haley had sung at Bin 46 and I could still smell the lingering fragrance of her perfume. It had killed me to leave her at the hospital, especially when she'd been so badly beaten, her voice so hoarse it had been barely audible. But she had her mom and Paige, and I knew her friends would rally around her. She was surrounded by love. She didn't need me.

"We're putting a different spin on it," she said, thankfully not noticing that my hand was clenched around the hanger so hard it had imprinted into my palm. "The contaminated water isn't coming from a factory. We're an unwitting part of a government experiment, and I go undercover to expose them. There's drama with the sick kid, of course, lots of emotion, crying and such, but also action and suspense. I had to learn how to fight."

"Always a useful skill." I had planned to teach Haley some basic self-defense moves at a local fight club where we could practice with matting on the floor so she wouldn't get bruised. The irony was almost too much.

"You seem distracted," she said. "Is everything okay?"

"Of course." I closed the door on the memories and tried to focus on the here and now. "Where are we going this evening?"

"Dash just got its second Michelin star so I'm having dinner there with a few friends. I spoke to the chef, and he'll have a plate waiting for you. I hope you're not hungry. Everything is miniaturized. It will be a big change from Chicago. I grew up there and I still miss the food. I get tired of all the deconstructed terrines, the foie gras served with foam or reduction, and all the fermented or sublimated vegetables. Sometimes you just want a burger or a real slice of pie."

Her face fell when I didn't laugh with her. "Are you sure you're okay, Ace?"

"I'm good, Jessica. Let's get you to dinner."

Chad texted me a few days later to let me know he needed to speak in person. I managed to find some time when Jessica was in her trailer on set to give him a call.

"I'm here with Theo," Chad said. "I know two of the guys who kidnapped Haley are dead and the FBI have the other two in custody, but before that happened, Theo had gone on the dark web and found a listing for what he's pretty sure was the job to disable the cameras on Michigan Avenue. The timing was right, and the skills needed for the job were the same. He messaged the poster and said he was looking for someone to do a similar job and if the dude found someone good to let him know. And get this. Last night, someone answered and gave him a name. He told Theo it was a friend of his and their last job went south so his friend was looking for work."

My blood ran cold. "That means there are more of them out there. The FBI were certain no one else was involved."

"We're working on getting an ID, but we have to be careful. I did some research into the political angle and the election stakes are high. The entire Senate will flip if Haley's mom gets reelected, and it means some of the controversial bills she's been spearheading will likely go through."

"Why wouldn't they just go after her?"

"It's too obvious," Chad said. "It's much more effective if she steps down and endorses someone else, and the best way to get her to do that is to threaten her family."

"So, you're pretty sure this isn't just a small group of people who were pissed about her position on a volatile issue?"

"You'd need a lot of money to do what they did—four guys,

guns, burner phones, vehicles, surveillance, planning . . . and then there was the CCTV. Whoever hacked the system to erase all the footage had some serious connections and hired people with a lot of skill. The big question is whether it's the opposing party trying to preserve their Senate majority and stop the senator from joining the presidential ticket, or whether it's someone from the senator's own party who wants that seat and the power that comes with it. The only problem with the latter is that even if she drops out, it's up to the state committee to appoint a replacement, and with only a few days until the election, it seems unlikely."

"Either way it sounds like some serious corruption," I said. "You need to talk to the FBI and let them know what you found."

"I already called the local field office," he said. "Special Agent Fernandez is in charge. He told me to call back when I had some concrete evidence. I don't think he took me seriously, since I'm just a student. Just wait until I blow this thing out of the water."

My pulse kicked up a notch. "Do you think Haley is still in danger?"

"I asked Fernandez that question and he said that the dark web guys we'd found were low-level contractors, and he was confident that the real threat had been neutralized."

"But you don't believe him," I said picking up on the hesitation in Chad's tone.

I heard some banging in the trailer and Jessica opened the door, yawning. "Hair and makeup are coming to fix me up before I go back on set. You can just let them in."

I nodded and returned to the call. "You need to be careful. Look what they did to Haley. If they find out you're poking around, they might come after you."

"We're being careful," Chad said. "Theo's an expert at moving through the internet without being traced and my contacts are discreet."

"Who are these contacts?"

"I might have met a few interns at a recruitment event," Chad said, chuckling. "And they might be the kind of interns who like to do things together, if you know what I mean. Did you know Cleveland is about halfway and you can drive there in under six hours?"

"Sounds like you're really sacrificing for the cause," I said dryly.

Chad laughed. "If you weren't with Haley, I would have invited you to join us."

My moment of amusement disappeared in a heartbeat. "We're not—"

"Then you need to haul ass back to Chicago and fix whatever you broke," he interjected. "And I'm saying this as a friend to both of you."

My stomach tightened in a knot. "I've got a new assignment. But if there's any chance Haley is in danger . . ."

"I'll let you know."

CHAPTER 32

Haley

A few days after the gig with Dante's Inferno at the Backstop Bar, Paige got the call. Her mother had been accepted for her clinical trial and she needed Paige to help her through what was expected to be a very rough first week.

I met Paige in the downstairs hallway just before the cab was due to arrive to take her to the airport. She took one look at my suitcase and frowned. "Where are you going?"

"I'm coming with you." I pulled my warmest jacket from the closet. Riverstone had already had their first few snowfalls of the season.

"You already missed a week of classes. You can't miss any more."

"I talked to my profs. Three of them post their lectures online, and I have friends in the other two classes who can give me their notes. My profs are going to waive the assignments for the week I missed so I don't have to play catchup, and I'm only going to miss one test, which I can make up afterwards."

Her mouth opened and closed again. "But . . ."

"Mom checked with the FBI and they didn't think I needed any more protection," I assured her. "The election is in a few days and then all the political drama will blow over. No one is after me, so I don't have to worry about grumpy bodyguards telling me what to do."

"What about your music?" she protested. "You need to get back out there. You haven't done an open mic in forever, and what about Stefan? Or other record execs? You might miss a chance to be discovered."

"One week isn't going to make a difference, and I still haven't figured out how to draw out the emotion Stefan was talking about," I said. "It will be good for me to get away."

Paige bit her lower lip, considering. We both knew it was all for show. If it had been my mom in the hospital, she'd have done the exact same thing.

"Work?" she asked.

"I've got people covering my shifts."

"Your show," she said firmly. "You already missed a show. You can't miss another."

I pulled open the front door. "I taped a show in advance and Chad is going to put it on for me. If you don't want to accept that I just want to be there for you, then tell yourself I'm coming because I really need to get out of Chicago and visit home to ground myself. Anything else?"

Paige dropped her bag and wrapped her arms around me. "Thank you."

I gave her a squeeze. "Someone has to be there to line up the medical staff. You set a high bar when I was in the hospital."

We cabbed it to O'Hare and then flew into Charleston where we rented a car for the two-hour drive to Riverstone. I hadn't been back since Matt's funeral, but nothing had changed. The sign on the highway was still slightly crooked, and no one had cleaned off the yellow spray-painted happy face over the *a*. Winter had arrived early and a blanket of snow covered the fields and forests, turning the town into a winter wonderland. From festive gardens to a magical open-air market and a decorative walking trail lit up from early November until early January revealing whimsical holiday decorations and themes, Riverstone was unparalleled for spirit at Christmas.

We drove straight to the hospital and were able to meet with her mom's doctor right away. "Everything is looking good," the doctor said to Paige. "We're just finalizing the paperwork and your mom should be able to start tomorrow. I'm glad she won't be alone. The side effects are significant for the first week, until the body adjusts."

"She'll be well looked after," I said. "And if anyone messes with her, Paige will whack them with an amp, or wrangle them into submission. I was in the hospital the other week and she had people lined up outside my door to treat me."

"She's exaggerating." Paige blushed. "I just wanted to make sure she had water and warm blankets and pillows, and she wasn't in any pain and they'd checked everything that should be checked and—"

"You're scaring her, babe," I said, laughing. "I think she gets it."

When I had Paige settled in her mom's room with candy, soda, and snacks, I drove across town to our family home. Mom had mentioned that she'd started paying someone to look after the house because she wasn't able to visit as often, and our sprawling two-story Arts and Crafts–style house looked tidy and well-kept. Even the Christmas lights that Matt and Ace had put up one winter were turned on, giving the house a festive glow.

I took a quick walk through the main level—dining room, living room, den, and bar all with warm hardwood floors and the same comfortable mismatched furniture that had been there forever. Mom had never been into decorating and Dad had an eclectic sense of style, except when it came to the kitchen, where everything was big, bold, and modern with granite countertops, stainless steel industrial appliances, and custom black-walnut cabinets. We never used his specialty equipment after he passed. Even Ace, who often came over to help with dinner, only used the basic kitchen supplies. It was a full year before I could even sit at the kitchen counter, much less attempt to make something more complicated than mac 'n' cheese.

Upstairs, I passed Mom's tidy bedroom and our shared family bathroom, bracing myself to pass Matt's room, when I saw the open door. I should have expected Mom to do to Matt's belongings what she'd done to Dad's, but it was still a shock when I saw that she'd stripped Matt's room bare. She hadn't left a stitch of clothing or even a pair of shoes. His model planes, books, and old toys were gone from the shelves, and she'd taken down his posters and even the covers from his bed. The only reason I knew he really existed was because one Christmas he'd carved his name into the wooden floor.

I dumped my bag in my bedroom. Over the years we'd redecorated as my interests had changed. Pink walls had become blue when I'd moved on from princesses to sea creatures. Posters of unicorns had given way to pictures of boy bands and inspirational sayings, and my final year of high school, I'd finally packed away the cheerful cotton candy bedspread on my white four-poster bed and replaced it with white and teal.

After making up Matt's room for Paige and changing my bed linen, I checked all the windows and doors and then made my way to the garage to open it up for my car.

Although our neighbor had turned on the heat when I called to say I was coming, the garage was cold enough to make me shiver. I reached for the button to raise the door when I noticed five large black containers stacked near the stairs, all sealed up with tape. The sender address was the Joint Personal Effects Department at Dover Air Force Base.

Matt's belongings.

Again, I shouldn't have been surprised they hadn't been opened. Mom had packed all Dad's things away in containers the week after he died and never opened them. Covered in dust, they took up most of the shelving on one side of the garage.

I'd come home to support Paige and to ground myself, not to stir up painful emotions, but my conversation with Chad kept playing over in my mind, and the memory that I'd let slip free was still there, painful edges dulled to leave warmth behind.

"I'm not going to open them," I said out loud. Still, I didn't move. Matt was in there. Pictures, clothes, the instant camera I'd given him in case he ever lost his phone, maybe even the old MP3 player with all the songs I'd helped him choose to deal with the pressure when he was away.

I don't know if I changed my mind because I'd thought I was going to die in that warehouse and now I had a second chance to do things right. Or maybe it was because I'd lost Ace again and there was no room left in the black box where I'd put all my pain. I don't even know if it was because Mom had tried to erase Matt's memory, but he'd stubbornly refused to leave. He was still there, etched into the floorboards like he was etched into my heart, and now he was waiting to see me again in a stack of black boxes by the stairs.

I went back inside, pulled on my jacket and hat, grabbed a knife from the kitchen, and returned to cut the tape and open the top container.

And there he was.

I studied Matt's military picture, soaking in the familiar smile, the blue eyes, and the dimple at the corner of his cheek. A wave of sadness swelled inside me, stealing my breath away. *Breathe. Breathe. You're fine.*

This time I didn't lock the feeling away. This time I let it fill me, take me into the darkness, tumble me around and pull me under again. I drew in a breath and then another, feeling the pain and loss eddy and swirl through my body until I was floating, calm in the dark sea.

I put aside a letter addressed to Ace and went through the pictures of Matt and Ace with their military buddies, one of him and Ace at their high school graduation, and an old family picture from one of our camping trips. I couldn't remember the last time I'd seen a picture of my dad, but he looked exactly as I remembered him with his ear-to-ear smile, the blue eyes that crinkled at the corners, and the strong arms that had always made me feel safe. A wave of nostalgia washed over me, and I was back in the darkness struggling against the current until I stopped fighting and let it carry me to a time when I was safe and loved and I was my daddy's baby girl.

I managed to get through the first box—clothes and shoes, a few odd items that must have held meaning for him, the instant camera and his MP3 player, and at the bottom, in a velvet pouch, Dad's high school ring. I remembered fighting with Matt over who would get the ring when Dad died, never imagining that only a few years later he'd be gone and the loss would be so overwhelming, something so trivial wouldn't matter.

But now, for some reason, it did.

I wanted Dad. I wanted his memories. I wanted to touch his things and smell his scent and see the things that had been important to him.

I made my way over to the shelf and pulled out one of the gray boxes that held my dad's things, dragging it across the concrete floor into the light before I pulled off the lid. Inside I found his aprons, recipe books, certificates, potholders, and some of his clothes. I pressed his favorite camping shirt to my face, and I smelled him—pine and barbecue sauce, campfire smoke, and the lingering spicy scent of the cheap cologne I'd given him one Christmas. He always wore it camping to scare off the bears.

This time the darkness roared like a monster wave sweeping me off my feet and crushing me under. My shoulders heaved and my lungs burned as I fought for breath. Tears spilled from my eyes and a sound ripped from my throat, a sob that was more a howl, eight years of pain rendering my soul in two.

"I've got you, bug."

Soft arms wrapped around me, a warm breath on my cheek, my nickname a whisper that I could hear despite the crashing waves, a voice deep and soothing. Familiar. It grounded me. My feet found earth and I held fast as the water swirled around me, through me, washing my soul clean and taking the darkness with it.

I didn't ask Ace why he was there.

He just was, like he had always been when I truly needed him.

CHAPTER 33

Haley

Ace hadn't come to Riverstone alone. He'd brought Maverick as backup, and Paige hadn't stopped drooling since she'd come from the hospital.

"You're embarrassing yourself," I whispered as Ace and Mav walked through the house, checking the doors and windows I'd already checked. "At least try to pretend you don't want to rip off his clothes and jump into bed with him."

"I mean . . ." She waved vaguely in Mav's direction, unable to even finish her sentence. "It's like someone jumped into my head, plucked out my fantasy man, and created him in real life."

"I still think this is overkill," Mav said after they'd finished their security check. "You think Haley is in danger because a journalism student and his student hacker sidekick put together some crazy conspiracy theory based on a posting they found on the dark web and information your wannabe journo got from threesomes he had with some White House interns?"

"Chad's been having threesomes with White House interns?" Paige laughed. "I thought his weekend trips were for his investigative journalism project."

"This is his investigative journalism project," Ace said. "I just can't believe the FBI wouldn't take him seriously."

"I can't believe Tony and Jordan took it seriously." Mav added another log to the fire Ace had built to warm me up after I'd gotten a chill in the garage. "But I'm not complaining. I've never been to Virginia before. Now I can check it off my list of states to visit. Your town is very festive. I've never seen so many lights.

You've even got lights on your roof and no one is living in the house."

"My dad put ours up a few years before he passed away," I said. "Ace and my brother helped him. It was so much work, he decided to just leave them up year-round. Mom didn't like the idea of Christmas lights in summer, but you can barely see them, and she did like just having to flick a switch in November when the town lights go on." It was a memory an ordinary person might share about someone who passed, but I'd never been able to talk about Dad before, and the words, as they dropped from my lips, felt shiny and new.

Ace adjusted the damper in the fireplace. "I would have liked more backup. There's a lot of property here, and a lot of house to protect."

"Maybe we have no backup because the danger is minimal," Mav countered. "Two of the kidnappers are dead. Two are in custody. Maybe there is another dude out there, but he's not going to have the resources to act alone, much less follow Haley to Virginia. No one knows she's here."

"Chad thought it was organized by a group at a high level." Ace shot me a worried look. "Even if they weren't watching Haley's house, it wouldn't be hard to figure out where she is. This was her mother's constituency. The house is in her name. Haley just went through a traumatic event. Where else would she be?"

"I dunno. Sitting on a beach in Mexico to get away?"

"Haley's not really a sit-on-the-beach kind of girl," Paige said. "Every time I've tried to get her to suntan with me, she lasts two minutes and then she's out on the water parasailing or waterskiing or engaging in any number of adrenaline-inducing water sports that are the complete opposite of relaxing."

"I suntanned on Mr. Dixon's motorboat during that school trip in eleventh grade," I reminded her.

"And then five minutes later you were beside him at the wheel, urging him to go full throttle."

"They'll be desperate," Ace said. "There are only two days until the election. Haley's mom has full-time security. They need Haley to force her mother out of the race. My guess is that they're already on their way."

"Are you sure you're not here for another reason?" Mav tipped his head in my direction. I wasn't sure if he meant for me to see, but his meaning was clear.

"I'm just doing my job," Ace said, his voice tight.

"Except it isn't your job. I heard you already had a new assignment in LA, and you took time off to come out here."

Ace gave Mav a warning shake of his head. I didn't understand what was happening between them, but I shrugged it off. I was still emotionally exhausted. I didn't know how long I'd stayed in the garage, but the tears kept coming for what seemed like forever. I cried for Dad and for Matt. I cried for Paige and her mom. I cried for me and the girl I was who had loved so deeply she was afraid to love again. Ace didn't say anything. He just held me until finally the pain washed away.

"I have faith in Chad and Theo," Paige said. "If they think there's some kind of political conspiracy, then I believe them. The question is, what do we need to do? Should we take Haley to a hotel? Wouldn't that be safer? There are so many ways someone could get into this house."

"I think we should stay here and draw them out," Mav said. "You need to end this so you're not constantly looking over your shoulder. And your mom needs to know who's behind it, because the threat might get worse if she is elected."

"So, I get to be bait?" I shrugged off the blanket Ace had wrapped around me, warm now from the roaring fire. "Should I put on some lingerie and run screaming into the dark forest?"

"It's not a horror movie, babe." Paige patted my knee. "No one is going to come at you with a mask and a chain saw."

"No, they'll be disguised as record executives and wear expensive clothing and seduce me with promises of making me famous." I couldn't hide the bitterness in my tone. How could I have been so stupid? Why would an EMI record exec come to see me at a karaoke bar? Stefan worked for a smaller record label, and he hadn't thought I was ready. I should have known I wasn't big-time material.

"Mav and I brought some surveillance equipment we're going to set up around the house to let us know if anyone comes into the yard," Ace said. "Why don't you two get some rest?"

It had been a long day, and I was more than happy to go upstairs. Paige and I made up my mom's bed for Maverick, and then she came into my room with a thin blanket and a pillow. "Are we setting up the spare room for Ace? I forgave him for five minutes after he saved you, but now I hate him again for walking away, so I think he should sleep alone in a cold, hard bed that has thumbtacks between the sheets."

I laughed out loud. "Your mama bear claws are showing."

"He should be afraid. I think I told him I would claw out his eyes if he hurt you again."

She looked so serious; I almost believed her. "He blamed himself for what happened, Paige. You should have seen him at the hospital. He was devastated. And he is here now even though Mav said he's in the middle of another job."

Paige sniffed in derision. "That is the least he could do."

"He did save me from the kidnappers," I offered. "He got into a gunfight and had to shoot two men. That couldn't have been easy."

"That was the job." Paige folded her arms and leaned against the wall. "I'm hearing a lot of excusing his behavior, and not a lot of being angry about his inability to make any kind of commitment."

I'd never thought of it that way. Ace and I had never been in an actual relationship, so the issue had never come up, but commitment could take many forms. "I was angry at him for years, and then he came back into my life, and for a while it was like it used to be between us. I always feel comfortable around him. I never feel like I have to be anyone other than myself. He never judges me; never tells me I talk too much or that I'm too energetic or crazy. He makes me feel calm, Paige. He makes all the noise in my head go away. I know that if I go too far, or I'm about to fall, he'll be there to catch me."

"Oh God." Paige tipped her head back and groaned. "You've fallen for him again."

I took the blanket and pillow from her and added them to my bed. "Would that be so bad?"

"It would if you're just pretending to yourself that he didn't hurt you, just like you've done with all the other terrible things that have happened to you in your life."

"I didn't pretend today," I said. "While you were at the hospital, I opened one of Matt's boxes from the air force and I let myself feel everything—the pain and loss and the memories. I thought about Dad and how much I missed him, so I opened one of his boxes, too. It hurt but it was beautiful, and I cried for them for the first time and I couldn't stop and then Ace was there."

"He always did have a good sense of timing," she said, not unkindly.

"He just held me until I was done. Now I feel different. Empty, but not in a bad way. I don't want to hide from how I feel anymore—not about them and not about Ace. I care about Ace, and I think he cares about me. I wish he hadn't left, but I understand why he did, and it doesn't change how I feel. He left, but he came back when I needed him. That's enough commitment for me."

"I guess we're not making up the spare room," she said. "At least I won't have to sneak in there tonight and make good on my promise to avenge you." She put her hand in her pocket and pulled out a container of thumbtacks. "What am I going to do with these?"

Ace joined me in bed an hour later, slipping between the covers and curling his warm body around me. "I didn't know if you'd want me here," he murmured. "I didn't check my messages until I went to the guest room and saw you hadn't made the bed."

"The heat has never worked well in that room." I snuggled against him. "I didn't want you to be cold."

"So thoughtful." He chuckled and put his arm around me. "You're definitely warming me up."

"I hope so. It's been a long time."

"Too long." He hesitated. "I'm sorry I left the way I did. I know it was the wrong thing to do, especially when you were hurting, and after you told me how you felt when I deployed, but I honestly thought you wouldn't want me around after I'd failed you. I didn't even want to be around me. If you'd been any other client, I wouldn't have left you in the bar to go back for Paige. My job was to keep you safe, and I didn't do that. I'll carry that guilt with me for the rest of my life."

"You carry too much guilt, and often for things that aren't your fault." I reached over to my nightstand, turned on the light, and grabbed the grad picture of him and Matt that I'd pulled out of the box, along with the other things I'd saved for him. Turning to face him, I pushed myself up on my elbow. "Look what he's holding."

Ace studied the picture. "That's the model plane your dad gave him for his sixteenth birthday."

"A plane." I gave him the model I'd found in the box. "Not a model tooth or a pair of dentures. He loved to fly, Ace. You know that. It's all he ever wanted to do."

"You should have this." Ace offered the plane to me. "He was your brother."

"I have his things, and I have this house, and I have his memories. Mom didn't give anything away. It's all there, and when this is over, I'm going to sit down with her and go through all the boxes, because I've realized that she buries her pain deep just like me." I handed him the letter. "He left this for you. I hope whatever he wrote in there helps you the way opening that box helped me."

"I have some work to do on myself," he admitted. "Tony sent me to see a psychologist. Apparently I'm not as unaffected by my childhood as I thought I was."

"Neither am I." I leaned over and kissed him. "You should try having a good long sob fest in a freezing garage and cry eight years' worth of tears. It's very cathartic."

His arms wrapped around me, and he pulled me close. "I know something else that's very cathartic."

"Do you seriously want to have sex when there are bad guys closing in?"

"Mav and I set up enough surveillance tech that the moment anything gets near the house, we'll know. It already went off when a rabbit hopped across the yard."

I slipped my hand into his boxers and stroked his hardened length. "What if they come at an inappropriate time? You'd better not stop."

"I wouldn't dream of leaving my girl unsatisfied. I'll send Mav to take care of them until I'm done with you."

A smile tugged at my cheeks. "Am I your girl?"

"You've always been my girl, Haley." His deep voice rumbled in his chest. "I've just never thought I was good enough for you." He flipped me on my back and tugged my nightdress over my head. "I'm going to make you forget every man you've ever had in this bed."

"That would just be you," I admitted.

He pushed to one arm and frowned. "I thought you said—"

"We didn't make it to the bed. He heard you and Matt talking downstairs and he got performance anxiety."

Ace threw back his head and laughed. "I promise you will not have that problem with me." His hand slipped between my legs and he pushed my panties aside with a thick finger. "In fact, I promise the opposite."

Ace made good on that promise. Multiple times. We could have probably gone all night, reconnecting physically and emotionally, but around 3:00 A.M., when we were lying exhausted in each other's arms, an alarm sounded on his phone.

"Stay here." He jumped out of bed and pulled on his clothes. "Mav and I will check it out. Hopefully it's just another rabbit.

I'll send Paige in so you're together. Lock the door after she's here."

"I'm not going to let you put yourselves at risk for me while I hide upstairs," I said, grabbing my jeans from the floor. "I've spent my whole life hiding—hiding from pain and loss, hiding from myself, hiding from the past. I trust you, Ace. I'm not going to do anything stupid. I'll stay upstairs with Paige, but if something doesn't sound right, I'm coming down. I've never been a coward and I'm not about to start now."

I thought he would protest, but instead he nodded. "Do you have a weapon?"

"Not up here, but if I make it to the kitchen, I'm sure I can find a knife."

He shook his head. "Stay away from knives. It's too easy to lose them to someone with any sort of training."

"So what? I get a frying pan?"

"It works in cartoons."

He left and returned with Paige a few moments later. We turned off my light and crouched by the window, looking for whoever might have triggered the alarm.

"So . . ." She smirked. "Good night?"

I returned her smirk with one of my own. "The best."

Five minutes later, I heard the shatter of glass followed by the crash of the door. Ace shouted for Maverick and the house shook with a thud.

"That doesn't sound like a rabbit," I whispered, hugging Paige as she hyperventilated beside me.

Shouts echoed up the stairs, followed by the sickening sound of flesh meeting flesh. I heard wood breaking, and the house vibrated and shook with what sounded like fighting downstairs. A gunshot echoed through the house, and then another, followed by silence.

"I have to go," I whispered after a few minutes. "I can't just sit here. I need to see if they're okay."

"I'll come with you."

We crawled down the hallway to the stairs and cautiously made our way to the ground level. After checking the foyer, I motioned to the kitchen, and we ran and huddled behind the counter.

"I didn't see anyone in the living room," Paige whispered. "But it's totally trashed."

"They must be in the back of the house or maybe the garage." I grabbed the cast-iron frying pan from the stove, the heavy metal cool and reassuring in my hand. I was about to try the garage door when a floorboard creaked outside the kitchen. Scrambling back behind the counter, I saw Ace in the doorway, his weapon ready in his hand. His eyes widened when he saw us but there was no time for words. A man dressed in black burst into the room. Before he could even turn his head and register Ace's presence, Ace had grabbed his shirt and yanked him forward, throwing him off-balance. Their struggle became a blur of fists and grunts as they fell to the kitchen floor. I peered around the island and saw a second man entering the kitchen through the garage door.

Fear threatened to paralyze me, but I pushed through it. As he passed the kitchen island, I shot to my feet and swung the frying pan at the back of his head. It connected with a sickening thud, and he stumbled forward to his knees. Reaching behind his back, he pulled his gun from its holster.

"Haley, down!" Ace's voice cut through the chaos. I dropped to the floor just as a shot rang out. The second intruder collapsed, and Paige slapped a hand over her mouth to cover her scream.

I scrambled to my feet, adrenaline coursing through me. Ace was still grappling with the first man, who had him pinned against the counter. Without thinking, I charged forward, ramming my shoulder into the attacker's side. The unexpected impact threw him off-balance and Ace seized the opportunity, flipping their positions and subduing the man with a swift strike.

Panting, we locked eyes. "Are you okay?" he asked, his voice rough.

I nodded, surprised to find I was trembling not from fear,

but from a surge of empowerment. "Paige and I are both fine. Where's Mav?"

"He's dealing with a guy outside who's built like a tank. Mav thought he'd have a bit of fun before he tied him up for questioning."

I helped Paige to her feet and realized something had shifted inside me. I'd faced my fear head-on and come out stronger. Ace had been there, not as a shield, but as a partner. For the first time in forever, I didn't need to tell myself to breathe. Whatever came next, I would have the strength to face it.

I was fine.

CHAPTER 34

Ace

I had always loved visiting Haley's house. Not just because of her family, but because it was always full of people. Neighbors were constantly dropping by, usually to talk to her dad over a new gourmet treat he'd just whipped up in the kitchen, but sometimes to chat with her mom about everything from legal issues to PTA meetings or costumes for the school play. Paige was always there, and Matt often invited friends over to game with him in the basement. I'd grown up mostly in silence and I was drawn by the constant hustle and bustle, the music and chatter, the endless activity, and Haley, at the center of it all.

Over the course of the next day, the house came alive again. The local sheriff came first, followed by Haley's mom and stepfather, and then the state police and finally the FBI. Her mother's campaign team showed up in a convoy of black SUVs and organized a press conference in the town square to urge her constituents to vote, and to keep any attention off the drama going on at the house.

Mav and I spent half a day giving statements and filling in paperwork. We put the authorities in touch with Chad and Theo, who shared the information they had uncovered. Theo was given immunity for his illegal hacking activities because his actions had contributed to the arrest of the people who had conspired to interfere with a Senate election. Chad managed to keep his "sources" confidential with a little help from his journalism professor. He was given the green light to publish a heavily redacted version of his story after the election was over, although his professor hinted that he could expect to lose a few marks on his final project for sleeping with his sources.

By the time the police and FBI were finished with me, the afternoon light was just beginning to fade. I pulled on my jacket and boots and took a walk through the forest behind the house. Snow crunched under my feet silencing the birds and forest creatures as I made my way to the creek. I still hadn't been able to bring myself to look at Matt's letter, but I was booked on the red-eye back to my job in LA with Jessica, and I wanted to read it before I left.

Hands shaking, and not from the cold, I studied the familiar writing on the envelope. I'd written a letter to Matt before I deployed and burned it the day I heard he'd died. For a moment, I was tempted to burn his letter, too. But Haley had been brave enough to open his boxes and let him back into her life. How could I not do the same?

Dear Ace

I hope when you read this letter you've made it back home safe. Maybe you're in Riverstone down by the creek, or in the forest behind my house walking the trails like you used to do. Or maybe you're fishing at Smith Mountain Lake, and if you are, catch a big one for me.

I'll have been gone months, maybe even years by the time you receive this letter. I know my family. My tough boxes will have been sitting in the garage unopened because Haley and Mom won't be able to accept that I'm gone. But one day something will change, and I'll finally be able to tell you what I need you to hear.

First, whatever happened to me is not your fault.

I don't know how you will have rationalized it, but I know you will have convinced yourself that you are to blame for my death. But I was exactly where I wanted to be, and I died doing what I always wanted to do.

Yes, you read that right. I always talked about applying to dentistry because my dad desperately wanted me to get a professional degree. It was the one regret he had in life and the only thing he wished he could have changed, and I wanted to honor his wish for me. In my heart, though, I always wanted to be an airman, and when you enlisted, I realized that he would want me to be true to myself. You inspired and encouraged me. You made me believe that anything is possible. Thank you for giving me the courage to follow my dream.

It was an absolute privilege being your best friend. You were my brother in all but name. You made me see beauty in a world that had lost its color after my dad died, and you gave me hope in my darkest days. If I had a wish, it would have been that we'd met earlier and you would have been spared the pain of your past, but that childhood led you to Riverstone and brought you into my family and that's something I would never change.

Don't be sad or angry for me. I have been blessed with the best friend a man could have, a wonderful family and the honor of serving my country doing something that gave meaning to my life. I found my true path because of you. My only regret is that it caused you to suffer, and for that I am truly sorry.

Let me go in peace, and don't waste any more time mourning me or feeling guilty for something that I freely chose to do. Live your life, Ace. Live it well. I would tell you to follow your dreams, but I know what's in your heart and now it's time to go and find her.

You and Haley have always had a connection. I knew it from the first day you met. You were the calm to her chaos, the port in her storm, and she was the sparkle and sunshine in your life. She is warm, generous, selfless, funny and when she loves, she loves deeply and with all her heart. She buried all her emotions after our dad died, and my death will just make that worse. She'll lose herself to grief just as you'll lose yourself to guilt, but you can help each other find the way back.

She needs you, Ace, and you need her.

I know you love her, and you held back out of respect. I'm grateful for that because it meant that I wasn't put in a position of having to choose before I was mature enough to understand that the heart wants what the heart wants and not even a bro code can change that. I cannot imagine a better man for Haley, and I cannot imagine a better woman for you.

Be strong. Be brave. Be free. Find your heart's desire. And when you do, give her a hug for me.

Your friend always,
Matt

Haley

Good morning, Chicago. This is Hidden Tracks *on* WJPK, *and I'm Haley Chapman. Today's show is a very personal one. It's about the times life throws you a curveball. You find yourself opening doors you've kept locked for years and letting the music that's been trapped inside finally break free. That's what happened to me, and I want to share it with you.*

We'll be exploring songs about new beginnings, about finding your voice when you thought it was lost forever. We'll hear from artists who've turned their pain into poetry, their silence into symphonies. I also have an announcement to make. For the first time ever, I'll be performing my own original songs. I'll be at the Blue-bird Café next Friday night and I hope to see you there to share this journey with me. It's terrifying and exhilarating all at once, kind of like life.

Today's playlist is for anyone who's ever felt stuck, anyone who's reopened old wounds only to find unexpected healing, anyone who's standing at the threshold of something new and scary and beautiful. It's for those of us learning to sing our own songs, even when the harmony isn't quite perfect.

We'll kick things off with a song I wrote to remind myself that sometimes, the bravest thing we can do is simply show up and be honest. Stay with us and remember—every ending is just a new be-ginning in disguise. This is "Echoes of the Heart" by Haley Chapman.

My heart pounded as hard as it had when I'd been hiding upstairs from the intruders in Riverstone. My first original song was going out into the world, and I had no idea what people would think. I'd written an entire album's worth of music in only two weeks and recorded "Echoes of the Heart" at a nearby studio before reaching out to local bars to see if they would be interested in booking me for a gig. My roommates, who had heard me practicing it dozens of times, had only nice things to say, but I wanted feedback from people who weren't worried about hurting my feelings. I also wanted to hear from Ace, because I'd written that song for him.

Ace had returned to LA the day after the election. For some reason, I'd thought he would transfer to Chicago, and we would be together and live happily ever after. But he'd gone for a walk in the forest before his cab arrived and when he'd returned, I knew something wasn't right. When I raised the issue of our relationship, he told me he had some things to figure out and some work to do on himself, but he promised he'd come back. I'd given him the benefit of the doubt, but it had been two weeks, and he hadn't even sent me a text.

I kept busy catching up on schoolwork, taking makeup tests, touching base with my clubs, but mostly I sat on my floor writing new songs. I'd looked at the mess of papers on my floor when I'd returned from Riverstone and immediately knew what was missing. Paige had been shocked when I dumped everything in the recycling bin—two years' worth of lyrics, two years of repressed emotion, two years of pain. Something had changed in me when I'd opened Matt's box. I finally felt free and ready to share the feelings inside me, no matter how painful they were. They were my stories. Real stories. The stories of my heart.

Chad thumped on the glass outside the studio and held up his phone. "Line is blowing up," he mouthed. I'd stopped checking messages during my shows after I'd received the threats and I had to steel myself to look at the screen.

Why haven't you been playing your music before?

Love this song

Amazing

Gave me all the feels

Definitely coming to your gig

Why aren't you signed? Or are you?

I responded to the last message with a hopeful Not yet and some cheerful emojis. I'd reached out to Stefan after the Bluebird had booked me, to let him know I was performing. I'd also sent him a download link to my new music, but a week had gone by and he hadn't responded so I figured I still had some work to do.

Dante and Chad were talking in the hallway when I left the studio after the show.

"That was a great track," Dante said. "I mean really great. Do you have more?"

"Enough for an album. I came back from Virginia, and it was like I was possessed. I couldn't stop writing, and then I did all the arrangements and suddenly I had a story in songs."

"Why aren't you in a recording studio right now?" he said. "I've always thought you had talent, but that track was next level."

Dante liked my song. I respected the hell out of him as a musician, and his praise meant the world to me. "I wanted to do a gig and get some live feedback. I've only ever sung covers in public. I just have no idea whether my original tracks are any good so I just recorded the one song."

"Haley." Dante shared a look with Chad, who had a grin from ear to ear. "It's fucking amazing. You don't need any more feedback. Have you seen the messages?"

My lips quivered at the corners. "Some."

"Read them. All of them." He pulled out his phone. "I've texted you the name of a guy I know who runs a recording studio in the Loop. Tell him I sent you and he'll give you a substantial discount.

Get that album recorded and then I can put you in touch with a PR team to get the word out."

"Fifty bucks says Haley is signed within three months of recording her album," Chad interjected.

"One hundred says two months." Dante shook his hand.

Chad grinned. "One fifty says one month and I'll donate the money you're going to give me to the Haley Recording Fund."

"Hey guys." I waved my hand in front of them. "I'm standing right here. I'd rather you just come out to my gig at the Bluebird and show support that way than trying to beat each other in a betting pool."

"I'm back for a few weeks and I was going to get the band together again," Dante said after shaking Chad's hand to confirm the last bet. "I could probably get another gig for us this weekend if you're interested."

"Thanks," I said. "But I think I'll go it alone."

CHAPTER 36

Ace

"I'm exhausted." Jessica collapsed on her oversize white leather couch after a long day on the set. "This movie better win me an Oscar because I'm utterly drained, emotionally and physically. I don't know how method actors do it. The more time I spend on set, the more I get into my character's head, and sometimes I forget that I'm me."

"You're still you," I assured her. "I don't think you'll be picking up a gun and blasting your way through any corporate offices anytime soon."

"That's sweet of you to say." She gestured to the seat across from her. "Sit down. Relax. We've hardly had a chance to catch up since you got back. Did you sort out your personal matter in Virginia?"

"I did. Thanks very much for giving me the time off."

"No problem. They sent Jorge to replace you," she said. "I swear that man never slept. He was awake when I went to bed, and when I got up, and anytime I got out of bed at night for a glass of water."

"You must have felt very safe."

"It was weird," she said. "We weren't a good fit. I like my body-guards to reflect me. They need to look good, be well-dressed, and have mad protection skills."

"I'm glad I made the cut."

"You very much made the cut." She gave me a calculated look. "How is your friend doing? The singer?"

"Very well."

"Any new gigs? I'd like to hear her sing again."

I knew I shouldn't say anything. My personal life was personal.

But I'd just heard Haley's song on her radio show—I never missed it—and I was so damn proud, and still reeling from the message it conveyed. "She just debuted a new track on her radio show, and she's posted her song online. She's doing her first live performance of her original music the day after tomorrow."

"She sings, performs, and she has a radio show." Jessica ran a hand through her long blond hair. "Let's take a listen."

I streamed the song on my phone, letting Haley's beautiful voice carry me back to Riverstone and the night by the creek when I'd cried for her father. I didn't realize Jessica was watching me until the song ended and I looked up for her reaction.

"That was beautiful," Jessica said, her voice curiously flat. "How do you know her?"

"We grew up together," I offered. "I was friends with her brother and we served in the air force together. He died on active duty a few years ago."

Sympathy creased her face. "I'm so sorry, Ace. I didn't mean to bring up bad memories. It's just, when you talk about her, and when we watched that video of her gig, and now when you listened to her music, your face changes. It makes me think she's more than a friend."

I opened my mouth to protest, and she held up her hand. "I know it's none of my business and you've been very careful to maintain that professional boundary, but I'm attracted to you, and you're the only man that I've been attracted to who hasn't been interested. I'm not counting the ones who were married or in a serious relationship, and for some of them even that wasn't an issue."

"I'm flattered, Jessica, but I don't want to cross that professional line."

"I'm not buying it," she said. "I've had many bodyguards and other professionals working for me, and that line is not etched in stone. But you're different, and I couldn't figure out the reason until you showed me the video of that gig. And now, after watching you listen to her sing, I know."

I shifted in my seat. "What do you know?"

"You're in love with her."

Pushing to stand, I crossed the room to the bar. I didn't usually drink on the job, but I needed something to settle my nerves. "I don't really think this is an appropriate conversation to have."

"Come on, Ace." She twisted on the couch so she could see me. "You've worked for me longer than any of my other bodyguards. You know things about me that no one else does, and although you've always kept your cards close to your chest, I've always considered us friends. Your feelings are written all over your face. If I had to guess, I think your trip to Virginia also had to do with her, and your grumpiness since you came back has to do with her as well."

I poured myself a shot of whiskey and downed it in one gulp. "I haven't been grumpy."

"Okay, how about brooding? Reflective? Unhappy? Take your pick."

The whiskey bottle was looking pretty good, so I poured myself another shot. "I'd better go and do a security check."

"I'll come with you." She jumped off the couch. "You can tell me what you're doing in LA when the woman you love is in Chicago."

I finished the second shot and seriously thought about having a third. "It's complicated."

"Love is not complicated," she said. "It's a gift. It's precious and rare, and I'm not going to let you throw it away. I spend my life pretending to be in love and wishing it would really happen to me. And here you are literally in love and pining away—"

Third shot going down. "I don't pine."

"Yes, you do," she said. "And it's sweet and it's beautiful and I wish you were pining for me, but she's got your heart and the only reason you're here is because you've clearly messed things up, so you need to go back to Chicago and make it right."

The whiskey loosened my tongue and I spoke my fear out loud. "I'm not—"

"Good enough?" she interjected. "Worthy? You think she could do better? I know those feelings, Ace. I've struggled with them all my life, and I recognize the signs in you. Fifteen years of therapy and I still have to fight them. But if you weren't good enough, she wouldn't love you, and that's what she's saying in her song, isn't it? That song is about you." Her eyes welled up with tears. "God, I wish someone would write me a song like that. I sure as hell wouldn't be on the other side of the country. I'd be on the first plane to Chicago and I'd never look back."

Something niggled at the back of my mind. "Aren't those the closing lines from your last movie?"

"I never said I was original." Jessica pulled out her phone. "I'll call my assistant and get her to book some flights. I feel like going to Chicago. There's a show I want to see."

Find your heart's desire.

"Actually, Jessica . . . I already have a ticket."

CHAPTER 37

Haley

"Oh my God. Why are there so many people?" I peeked out from the back hallway of the Bluebird Café. I'd approached the manager of the popular West Side bar because it was small and intimate. I'd never imagined it could hold such a big crowd.

"I might have told a few people about your gig." Paige shrugged. "All our friends are here. And everyone from the station, of course. And then there are people who heard your song on the radio. Dante may have told some people in the industry. Skye might have put up some flyers around the coffee shop and in the buildings where she has classes. Ben saw them and asked for copies to take to the athletic center . . ."

"It was supposed to be a small, intimate setting so I could get some feedback on my original songs," I moaned. "I got lots of positive responses about 'Echoes of the Heart' after I played it on my show, but I don't know if the rest of my music is any good. I've made a second set list of covers in case I don't get a good reception."

"You're not going to need it," she said. "I've been listening to you practice around the house. I'm no music expert, but I know you're going to kick ass tonight."

"I'm so nervous I can't breathe." I swallowed hard. "I don't usually get this nervous before I go on stage."

"This is a whole new you," she said. "And new you does get this nervous, because you're baring your soul with these new songs. They're real and they're raw and they're coming from the heart. You're incredibly brave."

"You're an okay friend," I told her, smiling for the first time since we'd left the house.

"So are you." Paige gave me a quick hug and checked her watch. "I don't know why they haven't called you up yet. I sent Skye to check if there was a problem and—"

"Sorry I took so long." Skye raced down the hallway. "I spoke to the manager. Apparently he was notified at the last minute that an A-list celebrity is coming to the bar tonight and there are security issues that have to be sorted out, and of course someone tipped off the press so now he's trying to find room for the paparazzi, too."

My heart sank in my chest. "Does that mean my gig has been canceled?"

"That's outrageous," Paige shouted. "I don't care if it's Beyoncé or Ed Sheeran. This is Haley's night. Who do I talk to?"

"No one." Skye laughed. "The show is still going on. Apparently, the celebrity was visiting Chicago and heard Haley's track online, and wanted to see her live."

"Now I'm really going to be sick." I doubled over as a wave of nausea washed over me.

Skye's phone buzzed and she checked the message. "Dante says she's here and the bar is absolutely packed. Lots of friends. Lots of press. The celebrity has brought an entourage . . ."

My hands found my knees and I moaned.

"Up." Paige grabbed the back of my shirt and yanked me upright. "Get yourself together. The manager is walking across the stage."

"Thanks everyone for coming out tonight," the manager said into the microphone. "We've got a special guest in the bar tonight. I thought she wanted to keep it under the radar, but I've just been informed she wants to say a few words. I give you Jessica Swanson."

My stomach clenched and I doubled over again. "Look at her. She's gorgeous. And famous. How am I going to follow an A-list movie star?"

"You'll start by being upright." Paige yanked me up again. "She probably just wants to plug her next movie."

"Hi, everybody!" Jessica waved from the stage. She looked impossibly elegant and yet perfectly dressed for an upscale dive bar in a black one-piece catsuit draped in an elegant scarf and accentuated with black patent stilettos. "As I'm sure you all know, I'm a South Side girl, and although I moved out to LA for my career, I make a point of coming back as often as I can to reconnect with my friends and family and to eat some real food." She paused while the audience cheered. "I first heard about Haley when she was singing with a band called Dante's Inferno, but when I heard her song online, I just had to come out and see her. If you haven't downloaded it, what are you waiting for? She's definitely going to be one of the top new artists in the coming year. Ladies and gentlemen, let's hear it for Haley Chapman."

Stunned, I couldn't move. Jessica Swanson saw me playing with Dante's Inferno? She'd listened to my song? How was that even possible?

"Go." Paige gave me a gentle shove and I stepped out onto the stage, blinking under the overhead lights. It was just me and my guitar and a sea of expectant faces, but I wasn't afraid anymore.

"Wow . . . I don't even know what to say." I gripped the mic. "Thank you, Jessica. I'm still trying to wrap my head around the fact that you've even heard my music, let alone liked it! This means . . . everything. And, um, I hope you all like what you hear tonight."

I opened with "Echoes of the Heart," putting everything I had into the song. It was about transformation and my emotional journey from repression to expression. It was about love and forgiveness. It was about Ace.

As the last notes of the song faded away, the stage lights dimmed and I saw two familiar faces at the back of the bar.

Ace and my mom.

And in my heart I saw Matt and my dad, waving proudly from

the shadows the way they'd done the very first time I'd sung on stage.

I gave my best performance ever. For them. For me. And for Ace, who had helped me find them again.

CHAPTER 38

Haley

The bar was alive with energy when I finally stepped off the stage. Adrenaline pumped through my veins, giving me a high like nothing I'd ever felt before. I could hardly believe I had finally shared the music that had been trapped inside me for so long. Ace had been there. And my mom. And then there was Jessica. *Jessica Swanson.* An A-list celebrity had actually stood in front of the cameras and told the world she loved my music.

I tried to stay in the moment, smiling and chatting with my friends until my mom joined us with her protective detail hovering not-so-discreetly behind her.

"I'm so proud of you." She squeezed me in a hug. "I've never heard you sing so well, and those songs . . ." Her eyes teared and she pressed a hand to her heart. "There was so much history there, so many stories, so much pain. I wish your dad had been here."

"He was."

A soft smile tugged at Mom's lips. "I imagine you're right. He would never miss a performance."

We chatted briefly before she left to catch a flight back to Washington. My friends bought me more drinks and then Jessica joined our little circle. She was as beautiful and elegant as she appeared in the movies, but genuinely friendly and down to earth in a way I had come to identify with the born-and-bred Chicagoans I'd met in the time I'd lived in the city.

"I knew you had something when Ace showed me that video of you singing with Dante's Inferno," Jessica said after we'd chatted about her latest movie, my music, and her favorite hidden-gem restaurants that we just had to try. "I pretty much knew the minute he showed it to me that I'd have no chance with him."

"Wait. What?" Paige frowned. "You and Ace?"

"I wish." Jessica shook her head and laughed lightly, seemingly unaware that Paige was only seconds away from defending my honor with a well-aimed punch. "He's my bodyguard and, unfortunately, a consummate professional who would never cross that line, especially because he's in love with someone else." She sighed. "I thought maybe I'd have a chance when he came back after his emergency trip to Virginia, but then he played your song for me, and I knew he wouldn't be staying for long."

My face heated to what felt like one hundred degrees. "I don't think that's—"

"He arranged for another bodyguard to take his place when we got to Chicago," she said. "I think it's because he wasn't planning to take his eyes off you for the rest of the night. You're a lucky girl. When a guy like that falls, he's yours for life."

Jessica's assistant whisked her away to talk to the press and I tried to get back to the celebration, but no matter how hard I tried, I couldn't focus. My mind kept wandering. Kept pulling me back to Ace. His presence was a constant, a reassuring weight in the back of my mind, but tonight, it was more than that. Tonight, it felt like something had shifted between us.

When Ace finally caught my eye from across the room, there was something in his expression that made my chest tighten—his walls were down, and for once he looked . . . exposed. He nodded toward the door, a silent signal, and I followed him out into the alley.

The cool night air hit me like a splash of water, grounding me after the chaos of the bar. Ace led me to a quiet corner where the glow of the streetlamp cast a warm circle of light around us. I stuffed my hands into my pockets, unsure of what to say.

"That was you," he said after a long silence. "You were incredible."

"That was me." I didn't want to dance around our issues anymore. Getting my songs out there had freed me from the past and I wasn't holding back my emotions anymore. "Why did you leave?"

He hesitated, eyes searching mine as if trying to gauge whether I was ready to hear what he had to say.

"I thought you'd be better off without me," he said, finally.

My heart squeezed in my chest. "But I told you—"

He cut me off with a shake of his head. "I've carried a lot of stuff with me. Growing up . . . my parents didn't just *ignore* me—they straight up told me they didn't want me. They told me again and again that if not for the money they got from the state, they would have given me away. You hear something like that enough times, you start to believe it. That you're a burden, worthless, that your existence is some kind of mistake. And it messes you up. I spent my whole life feeling like I was nothing. Disposable." He looked away, his jaw tightening for a moment before he continued.

"When I came to Riverstone, everything changed. I loved my grandmother. She saved me from a terrible situation and gave me a home, but you and Matt and your parents, you gave me a family. You shared all your love and joy with me. You made me feel useful, needed, wanted, and valued. Being part of your lives—it was the first time I felt like I actually belonged somewhere. Like maybe I wasn't as worthless as I thought. But even then, I couldn't shake that feeling. That voice in the back of my head telling me I didn't really deserve any of it."

"Ace . . ." I moved to touch him, and he backed away.

"I won't be able to finish if you touch me. It's a lot to get out but I need you to know who I really am." He ran a hand through his hair, his frustration evident as he wrestled with the demons that haunted him.

"When I fell for you, I was terrified. I was afraid that if I told you how I felt, I'd ruin everything. I didn't want to lose our friendship. I didn't want to come between you and your brother. I didn't want to mess up your family dynamics. But more than that, I didn't feel like I was good enough for you. I looked at you—this bright, beautiful, talented girl—and I thought, 'There's no way someone like her could ever really want someone like me.' I didn't even believe I was worthy of loving you."

His voice softened, the raw honesty in his tone making my heart ache. "And then that night before I deployed . . . I was ready to die for my country, to do something honorable and meaningful and worthy with my life. I was sure I would never come back, and I just wanted one thing for myself. I wanted you."

"I wanted you, too," I said quietly. "I always did."

"I thought I'd be able to kiss you and move on." His voice wavered. "But I couldn't. From the moment I held you in my arms, I knew that you were the only one for me. That I'd never want anyone else. But that scared the hell out of me too. Because if I let myself feel that, and you realized I wasn't enough . . . it would destroy me." He glanced down at me, his expression conflicted, as if sharing his heart with me was both a relief and a burden. "I didn't mean to hurt you, Haley. It was the last thing I ever wanted to do, and it made me feel even less worthy of you."

A wave of raw emotion swelled up inside me, and before I could stop myself, I put my arms around him and pulled him close, pressing my cheek against his chest. "I'm going to hold you now. You don't have to look at me, but don't stop. I'm not going anywhere." I felt his lips brush the top of my head, his body shudder in my arms.

"When I came back for Matt's funeral," he continued, "I was a mess. I couldn't even look at you. I felt responsible for what happened. I thought I'd talked Matt into joining the air force instead of pursuing his dream of becoming a dentist. I kept thinking, if I hadn't pushed him, maybe he'd still be here. And then . . . there you were, sobbing, utterly wrecked, and all I could feel was guilt. You'd lost your dad and I'd taken Matt away. I didn't know what to say. I didn't know how to face you." He put his arms around me and held me against him. "So, I did the cowardly thing and ran away, and then after we found each other, I ran again."

"But you're here now," I whispered. "What changed your mind?"

"I read Matt's letter." His arms tightened around me. "He said what you said. That he'd always wanted to be an airman, and instead of pushing him, I'd helped him find that dream. He told me he was exactly where he wanted to be, and he told me where I needed to go." His voice thickened. "He told me to go to you."

I swallowed hard, blinking away the tears. "Sometimes he wasn't a bad big brother."

Ace's tone lightened just the tiniest bit. "Being back in your life, spending time with you again, I see you for who you are. Not just the girl I kissed years ago, but the strong, amazing woman you've become. You don't need me to protect you but I want to. Not because I think you can't handle yourself, but because I care about you more than anything else in this world." He released me and pulled back just enough so I could see his face. His eyes met mine, and there was an intensity in them, a vulnerability I'd never seen before.

"I love you. I've always loved you. And I'm done running from that. I'll be here for you, no matter what happens and for as long as you'll have me."

"That would be forever."

And then he kissed me. Free of guilt and pain and the burden of the past. It was wonderful and beautiful and perfect. Just like I'd always imagined.

EPILOGUE

Haley

TWO MONTHS LATER

Good morning, Chicago. This is Hidden Tracks *on WJPK, and I'm Haley Chapman. Welcome to a brand-new year. We've been through a lot together, from the darkest of days to the moments that steal your breath away. And through it all there's been music. The soundtrack to our lives, the beat of our hearts, the songs that give voice to our hidden emotions.*

We're going to kick off with a celebration of journeys—of the paths we take, the detours we make, and the destinations we never expected to reach.

When I started this show, I thought I was just sharing music. But somewhere along the way, I realized I was also finding my own voice. We'll be exploring songs about growth and change, the courage it takes to face our fears, and the beauty we find when we finally let ourselves be heard.

Today's playlist is for anyone who's ever felt stuck and found a way to break free. For those who've learned that sometimes, the bravest thing we can do is simply allow ourselves to feel. It's for the wounded and the healing, for the silent and the people who have finally found their voice.

Our first track is a song about courage and hope and reminding ourselves that every ending is a new beginning. That even when the music stops, there's always another song waiting to be sung. Stay with us and remember—life's greatest compositions are often the ones we never saw coming.

I cued up my next few songs and sat back in my chair. Paige had wanted me to announce that I'd just been signed by Atlantic Records, the home of some of my dad's favorite R&B and jazz artists, but I wanted to keep my show focused on giving voice to new and emerging artists who, until Stefan called to tell me he'd been at the Bluebird and wanted to make me an offer, had been me.

It was hard to believe that five months ago, I'd thought my dream of making it as a singer was over. Now I was in the recording studio every day and my baby album was being turned into something big. I had an agent, Lily, who fought so hard for me she made Paige seem like a puppy, and a producer who couldn't have been more excited about my music.

I was still committed to finishing my degree—for me and for Dad and because all that psychology stuff was pretty useful when it came to exploring feelings and writing songs. I'd also reconnected with my mom from a place of shared understanding about the unhealthy way we'd dealt with our emotions. Over Christmas, we'd gone through all Dad's boxes in the garage and Matt's tough boxes and pulled out the things we wanted to put up in the house to remember them by. Our house had been full of love, friends, and family over the holidays, and it almost felt like Dad and Matt were with us again.

I saw Ace talking to Chad in the hallway after I finished my show and crept up behind him to give him a hug.

"How was your first day as a lowly engineering student?"

Ace pulled me around and gave me a soft kiss. "I killed it. No one read the course syllabus as hard as me."

Ace had decided to give up his work in security and make good his dream of becoming an engineer. With a little help from a friend in the army who assisted vets in pursuing post-secondary education, he'd managed to get second-semester admission, and of course, he already had a place to stay.

"We're going to be studying building structure in one of my classes," he said. "It will be helpful when I cut a door between our rooms."

"Not so sure the landlord will be up for that," Chad said. "Have you ever considered just alternating beds?"

"Is that what you do when you're visiting your White House sources?" Ace laughed. "Or are there hotels that will accommodate everyone at once?"

"I'm a gentleman." Chad mocked a huff. "I don't kiss and kiss and kiss and tell."

Ace walked me across campus to the coffee shop. "I was thinking . . ."

"That's a useful skill."

He gave me an amused smile. "I was thinking that as much as I enjoy hanging out with your roommates, I would like to have a bigger kitchen to practice my formidable cooking skills. Aditi said I'm an amazing cook and Paige used the word 'fantastic.' Theo and Chad said 'fucking awesome' several times when I made a roast."

"I'll be sure to let them know their compliments have gone to your head," I said dryly. "Is renovating the kitchen next on your agenda after you cut a hole in the wall?"

"Instead of renovating, I thought you might want to move in with me." He handed me his phone. "I found this place. It's modern, close to campus, has lots of light, an extra room that can be soundproofed as a music studio, and look at the size of the kitchen."

"I can't scroll with gloves on," I said. "And since it is well below zero, I am not even tempted to take them off. I'm sure it's very nice but it also looks expensive. It's not something I can afford."

"But I can." He whipped off his glove to scroll through the pictures. "In fact, I just bought it."

"You bought a condo?" I stared at him, aghast. "I didn't know security paid that well."

"It doesn't, but my grandmother left me a lot of money and I've had an offer on her house. There is nothing left in Riverstone for me. Everything I need is right here, all wrapped up in Janice's wooly scarf that is giving me ideas that I don't want to be having in below-freezing weather."

"So . . ." I studied the pictures on his phone. "This is all yours?"

"And yours, if you want. I don't smoke or vape or do drugs. I drink occasionally, usually when I'm stressed. I am very tidy and I'm good in bed. In fact, people have described my bedroom performance in the same words they have used for my cooking skills."

My lips quivered with a smile. "There is no bed in these pictures."

"I am very much looking forward to bed shopping with you. Did you know they let you try them out for ten minutes?"

"Naughty." I gave him a playful slap on the arm. "You'll get us arrested."

"It would be worth every one of those ten minutes," he said, nuzzling my frozen nose. "But you are about to be a mega-star, so I'll have to hold off until the bed is delivered. I'm thinking something with posts for decorating with scarves."

"I do like scarves," I said, musing. "And I do like the idea of having our own space. And I do like you."

Ace frowned. "Just like?"

"Love," I said. "If you don't believe me, I can give you my middle and high school notebooks with 'I love Ace' and 'Ace plus Haley' written in hearts all over them. But I thought you knew I loved you because I wrote you a song."

"It's my most played track," he said. "But I still like to hear it in real life, and I definitely want to see those notebooks. Does that mean you're saying yes?"

My cheeks flamed when I remembered all the times I'd written my name and Ace's name on my notebooks. But it was a good memory, a sweet memory, and a wish that had come true.

"Yes." I wrapped my arms around him. "I love you, Ace."

"I love you, too, bug." He kissed my frozen lips, and I felt his love like a warm blanket around my heart.

ACKNOWLEDGMENTS

This book is a college romance, but it's also a book about family. Whether they are ours through birth, circumstance, or we find them along the way, they ground us, motivate us, support us, and inspire us. I would never have been able to write Haley and Ace's story without my families near and far.

To my Bramble family: editors Monique Patterson and Erika Tsang for seeing the heart of my stories and making them shine. Special thanks to Mal Frazier, Tessa Villanueva, Ariana Carpentieri, and Laura Etzkorn. At Macmillan Audio my gratitude goes to Katy Robitzski, Isabella Narvaez, and Maria Snelling for an audiobook that brought Haley and Ace to life and to the ears of so many listeners.

My longtime agent, Laura Bradford, thank you for standing by my side with your constant encouragement and support when I ventured into new waters.

Debra Aikins, you are an assistant beyond compare. Thank you for keeping me sane and helping me get my story out into the world.

To my loyal readers who have followed me from lawyers to fighters and from bikers to mob bosses. Thank you for believing in me and taking a chance on a slightly less bad-boy hero.

To Sharon, Rana, Tarick, and Adele, thank you for keeping me entertained and bringing light to cloudy days. Mom and Dad, thank you for the memories and the stories and for teaching me the true meaning of family.

My children, Jamie, Sapphira, and Alysha. You have made life a beautiful thing.

And John, for carrying the wood, fixing the cars, raking the leaves, driving the monsters, and being my port in the storm.

ABOUT THE AUTHOR

Linda Mackie Photography

SARAH CASTILLE is the *New York Times* and *USA Today* best-selling author of over twenty romance novels featuring sexy fighters, rugged bikers, dangerously seductive mafia bosses, and tattooed bad boys. She is known for her steamy love scenes, heart-wrenching stories, and swoon-worthy happy endings.

A former bouncer, radio DJ, librarian, historian, and lawyer, Castille lives on Vancouver Island with her lively and energetic family. When she's not tormenting imaginary alpha heroes or wrangling kids, she's probably in her little red kayak, paddling out to sea.

For more information about Castille and her books, visit www .sarahcastille.com.